ALSO BY MARGARET TRUMAN:

Bess Truman
Souvenir
Women of Courage
Harry S. Truman
Letters from Father: The Truman Family's Personal Correspondence

Murder in Georgetown
Murder at the FBI
Murder on Embassy Row
Murder in the Supreme Court
Murder in the Smithsonian
Murder on Capitol Hill
Murder in the White House

MURDER IN THE CIA

MURDER IN THE CIA

MARGARET TRUMAN

RANDOM HOUSE
NEW YORK

 Published in the United States by Random House, Inc., New York, and simultaneously in Canada by Random House of Canada Limited, Toronto.

Library of Congress Cataloging-in-Publication Data

Truman, Margaret, 1924–
Murder in the CIA.

I. Title.
PS3570.R82M7557 1987 813'.54 87-42654
ISBN 0-394-55795-6

Manufactured in the United States of America
24689753
First Edition

MURDER IN THE CIA

CHAPTER 1

THE BRITISH VIRGIN ISLANDS, NOVEMBER 1985

Her name was Bernadette, eighteen, tall, a classic island "smooth skin," as they say there—very dark and with a velvety texture—hair the color of ink and falling to her shoulder blades, a full, rounded body defined beneath a clinging maroon jersey dress, a true *mantwana*, the island word for voluptuous woman.

They'd been teasing her since the launch left Anguilla Point on Virgin Gorda for its morning run to Drake's Anchorage on Mosquito Island. She'd started seeing a popular young man from Virgin Gorda, which prompted the gentle ribbing. Although she protested, she enjoyed it. She was proud of her new boyfriend and knew the other girls were jealous. "Gwan tease me, marrow deh," she said, a defiant smile on her lips. Tease all you want; tomorrow will be my day.

There were fifteen of them on board; waiters and waitresses, the bartender, kitchen help, chambermaids, and gardeners. Most of the help lived on Virgin Gorda and were brought in by launch. Drake's Anchorage was the only resort on Mosquito Island (named for a Colombian Indian tribe, not the dipterous insect), and there was only one house for staff, which was occupied by two engineers.

Bernadette was the assistant manager. Her English was excellent; so were her number skills. Her father, a bone fisherman, waded out into the shallow flats of Murdering Hole at dawn each morning in search of the indigenous fish, the so-called ladyfish. Her parents had a hard life, one they hoped she wouldn't inherit. She was their only child.

She turned her face into the wind and thought of last night with her new love. Spray from the intensely blue water stung her face. Life was good now. Last week she'd been depressed, wondered whether she would have to spend the rest of her life in this one place, as beautiful as it might be. Now, *he* was there and the glass was half full again.

The resort had been booked exclusively for two days by a Canadian businessman who'd done the same thing three months earlier, to hold seminars for key people, his assistant had said. The top echelon stayed in two magnificent villas overlooking Lime Tree Beach. Lesser managers occupied ten white-clapboard oceanfront cottages built on stilts and facing Gorda Sound. They all ate together in the thatch-roofed, open-air restaurant where the chef served up vol-au-vent stuffed with escargots, dolphin baked with bananas, West Indian grouper done with spices, herbs, and white wine, and deeply serious chocolate mousse from a guarded recipe.

Bernadette remembered the rules that had been laid down by the Canadian the last time he'd been there. The two villas were to be off-limits to everyone except his people, and resort workers were to come to them only when specifically invited. The villas were to be cleaned while their occupants were breakfasting. Always, the younger men who occupied the smaller cottages would be present in the villas when the chambermaids cleaned, or when busboys delivered food and whiskey.

Although secrecy had been the byword during the Canadians' first visit on Mosquito Island, there were those inevitable, human moments when the shroud was lifted, like the day on the beach when Bernadette saw one of the younger men sitting in a brightly striped canvas chair while cleaning a handgun. When he realized she was watching, he returned the weapon to its holster and quickly entered his cottage.

After that, Bernadette's friends noticed that others in the party carried revolvers in armpit holsters, although they took pains to conceal them. "Businessmen," the chef had said to her. "Serious business, I would say."

While the Canadian and his three senior colleagues had met in the villas, the younger men, always dressed in suits, sat on terraces surrounding the villas, saying nothing, their eyes taking in everything. They seemed pleasant enough men but kept to themselves. One had been a little more open and Bernadette had had a few friendly conversations with him. He was handsome and had a nice smile. Bernadette assumed he was in charge of communications because he frequently talked into a small portable radio to two yachts anchored offshore. Three of the four older men had arrived on those yachts. A float plane had delivered the fourth.

The radioman seemed to enjoy talking to Bernadette and she'd openly flirted with him. Once, she'd asked why there was so much secrecy surrounding a business meeting. She'd asked it lightly, giggled actually, and touched his arm. He'd smiled and said quietly, matter-of-factly, "We're about to launch a new product that our competitors would love to learn more about. That's all. Just taking precautions."

Bernadette didn't ask about the guns because it was none of her business, but she and other staff gossiped about them, speculated, eventually came to the conclusion that big mucky-mucks from up north attached more importance to themselves and to what they did than was necessary. "Silly boys," they said. One thing was certain: The silly boys tipped big. Everyone from Drake's Anchorage was happy to see them return.

■ ■ ■

On this day, a single yacht carrying three of the group's leaders arrived a few minutes past two. The float plane touched down a half hour later and slowly taxied toward the long, thin dock.

Bernadette had greeted those who'd disembarked from the yacht, and had been disappointed when the handsome young radioman wasn't among them.

Now, as she waited for the float plane's three passengers to step onto the dock, she saw his face through a window. He was the last one out of the aircraft, and she gave him her biggest welcome. He simply nodded and got into a motorized cart with the two older men. The native driver pulled away from the dock and proceeded along a narrow path that followed the contour of the sea. Bernadette watched it disappear around the curve of a hill and wondered why he'd been so curt. "Strange people," she told herself, happy that she had her new boyfriend back on the bigger island.

The arrival of the yacht and plane had been witnessed, and generally ignored, by people on yachts in the surrounding waters. Yachts in the British Virgins are as common as yellow cabs on New York City streets. One man, however, watched the comings and goings through a telescope from his 46-foot Morgan. He'd been anchored a mile offshore since early morning and had cooked breakfast on board. He had sandwiches for lunch accompanied by a Thermos of rum punch, and had just put on a pot of coffee. A pad of paper at his side was filled with notes. He wore cut-off jeans, brown deck shoes, a T-shirt that said EDWARDS YACHT CHARTERS, and a white canvas hat with a large, floppy brim on which was sewn a blue, red, and yellow patch—BRITISH NAVY: PUSSER'S RUM

He looked up and checked wind conditions. It'd be slow going back to base on Tortola. No sense raising the sails. It'd be engine all the way. He debated staying longer, decided there was nothing to be gained, hauled in the anchor, took a last look toward Mosquito Island, and headed home on a course that took him past a tiny island on which a single structure stood, an imposing, three-story concrete house surrounded by a tall chain-link fence. Two Doberman pinschers ran on the beach. A float plane and a pair of large, fast powerboats bobbed in a gentle swell against a private dock.

The man on the Morgan with his name on his T-shirt smiled as his boat slowly slid by the island. He poured rum into his coffee, lifted the cup toward the island, and said, "*Za vashe zdarov'ye!*" He laughed, put his cup down, and extended the middle finger of his right hand to the island.

CHAPTER 2

WASHINGTON, D.C., OCTOBER 1986

"What's new with the audio rights on Zoltán's new book?" Barrie Mayer asked as she entered her office on Georgetown's Wisconsin Avenue.

Her assistant, David Hubler, looked up at her from a desk piled high with manuscripts and said, "Not to worry, Barrie. We'll have contracts this week."

"I hope so," Mayer said. "You'd think we were negotiating for a million the way they drag their feet drawing papers. A lousy thousand bucks and they treat it like they were buying rights to Ronald Reagan's guide to sex after seventy."

She entered her inner office, tossed her attaché case onto a small couch, and opened the blinds. It was gray outside, threatening. Maybe a storm would clear out the hot, humid Washingtonian weather they'd been having the past few days. Not that it mattered to her. She was on her way to London and Budapest. London was always cool. Well, *almost* always cool. Budapest would be hot, but the Communists had recently invented air conditioning and introduced it to their Eastern bloc countries. With any luck she could spend her entire stay inside the Hilton.

She sat behind her desk and crossed long, slender, nicely molded legs. She wore a favorite traveling outfit: a pearl gray pants suit that had lots of give and barely wrinkled. Sensible burgundy shoes and a shell-pink button-down blouse completed the ensemble. Hubler poked his head through the door and asked if she wanted coffee. She smiled. Not only was he remarkably talented and organized, he didn't mind serving his boss coffee. "Please," she said. He returned a minute later with a large, steaming blue ceramic mug.

She settled back in her leather chair, swiveled, and took in floor-to-ceiling bookcases that lined one wall. The center section contained copies of many books written by the writers she represented as literary agent. There were twenty writers at the moment; the list swelled and ebbed as their fortunes shifted, but she could count on a hard core of about fifteen, including Zoltán Réti. Réti, the Hungarian novelist, had recently broken through and achieved international acclaim and stunning sales due, in no small part, to Barrie Mayer's faith in him and the extra effort she'd put into his latest book, *Monument*, a multigenerational novel that, according to the *New York Times* review, "touches the deepest aspects of the Hungarian, indeed the human, spirit."

Timing had been on the side of Réti and Mayer. The Soviets had recently loosened restrictions on Hungarian writers and artists, including travel. While Réti's manuscript had gone through a review by officials of the Hungarian Socialist Workers' Party under the leadership of János Kádár, it had emerged relatively unscathed. Réti had skillfully wrapped criticism of Hungary since its "liberation" in 1945 by the Soviet Union into innocuous passages, and reading between the lines said more than his Socialist readers had caught.

Monument was snapped up by publishers around the world and sat on best-seller lists for weeks. It was gratifying to Barrie Mayer because she'd put her all into the book. Now the major dilemma was what to do with the large sums of money Réti was earning from its success. That problem was still being addressed, and one of the reasons for Mayer's trip to Budapest was to confer with Réti and with a ranking member of the Hungarian Presidium who, according to Réti, "could be persuaded" to bend some rules.

Barrie had to smile when she thought of what "could be persuaded" meant. It translated into graft, pure and simple, money under the table to the right Hungarian officials, New York City style, a capitalist solution to a Socialist problem.

On a previous trip to Budapest, Barrie had been introduced to the Presidium member with whom she would meet again this time. He'd sustained a hard, incorruptible façade throughout most of that initial confab, referring to Réti as "a writer for the Hungarian people, not motivated by commercial success." To which Barrie had responded, "If that's the case, sir, we'll keep his millions in our account until there is a shift in policy."

"We have restrictions on foreign currency entering Hungary," said the official.

"A shame," said Mayer. "We're potentially talking millions of U.S. dollars. That would be good for your economy—*any* economy."

"Yes, a good point, Miss Mayer. Perhaps . . ."

"Perhaps we can pursue this another time." She got up to leave.

"I might be able to think of a way to create an exception in this case."

Barrie smiled. What did he want for himself, one of the new condos going up in the Buda hills that only went to Hungarians with a fistful of hard currency, a new car in months instead of the usual four-year wait, a bank account of his own in Switzerland?

"When will you return to Budapest?" he asked.

"Whenever you've . . . 'created your exception.' "

That meeting had taken place a month ago. The official had informed Réti that he'd "smoothed the way for Réti's funds to reach him in Budapest." He'd added, "But, of course, Mr. Réti, there must be some consideration for the time and effort I have expended in your behalf, to say nothing of the risk in which I place myself."

"Of course," Réti said.

"Of course," Barrie Mayer said to Réti when he relayed the official's message.

"Of course," she said to herself, grinning, as she sipped the hot, black coffee in her Washington office and allowed her eyes to wander to other books on the shelves written by foreign authors. Funny, she thought, how things in life take their own natural course. She'd never intended to become a literary agent specializing in foreign writers, but that's what had happened. First one, then another, and soon a blossoming reputation as an agent especially sensitive to the needs of such artists. She enjoyed the status it gave her within the publishing industry and in Washington, where she'd become a "hot name" on party invitation lists, including foreign embassies. There was the extensive travel, which, at times, was fatiguing but stimulating as well. She seemed to live out of suitcases these days, which displeased people like her mother who made no effort to conceal her disappointment at seeing so little of her only child.

Barrie's mother lived in a town house in Rosslyn, far enough away for Barrie's sanity, but close enough to see each other occasionally. Mayer had stayed at her mother's last night, an accommodation because of the trip she was about to begin that morning. They'd had a pleasant dinner at Le Lion d'Or, then sat up talking at her mother's house until almost 2:00 A.M. Barrie was tired; it would be good to get on the Pan Am flight from New York to London, sink into a first-class seat, and nap.

She pulled a box of scented pink notepaper from her desk and wrote quickly in broad, bold strokes:

> I know I shouldn't bother writing because in the frame of mind you've been in lately, the sentiment behind it won't register. But, that's me, always willing to take another shot and lay *me* on the line. You've hurt me again and here I am back for more. The only reason you're able to hurt me is because I love you. I also suspect that the *reason* you hurt me is because you love me. Fascinating creatures, men and women. At any rate, I'm about to leave and I wanted to say that when I get back we should book some private time, just the two of us, go away for a few days and talk. Maybe this time the words won't get in the way. London and Budapest beckon. Be good, and miss me, damn you.

Hubler came in again. "Got everything?"

"I think so," Mayer said, putting the pages in an envelope, sealing and addressing it, and slipping it into her purse. "Thanks to you."

"You'll be gone a week?"

"A day shy. I'll be at Eleven, Cadogan Gardens in London, and the Hilton in Budapest."

Hubler laughed. "So, what else is new?"

Mayer smiled and stood, stretched, blinked green eyes against sleepiness. "Is the car here?"

"Yeah." The agency had a corporate account with Butler's Limousine, and a stretch was waiting downstairs. "Barrie, a question."

"What?"

"You uncomfortable with this meeting with the Commie big shot in Budapest?"

"A little, but Zoltán says 'Not to worry.' " They both laughed. "He's been talking to you too much, David."

"Maybe he has. Look, I know *you* know your business, but greasing palms in a Socialist country might not be the smartest thing to do. You could be set up. They do it all the time."

Mayer grinned, then picked up her attaché case from the couch, came to where Hubler stood, and kissed him on the cheek. "You, David, are a dear. You also worry more than my mother does, which puts you in the Guinness class. Not to worry, David. Call me if you need me. I'll check in with you a couple of times. By the way, where's Carol?" Carol Geffin was one of two secretaries at the agency. The other, Marcia St. John, was on vacation. The only other two people on Mayer's staff were away on business, one in Hollywood following through on film rights to Réti's novel, the other in New York attending a conference.

"Must have been another heavy night at the Buck Stops Here," Hubler said. Carol Geffin's favorite disco closed at 6:00 A.M., sometimes.

Mayer shook her head. "You tell Carol that she's got to make a choice between working and dancing. One more late morning and she can dance all day on her money, not mine. Give me a hand, huh?"

Hubler carried her briefcase and a suitcase Mayer had dropped off in the reception area to the waiting limo. "See you in a week," she said as she climbed inside the back of the Fleetwood Brougham. The driver closed the door, got behind the wheel, and headed for National Airport and the shuttle to New York. She glanced back through the tinted glass and saw Hubler standing at the curb, his hand half raised in a farewell. One of many things Mayer liked about him was his disposition. He was always smiling, and his laugh was of the infectious variety. Not this day, however. His face, as he stood and watched the limo become smaller, was grim. It bothered her for a moment but quickly was displaced by thoughts of the day ahead. She stretched her legs out in front of her, closed her eyes, and said to herself, "Here we go again."

Her suitcase had been checked through to London, leaving her free to grab a cab from La Guardia into the city, where she was let off at the corner of Second Avenue and 30th Street. She walked toward the East River on 30th until she reached a brownstone with a series of physicians' names in black-on-white plaques.

JASON TOLKER—PSYCHIATRIST. She went down the steps and rang the bell. A female voice asked through an intercom, "Who is it?"

"Barrie Mayer."

A buzzer sounded and Barrie opened the door, stepped into a small carpeted reception area, and closed the door behind her. She was the only person there except for a young woman who came from an office in the rear and said, "Good morning."

"Good morning," Mayer said.

"He's not here, you know," the nurse said.

"I know, a conference in London. He told me to . . ."

"I know. It's here." The nurse, whose face was severely chiseled and whose skin bore the scars of childhood acne, reached behind a desk and came up with a black briefcase of the sort used by attorneys to carry briefs. Two straps came over the top, and a tiny lock secured the flap to the case itself.

"He said you'd been told about this," the nurse said.

"That's right. Thank you."

The nurse's smile was a slash across her lower face. "See you again," she said.

"Yes, you will."

Mayer left, carrying the new briefcase as well as her attaché case, one in each hand. She checked into a room at the Plaza that David had reserved from Washington, had lunch sent up, and perused papers from her attaché case until three, when she placed a wake-up call for five, stripped naked, and took a nap. She got up at five, showered, dressed again, took a cab to Kennedy Airport, and checked in at the Clipper Club, where she had a martini and read a magazine before boarding Pan Am's seven o'clock 747 to London.

"Can I take those for you?" a flight attendant asked, indicating the two briefcases.

"No, thank you. Lots of work to do," Mayer said pleasantly.

She slid both cases under the seat in front of her and settled in for the flight. It left on time. She had another martini, and then caviar and smoked salmon, rare beef carved at her seat, and blueberry cheesecake; Cognac to top it off. The movie came on, which she ignored. She put on slippers provided by the flight attendant and a pair of blue eyeshades from a toiletry kit given to each first-class passenger, positioned a pillow behind her head, covered herself with a blue blanket, and promptly fell asleep, the toes of her left foot wedged into the handle of the briefcase she'd picked up at Dr. Jason Tolker's office.

The cabbie from Heathrow Airport to her hotel was an older man who took more delight in chatting than in driving. Mayer would have preferred silence but he was a charming man, as all the older London cab drivers seemed to be, and she thought of the difference between him and certain New York cabbies, who not only were rude and uncaring but malicious, nervous, opinionated, hyperactive, and who curbed any tendency toward humanity by driving insanely.

"Here we are, ma'am," the driver said as he pulled up in front of a row of brick houses on Cadogan Gardens. There was no indication of a hotel on the block. Only the number 11 appeared above a polished wooden door that Mayer went to. She rang a bell. Moments later a hall porter in a white jacket opened the door and said, "Welcome, Miss Mayer. Splendid to see you again. Your room is ready."

She signed the guest book and was led to the suite she usually reserved—Number 27. It consisted of a living room, bedroom, and bath. The white ceilings were high, the walls of the living room bloodred. Victorian furniture was everywhere, including a glass-fronted bookcase, an armoire, a dressing table in front of French windows in the bedroom that overlooked a private park across the street, and a gracefully curved chaise and chairs upholstered in gold.

"Would you like anything, ma'am?" the porter asked.

"Not this minute, thank you," Barrie said. "Perhaps tea at three?"

"Of course."

"I'll be leaving tomorrow for a few days," she said, "but I'll be keeping the room for my return."

"Yes, ma'am. Tea at three."

She slept, and later watched BBC-TV while enjoying scones with clotted cream and jam with her tea. She had dinner at seven at the Dorchester with a British agent, Mark Hotchkiss, with whom she'd been exploring a business link for the past few months, and was back in bed at the Cadogan by ten.

She arose at seven, had breakfast sent up to the room, dressed and left the hotel at eight. She arrived at Heathrow's Terminal Number 2 and joined a long line of people waiting to go through a security section leading to a vast array of flights by smaller foreign airlines, including Malev, the Hungarian National Airline.

She'd been through this before. How many trips had she taken to Budapest in the two or three years? Fifteen, twenty? She'd lost track. Only her accountant knew for certain. The line at Terminal 2 was always impossibly long and slow, and she'd learned to be patient.

She glanced up at a TV departure monitor. Plenty of time. An older man in front of her asked if she'd "protect" his place while he went to buy a pack of cigarettes. "Of course," she said. A woman behind her ran the wheel of a suitcase caddy into Mayer's heel. Mayer turned. The woman raised her eyebrows and looked away.

The line moved in spurts. Mayer carried her briefcases,

and pushed her suitcase along the ground with her foot.

A loud voice to her right caused Barrie, and everyone else in the line, to turn in its direction. A young black man wearing an open white shirt, black trousers, and leather sandals had gotten up on a trash container and began screaming a protest against British policy in South Africa. Everyone's attention remained on him as two uniformed airport-security officers pushed through crowds of people in his direction.

"Barrie."

She didn't immediately react. Because she, and everyone else in the line, had turned to her right, her back was to a row of counters. The mention of her name had come from behind her.

She turned. Her eyebrows went up. She started to say something, a name, a greeting, when the hand came up beneath her nose. In it was a metal tube that might have held a cigar. The thumb on the hand flicked a switch on the tube and a glass ampule inside it shattered, its contents blown into Mayer's face.

It all happened so quickly. No one seemed to notice . . . until she dropped both briefcases to the floor and her hands clutched at her chest as a stabbing pain radiated from deep inside. She couldn't breathe. The airport, and everyone in it, was wiped away by a blinding white light that sent a spasm of pain through her head.

"Lady, are you . . . ?"

Her face was blue. She sank to her knees, her fingers frantic as they tried to tear open her clothing, her chest itself in search of air and relief from the pain.

"Hey, hey, over here, this lady's . . ."

Mayer looked up into the faces of dozens of people who were crouching low and peering at her, in sympathy or in horror. Her mouth and eyes opened wide, and rasping sounds came from her throat, pleas without words, questions for the faces of strangers so close to her. Then she pitched forward, her face thudding against the hard floor.

There were screams now from several people who saw what had happened to the tall, well-dressed woman who, seconds before, had stood in line with them.

The man who'd gone to get cigarettes returned. "What's this?" he asked as he looked down at Mayer, sprawled on the floor of Terminal Number 2. "Good God," he said, "someone do something for her."

CHAPTER 3

BUDAPEST—TWO DAYS LATER

I just can't believe it," Collette Cahill said to Joe Breslin as they sat at an outdoor table at Gundel, Budapest's grand old restaurant. "Barrie was . . . she'd become my best friend. I went out to Ferihegy to meet her flight from London, but she wasn't on it. I came back to the embassy and called that hotel in Cadogan Gardens she always stays at in London. All they could tell me was that she left that morning for the airport. Malev wouldn't tell me anything until I got hold of that guy in operations I know who checked the passenger manifest. Barrie was listed as a reservation, but she hadn't boarded. That's when I really started worrying. And then . . . then, I got a call from Dave Hubler in her Washington office. He could barely talk. I made him repeat what he'd said three, four times and . . ." She'd been fighting tears all evening and now lost the battle. Breslin reached across the table and placed a hand on hers. A seven-piece roving Gypsy band dressed in bright colors approached the table but Breslin waved them away.

Collette sat back in her chair and drew a series of deep breaths. She wiped her eyes with her napkin and slowly shook her head. "A heart attack? That's ridiculous, Joe. She was, what, thirty-five, maybe thirty-six? She was in great shape. Damn it! It can't be."

Breslin shrugged and lighted his pipe. "I'm afraid it can, Collette. Barrie's dead. No question about that, sadly. What about Réti, her writer?"

"I tried his house but no one was there. I'm sure he knows by now. Hubler was calling him with the news."

"What about the funeral?"

"There wasn't any, at least nothing formal. I called her mother that night. God, I dreaded it. She seemed to take it pretty well, though. She said she knew that Barrie wanted immediate cremation, no prayers, no gathering, and that's what she had."

"The autopsy. You say it was done in London?"

"Yes. They're the ones who labeled it a coronary." She closed her eyes tightly. "I will not buy that finding, Joe, never."

He smiled and learned forward. "Eat something, Collette. You haven't had a thing for too long. Besides, I'm starved." Large bowls of goulash soup sat untouched in front of them. She took a spoonful and looked at Breslin, who'd dipped a piece of bread in the hearty broth and was savoring it. Cahill was glad she had him to lean on. She'd made many friends since coming to Budapest, but Joe Breslin provided a stability she needed at times like this, perhaps because he was older, fifty-six, and seemed to enjoy the role of surrogate father.

Breslin had been stationed with the American Embassy

in Budapest for just over ten years. In fact, Collette and a group of friends had celebrated his tenth anniversary only last week at their favorite Budapest night spot, the Miniatur Bar on Budai Läszlö Street, where a talented young Gypsy pianist named Nyári Károly played a nightly mix of spirited Hungarian Gypsy melodies, American pop tunes, Hungrian love songs, and modern jazz. It had been a festive occasion and they'd closed the bar at three in the morning.

"How's the soup?" Breslin asked.

"Okay. You know, Joe, I just realized there's someone else I should call."

"Who's that?"

"Eric Edwards."

Breslin's eyebrows lifted. "Why?"

"He and Barrie were . . . close."

"Really? I didn't know that."

"She didn't talk about it much but she was mad about him."

"Hardly an exclusive club."

The comment brought forth the first smile of the evening from her. She said, "I've finally gotten old enough to learn never to question a relationship. Do you know him well?"

"I don't know him at all, just the name, the operation. We had some dispatches from him this morning."

"And?"

"Nothing startling. Banana Quick is alive and well. They've had their second meeting."

"On Mosquito?"

He nodded, frowned, leaned across the table, and said, "Was Barrie carrying anything?"

"I don't know." They both glanced about to make sure

they weren't being overheard. She spotted a table four removed at which a heavyset man and three women sat. She said to Breslin, "That's Litka Morovaf, Soviet cultural affairs."

Breslin smiled. "What is he now, number three in the KGB here?"

"Number two. A real Chekist. Drives him crazy when I call him Colonel. He actually thinks not wearing a uniform obscures his military rank. He's a pig, always after me to have dinner with him. Enough of him. Getting back to Barrie, Joe, I didn't always know whether she was carrying or just here on business for her agency. She'd tightened up a lot lately, which made me happy. When she first got involved, she babbled about it like a schoolgirl."

"Did she see Tolker before leaving?"

"I don't know that, either. She usually contacted him in Washington but she had time to kill in New York this trip, so I assume she saw him there. I don't know anything, Joe—I wish I did."

"Maybe it's better you don't. Feel like dinner?"

"Not really."

"Mind if I do?"

"Go ahead, I'll pick."

He ordered *Fogasfile Gundel Modon,* the small filets of fish accompanied by four vegetables, and a bottle of Egri Bikavér, a good red Hungarian wine. They said little while he ate. Cahill sipped the wine and tried to shake the thoughts that bombarded her about Barrie's death.

They'd become friends in college days. Collette was raised in Virginia, attended George Washington University, and graduated from its law school. It was during her postgraduate work that she met Barrie Mayer, who'd come from Seattle to work on a master's degree in English literature at Georgetown University. It had been a chance meeting. A young attorney Cahill had been seeing threw a party at his apartment in Old Town and invited his best friend, another attorney who'd just started dating Barrie Mayer. He brought her to the party and the two young women hit it off.

That they became close friends surprised the attorneys who'd introduced them. They were different personalities, as different as their physical attributes. Mayer, tall, leggy, had a mane of chestnut hair that she enjoyed wearing loose. She seldom used makeup. Her eyes were the color of malachite and she used them to good advantage, expressing a variety of emotions with a simple widening or narrowing, a partial wink, a lift of a sandy eyebrow, or a sensuous clouding over that she knew was appealing to men.

Cahill, on the other hand, was short and tightly bundled, a succession of rounded edges that had been there since adolescence and that had caused her widowed mother sleepless nights. She was as vivacious as Mayer was laid-back, deep blue eyes in constant motion, a face punctuated by high cheekbones that belied her Scottish heritage, a face that seemed always ready to burst apart with enthusiasm and wonder. She enjoyed using makeup to add high color to her cheeks and lips. Her hair was black ("Where did that come from, for heaven's sake?" her mother often asked), and she wore it short, in a style flattering to her nicely rounded face.

Their initial friendship was rooted in a mutual determination to forge successful careers. The specific goals were different, of course. For Mayer, it was to eventually head up a major book-publishing company. For Cahill, it was government service with an eye toward a top spot in the Justice Department, perhaps even becoming the first female Attorney General. They laughed often and loudly about their aspirations, but they were serious.

They remained close until graduation, when the beginning stages of their work moved them away from each other. Cahill took a job with a legal trade journal published in Washington that kept tabs on pending legislation. She gave it a year, then took a friend's advice and began applying to government agencies, including Justice, State, and the Central Intelligence Agency. The CIA was first with an offer and she accepted it.

"You *what*?" Barrie Mayer had exploded over dinner the night Cahill announced her new job.

"I'm going to work for the CIA."

"That's . . . that's crazy. Don't you read, Collette? The CIA's a terrible organization."

"Media distortion, Barrie." She had smiled. "Besides, after training, they're sending me to England."

Now Mayer's smile matched Collette's. "All right," she said, "so it's not such a terrible organization. What will you be doing there?"

"I don't know yet, but I'll find out soon enough."

They ended the dinner with a toast to Collette's new adventure, especially to London.

At the time of Collette Cahill's decision to join the Pickle Factory, as CIA employees routinely referred to the agency, Barrie Mayer was working at a low-level editorial job with *The Washingtonian*, D.C.'s leading "city" magazine. Her friend's decision to make a dramatic move prompted action on her part. She quit the magazine and went to New York, where she stayed with friends until landing a job as assistant to the executive editor of a top book publisher. It was during that experience that she took an interest in the literary agent's side of the publishing business, and accepted a job with a medium-size agency. This suited her perfectly. The pace was faster than at the publishing house, and she enjoyed wheeling and dealing on behalf of the agency's clients. As it turned out, she was good at it.

When the founder of the agency died, Mayer found herself running the show for three years until deciding to strike out on her own. She ruled out New York; too much competition. With an increasing number of authors coming out of Washington, she decided to open Barrie Mayer Associates there. It flourished from the beginning, especially as her roster of foreign authors grew along with an impressive list of Washington writers.

Although their careers created a wide geographical distance between them, Barrie and Collette kept in touch through occasional postcards and letters, seldom giving much thought to whether they'd ever renew the friendship again in person.

After three years at a CIA monitoring station in an abandoned BBC facility outside of London, where she took raw intercepts of broadcasts from Soviet bloc countries and turned them into concise, cogent reports for top brass, Cahill was asked to transfer to a Clandestine Services unit in the Hungarian division, operating under the cover of the U.S. Embassy in Budapest. She debated making the move; she loved England, and the contemplation of a long assignment inside an Eastern European Socialist state did not hold vast appeal.

But there was the attraction of joining Clandestine Services, the CIA's division responsible for espionage, the *spy* division. Although space technology, with its ability to peek into every crevice and corner of the earth from miles aloft, had diminished the need for agents, special needs still existed, and the glamour and intrigue perpetuated by writers of spy novels lived on.

What had they said over and over during her training at headquarters in Langley, Virginia, and at the "Farm," the handsome estate a two-hour drive south of Washington? "The CIA is not essentially, or wholly, an espionage organization. It has only a small section devoted to espionage, and agents are never used to gain information that can be obtained through other means."

Her instructor in the course "Management of the Espionage Operation" had quoted from British intelligence to get across the same point. "A good espionage operation is like a good marriage. Nothing unusual ever happens. It is, and should be, uneventful. It is never the basis of a good story."

Her cover assignment would be the embassy's Industrial Trade Mission. Her real responsibility would be to function as a case officer, seeking out and developing useful members of Hungary's political, industrial, and intelligence communities into agents for the United States, to "turn" them to our side. It would mean returning to Washington for months of intensive training, including a forty-four-week language course in Hungarian at the Foreign Service Institute.

Should she take it? Her mother had been urging her to return home from England and to put her law training to the use for which it was intended. Cahill herself had been considering resigning from the Pickle Factory and returning home. The past few months in England had been boring, not socially but certainly on the job as her routine became predictable and humdrum.

It was not an easy decision. She made it on a train from

London after a weekend holiday of good theater, pub-crawling with friends she'd made from the Thames Broadcasting Network, and luxuriating in a full English tea at Brown's.

She'd take it.

Once she'd decided, her spirits soared and she enthusiastically prepared for her return to Washington. She'd been instructed to discuss it with no one except cleared CIA personnel.

"Not even my mother?"

An easy, understanding smile from her boss. "*Especially* your mother."

■ ■ ■

"You will hear two things from Hungarians," her language instructor at Washington's Foreign Service Institute told the class the first day. "First, they will tell you that Hungary is a very small country. Second, they will tell you that the language is *very* difficult. Believe them. Both statements are true."

■ ■ ■

Friday.

Cahill's first week of language classes had ended, and she'd made plans to spend the weekend with her mother in Virginia. She stopped in the French Market in Georgetown to pick up her mother's favorite pâté and cheese, and was waiting for her purchases to be added up when someone behind her said her name. She turned. "It can't be," she said, wide-eyed.

"Sure is," Barrie Mayer said.

They embraced, stepped apart, and looked at each other, then hugged again.

"What are you doing here?" Mayer asked.

"Going to school. I'm being transferred and . . . it's a long story. How are you? The agency's doing well? How's your . . . ?"

"Love life?" A hearty laugh from both. "That, too, is a long story. Where are you going now? Can we have a drink? Dinner? I've been meaning to . . . "

"So have I. I'm going home for the weekend . . . I mean, where my mother lives. God, I can't believe this, Barrie! You look sensational."

"So do you. Do you have to go right now?"

"Well, I—let me call my mother and tell her I'll be late."

"Go tomorrow morning, early. Stay with me tonight."

"Ah, Barrie, I can't. She's expecting me."

"At least a drink. My treat. I'm dying to talk to you. This is incredible, bumping into you. Please, just a drink. If you stay for dinner, I'll even send you home by limo."

"Things are good, huh?"

"Things are *fantastic*."

They went to the Georgetown Inn where Cahill ordered a gin and tonic, Mayer an old-fashioned. There was a frenetic attempt to bring each other up to date as quickly as possible, which resulted in little information actually being absorbed. Mayer realized it and said, "Let's slow down. You first. You said you were here to take classes. What kind of classes? What for?"

"For my job. I'm"—she looked down at the bar and said sheepishly—"I can't really discuss it with . . . with anyone not officially involved with the Company."

Mayer adopted a grave expression. "Heavy spy stuff, huh?"

Cahill laughed the comment away. "No, not at all, but you know how things are with us."

"Us?"

"Don't make me explain, Barrie. You know what I mean."

"I sure do."

"Do you?"

Mayer sat back and played with a swizzle stick. She asked, "Are you leaving jolly old England?"

"Yes."

"And?"

"I'll be . . . I've taken a job with the U.S. Embassy in Budapest."

"That's wonderful. With the embassy? You've left the CIA?"

"Well, I . . ."

Mayer held up her hand. "No explanations needed. I read the papers."

What had been an exuberant beginning to the reunion deteriorated into an awkward silence. It was Cahill who broke it. She clutched Mayer's arm and said, "Let's get off the cloaks and daggers. Barrie, your turn. Tell me about *your* agency. Tell me about, well . . ."

"My love life." They giggled. "It's stagnant, to be kind, although it has had its moments recently. The problem is that I've been spending more time on airplanes than anywhere else, which doesn't contribute to stable relationships. Anyway, the agency is thriving *and*, coincidentally, you and I will probably see more of each other in Budapest than we have for the past five years."

"Why?"

She explained her recent success with foreign authors, including the Hungarian, Zoltán Réti. "I've been to Budapest six or eight times. I love it. It's a marvelous city despite Big Red Brother looking over your shoulder."

"Another drink?"

"Not for me. You?"

"No. I really should be heading off."

"Call your mother."

"All right."

Cahill returned and said, "She's such a sweetness. She said, 'You spend time with your dear friend. Friends are important.' " She delivered the words with exaggerated gravity.

"She sounds wonderful. So, what is it, dinner, stay over? You name it."

"Dinner, and the last train home."

They ended up at La Chaumière on M Street, where Mayer was given a welcome worthy of royalty. "I've been coming here for years," she told Cahill as they were led to a choice table near the center fireplace. "The food is scrumptious and they have a sense of when to leave you alone. I've cut some of my better meals and deals here."

It turned into a long, leisurely, and progressively introspective evening, aided by a second bottle of wine. The need to bombard each other with detailed tales of their lives had passed, and the conversation slipped into a comfortable and quiet series of reflective thoughts, delivered from their armchairs.

"Tell me more about Eric Edwards," Cahill said.

"What else is there to say? I was in the BVI meeting with an author who'd recently hit it big. Besides, never pass up a chance at the Caribbean. Anyway, he took me on a day cruise, and the charter captain was Eric. We hit it off right away, Collette, one of those instant fermentations, and I spent the week with him."

"Still on?"

"Sort of. It's hard with my travel schedule and his being down there, but it sure ain't dead."

"That's good."

"And . . ."

Cahill looked across the candlelit table and smiled. "That's right," she said, "there was something you were dying to tell me."

"Eric Edwards isn't enough?"

"Only if you hadn't hinted that there was something even bigger. Lay it on me, lady literary agent. That last train home isn't far off."

Mayer glanced around the restaurant. Only two other tables were occupied, and they were far away. She put her elbows on the table and said, "I joined the team."

Cahill's face was a blank.

"I'm one of you."

It dawned on Cahill that her friend might be referring to the CIA but, because it didn't make much sense—and because she had learned caution—she didn't bring it up. Instead, she said, "Barrie, could you be a little more direct?"

"Sure. I'm working for the Pickle Factory." There was mirth in her voice as she said the words.

"That's . . . how?"

"I'm a courier. Just part time, of course, but I've been doing it fairly regularly now for about a year."

"Why?" It was the only sensible question that came to Cahill at the moment.

"Well, because I was asked to and . . . I like it, Collette, feel I'm doing something worthwhile."

"You're being paid?"

Mayer laughed. "Of course. What kind of an agent

would I be if I didn't negotiate a good deal for myself?"

"You don't *need* the money, do you?"

"Of course not, but who ever has too much money? And, finally, some earnings off the books. Want more specifics?"

"Yes and no. I'm fascinated, of course, but you really shouldn't be talking about it."

"To *you?* You're cleared."

"I know *that,* Barrie, but it's still something you don't chit-chat about over dinner and wine."

Mayer adopted a contrite expression. "You aren't going to turn me in, are you?"

Collette sighed and looked for a waiter. Once she'd gotten his attention, she said to Mayer, "Barrie, you have ruined my weekend. I'll spend it wondering about the strange twists and turns my friend's life has taken while I wasn't around to protect her."

They stood outside the restaurant. It was a crisp and clear evening. The street had filled with the usual weekend crowds that gravitated to Georgetown, and that caused residents to wring their hands and to consider wringing necks, or selling their houses.

"You'll be back Monday?" Mayer asked.

"Yup, but I'll be spending most of my time out of town."

"At the Farm?"

"Barrie!"

"Well?"

"I have some training to take. Let's leave it at that."

"Okay, but promise you'll call the first moment you're free. We have a lot more catching up to do."

They touched cheeks, and Collette flagged a cab. She spent the weekend at her mother's house thinking about Barrie Mayer and the conversation at the restaurant. What she'd told her friend was true. She *had* spoiled her weekend, and she returned to Washington Monday morning anxious to get together again for another installment of Barrie Mayer's "other life."

▪ ▪ ▪

"This restaurant isn't what it used to be," Joe Breslin said as he finished his meal. "I remember when Gundel was . . ."

"Joe, I'm going to London and Washington," Cahill said.

"Why?"

"To find out what happened to Barrie. I just can't sit here and let it slide, shrug and accept the death of a friend."

"Maybe you should do just that, Collette."

"Sit here?"

"Yes. Maybe . . ."

"Joe, I know exactly what you're thinking, and if what you're thinking bears any relationship to the truth, I don't know what I'll do."

"I don't know anything about Barrie's death, Collette, but I do know that she assumed a known risk once she got involved, no matter how part time it might have been. Things have heated up since Banana Quick. The stakes have gotten a lot bigger, and the players are more visible and vulnerable." He added quickly, in a whisper, "The schedule's been moved up. It'll be sooner than planned."

"What are you saying, Joe, that this could have been a Soviet wet affair?" She'd used Russian intelligence slang for blood, for an assassination, which had been picked up by the intelligence community in general.

"Could be."

"Or?"

"Or . . . your guess. Remember, Collette, it might have been exactly what it was labeled by the British doctors, a coronary pure and simple."

A lump developed in Cahill's throat and she touched away a tear that had started down her cheek. "Take me home, Joe, please. I'm suddenly very tired."

As they left Gundel, the Soviet intelligence officer at the table with three women waved to Collette and said, "*Vsyevó kharóshevo*, Madam Cahill." He was drunk.

"Good night to you, too, Colonel," she responded.

Breslin dropped her at her apartment on Huszti út, on the more fashionable Buda side of the Danube. It was one of dozens of apartments the U.S. government had leased to house its embassy personnel, and although it was extremely small and three flights up, it was light and airy and featured a remodeled kitchen that was the best of all the kitchens her embassy friends had in their subsidized apartments. It also came with a telephone, something Hungarian citizens waited years for.

A flashing red light indicated Cahill had two messages on her answering machine. She rewound the tape and heard a familiar voice, his English heavily laden with his Hungarian birthright. *"Collette, it is Zoltán Réti. I am in London. I am shocked at what I have heard about Barrie. No, shocked is not the word to describe my feelings. I read about it in the paper here. I am attending a conference and will return to Budapest tomorrow. I am sorry for the loss of your good friend, and for my loss. It is a terrible thing. Goodbye."*

Cahill stopped the machine before listening to the second message. London? Hadn't Réti known Barrie was coming to Budapest? If he hadn't—and if she knew he wouldn't be here—she had to be on CIA business. But that broke precedent. She'd never traveled to Budapest without having him there as the reason for her visit which, in fact, was legitimate. He was a client. The fact that he happened to be Hungarian and lived in Budapest only made it more plausible and convenient to perform her second mission, carrying materials for the Central Intelligence Agency.

She started the second message:

"Collette Cahill, my name is Eric Edwards. We've never met, but Barrie and I were quite close, and she talked about you often. I just learned about what happened to her and felt I had to make contact with someone, anyone who was close to her and shares what I'm feeling at this moment. It seems impossible, doesn't it, that she's gone, like that, this beautiful and talented woman who . . ." There was a pause, and it sounded to Cahill as though he were trying to compose himself. *"I hope you don't mind this long and convoluted message but, as I said, I wanted to reach out and talk to her friend. She gave me your number a long time ago. I live in the British Virgin Islands but I wondered if . . ."* The line went dead. He was cut off, and the machine made a series of beeping noises.

His call set up another set of questions for her. Didn't he know that *she* would know who he was, that he lived in the British Virgins, was a CIA operative there whose primary mission had to do with Hungary? Was he just being professional? Probably. She couldn't fault that.

She made herself a cup of tea, got into her nightgown, and climbed into bed, the tea on a small table beside her. She decided three things: She would request time off immediately to go to London and Washington; she would look up everyone who was close to Barrie and, at least, be able to vent her feelings; and she would, from that moment forward, accept the possibility that her friend Barrie Mayer had died prematurely of a heart attack, at least until there was something tangible to prove otherwise.

She fell asleep crying silently after asking in a hoarse, low voice, "What happened, Barrie? What *really* happened?"

CHAPTER 4

C*ollette: Please see me as soon as you come in. Joe.*

The note was taped to the telephone in her office on the second floor of the embassy. She got a cup of coffee and walked down the hall to Breslin's office. "Come in," he said. "Close the door."

He took a sip of his coffee which, Cahill knew, contained a healthy shot of akvavit, compliments of a buddy in the U.S. Embassy in Copenhagen who always included a bottle in his diplomatic pouch. "What's up?" she asked.

"Feel like a walk?"

"Sure." He wasn't suggesting it because he needed exercise. What he had to say was important and private, and Breslin was a notorious paranoid when it came to holding such conversations inside the embassy.

They went down a broad staircase with worn red carpeting, through a door tripped electronically by a young woman at the front desk, past a Hungarian Embassy employee who was running a metal detector over a visitor, and out into bright sunshine that bathed Szabadság tėr and Liberation Square.

A group of schoolchildren gathered at the base of a huge memorial obelisk dedicated to Soviet soldiers who'd liberated the city. The streets were bustling with people on their way to work, or heading for Váci utca and its parallel shopping boulevard from which all vehicles were banned. "Come on," Breslin said, "let's go down to Parliament."

They walked along the Danube's shoreline until they reached the domed, neo-Gothic Parliament building with its eighty-eight statues depicting Hungarian monarchs, commanders, and famous warriors. Breslin looked up at it and smiled. "I would have liked being around here when they really did have a Parliament," he said. Since the Soviets took over, the Parliament continued to function, but in name only. The *real* decisions were made in an ugly, rectangular building farther up the river where the MSZMP—the Hungarian Socialist Workers' Party—sat.

Cahill watched boat traffic on the Danube as she asked, "What do you want to tell me?"

Breslin pulled his pipe from his jacket, tamped tobacco into its bowl, and put a wooden match to it. "I don't think you'll have to ask for time off to chase down what happened to your friend Barrie."

"What do you mean?"

"Based upon what Stan told me this morning, you're going to be asked to do it officially." Stanley Podgorsky was chief-of-station for the CIA unit operating out of the embassy. Of two hundred Americans assigned there, approximately half were CIA people reporting to him.

"Why me?" Cahill asked. "I'm not a trained investigator."

"Why not? How many Company investigators have you known who were trained?" It caused her to smile. "You know how it works, Collette, somebody knows somebody who's been compromised and they get the assignment, instant investigator. I think that's you this time around."

"Because I knew Barrie?"

"Exactly."

"And it wasn't a heart attack?"

"Not from what I hear."

They approached a construction crew that was using jackhammers to tear out an old dock. When they were close enough so that even sophisticated, long-range microphones would fail to distinguish their words from the din, Breslin said, "She *was* carrying, Collette, and evidently it was important."

"And it's gone?"

"Right."

"Any ideas?"

"Sure. It was either us or them. If it was them, they have the material and we're in a panic. If it was us, one of our people has what she had in her briefcase and maybe is looking to sell it to the other side." He drew on his pipe and said, "Or . . ."

"Or wanted what she had for other reasons, personal maybe, incriminating, something like that."

"Yes, something like that."

She squinted against the sun that popped out from a fast-moving cloud and said, "Joe, we're down here for more than just a preliminary warning to me that Stan might ask me to look into Barrie's death. He told you to feel me out, didn't he?"

"Not in so many words."

"I'll do it."

"Really? No hesitation?"

"None. I wanted to do it on my own time anyway. This way I don't blow what leave I have coming to me."

"That's pragmatic."

"That's working for the Pickle Factory too long. Do I go back and tell him, or do you?"

"You. I have nothing to do with this. One final bit of advice, Collette. Stan and the desk people back at Langley really don't give a damn how Barrie died. As far as they're concerned, she had a heart attack. I mean, they know she didn't but *she* doesn't count. The briefcase does."

"What was in it? Who was it from?"

"Maybe Stan will tell you, but I doubt it. Need-to-know, you know."

"If I'm trying to find out who ended up with it, I'll need to know."

"Maybe, maybe not. That's up to Stan and Langley. Let them lay out the rules and you stay within them." He looked over half-glasses to reinforce his point.

"I will, and thanks, Joe. I'll go see Stan right now."

Podgorsky occupied an office that had a sign on the door that read TYPEWRITER REPAIR. Many CIA offices within the embassy had such signs which, the thinking went, would discourage casual visitors. They usually did.

He sat behind a battered desk with a row of burn marks from too many cigars perched on the edge. Stanley was short and stocky, with a full head of gray hair of which he was inordinately proud. Cahill liked him, had from the first day she arrived in Budapest. He was shrewd and tough but had a sentimental streak that extended to everyone working for him.

"You talked to Joe?" he asked.

"Yes."

"Make sense to you?"

"I guess so. We were close. I was supposed to meet her flight."

He nodded and grunted, rolled his fingertips on the desk. "Were you meeting her for us?"

"No, strictly personal. I didn't know whether she was carrying or not."

"She ever talk to you about what she was doing?"

"A little."

"Nothing about this trip."

"Nothing. She never got specific about any trip she took here. All she ever got into was her meetings with her agency clients like Zoltán Réti."

"He's not here."

"I know. He called me last night from London and left a message on my machine."

"You find it strange he isn't here?"

"As a matter of fact, yes."

"She was supposed to meet with him and a Party big shot about clearing Réti to get the money his books are making in the West."

"How much was *that* going to cost?"

Podgorsky laughed. "Whatever the *papakha* needed to buy one of those condos up on the hill, or to get himself a fancy new car quick."

"Palms are all the same."

"So's the grease and the way it goes on." His face became grim. "We lost a lot, Collette."

"What she was carrying was that important?"

"Yeah."

"What was it?"

"Need-to-know."

"*I* need to know if I'm going to be digging into what led up to her death."

He shook his head. "Not now, Collette. The assignment is clear-cut, no ambiguities. You go home on leave and touch base with everybody in her life. You're grieving, can't believe your good friend is dead. You find out what you can and report it to a case officer at Langley."

"How cynical. I really do care what happened to my friend."

"I'm sure you do. Look, you don't have to do this. It's not in your area, but I'd suggest you think six times before turning it down. Like I said, the stakes are big here."

"Banana Quick?"

He nodded.

"Am I really taking leave?"

"It'll be on the books that way in case somebody wants to snoop. We'll make it up to you later. That's a promise from me."

"When do you want me to start?"

"Leave in the morning."

"I can't. You know I have a meet set up with Horgász."

"That's right. When?"

"Tomorrow night."

Podgorsky thought for a moment before saying, "It's important?"

"I haven't seen him for six weeks. He left word at one of the drops that he had something. It's been set, can't be changed."

"Then do it, leave the next morning."

"All right. Anything else?"

"Yeah. Go easy. Frankly, I tried to veto having you assigned to this. Too close. Good friends usually get in the way. Try to forget who she was and concentrate on business. A briefcase. That's all anybody cares about."

She stood and said, "I really do hate this place, Stan."

"Gay ol' Budapest?" He laughed loudly.

"You know what I mean."

"Sure I do. Everything set for Horgász?"

"I think so. We're using the new safehouse."

"I still don't like that place. I should have stuck to my guns and killed it when it was suggested. Too close to too many other things."

"I'm comfortable with it."

"That's good. You're a trouper, Collette."

"I'm an employee. You said I'll be on leave, which means no official status. That makes it tough."

"No it doesn't. The only thing having status would give you is access to our people. You don't need them. They don't have any answers. They're *looking* for answers."

"I want to retrace Barrie's steps. I'll go to London first."

He shrugged.

"I want to talk to the doctors who did the autopsy."

"Nothing to be gained there, Collette. They used cleared personnel."

"British SIS?"

"Probably."

"How was she killed, Stan?"

"Beats me. Maybe prussic acid if it was the Soviets."

"We use it, too, don't we?"

He ignored the question by going through a slow, elaborate ritual of clipping, wetting, and lighting a cigar. "Forget the British doctors, Collette," he said through a cloud of blue smoke.

"I still want to go to London first."

"Nice this time of year. Not many tourists."

She opened the door, turned, and asked, "How's the typewriter repair business?"

"Slow. They make 'em too good these days. Take care, and keep in touch."

She spent the remainder of the day, much of the night, and all of the next day preparing for her meet with a man, code name Horgász, Hungarian for "Fisherman." He represented Collette Cahill's coup since being in Budapest. Horgász, whose real name was Árpád Hegedüs, was a high-ranking psychologist within the KGB's Hungarian intelligence arm.

■ ■ ■

Cahill had met Árpád Hegedüs the first week she was in Budapest at a reception for a group of psychologists and psychiatrists who'd been invited to present papers to a Hungarian scientific conference. Three Americans were among the invited, including Dr. Jason Tolker. Cahill's dislike for Tolker was instantaneous, although she hadn't thought much about it until Barrie Mayer confided in her that he was the one who'd recruited her into the part-time role of CIA courier. "I didn't like him," Cahill had told her friend, to which Mayer replied, "You're not supposed to like your shrink." Mayer had been his patient for a year before hooking up with Central Intelligence.

Árpád Hegedüs was a nervous little man, forty-six years old, who wore shirt collars that were too tight and wrinkled suits that were too large. He was married and had two children. Most of his training in psychology had been gained at the Neurological and Psychiatric Clinic on Balassa utca, near the Petőfi Bridge linking the Pest and Buda sides of the Grand Boulevard. He'd come to the attention of Soviet authorities after he'd developed and instituted a series of psychological tests for workers in sensitive jobs that were designed to flag personality traits that could lead to dissatisfaction, and perhaps even disloyalty. He was taken to Moscow, where he spent a year at VASA, the Soviet military intelligence school that constitutes a special department of the prestigious Military Diplomatic Academy. His intellect shone there and he was brought into the Sovietskaya Kolonia, the KGB's arm responsible for policing the loyalty of the Soviet's colonies abroad, in this case its Hungarian contingent. That was the job he held when Cahill met him at the reception, although his official position was with the teaching staff of his Hungarian alma mater.

Cahill bumped into him a few more times over the ensuing months. One night, as she ate dinner alone in Vigadó, a downtown brasserie on Vigadó Square, he approached the table and asked if he might join her. They had a pleasant conversation. He spoke good English, loved opera and American jazz, and asked a lot of questions about life in the United States.

Cahill didn't attach any significance to the chance meeting. It was two weeks later that the reason for his approach became obvious.

It was a Saturday morning. She'd gone for a run and ended up at the former Royal Palace on Castle Hill. The palace had been completely destroyed during World War II. Now the restoration was almost completed and the baroque palace had been transformed into a vast museum and cultural complex, including the Hungarian National Gallery.

Cahill often browsed in the museum. It had become, for her, a peaceful refuge.

She was standing in front of a huge medieval ecclesiastical painting when a man came up behind her. "Miss Cahill," he said softly.

"Oh, hello, Mr. Hegedüs. Nice to see you again."

"You like the paintings?"

"Yes, very much."

He stood next to her and gazed up at the art work. "I would like to speak with you," he said.

"Yes, go ahead."

"Not now." He looked around the gallery before saying so softly she almost missed it, "Tomorrow night at eleven, at the St. Mary Magdalene Church in Kapisztrán tėr."

Cahill stared at him.

"In the back, behind the tower. At eleven. I will wait only five minutes. Thank you. Goodbye." Cahill watched him cross the large room, his head swiveling to take in the faces he passed, his short, squat body lumbering from side to side.

She immediately returned to her apartment, showered, changed clothes, and went to Stan Podgorsky's apartment.

"Hi, Lil," Cahill said to his wife when she answered the door. "Sorry to barge in but . . ."

"Just a typical Hungarian Saturday at home," she said. "I'm baking cookies and Stan's reading a clandestine issue of *Playboy*. Like I said, just your run-of-the mill Hungarian weekend."

"I have to talk to you," Cahill told him in the crowded little living room. "I've just had something happen that could be important."

They took a walk and she told him what had transpired in the museum.

"What do you know about him?" he asked.

"Not much, just that he's a psychologist at the hospital and . . ."

"He's also KGB," Podgorsky said.

"You know that for certain?"

"I sure do. Not only is he KGB, he's attached to the SK, the group that keeps tabs on every Russian here. If he's making an overture to us, Collette, he could be playing games—or he could be damn valuable. No, Christ, that's an understatement. He could be gold, pure gold."

"I wonder why he sought me out," she said.

"It doesn't matter. He liked the way you looked, sensed someone he could trust. Who knows? What matters is that we follow up on it and not do anything to scare him off, on the long shot that he might be turned—or *has* turned." He looked at his watch, said, "Look, go on home and pack a small overnight bag. I'll meet you at the embassy in two hours, after I get hold of some others we need on this. Take a circle route to the embassy. Make sure nobody's tailing you. Anybody look interested in your conversation with him at the museum?"

"I really wasn't looking for anyone, but he sure was. He was a wreck."

"Good. And for good reason. Okay, two hours, and be ready for a marathon."

The next thirty-six hours were intense and exhausting. By the time Cahill headed for the square of St. John Capistrano, she'd had a complete briefing on Árpád Hegedüs provided by the station's counterintelligence branch, whose job it was to create biographical files on everyone in Budapest working for the other side.

A gray Russian four-door Zim with two agents was assigned to follow her to the street-meet with Hegedüs.

The rules that had been laid down for her were simple and inviolate.

She was to accept nothing from him, not a scrap of paper, not a matchbook, *nothing*, to avoid being caught in the standard espionage trap of being handed a document from the other side, then immediately put under arrest for spying.

If anything seemed amiss ("*Anything!*" Podgorsky had stressed), she was to terminate the meeting and walk to a corner two blocks away where the car would pick her up. The same rule applied if he wasn't alone.

The small Charter Arms .38-caliber special revolver she carried in her raincoat pocket was to remain there unless absolutely necessary for her physical protection. If that need arose, the two agents in the Zim would back her up with M-3 submachine guns with silencers.

She was to commit to nothing to Hegedüs. He'd called the meet, and it was her role to listen to what he had to say. If he indicated he wished to become a double agent, she was to set another meeting at a safehouse that was about to be discarded. No sense exposing an ongoing location to him until you were sure he was legit.

Cahill lingered in front of a small café down the street from the Gothic church. She was grateful for its presence. Her heart was beating and she drew deep breaths to calm down. Her watch read 10:50. He said he'd wait only five minutes. She couldn't be late.

The gray Zim passed, the agents looking straight ahead but taking her in with their peripheral vision. She walked away from the café and approached the church, still in ruins except for the meticulously restored tower. She had a silly thought—she wished there were fog to shroud the scene and to give it more the atmosphere of spy-meeting-spy. There wasn't; it was a pristine night in Budapest. The moon was nearly full and cast a bright floodlight over the tiny streets and tall church.

She went behind the church, stopped, looked around, saw no one. Maybe he wouldn't show. Podgorsky had raised that possibility. "More times than not they get cold feet," he'd told her. "Or maybe he's been made. He's put his neck way out on a limb even talking to you, Collette, and you may have seen the last of him."

She had mixed emotions. She hoped he wouldn't show up. She hoped he would. After all, that's what her new job with the CIA in Budapest was all about, to find just such a person and to turn him into a successful and productive counterspy against his own superiors. That it had happened so fast, so easily, was unlikely, was . . . "Life is what happens while you're making other plans," her father had always said.

"Miss Cahill."

His voice shocked her. Although she was expecting him, she was not ready for his voice, any voice. She gasped, afraid to turn.

Hegedüs came out of the shadows of the church and stood behind her. She slowly turned. "Mr. Hegedüs," she said in a shaky voice. "You're here."

"*Igen*, I am here, and so are you."

"Yes, I . . . "

"I will be brief. For reasons of my own I wish to help you and your country. I wish to help Hungary, my country, rid itself of our most recent conquerors."

"What sort of help?"

"Information. I understand you are always in need of information."

"That's true," she said. "You realize the risk you take?"

"Of course. I have thought about this for a very long time."

"And what do you want in return? Money?"

"Yes, but that is not my only motivation."

"We'll have to talk about money. I don't have the authority to . . . " She wished she hadn't said it. It was important that he put his complete trust in her. To suggest that he'd have to talk to others wasn't professional.

It didn't seem to deter him. He looked up at the church tower and smiled. "This was a beautiful country, Miss Cahill. Now it is . . . " A deep sigh. "No matter. Here." He pulled two sheets of paper from his raincoat pocket and thrust them at her. Instinctively, she reached for them, then withdrew her hand. His expression was one of puzzlement.

"I don't want anything from you now, Mr. Hegedüs. We'll have to meet again. Is that acceptable to you?"

"Do I have a choice?"

"Yes, you can reconsider your offer and withdraw it."

It was a rueful laugh. "Pilots reach a point in their flight that represents no return. Once they pass it, they are committed to continuing to their final destination—or crashing. It is the same with me."

Cahill pronounced slowly and in a clear voice the address of the safehouse that had been chosen. She told him the date and time: exactly one week from that night, at nine in the evening.

"I shall be there, and I shall bring what I have here to that meeting."

"Good. Again, I must ask whether you understand the potential ramifications of what you're doing?"

"Miss Cahill, I am not a stupid man."

"No, I didn't mean to suggest that. . . . "

"I know you didn't. You are not that kind of person. I could tell that the moment I met you, and that is why it was you I contacted."

"I appreciate that, Mr. Hegedüs, and I look forward to our next meeting. You have the address?"

"Yes, I do. *Viszontlátásra!*" He disappeared into the shadows. Somehow, his simple "Goodbye" was inadequate for Collette.

If the meet went smoothly, she was not to get into the Zim but return to her apartment by public transportation. A half hour after she'd arrived, there was a knock on the door. She opened it. It was Joe Breslin. "Hey, just in the neighborhood and thought I could buy you a drink."

She realized he was there as part of what had gone on at the church. She put on her coat and they went to an outdoor café, where he handed her a note that read, *"Tell me what happened without mentioning names or getting specific. Use a metaphor—baseball, ballet, whatever."*

She recounted the meeting with Hegedüs as Breslin lighted his pipe and used the match to incidentally ignite the small slip of paper he'd handed her. They both watched it turn to ash in an ashtray.

When she was done, he looked at her, smiled his characteristic half-smile, touched her hand. "Excellent," he said. "You look beat. These things don't take a hell of a lot of time, but they drain you. So drain a *hosszúlépés* and I'll take you home. If anyone's tail is on us, they'll think we're having just another typical, torrid, capitalistic affair."

Her laugh caught, became almost a giggle. "After what I've been through, Joe, I think we should make it a *fröccs*."

Two parts wine to one part soda, the reverse of what he'd suggested.

■ ■ ■

Now, two years later, she prepared for another meet with the Fisherman. How many had there been, fifteen, twenty, maybe more? It had gotten easier, of course. She and "her spy" had become good friends. It was supposed to end up that way, according to the handbook on handling agents-in-place. As Árpád Hegedüs's case officer, Cahill was paid to think of everything that might compromise him, threaten him, *anything* that conceivably could jeopardize him and his mission. So many rules she had to remember and remind herself of whenever a situation came up.

Rule One: The agent himself is more important than any given piece of information he might be able to deliver. Always consider the long haul, never the immediate gain.

Rule Two: Never do anything to jog his conscience. Never ask for more than his conscience will allow him to deliver.

Rule Three: Money. Small and steady. A change in basic lifestyle tips off the other side. Make him come to depend upon it. No bonuses for delivering an especially important piece of information, no matter how risky it was to obtain. Among other reasons, don't reveal how important any one piece of information might be.

Rule Four: Be alert to his moods and personal habits. Be his friend. Hear him out. Counsel when it's appropriate, hear his confessions, help him stay out of trouble.

Rule Five: Don't lose him.

This meet had been arranged like all the others. When Hegedüs had something to pass on, he left a red thumbtack in a utility pole around the corner from his home. The pole was checked each day by a Hungarian postman who'd been on the CIA payroll for years. If the tack was there, he called a special number at the American Embassy within ten minutes. The person answering the phone said, "International Wildlife Committee," to which the postman would respond, "I was thinking of going fishing this weekend and wondered about conditions." He would then abruptly hang up. The person who'd taken the call would inform either Stan Podgorsky, Collette Cahill, or the station's technical coordinator and second-in-command, Harold "Red" Sutherland, a hulk of a man with sparse red hair, feet that had broken down years ago beneath his weight, and who was fond of red suspenders and railroad handkerchiefs. Red was an electronics genius, responsible for video and audio eavesdropping for the Budapest station, including an elaborate recording operation in the safehouse where Cahill and Hegedüs met.

It was understood that a meet would take place exactly one week from the day the tack was found, at a predetermined time and place. Cahill had informed Hegedüs at their last get-together of the change in safehouses, which was acceptable to him.

Cahill arrived an hour before Hegedüs. The recording and photographic equipment was tested, and Cahill went over a set of notes she and others at the station had developed. Hegedüs's desk officer back at Langley, Virginia, had transmitted a series of "RQMs," intelligence requirements, that they wanted met from this most recent meet. They all involved the operation known as Banana Quick. Primarily, they needed to know how much the

Soviets knew about it. Cahill had given the requirement to Hegedüs at their last meeting and he'd promised to come up with whatever he could.

When Árpád Hegedüs walked into the room, he chuckled. A table was set with his favorite foods, which had been brought in that afternoon—*libamáj*, goose liver; *rántott gombafejek*, champignon mushroom caps that had been fried in the kitchen by Red Sutherland shortly before Hegedüs's arrival; a plate of cheeses, Pálpusztai, Márványsajt, and a special Hungarian cream cheese with paprika and caraway seeds known as körözött. For dessert there was a heaping platter of *somlói galuska*, small pieces of sponge cake covered with chocolate and whipped cream—they were a passion for Hegedüs. Everything would be washed down with bourbon. He'd been served vodka early in the game, but one night he expressed a preference for American bourbon and Red Sutherland arranged for Langley to ship in a case of Blanton's, the brand Sutherland, a dedicated bourbon drinker, claimed was the best. An hour-long meeting on the subject of which bourbon to sneak into Hungary had been held behind embassy closed doors and, as often happened, it became a project with a name—"Project Abe," referring to Abraham Lincoln's pre-political career as a bourbon distiller.

"You look well, Árpád," Cahill said.

He smiled. "Not nearly as good as you, Collette. You're wearing my favorite outfit." She'd forgotten that at a previous meeting he'd complimented her on the blue and gray dress she had on again this night. She thanked him and motioned toward a small bar in the corner of the room. He went to it, rubbed his hands, and said, "Splendid. I look forward to these evenings for seeing Mr. Blanton almost as much as for seeing you."

"As long as I'm still the most important, the highest proof, you might say" she said. He seemed puzzled; she explained. He grinned and said, "Ah, yes, the proof. The proof is always important." He poured himself a full glass and dropped an ice cube from a silver bucket into it, causing the amber liquid to spill over the sides. He apologized. Cahill ignored him and poured herself an orange juice, almost as rare in Budapest as bourbon.

"Hungry?" she asked.

"*Always*," he answered, his eyes lighting up as if there were candles on the table. He sat and filled a plate. Cahill took a few morsels and sat across from him.

Hegedüs looked around the room, as though suddenly realizing he was in a new place. "I like the other house better," he said.

"It was time to change," Cahill said. "Too long in one place makes everyone nervous."

"Except me."

"Except you. How are things?"

"Good . . . bad." He waved his pudgy hand over his plate. "This will be our last meeting."

Cahill's heart tripped. "Why?" she asked.

"At least for some time. They are talking of sending me to Moscow."

"What for?"

"Who knows how the Russian mind works, what it's for? My family packs now and will leave in three days."

"You won't be with them?"

"Not immediately. It had occurred to me that sending them has other meanings." He answered her eyebrows. "It has been happening to others recently. The family is sent to Russia and the man stays behind expecting to join them but . . . well, he never does." He devoured two of the mushrooms, washed them down with bourbon, put his elbows on the table, and leaned forward. "The Soviets become more paranoid every day here in Hungary."

"About what?"

"About what? About security, about leaks to your people. Having the families in Russia is a way to control certain . . . how shall I say? . . . certain questionable individuals."

"Are you now considered 'questionable'?"

"I didn't think so, but this move of my family and talk of moving me . . . Who knows? Do you mind?" He indicated his empty glass.

"Of course not, but put the ice in first," she said lightly. She'd been growing increasingly concerned about his drinking. Almost the entire bottle had been consumed last time, and he was quite drunk when he left.

He returned to the table and sipped from his fresh drink. "I have news for you, Collette. What did you call your request last time—an RQM?"

"Yes, a requirement. What is the news?"

"They know more than your people perhaps realize."

"About Banana Quick?"

"Yes. That island they've taken has been doing its job. The surveillance equipment on it is their best, and they've recruited native people who have been passing on information about your activities."

The Russians had leased the private island in the British Virgins from its owner, a multimillionaire British real estate developer who was told it was to be used as a rest-and-recreation area for tired, high-ranking Soviet bureaucrats. The U.S. State Department, upon learning of this and after hurried conferences with the CIA, approached him and asked that he reconsider. He wouldn't. The deal went through and the Russians moved in.

A further assessment was made then by State and Central Intelligence. Their conclusion: The Soviets could not move in enough sophisticated equipment and staff in time to effectively monitor Banana Quick, nor had they enough agents in place to build an effective corps of citizen-spies.

"Can you be more specific?" Cahill asked.

"Of course." He pulled papers from his rumpled black suit jacket and handed them to her. She laid them flat on the table and started reading. When she was done with the first page, she looked up at him and allowed a tiny whistle to come through her lips. "They know a lot, don't they?"

"Yes. These dispatches arrived from the island outpost. It was all I felt I could safely take—and bring with me. I return them in the morning. However, I have seen many more and have done my best to commit them to memory. Shall I begin?"

Cahill looked to the wall that concealed the cameras and recorders. Hegedüs knew they were there and often joked about them, but they remained shielded from his view, the sight of such instruments providing neither inspiration nor incentive. She prompted him to start before more of the bourbon disappeared and his memory with it.

He talked, drank, ate, and recalled for three hours. Cahill focused on everything he said, making notes to herself despite knowing every word was being recorded. Transcripts seldom provide nuance. She pushed him for details, kept him going when he seemed ready to fade, complimented, cajoled, stroked, and encouraged.

"Anything else?" she asked once he'd sat back, lighted a cigarette, and allowed a permanent smile of satisfaction to form on his thick lips.

"No, I think that is all." He suddenly raised his index finger and sat up. "No, I am wrong, there is more. The name of a man you know has come up."

"What man? I know him?"

"Yes. The psychiatrist who is involved with your *Company.*"

"You mean Tolker?" She was instantly furious at herself for mentioning the name. Maybe he didn't mean him. If so, she'd given the name of a CIA-connected physician to the other side. It was a relief to hear him say, "Yes, that is the one. Dr. Jason Tolker."

"What about him?"

"I'm not really sure, Collette, but his name was mentioned briefly in connection with one of the dispatches from our island listening post about Banana Quick."

"Was it positive? I mean, were they saying that . . . ?"

"They said nothing specific. It was the tone of the voices, the context in which it was said that led me to believe that Dr. Tolker might be . . . *friendly.*"

"To you. To the Soviets."

"Yes."

Cahill had forgotten about Barrie during the session. Now her image filled the room. She wasn't sure how to respond to what Hegedüs had said, so said nothing.

"I am afraid I am becoming an expensive friend to you and your people, Collette. Look, the bourbon is all but finished."

She resisted mentioning that it always was, said instead, "There's always more to replace it, Árpád. But not to replace you. Tell me, how are things with you personally?"

"I shall miss my family but . . . perhaps this is the time to bring up what is on my mind."

"Go ahead."

"I have been thinking, I have been feeling lately that the time might be approaching for me to consider becoming one of you."

"You are. You know that. . . ." She observed him shaking his head. He was smiling.

"You mean time to defect to our side?"

"Yes."

"I don't know about that, Árpád. As I told you when that subject came up before, it isn't something I deal with."

"But you said you would talk to those in charge about the possibility."

"Yes, I did." She didn't want to tell him that the discussion with Podgorsky and with two people from Langley had resulted in a flat denial. Their attitude was that Árpád Hegedüs was valuable to them as long as he remained ensconced in the Hungarian and Soviet hierarchy and could provide information from the inner councils. As a defector, he was useless. Of course, if it meant saving him in the event he'd been uncovered by his superiors, that would create a different scenario; but Cahill had been instructed in no uncertain terms that she was to do everything in her power to dissuade him from such a move, and to foster his continued services as an agent.

"It was not met with enthusiasm, I take it," he said.

"It isn't that, Árpád, it's just that—"

"That I am worth more where I am."

She drew a breath and fell back in her chair. It was naive of her to think he wouldn't know exactly the reason without being told. He worked for an organization, the KGB, that played by the same rules, operated from the same set of needs and intelligence philosophies.

"Don't look worried, Collette. I do understand. And I

intend to continue functioning as I have. But, if the need arises, it would be comforting to me and my family to know that the possibility was there."

"I appreciate your understanding, Árpád, and I shall bring it up with my people again."

"I am grateful. Well, what do you say, 'One for the road'? I shall have one, and then the road, and then home."

"I'll join you."

They sat in silence at the table and sipped from their drinks. His smile was gone; a sadness that pulled down the flesh of his face had replaced it.

"You're more upset about your family going to Moscow than you want to admit," she said.

He nodded, eyes on his glass. He grunted, looked up, and said, "I have never told you about my family, about my dear children."

Collette smiled. "No, you haven't, except that your daughter is very beautiful and sweet, and that your son is a fine boy."

There was a flicker of a smile, then gloom again. "My son is a genius, a very bright boy. He is sensitive and loves artistic things." He leaned forward and spoke with renewed animation. "You should see how the boy draws and paints, Collette. Beauty, always such beauty, and the poetry he writes touches me so deeply."

"You must be very proud," Collette said.

"Proud? Yes. And concerned for his future."

"Because—"

"Because in Russia, he will have little chance to develop his talents. For the girl, my daughter, it is not so bad. She will marry because she is pretty. For him . . ." He shook his head and finished his drink.

Cahill was tempted to come around and hug him. Any initial thoughts of the chauvinistic attitude he'd expressed were tempered by her understanding of the society in which he, and his family, functioned.

She thought, then said, "It would be better for your son here in Hungary, wouldn't it?"

"Yes, there is more freedom here, but who knows when that will end? America would be best. I am not a religious man, Collette, but I sometimes pray to someone that my son will be allowed to grow up in America."

"As I said before, Árpád, I'll try to . . ."

He wanted to continue, and did. "When I first came to you and offered my services, I talked about how my beloved Hungary had been destroyed by the Soviets. I talked of disgust with their system and ways, of how this wonderful country has been forevermore changed by them." He sighed deeply, sat back, and nodded in agreement with whatever he was thinking at the moment. "I was not completely honest, Collette. I came to you because I wanted to find a way to see my family—my son—reach America. Instead, he goes to Moscow."

Cahill stood. "Árpád, I will make every effort to help bring that about. No promises, but a decent effort."

He stood, too, and extended his hand. She took it. "Thank you, Collette. I know you will do what you say. I have been here a long time. I must go."

He was paid and she escorted him to the door. She said, "Árpád, be careful. Don't take risks. Please."

"Of course not." He looked back to the center of the room. "The tape and camera are off?"

"I assume they are. The main show is over."

He motioned her into the hall and spoke in a whisper, so close to her ear that his lips touched it. "I am in love."

"In . . . love?"

"I have met a wonderful woman recently and . . . "

"I don't think that's a good idea," Cahill said.

"Good idea, bad idea, it has happened. She is very beautiful and we have commenced . . . an affair."

Collette wasn't sure what to say, except, "What about your family, Árpád? You say you love them so much and . . . "

His grin was sheepish, a little boy caught in a quandary. His eyes averted her and he shuffled his feet. Then he looked at her and said, "There are different forms of love, Collette. Surely, that reality is not a Socialist aberration." He cocked his head and waited for a response.

Cahill said, "We should meet again soon and discuss this. In the meantime, take extra care. Discuss what you're doing with no one. No one, Árpád."

"With her?" His laugh was guttural. "We have so little time together that discussion is the last thing on our minds. *Köszönöm*, Collette."

"Thank *you*, Árpád."

"Until the next time a tack appears in the pole. *Viszontlátásra!*"

▪ ▪ ▪

Rule Six: Do anything you can to keep your agent from having an affair—at least with anyone else.

CHAPTER 5

Collette Cahill got off a Malev flight in London, went to a phone booth, and dialed a number. A woman answered, "Eleven, Cadogan Gardens."

"My name is Collette Cahill. I was a close friend of Barrie Mayer."

"Oh, yes, what a tragedy. I'm so sorry."

"Yes, we were all terribly shocked. I've just arrived in London for a few days' vacation and wondered if you had any available rooms?"

"Yes, we do, a few suites as a matter of fact. Oh, goodness."

"What?"

"Number 27 is available. It was Miss Mayer's favorite."

"Yes, that's right, she always talked about it. That would be fine with me."

"You wouldn't mind . . . ?"

"Staying where she'd stayed? No, not at all. I'll be there within the hour."

She spent the first hour sitting in the Victorian living room and imagining what Barrie had done the last day and night of her life while in London. Had she watched television, gone across to the private park, read, called friends, napped, walked the pretty, quiet streets of Chelsea and Belgravia, shopped for relatives back home? It eventually became too sad an exercise. She went downstairs to the main drawing room and flipped through an array of magazines and newspapers, then caught the attention of one of the hall porters. "Yes, ma'am?" he said.

"I was a very good friend of Miss Mayer, the lady who'd stayed in Number 27 and who recently died."

"Poor Miss Mayer. She was my one of my favorite guests whenever she was here, a real lady. We're all terribly sad at what happened."

"I was wondering whether she did anything special the day she arrived, the day before she died?"

"Special? No, not really. I brought her tea at three . . . let me see, yes, I'm quite certain it was three o'clock the afternoon she arrived. We made a reservation for her that evening at the Dorchester for dinner."

"For how many people?"

"Two. Yes, for two. I can check."

"No, that's all right. Did she take a taxi, or did someone pick her up?"

"She took the limousine."

"*The* limousine?"

"Ours. It's available to our guests twenty-four hours a day."

"Did the limousine pick her up at the Dorchester?"

"I don't know, madam. I wasn't here that evening when she returned, but I can ask."

"Would you mind?"

"Of course not."

He returned a few minutes later and said, "To the best

of recollection, Miss Mayer returned a little before ten that evening. She arrived by taxi."

"Alone?"

He looked at the floor. "I'm not sure, madam, whether that would be discreet to comment upon."

Cahill smiled. "I'm not snooping. It's just that we were such good friends and her mother back in the States asked me to find out what I could about her daughter's last hours."

"Of course. I understand. Let me ask."

He returned again and said, "She was alone. She announced she was going straightaway to bed and left an early call. That was the morning she was leaving for Hungary, I believe."

"Yes, that's right, to Budapest. Tell me, didn't the police come and ask questions about her?"

"Not to my knowledge. They came and took her things from the room and . . ."

"Who's *they*?"

"Friends, business colleagues, I think. You'd have to ask the manager about that. They spoke to her. They took everything and were gone within ten minutes. The other one . . . there were three chaps . . . he stayed behind for at least an hour. I remember he said he wanted to sit where Miss Mayer had spent her last hours and think. Poor chap, I felt terrible for him."

"Did any of them have names?"

"I feel like I'm getting a proper interrogation," he said, not angrily but with enough of an edge to cause Cahill to back off. She smiled. "I guess so many people knew and loved her that we're not behaving in our usual manner. Sorry, I didn't mean to ask so many questions of you. I'll check with the manager a little later."

He returned the smile. "No problem, madam. I understand. Ask me anything you wish."

"Oh, I think I've asked enough. Did they have names, the men who came here and took her things?"

"Not that I recall. They might have muttered something or other but . . . Yes, one of them said he was a business associate of Miss Mayer. I believe he said his name was Mr. Hubler."

"David Hubler?"

"I don't think he used a first name, madam."

"What did he look like? Was he fairly short, dark, lots of black curly hair, handsome?"

"That doesn't quite fit my memory of him, madam. Tall and sandy would be more like it."

Cahill sighed and said, "Well, thank you so much. I think I'll go back upstairs and take a nap."

"May I bring you anything? Tea at three?"

Like Barrie, Cahill thought. "No, make it four," she said.

"Yes, madam."

She called David Hubler a few minutes before tea was scheduled to arrive. It was almost eleven in the morning in Washington. "David, Collette Cahill."

"Hi, Collette."

"I'm calling from London, David. I'm staying in the same hotel Barrie always used."

"Eleven, Cadogan. What are you doing there?"

"Trying to sort out my mind about what happened. I took a vacation and am heading home, but thought I'd stop here on the way."

There was silence.

"David?"

"Yeah, sorry. I was just thinking about Barrie. Unbelievable."

"Have you been here in London since she died?"

"Me? No. Why?"

"Someone at the hotel thought you might have been the one who picked up her things from the room."

"Not me, Collette."

"Were any of her things sent back to you at the office?"

"Just her briefcase."

"Her briefcase. Was it the one she usually carried?"

"Sure. Why?"

"Oh, nothing. What was in it?"

"Papers, a couple of manuscripts. Why are you asking?"

"I don't know, David. My mind just hasn't functioned since you called me with the news. What's happening back there? The agency must be in chaos."

"Sort of, although not as bad as you might think. Barrie was incredible, Collette, but you know that. She left everything in perfect order, right down to the last detail. You know what she did for me?"

"What?"

"She had me in her will. She left me insurance money, one of those key-man policies. In effect, she left me the agency."

Cahill was surprised, enough so that she wasn't quite sure what to say. He filled the gap with, "I don't mean she left it all to me, Collette. Her mother benefits from it, but she structured things so that I'm to run it for a minimum of five years and share in the profits. I was flabbergasted."

"That was wonderful of her."

"Typical of her is more like it. When will you be back in Washington?"

"A day or two. I'll stop by."

"Please do, Collette. Let's have lunch or dinner. There's a lot we can talk about."

"I'd like that. By the way, do you have any idea who she might have seen here in London before . . . before it happened?"

"Sure, Mark Hotchkiss. They were scheduled for dinner the night she arrived."

"Who's he?"

"A British literary agent Barrie liked. Why, I don't know. I think he's a swine and I told her so but, for some reason, she kept talking to him about linking up. With all Barrie's brights, Collette, there were certain people who could con her, and Hotchkiss is one."

"Know how I can reach him while I'm here?"

"Sure." He gave her an address and phone number. "But watch out for him, Collette. Remember, I said swine, *cochon*."

"Thanks, David. See you soon."

She replaced the phone in its cradle as the porter knocked. She opened the door. He placed the tea tray on a coffee table and backed out of the suite, leaving her sitting in a gold wingback chair. She wore a light blue robe; shafts of late-afternoon sunlight sliced through gaps in the white curtains and across the worn Oriental rug that took up the center of the room. One beam of light striped her bare foot and she thought of Barrie, who was always so proud of her feet, gently arched and with long, slender toes that were perfectly sized in relation to each other. Cahill looked at her own foot, short and stubby, and smiled, then laughed. "God, we were different," she said aloud as she poured her tea and smeared clotted cream and black cherry jam over a piece of scone.

She caught Mark Hotchkiss just as he was leaving his office, introduced herself, and asked if he were free for dinner.

"Afraid not, Miss Cahill."

"Breakfast?"

"You say you're Barrie's friend?"

"Yes, we were best friends."

"She never mentioned you."

"Were you that friendly that she would have?"

His laugh was forced. He said, "I suppose we could meet for something in the morning. You have a decent place near you on Sloane Street, right around the corner. It's a café in back of the General Trading Company. Nine?"

"Fine. See you then."

"Miss Cahill."

"Yes?"

"You do know that Barrie and I had entered into a partnership arrangement just prior to her death?"

"No, I didn't know that, but I was aware it was being discussed. Why do you bring it up now?"

"Why not bring it up *now*?"

"No reason. You can tell me all about it in the morning. I look forward to it."

"Yes. Well, cheerio. Pleasant evening. Enjoy London. The theater season is quite good this year."

She hung up agreeing with David Hubler. She didn't like Hotchkiss, and wondered what aspect of him had seduced Barrie into entering a "partnership agreement," if that claim were true.

She called downstairs and asked if they could get her tickets to a show. Which one? "It doesn't matter," Cahill said, "something happy."

The curtain went up on *Noises Off* at seven-thirty, and by the time the British farce was over, Cahill's sides hurt from laughing, and the unpleasant reason for her trip had been forgotten, at least for the duration of the show. She was hungry, had a light dinner at the Neal Street Restaurant, and returned to the hotel. A porter brought Cognac and ice to her room and she sat quietly and sipped it until her eyes began to close. She went to bed, aware as she fell asleep of the absolute quiet of this street and this hotel, as quiet as the dead.

CHAPTER 6

Cahill arrived on time at the General Trading Company, whose coat of arms heralded the fact that it had provided goods to at least one royal household. She took a table in the rear outdoor area. The morning had dawned sunny and mild. A raincoat over a heather tweed suit made her perfectly comfortable.

She passed the time with a cup of coffee and watching tiny birds make swooping sorties on uncovered bowls of brown sugar cubes on the tables. She glanced at her watch; Hotchkiss was already twenty minutes late. She'd give it ten more minutes. At precisely nine-thirty, he came through the store and stepped onto the terrace. He was tall and angular. His head was bald on top, but he'd combed back long hair on the sides, giving him the startling appearance of—not swine, David, she thought, duck—he looked like a duck's rear end. He wore a double-breasted blue blazer with a crest on its pocket, gray slacks, a pair of tan Clark's desert boots, a pale blue shirt with white collar, and a maroon silk tie. He carried a battered and bulging leather briefcase beneath his arm. A similarly well-worn trench coat was slung over his shoulder.

"Miss Cahill," he said with energy. He smiled and extended his hand, his teeth markedly yellow, and she noticed immediately that his fingernails were too long and needed cleaning.

"Mr. Hotchkiss," she said, taking his hand with her fingertips.

"Sorry I'm late but traffic is bastardly this hour. You've had coffee. Good."

Cahill stifled a smile and watched him ease into a white metal chair with yellow cushions. "Not chilly?" he asked. "Better inside?"

"Oh, no, I think it's lovely out here."

"As you wish." He made an elaborate gesture at one of the young waitresses, who came to the table and took their order for coffee and pastry. When she'd gone, he sat back, formed a tent beneath his chin with his fingers, and said, "Well, now, we're obviously here to discuss Barrie Mayer, poor dear, may she rest in peace. You were friends, you say?"

"Yes, close friends."

"She never mentioned you, but I suppose someone like Barrie had so many friends or, at least, acquaintances."

"We were close *friends*," Cahill said, not enjoying his inference.

"Yes, of course. Now, what was it you wished to discuss with me?"

"Your relationship with Barrie, what she did the night before she died, anything that might help me understand."

"Understand? Understand *what*? The poor woman dropped dead of a heart attack, coronary thrombosis, premature certainly but Lord knows what life has in store for any of us."

Cahill had to remind herself of her "official" role in looking into Mayer's life. She was a grieving friend, not an investigator, and her approach would have to soften to reflect that. She said, "I'm actually as interested for Barrie's mother's sake as I am for my own. We've been in contact and she asked me to find out anything that would . . . well, comfort her. I'm on my way to Washington now to see her."

"What do you do for a living, Miss Cahill? I know that's hardly a British question, more what you Americans seem always to ask at first meeting, but I am curious."

"I work for the United States Embassy in Budapest."

"Budapest! I've never been. Is it as gray and grim as we hear?"

"Not at all. It's a lovely city."

"With all those soldiers and red stars."

"They fade into the background after a while. You had dinner with Barrie the night before she died."

"Indeed, at the Dorchester. Despite the Arabs, it still has London's finest chef."

"I wouldn't know."

"You must let me take you. Tonight?"

"I can't, but thank you. What mood was Barrie in that night? What did she say, do? Did she seem sick?"

"She was in the pink of health, Miss Cahill. May I call you Collette? I'm Mark, of course."

"Of course." She laughed. "Yes, call me Collette. You say she seemed healthy. Was she happy?"

"Irrepressibly so. I mean, after all, we forged a partnership that evening. She was bubbling."

"You mentioned on the phone that you'd become partners. I spoke with David Hubler in Barrie's Washington office. He had no idea it had gone that far."

"David Hubler. I dislike being indiscreet but I must admit Mr. Hubler is not my favorite person. Frankly, I thought he was a stone about Barrie's neck, and I told her so."

"I like David. I always understood from Barrie that she was extremely fond of him, and had great professional respect for him."

"Besides being a consummate businesswoman, Barrie Mayer was also gullible."

Cahill thought of Hubler saying the same thing. She said to Hotchkiss, "Mark, are you aware of Barrie's will and what it contains relative to David Hubler?"

"No." He laughed loudly, revealing the yellowed teeth. "Oh, you mean that nonsense about ensuring that Hubler runs the Washington office if she should die. A bone, that's all, a bone tossed at him. Now that the agency . . . *all of it* . . . passes to me, the question of Mr. Hubler's future has little to do with a piece of worthless paper."

"Why?"

"Because the agreement Barrie and I entered into takes precedence over what was decreed before." He smiled smugly and formed the finger tent again. The waitress delivered their coffee and pastry and Hotchkiss held up his cup. "To the memory of a lovely, talented, and beautiful woman, Barrie Mayer, and to you, Miss Collette Cahill, her dear friend." He sipped his coffee, then asked, "Are you truly not free this evening? The Dorchester has a very nice dance band and, as I said, the chef is without parallel in London these days of mediocre food. Sure?" He cocked his head and elevated one bushy eyebrow.

"Sure, but thank you. You signed a paper with Barrie that night?"

"Yes."

"May I . . . I know this is none of my business, but . . ."

"I'm afraid it would be inappropriate at this time for me to show it to you. Are you doubting me?"

"Not at all. Again, it's just a matter of wanting to know *everything* about her just before she died. Did you go to the airport with her the next morning?"

"No."

"I just thought . . ."

"I dropped Barrie back at the hotel. That was the last time I saw her."

"In a taxi?"

"Yes. My goodness, I'm beginning to feel as though you might have an interest beyond that of a close friend."

Cahill grinned. "The hall porter at the hotel said the same thing. Forgive me. Too many years of asking stranded American tourists where they might have lost their passports."

"Is that what you do at the embassy?"

"Among other things. Well, Mark, this was extremely pleasant."

"And informative, I trust. I'll be coming to Washington soon to tidy up things at the agency. Do you know where you'll be staying?"

"With my mother. She lives outside the city."

"Splendid. I shall call you there."

"Why not contact me through David Hubler? I'll be spending considerable time with him."

"Oh, I think I've placed one foot in one very large mouth."

"Not at all." She stood. "Thank you."

He stood, too, and accepted her hand. They both looked down at the check the waitress had placed on the table. "My treat," Cahill said, knowing it was what he wanted her to say.

"Oh, no, that would be . . ."

"Please. I initiated this. Perhaps I'll see you in Washington."

"I certainly hope so."

Hotchkiss left. Cahill stopped on her way through the large store to buy her mother a set of fancy placemats, and a book for her nephew. She walked around the corner to the hotel, where she made a series of calls to the physicians who'd performed the autopsy on Barrie and whose names she'd gotten from Red Sutherland before leaving Budapest. The only one she reached was a Dr. Willard Hymes. She introduced herself as Barrie Mayer's closest friend and asked if she could arrange to meet with him.

"Whatever for?" he asked. He sounded young.

"Just to put my mind, and her mother's mind, at rest."

"Well, Miss Cahill, you know I'm not at liberty to discuss autopsy findings except with designated authorities."

Pickle Factory authorities, Cahill thought. She said, "I understand that, Dr. Hymes, but it wouldn't breach any confidences if you were to tell me the circumstances of the autopsy, your informal, off-the-record reactions to her, what she looked like, things like that."

"No, Miss Cahill, that would be quite out of the question. Thank you for calling."

Cahill said quickly, "I was concerned about the glass that was found in her face."

"Pardon?"

Cahill continued. She'd read up on past cases in which prussic acid had been used to "terminate" agents on both sides. One of the telltale signs was tiny slivers of glass blown into a victim's face along with the acid. "Dr. Hymes, there was glass in her face."

She was guessing, but had drawn blood. He made a few false starts before getting out, "Who told you about the glass?"

That was all she needed, wanted. She said, "A mutual friend who'd been at the airport and saw her just after she died."

"I didn't know there was a friend with her."

"Were you at the airport?"

"No. She was brought here to clinic and . . ."

"Dr. Hymes, I really appreciate the chance to talk with you. You've been very generous with your time and I know Barrie's mother will appreciate it."

She hung up, sat at a small desk near the French windows, and wrote a list of names on a piece of the hotel's embossed buff stationery:

KNEW BARRIE CARRIED FOR THE CIA

Dr. Jason Tolker
Stanley Podgorsky
Red Sutherland
Collette Cahill
Langley Desk Officer
Dr. Willard Hymes
Mark Hotchkiss ???
David Hubler ???
Barrie's mother ???
Eric Edwards ???

Zoltán Réti ???
KGB ???
Others ??? Other boyfriends—Others at literary agency—Others at Budapest station—The World.

She squinted at what she'd written, tore the paper into tiny pieces and ignited them in an ashtray. She called downstairs and told the manager on duty that she'd be leaving the following morning.

"I hope you've enjoyed your stay," the manager said.

"Oh, yes, very much," Cahill said. "It's every bit as lovely as Miss Mayer always said it was."

CHAPTER 7

TORTOLA, BRITISH VIRGIN ISLANDS

The twin-engine turboprop Air BVI plane from San Juan touched down on Beef Island and taxied to the small terminal. Thirty passengers deplaned, including Robert Brewster and his wife, Helen. Both looked tired and wilted. There had been a delay in San Juan, and the Air BVI flight had been hot; tiny fans installed in the open overhead racks had managed only to stir the warm, humid cabin air.

The Brewsters passed through passport control and Customs, then went to a yellow Mercedes parked behind the terminal. Helen Brewster got in. Her husband said to the native driver, "Just a few minutes." He went to a pay phone, took out a slip of paper, and dialed the number on it. "I'm calling Eric Edwards," he told the woman who answered. "He's dining with you tonight."

A few minutes later, Edwards came on the line.

"Eric, it's Bob Brewster."

"Hello, Bob. Just get in?"

"Yes."

"Pleasant trip?"

"Not especially. Helen isn't feeling well and I'm beat. The heat."

"Well, a nice week's vacation down here will straighten you out."

"I'm sure it will. We're looking forward to seeing you again."

"Same here. We must get together."

"I was thinking we could catch up for a drink this evening. We'll go to the hotel and freshen up and . . ."

"I'm tied up this evening, Bob. How about tomorrow? I have a free day. We'll take a cruise, my treat."

Brewster didn't bother, nor did he have the energy to argue. He said, "I can't speak for Helen. Call me in the morning. We're staying at Prospect Reef."

"Give my best to the manager there," Edwards said. "He's a friend, might even buy you a welcoming drink."

"I'll do that. Call me at eight."

"It'll have to be later. I'm in for a long evening."

"Eric."

"Yes?"

"Life has become very complicated lately."

"Has it? That must be why you and Helen are so tired. Simplicity is far less fatiguing. We'll talk about it tomorrow."

Eric Edwards returned to a candlelit table in the Sugar Mill Restaurant, part of a small and exclusive resort complex on Apple Bay. Across from him sat a tall, stately blond woman of about thirty-five who wore a low-cut white silk dress. Because her skin was deeply tanned, it contrasted sharply with the white dress, like teeth against the natives' dark skin. It had taken her many hours in the sun to become that color. Her skin, especially the tops of her breasts, hinted at the leathery texture it would turn to by sixty.

Her nails were long and painted an iridescent pink. Her fingers held large rings, and ten slender gold bracelets covered each wrist.

Edwards was dressed in white duck slacks, white loafers sans socks, and a crimson shirt worn open to his navel. His hair—sun-bleached blond with gray at the temples so perfectly blended that it might have come from a Hollywood makeup expert—swirled casually over his forehead, ears, and neck. The features on his tanned face were fine and angular, yet with enough coarseness to keep him from being pretty. There was sufficient worldly weariness and booze in his gray eyes to give them substance and meaning.

Eric Edwards was a handsome man, no matter what the criterion. Ask Morgana Wilson who sat across from him. Someone had, recently. "He's the most sensuous, appealing male animal I've ever known," she told a friend, "and I've known a few in my day."

Edwards smiled up at the waiter as he removed bowls that had contained curried banana soup, a house specialty. Edwards ordered another rum punch, reached across the table, and ran his fingers over the top of Morgana's hand. "You usually look beautiful. Tonight, you look spectacular," he said.

She was used to such compliments and simply said, "Thank you, darling."

They said little as they enjoyed their entrees—pasta with lime cream and red caviar, and grilled fish with fennel butter. There was little to say. Their purpose was not to exchange thoughts, only to establish an atmosphere conducive to the mating game. It wasn't new to them. They'd spent a number of intimate evenings together over the past four or five years.

She'd met Edwards during a trip to the BVI with her husband, a successful New York divorce lawyer. They'd chartered one of Edwards's yachts for an overnight cruise. Her husband returned to New York after only a few days in the islands, leaving Morgana behind to soak up a few additional days of sun. She spent them with Edwards on one of his yachts.

Six months afterward, she was divorced, and Edwards was cited as having been caught in *particeps crimini*—a corespondent to the action. "Ridiculous," he'd told her. "Your marriage was damn near over anyway." Which was true, although his powerful attraction had certainly played a role.

They saw each other no more than three or four times a year, always when she visited him in the BVI. As far as she knew, he never came to New York. In fact, he never called her when he was there. There were others to contact on those trips.

"Ready?" he asked, when she'd finished the soursop fruit ice cream and coffee.

"Always," she said.

The alarm clock next to Edwards's bed buzzed them awake at six the next morning. Morgana sat up, folded her arms across her bountiful bare breasts, and pouted. "It's too early," she said.

"Sorry, love, but I've got a charter today. I have to provision it and take care of some other things before my guests arrive." His voice was thick with sleep, and raspy from too many cigarettes.

"Will you be back tonight?"

"I think so, although you never know. Sometimes they

fall in love with the boat and decide to stay out overnight."

"Or fall in love with you. Can I come?"

"No." He got out of bed and crossed the large bedroom, tripping over her discarded clothing on the floor. She watched him as he stood before one of two large windows with curved tops, the first rays of sunrise casting interesting patterns over his long, lean naked body.

"I have to leave tomorrow," she said in a little girl's voice that always grated on him.

"Yes, I know. I'll miss you."

"Will you?" She joined him at the window and they looked down from his hilltop villa to Road Harbor, the site of his chartering operation. Edwards Yacht Charters was a small company compared to the Moorings, the reigning giant of island chartering, but it had managed to do well, thanks to some innovative PR a one-man agency in New York had conceived and implemented for it. Edwards currently owned three yachts—a Morgan 46, a Gulfstar 60, and a recently purchased, Frers-designed 43-foot sloop. Finding customers in season for them wasn't difficult. Finding experienced, trustworthy captains and mates was.

She turned him so they faced and wrapped her arms about his body. She was tall; the top of her head reached his nose, and he was over six feet. The warmth of her naked body, and the damp, sweet smell of sex in her hair radiated powerfully in surges through him. "I really have to go," he said.

"So do I. I'll be back in a flash," she said, heading for the stone bathroom that was open to the sky. When she returned, he was back in bed and ready for her.

■ ■ ■

Edwards's mechanic, a skinny Tortolian named Walter who was capable of fixing anything, was on board when Edwards arrived. Native *kareso* music blared from a large portable cassette recorder. As Edwards poked his head down into the engine room, Walter said, "*Laam,* I work on this engine all night long."

Edwards laughed and mimicked him. "*Laam,* I really don't care, and I'm not paying you extra. How about that, my conniving friend?"

Walter laughed and closed a cover over the engine. "How about the boat don't run so good today, huh? How about that, my rich boss?"

"*Laam,* or Lord, or whatever it is you say, don't do that to me, and turn down the bloody radio."

The good-natured banter was standard. Edwards knew that Walter would turn himself inside out to please him, and Walter knew that Edwards appreciated him, and would slip him extra pay.

Edwards had called Robert Brewster and arranged to meet him at the dock at ten. Brewster arrived wearing madras Bermuda shorts, a white button-down shirt, high-top white sneakers, and black ankle socks. He carried a canvas flight bag. His legs were white; this would be the first exposure to sunlight they'd received all year.

"No snorkeling equipment today, huh?" Walter said to Edwards after observing the new arrival.

"No, not today," Edwards said. "Where's Jackie?"

"I see her at the coffee shop. She be down." Jackie was a native girl Edwards sometimes used to crew smaller charters. She was willing, energetic, a good sailor, and almost totally deaf. They communicated through a pidgin sign language they'd developed. She arrived a few minutes later and Edwards introduced her to Brewster, who seemed distinctly uncomfortable standing on the deck. "She doesn't hear anything," Edwards said. "If her father only owned a liquor store I'd be tempted to . . ."

"Could we get on with it?" Brewster said. "I want to get back to Helen."

"Sure. She still under the weather?"

"Yes. The heat."

"I like heat," said Edwards. "It makes you sweat—for the right reasons. Let's get going."

Fifteen minutes later, after they'd cleared the channel, Edwards hoisted sail with Jackie's help. Once everything was trimmed, he turned to Brewster, who sat next to him at the helm, and said, "What's up? What did you mean things are getting complicated?"

Brewster smiled at Jackie as she delivered a steaming cup of coffee from the galley. Edwards shook his head when she offered one to him and told her with his hands that he and his guest needed time to be alone. She nodded, grinned at Brewster, and disappeared down the galley ladder.

Brewster tasted his coffee, made a face, and said, "Too hot and too strong, Eric . . . and I don't intend to say it reflects you. All right, what's going on down here?"

"With what?"

"You know what I mean. With Banana Quick."

"Oh, *that.*" He laughed and turned a winch behind him to take up slack in a sail. "As far as I'm concerned, everything's just wonderful with Banana Quick. You hear otherwise?"

"It isn't so much what I hear, Eric, it's more a matter of what's blatantly visible. The death of Miss Mayer has a lot of people upset."

"None more than me. We were close."

"Everyone knows that, and that's exactly what has people back at Langley wondering."

"Wondering about what? How she was in bed?"

Brewster shook his head and shifted on his seat so that his back was to Edwards. He said over the gentle rush of wind and whoosh of water against the keel, "Your cuteness, Eric, doesn't play well these days."

Edwards had to lean close to him to hear. Brewster suddenly turned and said into his face, "What was Barrie Mayer carrying to Budapest?"

Edwards leaned back and frowned. "How the hell would I know?"

"It's the opinion at Langley, Eric, that you damn well might know. She'd been down here to see you just before she died, hadn't she?"

Edwards shrugged. "A couple of days, something like that."

"One week exactly. Would you like her itinerary?"

"Got videos of us making love, too?"

Brewster ignored him. "And then *you* disappeared."

"Disappeared where?"

"You tell me. London?"

"As a matter of fact I did pop over there for a day. I had a . . ." He smiled. "I had an appointment."

"With Barrie Mayer?"

"No. She didn't know I was there."

"That's surprising."

"Why?"

"It's our understanding that you had become serious."

"You understand wrong. We were friends, close friends, and lovers. End of story."

Brewster chewed his cheek and said, "I don't want to be the rude guest, Eric, but you'd better listen to what I have to say. There is considerable concern that Banana Quick might have been compromised by Barrie Mayer, with your help."

"That's crap." Edwards pointed toward the private island on which the Russians had established their supposed R & R facility. "Want to stop in and ask them what's going on?"

Brewster moved to the side of the yacht and peered at the island. Edwards handed him a pair of binoculars. "Don't worry," he said, "they're used to me looking down their throats. See all that rigging on the roof? They can probably hear us better than we can hear each other." He laughed. "This game gets more ridiculous every day."

"Only for people like you, Eric." Brewster held up the binoculars and watched the island slip past. He lowered them, turned, and said, "They want you back in Washington."

"What for?"

"For . . . conversation."

"Can't do it. This is the busy season down here, Bob. How would it look if I . . . ?"

"The end of the week, and don't give me 'busy season' dialogue, Eric. You're here because you were put here. This wonderful boat of yours, and the others, are all compliments of your employer. You're to be back by the end of the week. In the meantime, they want us . . . you and I . . . to spend a little time together going over things."

"What things?"

"What's been going on in your life lately, the status of your mission here, the people you've been seeing . . ."

"Like Barrie Mayer?"

"Among others."

"How come they sent you down, Bob? You're a desk

jockey . . . what's it called, employee evaluation or some nonsense like that?"

"Helen and I decided to come here on vacation and they thought—"

"No, they thought you and Helen should come here on vacation and, while you're here, have these little talks. More accurate?"

"It doesn't matter. The fact is that I'm here, they want, and you are expected to give. What do you think, Eric—that the Company set you up here in the British Virgin Islands because it likes you, felt it owed you something? You pulled off what I consider the biggest coup . . . no, let's call it what it is, the biggest scam anyone has ever pulled on the agency."

Edwards's laugh was more forced this time.

"What did they put up to get you started, Eric, a half a million, three quarters of a million?"

"Somewhere around there."

"It hasn't been cost-effective."

"Cost-effective?" Edwards guffawed. "Name me one agency front that's cost-effective. Besides, how do you measure the return?"

Brewster stared straight ahead.

"Whose idea was it to use the BVI as headquarters for Banana Quick?" He didn't wait for Brewster's reply. "Some genius up there at Langley decides to direct an Eastern European operation from down here. Talk to me about cost-effective. The point is that once that decision was made, there had to be a surveillance unit in place, and that's me."

"You were here before Banana Quick."

"Sure, but I have to figure it was already in the planning stages when the deal was made to send me here. What was the original reason, to make sure that these idyllic islands weren't infiltrated by the bad guys? I had to laugh at that, Bob. What they really wanted was to keep tabs on our British cousins."

"You talk too much, Eric. That's something else that has them worried. You operate too loose, get close to too many people, drink too much. . . ."

"What the hell have they appointed you, Company cleric? I do my job and I do it well. I did twelve years of dirty work while you guys basked in air conditioning at Langley, and I keep doing my job. Tell them that."

"Tell them yourself at the end of the week."

Edwards looked up into a scrim of pristine blue sky, against which puffs of white clouds quickly moved across their bow. "You had enough?" he asked.

"I was just beginning to enjoy it," Brewster answered.

"I'm getting seasick," Edwards said.

"Want a Dramamine? I took one at breakfast."

"You're getting sunburned, Bob."

"Look at you, a prime candidate for skin cancer." The two men stared at each other before Edwards said, "Tell me about Barrie Mayer."

"What's to tell? She's dead."

"Who?"

"Mother Nature. A clogged artery to the heart, blood flow ceases, the heart cries out for help, doesn't get it, and stops pumping."

Edwards smiled. Jackie came up from the galley and gestured. Did they need anything? Edwards said to Brewster, "You hungry? I stocked a few things."

"Sure. Whatever you have."

"Lunch," Edwards said to the slender native girl, using his hands. "And bring the Thermos." He said to Brewster,

"It's full of rum punch. We can get drunk together and get candid."

"Too early for me."

"I've been up a while. Barrie Mayer, Bob. Why did you ask me what she was carrying? Her principal's the one to ask. It's still that shrink, Tolker."

"That bothers me."

"What bothers you?"

"That you know who her principal was. What else did she tell you?"

"Damn little. She never said a word about signing on as a courier until . . ."

"Until what?"

"Until somebody told her about me."

"That you're Company?"

"Yeah."

"Who was that?"

He shrugged.

■ ■ ■

Edwards thought back to the night Barrie Mayer told him she was aware that he was more than just a struggling charter boat owner and captain.

She'd come to the BVI for a week's vacation. Their affair had been in progress for a little more than a year and they'd managed to cram in a considerable amount of time together, considering the physical distance that separated them. Mayer flew to the BVI at every opportunity, and Edwards made a few trips to Washington to see her. They'd also met once in New York, and had spent an extended weekend together in Atlanta.

Seeing her get off the plane that day jolted him with

the same intense feelings she always raised in him. There had been many women in his life, but few had the impact on him she did. His first wife had had that effect. So did his second, come to think of it, but none since . . . until Barrie Mayer.

He recalled that Barrie was in a particularly giddy mood that day. He asked her about it in his car on their way to his villa. She'd said, "I have a secret to share with you." When he asked what it was, she said it would have to wait for a "very special moment."

The moment occurred that night. They'd gone out on one of his yachts and anchored in a cove where they stripped off their clothes and dove into the clear, tepid water. After their swim—more aquatic embracing than swimming—they returned to the yacht and made love. After that he cooked island lobsters and they sat naked on the bleached deck, legs crossed, knees touching, fingers dripping with melted butter, a strong rum swizzle burning their bellies and tripping the switches that cause incessant laughter.

They decided to spend the night on the yacht. After they'd made love again and lay side by side on a bundle of folded sails, he said, "Okay, what's this big, dark secret you have to share with me?"

She'd dozed off. His words startled her awake. She purred and touched his thigh. "Eurosky," she said, or something so softly that he couldn't catch it. When he didn't respond, she turned on her side, propped her head on her elbow, looked down into his face, and said, "You're a spy."

His eyes narrowed. Still, he said nothing.

"You're with the CIA. That's why you're here in the BVI."

He asked quietly, "Who told you that?"

"A friend."

"What friend?"

"It doesn't matter."

"Why would anyone tell you that?"

"Because . . . well, I told . . . this person . . . about you and me and . . ."

"What about you and me?"

"That we've been seeing each other, that I . . . really want to hear?"

"Yes."

"That I'd fallen in love with you."

"Oh."

"That seems to upset you more than my knowing about what you do for a living."

"Maybe it does. Why would this *friend* even bring it up? Does he know me?"

"Yes. Well, not personally, but knows of you."

"Who does your friend work for?"

She started to feel uncomfortable, hadn't expected the intense questioning from him. She tried to lighten the moment by saying with a laugh, "I think it's wonderful. I think it's silly and wonderful and fun."

"What's fun about it?"

"That we have a mutual interest now. You don't care about my literary agency, and I don't care about your boats, except for enjoying being on them with you."

His raised eyebrows asked the next question. Mutual?

"I work for the CIA, too."

His eyebrows lowered. He sat up and looked at her until she said, "I'm a courier, just part time, but it's for the Company." She giggled. "I like the Pickle Factory better. It's . . ." She realized he was not sharing her frivolity. She changed her tone and said, "I can talk about it to you because . . ."

"You can talk about it to nobody."

"Eric, I . . ."

"What the hell do you think this is, Barrie, a game, cops and robbers, an exercise to inject more excitement into your life?"

"No, Eric, I don't think that. Why are you so angry? I thought I was doing something worthwhile for my country. I'm proud of it and I haven't told anyone except you and . . ."

"And your friend."

"Yes."

"And your friend told you about me."

"Only because she knew I was seeing you."

"It's a woman?"

"Yes, but that doesn't matter."

"What's her name?"

"I think under the circumstances that . . ."

"Who is she, Barrie? She's breached a very important confidence."

"Forget it, Eric. Forget I even mentioned it."

He got up and sat on the cabin roof. They said nothing to each other. The yacht swayed in the soft evening breeze. The sky above was dark, the stars pinpoints of white light through tiny holes in black canvas. "Tell me all about it," Edwards said.

"I don't think I should," she said, "not after that reaction."

"I was surprised, that's all," he said, smiling. "You told me you had a big surprise to share with me at an appropriate time and you weren't kidding." She stood next to him. He looked into her eyes and said, "I'm sorry I sounded angry." He put his arm around her and kissed her cheek. "How the hell did you end up working for the CIA?"

She told him.

CHAPTER 8

SAN FRANCISCO

Dr. Jason Tolker sat in his suite at the Mark Hopkins and dialed his Washington office. "Anything urgent?" he asked his receptionist.

"Nothing that can't wait." She read him a list of people who'd called, which included Collette Cahill.

"Where did she call from?" he asked.

"She left a number in Virginia."

"All right. I'll be back on schedule. I'll call again."

"Fine. How's the weather there?"

"Lovely."

It was two in the afternoon. Tolker had until six before his meeting in Sausalito. He put on a white cable-knit sweater, comfortable walking shoes, tossed his raincoat over his arm, posed for an admiring moment before a full-length mirror, then strolled down California Street to Chinatown, where he stopped in a dozen small food shops to peruse the vast array of foodstuffs. Among many of his interests was Chinese cooking. He considered himself a world-class Chinese chef, which wasn't far from true, although, as with many of his hobbies, he tended to overvalue his accomplishments. He also boasted a large collection of vintage jazz recordings. But, as a friend and devoted jazz buff often said, "The collection means more to Jason than the music."

He bought Chinese herbs that he knew he'd have trouble finding in Washington, or even in New York's Chinatown, and returned to the hotel. He showered, changed into one of many suits he had tailored by London's Tommy Nutter, went to the Top of the Mark, sat at a window table with a glass of club soda, and watched the fog roll in over the Golden Gate Bridge on its way to obscuring the city itself. Nice, he thought; appropriate. He checked his watch, paid, got into his rented Jaguar, and headed for the bridge and his appointment on the other side.

He drove through the streets of Sausalito, the lights of San Francisco across the bay appearing, then disappearing through the fog, and turned into a street that began as a residential area, then slowly changed to light industry. He pulled into a three-car paved parking lot next to a two-story white stucco building, turned off his engine and lights, and sat for a moment before getting out and approaching a side door that was painted red. He knocked, heard footsteps on an iron stairway, and stood back as the door was opened by an older man wearing a gray cardigan sweater over a maroon turtleneck. His pants were baggy and his shoes scuffed. His face was a mosaic of lumps and crevices. His hair was gray and uncombed. "Hello, Jason," he said.

"Bill," Tolker said as he stepped past him. The door closed with a thud. The two men walked up a staircase to the second floor. Dr. William Wayman opened a door to his large, cluttered office. Seated in it was a woman who Tolker judged to be in her mid-thirties. She was in a shadowed corner of the room, the only light on her face coming through a dirty window at the rear of the building.

"Harriet, this is the doctor I told you about," Wayman said.

"Hello," she said from the corner, her voice small and conveying her nervousness.

"Hello, Harriet," Tolker said. He didn't approach her. Instead, he went to Wayman's desk and perched on its edge, his fingers affirming the crease in his trousers.

"Harriet is the person I told you about on the phone," Wayman said, sitting in a chair next to her. He looked at Tolker, who was illuminated by a gooseneck lamp.

"Yes, I was impressed," Tolker said. "Perhaps you'll tell me a little about yourself, Harriet."

She started to talk, then stopped as though the tone arm on a turntable had been lifted from a record. "Who are you?" she asked.

Waymen answered her in a calm, patient, fatherly voice. "He's from Washington, and is very much involved in our work."

Tolker got up from the desk and approached them. He stood over her and said pleasantly, "I think it's wonderful what you're doing, Harriet, very courageous and very patriotic. You should be extremely proud of yourself."

"I am . . . I just . . . sometimes I become frightened when Dr. Wayman brings other people into it."

Tolker laughed. It was a reassuring laugh. He said, "I'd think you'd find that comforting, Harriet. You're certainly not alone. There are thousands of people involved, every one of them like you, bright, dedicated, *good* people."

Tolker saw a small smile form on her face. She said, "I

really don't need a speech, Dr. . . . what was your name?" Her voice was arrogant, unfriendly, nothing like the sweet quality it had when they'd been introduced.

"Dr. James. Richard James." He said to Wayman, "I'd like to see the tests, Bill."

"All right." Wayman placed his hand on Harriet's hand, which was on the arm of her chair. He said, "Ready, Harriet?"

"As ready as I'll ever be," she said in a voice that seemed to come from another person. "It's showtime, Dr. J-a-m-e-s."

Wayman glanced up at Tolker, then said to her in a soothing voice, "Harriet, I want you to roll your eyes up to the top of your head, as far as you can." He placed his forefinger on her brow and said, "Look up, Harriet." Tolker leaned forward and peered into her eyes. Wayman said, "That's right, Harriet, as far as you can." Her pupils disappeared, leaving only two milky white sockets.

Tolker nodded at Wayman and smiled.

Wayman said, "Now, Harriet, I want you to keep your eyes where they are and slowly lower your eyelids. That's it . . . very slowly . . . there you are. You feel very relaxed now, don't you?" She nodded. "Now, Harriet, your arm, the one I'm touching, feels light, buoyant, as though a dozen helium-filled balloons were attached to it. Let it rise, let it float up. That's it, that's wonderful." Her arm drifted into the air and hung there as though suspended by an invisible wire.

Wayman turned to Tolker and said, "She's a perfect 'five,' the best I've ever seen."

Tolker grunted and leaned close to her face. "This is Dr. James, Harriet. How do you feel?"

"I feel good."

"I have something I want to ask you to do."

"I . . . I won't."

Wayman said, "She responds only to me. What do you want her to do?"

"Learn a phrase, and be told I'm the one she's to repeat it to."

"All right. Harriet, I want you to remember what I'm about to say to you. You'll never repeat it to anyone else except someone who says to you, 'The fog is thick.' All right?"

"Yes," she said in a dreamy voice.

"I want you to remember, 'There are four people. Two of them are good, and two of them are bad. The bad ones are Bill and Sally.' Do you understand?"

"Yes."

"When I tell you to come out of the pleasant, relaxed state you're enjoying now, you'll remember that phrase and only repeat it to someone who says, 'The fog is thick.' "

"Yes."

"I'm going to count backwards from five to one. When I reach one, you'll open your eyes and feel very good, very relaxed. Ready?"

"Yes."

"Five—four—three—two—one."

She blinked open her eyes and a placid smile crossed her face.

"Feel good?" Wayman asked.

"Yes. I feel good."

"You look very relaxed, at peace," Tolker said.

"Who are you?" she asked.

Tolker laughed. "You know who I am. I was introduced to you only a few minutes ago."

"Yes, I remember. You're Dr. James."

"That's right. I was wondering, Harriet, about the four people we've been discussing."

She looked at Wayman and frowned.

"You know who I mean," Tolker said, "the four people we're concerned about. We want to know which ones we can trust and which ones we can't trust."

"I don't understand," she said.

"Of course you don't," Wayman said. He looked at Tolker and said, "Go ahead."

Tolker said to her, "Harriet, the fog is thick."

She closed her eyes, opened them, and blinked rapidly.

"Did you hear me, Harriet? I said the fog is thick."

Her eyes continued to flutter. They rolled up in her head, and her arm began to tremble. She said in a halting, tentative voice, "There are . . . four people. Some of them are good and . . . two of them are bad. The bad ones are . . . Bill . . . and . . . Sally."

"Excellent," Wayman said. He sat back and looked to Tolker for approval. Tolker returned to the desk and resumed his seat on its edge.

Wayman said to Harriet, "That was very good, Harriet. You're not in your relaxed state anymore. You can open your eyes now. You've done a very good job."

Tolker watched her come out of her hypnotic state. She shook her head and rubbed her eyes.

"What do you remember?" Wayman asked her.

"I remember . . . I was feeling very good. Is there something else I should remember, *Doctor*?" It was the same angry, scornful voice she'd used earlier.

"No," Wayman said. He stood and held out his hand to her. "Why don't you wait in the other room. I won't be long. I just want to talk to my colleague for a few moments."

She got up and ran her hands over the front of her

dress. Tolker observed that she was attractive, a little overweight but with a frank sensuality she was used to displaying. She watched him, openly inviting him as she crossed the room, opened a door, and went out.

"Impressed?" Wayman said. He'd gone to his chair behind the desk and lighted a cigarette.

"Yes. She's good. I'm not sure she's a five, though."

"I test her that way," said Wayman.

"I'd have to look again. Her upgaze is, but the eye roll might not be."

"Does it really matter?" Wayman asked, not bothering to mask the amusement in his voice. "This search for the perfect five is probably folly, Jason."

"I don't think so. How long have you been working with her?"

Wayman shrugged. "Six months, eight months. She's a prostitute, or was, a good one, highly paid."

"A call girl."

"That is more genteel. We came across her by accident. One of the contacts arranged for her to bring men to the safehouse. I watched a few of the sessions and realized that what I was seeing in *her* was far more interesting than the way the men were behaving under drugs. I mentioned it to the contact and the next time she was up, we were introduced. I started working with her the next day."

"She was that willing?"

"She's bright, enjoys the attention."

"And the money?"

"We're paying her fairly."

Tolker laughed. "Is this the first time she's been put to the test?"

It was Wayman's turn to laugh. "For heaven's sake, no. I'd started planting messages with her and testing the recall process within the first month. She's never failed."

"I'll have to see more."

"Tonight?"

"No." Tolker walked to a window that was covered by heavy beige drapes. He touched the fabric, turned, and said, "There's something wrong with using a hooker, Bill."

"Why?"

"Hookers are . . . Christ, one thing they're *not* is trustworthy."

Wayman came up behind and patted him on the back. "Jason, if one's basic morality were a criterion for choosing subjects in this project, we'd all have abandoned it years ago. In fact, we'd all have been ruled out ourselves."

"Speak for yourself, Bill."

"Whatever you say. Shall I continue with her?"

"I suppose so. See how far you can take her."

"I'll do that. By the way, I was sorry to hear about Miss Mayer."

"I'd rather not discuss it."

"Fine, except it must rank as a loss, Jason. If I understood you correctly the last time we met at Langley, she represented one of your best cases."

"She was all right, a solid four, nothing special."

"I thought she was . . . "

"Just a solid four, Bill. I couldn't use her to carry mentally. She worked out as a bag carrier."

"Just that?"

Tolker glared at him. "Yes, just that. Anything else for me to see while I'm out here?"

"No. I have a young man in therapy who shows potential, but I haven't made up my mind yet."

Wayman showed Tolker out of the building and to his car. "You drive her home?" Tolker asked.

"Yes."

"She live in San Fran?"

"Yes."

"She still turn tricks?"

"Only for us. We have a session set up for tomorrow night. Care to join us?"

"Maybe I will. Same place?"

"Yes. Good night, Jason."

"Good night, Bill."

Dr. William Wayman closed the door behind him and muttered "Slime" as he climbed the stairs.

Tolker returned to the city, called his wife from the room at the Hopkins, had a brief conversation. Their marriage had deteriorated to an accommodation years ago. He called another number. A half hour later a young Oriental girl wearing a silk dress the color of tangerines knocked at the door. He greeted her, said, "It's been too long," and sprawled on the bed as she went into the bathroom. When she returned, she was nude. She carried a small plastic bag of white powder, which she placed on the bed next to him. He grinned and absently ran his hand over her small breast.

"I brought the best," she said.

"You always do," he said as he rolled off the bed and started to undress.

■ ■ ■

At eleven o'clock the next night Jason Tolker stood with Dr. William Wayman and two other men in a small apartment. A video camera was positioned against an opening through the wall into the adjoining apartment. A small speaker carried audio from the other apartment.

"Here we go," one of them said, as what had been a static picture of the next room on the monitor suddenly came to life. The door to the next room opened. Harriet, the woman from Wayman's office the night before, led a rotund man through the door. She closed and locked it, turned, and started to undo his tie. He was drunk. A large belly hung over the front of his pants, and his suit jacket was visibly wrinkled even in the room's dim light.

"Drink?" she asked.

"No, I . . . "

"Oh, come on, join me in a drink. It gets me in the mood."

She returned from the kitchen with two glasses.

"What's she using?" Tolker asked.

"That new synthetic from Bethesda," Wayman said.

It turned out to be a wasted evening, at least scientifically. The man Harriet had brought to the apartment was too drunk to be a valid subject, the effects of the drug she'd placed in his drink compromised by the booze. He was too drunk even to have sex with her, and fell asleep soon after they'd climbed into bed, the sound of his snoring rasping from the speakers. The men in the next room continued to watch, however, while Harriet pranced about the room. She examined her full body in a mirror, and even hammed for the camera after a cautious glance at the sleeping subject.

"Disgusting," Tolker muttered as he prepared to leave.

"Harriet?" Wayman asked.

"The fat slob. Tell her to pick better quality next time." He returned to the hotel and watched Randolph Scott in a western on TV before falling asleep.

CHAPTER 9

VIRGINIA, TWO DAYS LATER

It was good to be home.

Collette Cahill had slept off her jet lag in the room that had been hers as she grew up. Now she sat in the kitchen with her mother and helped prepare for a party in her honor that night, not a big affair, just neighbors and friends in for food and drinks to welcome her back.

Mrs. Cahill, a trim and energetic woman, had gone to an imported food store and bought things she felt represented Hungarian fare. "That's all I eat now, Mom," Collette had said. "We get a lot of Hungarian food."

To which her mother replied, "But we don't. It's a good excuse. I've never had goulash."

"You still won't have had it, Mom. In Hungary, goulash is a soup, not a stew."

"Pardon me," her mother said. They laughed and embraced and Collette knew nothing had changed, and was thankful for it.

Guests began to arrive at seven. There was a succession

of gleeful greetings at the door: "I can't believe it." "My God, it's been ages!" "You look wonderful." "Great to see you again." One of the last guests to arrive was, to Collette's surprise, her high school beau, Vern Wheatley. They'd been "a number" in high school, had dated right through graduation when they promptly went their separate ways, Collette staying in the area to attend college, Wheatley to the University of Missouri to major in journalism.

"This is . . . this is too much," Cahill said as she opened the door and stared at him. Her first thought was that he'd grown more handsome over the years, but then she reminded herself that every man got better-looking after high school. His sandy hair had receded only slightly, and he wore it longer than in his yearbook photo. He'd always been slender, but now he was sinewy slim. He wore a tan safari jacket over a blue button-down shirt, jeans, and sneakers.

"Hi," he said. "Remember me?"

"Vern Wheatley, what are you doing here? How did you . . . ?"

"Came down to Washington on assignment, called your mom, and she told me about this blast. Couldn't resist."

"This is . . ." She hugged him and led him to the living room where everyone was gathered. After introductions, Collette led him to the bar where he poured himself a glass of Scotch. "Collette," he said, "you look sensational. Budapest must be palatable."

"Yes, it is. I've had a very enjoyable assignment there."

"Is it over? You're coming back here?"

"No, just a leave."

He grinned. "You take leaves, I take vacations."

"What are you doing these days?"

"I'm an editor, at least for the moment. *Esquire*. It's my

fifth . . . no, seventh job since college. Journalists have never been known for stability, have we?"

"Judging from you, I guess not."

"I do some free-lancing, too."

"I've read some of your pieces." He gave her a skeptical look. "No, I really have, Vern. You had that cover story in the *Times* magazine section on . . ."

"On the private aviation lobby helping to keep our skies unsafe."

"Right. I really did read it. I said to myself, 'I know him.' "

"When."

"Huh?"

"I knew him when. I'm still in my when stage."

"Oh. Do you like New York?"

"Love it, although I can think of other places I'd rather live." He sighed. "It's been a while."

"It sure has. I remember when you got married."

"So do I." He chuckled. "Didn't last long."

"I know, Mom told me. I'm sorry."

"I was, too, but then I realized it was good it fell apart so soon, before there were kids. Anyway, I'm not here to talk about my ex-wife. God, I hate that term. I'm here to celebrate Collette Cahill's triumphant return from behind the Iron Curtain."

She laughed. "Everybody thinks Hungary is like being in the Soviet Union. It's really very open, Vern. I suppose that bothers the Soviets, but that's the way it is, lots of laughter and music, restaurants and bars and . . . well, that's not entirely true, but it's not as bad as people think. The Hungarians are so used to being conquered by one country or another that they shrug and get on with things."

"You're with the embassy?"

"Yup."

"What do you do there?"

"Administration, dealing with trade missions, tourists, things like that."

"You were with the CIA."

"Uh-huh."

"Didn't like it?"

"Too spooky for me, I guess. Just a Virginia country girl at heart."

His laugh indicated he didn't buy it but wasn't about to debate.

Collette drifted to other people in the room. Everyone was interested in her life abroad and she did her best to give them capsule responses.

By eleven, just about everyone had gone home, except for her Uncle Bruce who'd gotten drunk, a next-door neighbor who was helping Collette's mother to gather up the debris, and Vern Wheatley. He sat in a chair in the living room, one long leg casually dangling over the other, a beer in his hand. Collette went to him and said, "Nice party."

"Sure was. Feel like escaping?"

"Escaping? No, I . . ."

"I just figured we could go somewhere, have a drink and catch up."

"I thought we did."

"No we didn't. How about it?"

"I don't know, I . . . just a second."

She went to the kitchen and said she might go out for a cup of coffee with Wheatley.

"That's nice," said her mother, who then whispered, "He's divorced, you know."

"I know."

"I always liked him, and I could never understand what he saw in that other woman."

"He saw something—a ring, a marriage, a mate. Sure you don't mind?"

"Not at all."

"I won't be late. And, Mom, thanks for a wonderful party. I loved seeing everyone."

"And they loved seeing you. The comments, how beautiful you are, what a knockout, a world traveler . . ."

"Good night, Mom. You're spoiling me." She said goodbye to the neighbor and to her Uncle Bruce, who was hearing or feeling nothing, but would in the morning, and she and Wheatley drove off in his 1976 Buick Regal.

They went to a neighborhood bar, settled in a corner booth, ordered beers, and looked at each other. "Fate," he said.

"What?"

"Fate. Here we are, high school sweethearts separated by fate and together again because of fate."

"It was a party."

"Fate that I was here when the party was thrown, fate that you came home at the right time, fate that I'm divorced. *Fate*. Pure and simple."

"Whatever you say, Vern."

They spent two hours catching up on their lives. Cahill found it awkward, as usual, that there was much she couldn't talk about. It was one of the limitations to working for the CIA, particularly in its most clandestine division. She avoided that aspect of her recent life and told tales of Budapest, of the nights at the Miniatur and Gundel, of the Gypsy bands that seemed to be everywhere, of the friends she'd made and the memories she'd developed for life.

"It sounds like a wonderful city," Wheatley said. "I'd like to visit you there someday."

"Please do. I'll give you a special tour."

"It's a date. By the way, your former employer made a pass at me not too long ago."

Cahill tried to imagine someone she'd worked for doing that. A homosexual former boss?

"The Pickle Factory."

"The CIA? Really?"

"Yeah. Journalists used to be big with them. Remember? Then all the crap hit the fan back in '77 and it was 'cool it' for a while. Looks like they're back with us."

"What did they want you to do?"

"I was heading off for Germany on a free-lance assignment. This guy in a cheap suit and raincoat got to me through a friend who lives in the East Village and sculpts for a living. This guy wanted me to hook up with a couple of German writers, get to know them, and see what they knew about the current situation in Germany."

Cahill laughed. "Why didn't they just ask them themselves?"

"Not enough intrigue, I guess. Besides, I figured that what they really want is to have you in their pocket. Do them one favor, then another, collect a little dough for it and start depending upon more. You know what?"

"What?"

"I'm glad you aren't with them anymore. When I heard you'd taken a job with the CIA, all I could think of was what I wrote in your yearbook."

She smiled. "I remember it very well."

"Yeah. *'To the one girl in this world who will never sell out.'* "

"I really didn't understand it then. I do now."

"I'm glad." He sat up, rubbed his hand to signal that

that phase of the conversation was over, and asked, "How long will you be home?"

"I don't know. I have . . ." She had to think. "I have two weeks' leave, but I'm spending a lot of it trying to run down what happened to a very dear friend of mine."

"Anybody I know?"

"No, just a good friend who died suddenly a week or so ago. She was in her mid-thirties and had a heart attack."

He made a face. "That's rough."

"Yes, I'm still trying to deal with it, I guess. She was a literary agent in Washington."

"Barrie Mayer? I didn't know you were friendly."

"You know about it?"

"Sure. It made the New York papers."

"I didn't read anything about it," Cahill said with a sigh. "I know her mother real well and promised her I'd try to find out as much as I could about what Barrie was doing right up until she died."

"Not a great way to spend a vacation. Leave. I forgot."

"Holiday. I like the British approach."

"So do I, in a lot of things. I'm sorry about what happened to your friend. Having friends die is for . . . for older people. I haven't started reading the obits yet."

"Don't. You know, Vern, this was great but I'm pooped. I thought I was slept out but my circadian rhythms are still in chaos."

"Is that like menopause?"

"Vaguely." She laughed. "I should get home."

"Sure."

They pulled up in front of her mother's house. Wheatley turned off the engine and they both looked straight ahead. Cahill glanced over and saw that he was grinning. She thought she knew what he was thinking, and a grin broke out on her face, too, which quickly turned into stifled laughter.

"Remember?" he said.

She couldn't respond because now laughter took all her breath. She tried. "I . . . I remember that you . . ."

"It was you," he said with equal difficulty. "You missed."

"I did not. You had your coat collar turned up because you thought it was cool and when I went to kiss you good night, all I hit was . . . the . . . coat collar."

"You ruined the coat. I never could get the lipstick off."

They stopped talking until they'd gotten themselves under control. She then said to him, "Vern, it was great seeing you again. Thanks for coming to my party."

"My pleasure. I'd like to see you again."

"I don't know if . . . "

"If we should, or if you'll have time while you're home?" She started to reply but he placed his finger on her lips. "I've never forgotten you, Collette. I mean . . . I'd like to see you again, go out, have dinner, talk, just that."

"That'd be nice," she said. "I just don't know how much time I'll have."

"Give me whatever you can spare. Okay?"

"Okay."

"Tomorrow?"

"Vern."

"Are you staying here?"

"At the house? Another night, I think. Then I'm going to stay in the city. I really should have dinner with Mom tomorrow."

"Absolutely. I remember what a hell of a cook she is. Am I invited?"

"Yes."

"I'll call you during the day. Good night, Collette."

He made a deliberate gesture to flatten his jacket collar. She laughed and kissed him lightly on the lips. He tried to intensify the kiss. She resisted, gave in, resisted again, and opened the door. "See you tomorrow," she said.

CHAPTER 10

Jason Tolker's Washington office was located in a three-story detached house in Foggy Bottom, next to the George Washington University campus and with a view of the Kennedy Center from the third floor.

Cahill arrived precisely at 6:00 P.M. Tolker's secretary had told Cahill that he would see her after his last patient.

She rang, identified herself through an intercom, and was buzzed through. The reception area was awash in yellows and reds, and dominated by pieces of pre-Columbian and Peruvian art. Her first thought was to wonder whatever happened to the notion of decorating therapists' offices in soothing pastels. Her second thought was that Dr. Tolker was a pretentious man, not the first time she'd come to that conclusion. Her only other meeting with him, which occurred at the scientific conference in Budapest a week after she'd arrived there, had left her with the distinct impression that his ego was in direct proportion to the outward manifestations of his personality—movie-star handsome (Tyrone Power?), expensive clothing on a six-foot frame built for designer suits, money (it was as if he wore a sandwich board with a large green dollar sign on it). But, and probably more important, there was a self-assuredness that many physicians seemed to carry with them out of medical school but that was particularly prevalent with those who dealt with a patient's emotions and behavior, a godlike view of the world and fellowmen, knowing more, seeing through, inwardly chuckling at how the "others" live their lives, scornful and bemused and willing to tolerate the daily brush with the human dilemma in fifty-minute segments only, payment due at conclusion of visit.

The receptionist, a pleasant, middle-aged woman with a round face, thinning hair, her coat and hat on, ready to leave, told Cahill to be seated: "Doctor will be with you in a few minutes." She left, and Cahill browsed a copy of *Architectural Digest* until Tolker came through a door. "Miss Cahill, hello, Jason Tolker." He came to where she was sitting, smiled, and offered his hand. Somehow, his gregarious greeting didn't match up with what she'd remembered of him from Budapest. She stood and said, "I appreciate you taking time to see me, Doctor."

"Happy to. Come in, we'll be more comfortable in my office."

His office was markedly subdued compared to the waiting room. The walls were the color of talcum; a soothing pastel, she thought. One wall was devoted to framed awards, degrees, and photograhs with people Cahill didn't recognize at first glance. There was no desk; his wine leather swivel chair was behind a round glass coffee table. There were two matching leather chairs on the other side of the table. A black leather couch that gracefully curved up to form a headrest was against another wall. A small chair was positioned behind where the patient's head would lie.

"Please, sit down," he said, indicating one of the chairs. "Coffee? I think there's some left. Or maybe you'd prefer a drink?"

"Nothing, thank you."

"Do you mind if I do? It's been an . . ." A smile. "An interesting day."

"Please. Do you have wine?"

"As a matter of fact, I do. Red or white?"

"White, please."

She watched him open a cabinet, behind which was a bar lighted from within. Her reaction to him was different than it had been in Budapest. She began to like him, finding his demeanor courteous, friendly, open. She also knew she was responding to his good looks. For a tall man, he moved fluidly. He was in shirtsleeves; white shirt, muted red tie, charcoal gray suit trousers, and black Gucci loafers. His dark hair was thick and curly, his facial features sharp. It was his eyes, however, that defined him: large, saccadic raven eyes that were at once soothing and probing.

He placed two glasses of wine on the coffee table, sat in his chair, lifted his glass, and said, "Health."

She returned the salute and took a sip. "Very good," she said.

"I keep the better vintages at home."

She wished he hadn't said it. There was no need to say it. She realized he was staring at her. She met his gaze and smiled. "You know why I'm here."

"Yes, of course, Mrs. Wedgemann, my secretary, told me the nature of your visit. You were a close friend of Barrie Mayer."

"Yes, that's right. To say I was shocked at what happened to her is one of those classic understatements, I suppose. I've been in touch with her mother who, as you can imagine, is devastated, losing her only daughter. I decided to take . . . to take a vacation and see what I could find out about things leading up to Barrie's death. I promised her mother I'd do that but, to be honest, I would have done it for myself anyway. We *were* close."

He pressed his lips together and narrowed his eyes. "The question, of course, is why come to me?"

"I know that Barrie was in therapy with you, at least for a while, and I thought you might be able to give me some hint of what frame of mind she was in before she died, whether there was any indication that she wasn't feeling well."

Tolker rubbed his nose in a gesture of thoughtfulness before saying, "Obviously, Miss Cahill, I wouldn't be free to discuss anything that went on between Barrie and me. That falls under doctor-patient confidentiality."

"I realize that, Dr. Tolker, but it seems to me that a general observation wouldn't necessarily violate that principle."

"When did you meet Barrie?"

The sudden shift in questioning stopped her for a moment. She said, "In college. We stayed close until we each went our separate ways for a number of years. Then, as often happens, we got back in touch and renewed the friendship."

"You say you were close to Barrie. How close?"

"Close." She thought of Mark Hotchkiss, who'd exhibited a similar skepticism of the depth of her relationship with Mayer. "Is there some element of doubt about my friendship with Barrie or, for that matter, my reason for being here?"

He smiled and shook his head. "No, not at all. I'm sorry if I gave you that impression. Do you work and live in the Washington area?"

"No, I . . . I work for the United States Embassy in Budapest, Hungary."

"That's fascinating," said Tolker. "I've spent some time there. Charming city. A shame the Soviets came in as they did. It certainly has put a lid on things."

"Not as much as people think," Cahill said. "It's got to be the most open of Soviet satellite countries."

"Perhaps."

It dawned on Cahill that he was playing a game with her, asking questions for which he already had answers. She decided to be more forthright. "We've met before, Dr. Tolker."

He squinted and leaned forward. "I thought we had the minute I saw you. Was it in Budapest?"

"Yes. You were attending a conference and I'd just arrived."

"Yes, it comes back to me now, some reception, wasn't it? One of those abominable get-togethers. You're wearing your hair different, shorter, aren't you?"

Cahill laughed. "Yes, and I'm impressed with your memory."

"Frankly, Miss Cahill, when more than a year has passed since meeting a woman, it's always safe to assume she's changed her hair. Usually, it involves the color, too, but that isn't the case with you."

"No, it isn't. Somehow, I don't think I was born to be a blonde."

"No, I suppose not," he said. "What do you do at the embassy?"

"Administration, trade missions, helping stranded tourists, run-of-the-mill."

He smiled and said, "It can't be as dull as you make it sound."

"Oh, it's never dull."

"I have a good friend in Budapest."

"Really? Who is that?"

"A colleague. His name is Árpád Hegedüs. Do you know him?"

"He's . . . he's a colleague, you say, a psychiatrist?"

"Yes, and a very good one. His talent is wasted having to apply it under a Socialist regime, but he seems to find room for a certain amount of individuality."

"Like most Hungarians," she said.

"Yes, I suppose that's true, just as you must find room for other activities within the confines of your run-of-the-mill job. How much time do you devote to helping stranded tourists as opposed to . . . ?"

When he didn't finish, she said, "As opposed to what?"

"As opposed to your duties for the CIA."

His question startled her. Early in her career with Central Intelligence, it would have thrown her, perhaps even generated a nervous giggle as she collected her thoughts. That wasn't the case any longer. She looked him in the eye and said, "That's an interesting comment."

"More wine?" he asked, standing and going to the bar.

"No, thank you, I have plenty." She looked at her glass on the table and thought of the comment Árpád Hegedüs had made to her during their last meet in Budapest: "Jason Tolker might be friendly to the Soviets."

Tolker returned, took his seat, sipped his wine. "Miss

Cahill, I think you might accomplish a lot more, and we might get along much better, if you practiced a little more candor."

"What makes you think I haven't been candid?"

"It isn't a matter of thinking, Miss Cahill. I *know* you haven't been." Before she could respond he said, "Collette E. Cahill, graduated cum laude from George Washington University Law School, a year or so with a legal trade journal, then a stint in England for the CIA and a transfer to Budapest. Accurate? Candid?"

"Am I supposed to be impressed?" she asked.

"Only if your life to date impresses you. It does me. You're obviously bright, talented, and ambitious."

"Thank you. Time for me to ask you a question."

"Go ahead."

"Assuming the things you've said about me were correct, particularly my supposed continuing employment with the CIA, how would you know about that?"

He smiled, and it quickly turned into a laugh. "No argument, then?"

"Is that Shrink School 101, answer a question with a question?"

"It goes back further than that, Miss Cahill. The Greeks were good at it. Socrates taught the technique."

"Yes, that's true, and Jesus, too. As a learning tool for students, not to evade a reasonable question."

Tolker shook his head and said, "You're still not being candid, are you?"

"No?"

"No. You know, either through Barrie or someone else in your organization, that I have, on occasion, provided certain services to your employer."

Cahill smiled. "This conversation has turned into one

with so much candor that it would probably be upsetting to . . . to our employers, *if* we worked for them."

"No, Miss Cahill, your employer. I simply have acted as a consultant on a project or two."

She knew that everything he'd said up to that moment was literally true, and decided it was silly to continue playing the game. She said, "I'd love another glass of wine."

He got it for her. When they were both seated again, he looked at his watch and said, "Let me try to tell you what it is you want to know without you having to ask the questions. Barrie Mayer was a lovely and successful woman, as you're well aware. She came to me because there were certain aspects of her life with which she was unhappy, that she was having trouble negotiating. That, of course, is a sign of sanity in itself."

"Seeking help?"

"Of course, recognizing a problem and taking action. She was like most people who end up in some form of therapy, bright and rational and put together in most aspects of her life, just stumbling now and then over some ghosts from the past. We worked things out very nicely for her."

"Did you maintain a relationship after therapy was finished?"

"Miss Cahill, you know we did."

"I don't mean about what she might have done as a courier. I mean a personal relationship."

"What a discreet term. Do you mean did we sleep together?"

"It would be indiscreet for me to ask that."

"But you already have, and I prefer not to answer an indiscretion with an indiscretion. Next question."

"You were telling me everything I need to know without questions, remember?"

"Yes, that's right. You'll want to know whether I have any information bearing upon her death."

"Do you?"

"No."

"Do you have any idea who killed her?"

"Why do you assume someone killed her? My understanding is that it was an unfortunate, premature heart attack."

"I don't think that's really what happened. Do you?"

"I wouldn't know more about that than what I've read in the papers."

Cahill sipped her wine, not because she wanted it but because she needed a little time to process what had transpired. She'd assumed when she called and asked for an appointment with Tolker that she would be summarily turned down. She'd even considered seeking an appointment as a patient but realized that was too roundabout an approach.

It had all been so easy. A phone call, a brief explanation to the secretary that she was Barrie Mayer's friend—instant appointment with him. He'd obviously worked fast in finding out who she was. Why? What source had he turned to to come up with information on her? Langley and its central personnel files? Possible, but not likely. That sort of information would never be given out to a contract physician who was only tangentially associated with the CIA.

"Miss Cahill, I've been preaching candor to you without practicing it myself."

"Really?"

"Yes. I'm assuming that you're sitting here wondering how I came up with information about you."

"As a matter of fact, that's right."

"Barrie was . . . well, let's just say she didn't define close-mouthed."

Cahill couldn't help but laugh. She remembered her dismay at her friend's casual mention of her new, part-time job as courier.

"You agree," Tolker said.

"Well, I . . ."

"Once Barrie agreed to carry some materials for the CIA, she became talkative. She said it was ironic because she had this friend, Collette Cahill, who worked for the CIA at the American Embassy in Budapest. I found that interesting and asked questions. She answered them all. Don't misunderstand. She didn't babble about it. If she had, I would have ended the relationship, at least that aspect of it."

"I understand what you're saying. What else did she say about me?"

"That you were beautiful and bright and the best female friend she'd ever had."

"Did she really say that?"

"Yes."

"I'm flattered." She sensed that a tear might erupt and swallowed against it.

"Want my honest opinion about how and why she died?"

"Please."

"I buy the official autopsy verdict of a coronary. If that *isn't* why she died, I'd assume that our friends on the other side decided to terminate her."

"The Russians."

"Or some variation thereof."

"I can't accept that, not today. We're not at war. Besides, what could Barrie have been carrying that would prompt such a drastic action?"

He shrugged.

"What *was* she carrying?"

"How would I know?"

"I thought you were her contact."

"I was, but I never knew what was in her briefcase. It was given to me sealed, and I would give it to her."

"I understand that but . . ."

He leaned forward. "Look, Miss Cahill, I think we've gotten off onto a tangent that goes far beyond the reality of the situation. I know that you're a full-time employee of the CIA, but I'm not. I'm a psychiatrist. That's what I do for a living. It's my profession. A colleague suggested to me years ago that I might be interested in becoming a CIA-approved physician. All that means is that when someone from the agency needs medical help in my specialty, they're free to come to me. There are surgeons and OB-GYN men and heart specialists and many others who've been given clearance by the agency."

She cocked her head and asked, "But what about being a contact for a courier like Barrie? That isn't within your specialty."

His smile was friendly and reassuring. "They asked me somewhere along the line to keep my eye out for anyone who might fit their profile of a suitable courier. Barrie fit it. She traveled often to foreign countries, particularly Hungary, wasn't married, didn't have any deep, dark secrets that would jeopardize her clearance, and she enjoyed adventure. She also appreciated the money, off-the-books money, fun money for clothes and furniture and other frills. It was a lark for her."

His final words hit Cahill hard, caused her to draw a deep breath.

"Something wrong?" Tolker asked, observing the pain on her face.

"Barrie's dead. 'Just a lark.' "

"Yes. I'm sorry."

"Do you feel any . . . any guilt about having recruited her into a situation that resulted in her death?"

For a moment, she thought his eyes might mist. They didn't, but his voice had a ring of pathos. "I think about it often. I wish I could go back to that day when I suggested she carry for your employer and withdraw my offer." He sighed and stood, stretched, and broke his knuckles. "But that's not possible, and I tell my patients that to play the what-if game is stupid. It happened, she's dead, I'm sorry, and I must leave."

He walked her to the office door. They paused and looked at each other. "Barrie was right," he said.

"About what?"

"About her friend being beautiful."

She lowered her eyes.

"I hope I've been helpful."

"Yes, you have, and I'm appreciative."

"Will you have dinner with me?"

"I . . ."

"Please. There's probably more ground we could cover about Barrie. I feel comfortable with you now. I didn't when you first arrived, thought you were just snooping around for gossip. I shouldn't have felt that way. Barrie wouldn't have a very close friend who'd do that."

"Maybe," she said. "Yes, that would be fine."

"Tomorrow night?"

"Ah, yes, fine."

"Would you mind coming by here at seven? I have a six o'clock group. Once they're gone, I'm free."

"Seven. I'll be here."

She drove home realizing two things. One, he'd told her everything that she would have known anyway. Two, she was anxious to see him again. That second thought bothered her because she couldn't effectively separate her continuing curiosity about Barrie Mayer's death from a personal fascination with him as a man.

"Have a nice night?" her mother asked.

"Yes."

"You're staying in the city tomorrow night?"

"For the next few nights, Mom. It'll be easier to get things done. I'm seeing Barrie's mother tomorrow for lunch."

"Poor woman. Please give her my sympathy."

"I will."

"Will you be seeing Vern?"

"I don't know. Probably."

"It was fun having him at dinner last night, like when you were in high school and he used to hang around hoping to be invited."

Cahill laughed. "He's nice. I'd forgotten how nice."

"Well," said her mother, "the problem with pretty girls like you is having to pick and choose among all the young men who chase you."

Cahill hugged her mother and said, "Mom, I'm not a girl anymore, and there isn't a battalion of men chasing me."

Her mother stepped back, smiled, and held her daughter at arm's length. "Don't kid me, Collette Cahill. I'm your mother."

"I know that, and I'm very grateful that you are. Got any ice cream?"

"Bought it today for you. Rum raisin. They were out of Hungarian flavors."

CHAPTER 11

Cahill drove a rented car into the city the next morning and checked into the Hotel Washington at 15th and Pennsylvania. It wasn't Washington's finest, but it was nice. Besides, it had a sentimental value. Its rooftop terrace restaurant and bar offered as fine a view of Washington as any place in the capitol. Cahill had spent four glorious Fourth of Julys there with friends who, through connections, had been able to wangle reservations on the terrace's busiest night of the year, and were able to view the spectacular festivities that only Washington can provide on the nation's birthday.

She went to her room, hung up the few items of clothing she'd brought with her, freshened up, and headed for her first appointment of the day: CIA headquarters in Langley, Virginia.

The person she was seeing had been a mentor of sorts during her training days. Hank Fox was a grizzled, haggard, wayworn agency veteran who had five daughters, and who took a special interest in the increasing number of women recruited by the CIA. His position was Coordinator: Training Policy and Procedures. New recruits often joked that his title should be "Priest." He had that way about him—ignoring his five issue, of course.

She whizzed along the George Washington Memorial Parkway until reaching a sign that read CENTRAL INTELLIGENCE AGENCY. It hadn't always been marked that way. In the years following its construction in the late 1950s, a single sign on the highway read BUREAU OF PUBLIC ROADS. Frequent congressional calls for the agency to be more open and accountable brought about the new sign. Behind it, little had changed.

She turned off the highway and onto a road leading to the 125-acre tract on which the Central Intelligence Agency stood. Ahead, through dense woods, stood the modernistic, fortress-like building surrounded by a high and heavy chain-link fence. She stopped, presented her credentials to two uniformed guards, and explained the purpose of her visit. One of them placed a call, then informed her that she could pass through to the next checkpoint. She did, submitted her identity again to scrutiny, and was allowed to proceed to a small parking area near the main entrance.

Two athletic young men wearing blue suits and with revolvers beneath their jackets waited for her to approach the entrance. She noticed how short their hair was, how placid the expression on their faces. Again, a show of credentials, a nod, and she was escorted through the door by one of them. He walked slightly in front of her at a steady pace until coming to the beginning of a long, straight white tunnel that was arched at the top. Royal blue industrial-grade carpeting lined the floor. There was nothing in the tunnel except for recessed lights that created odd shadows along its length. At the far end was an illuminated area where two stainless-steel elevator doors caught the light and hurled it back into the tunnel.

"Straight ahead, ma'am."

Cahill entered the tunnel and walked slowly, her thoughts drifting back to when she was a new recruit and had first seen this building, had first walked this tunnel. It had been part of an introductory tour and she'd been struck by the casualness of the tour guide, a young man who demonstrated what Cahill, and others in her class, considered strangely irreverent behavior considering the ominous image of the CIA. He'd talked about how the contractor who'd built the building wasn't allowed to know how many people would occupy it, and was forced to guess at the size and capacity of the heating and air-conditioning system. The system turned out to be inadequate, and the CIA took him to court. He won, his logic making more sense to the judge than the "national security" argument presented by the agency's counsel.

The guide had also said that the $46-million building had been approved in order to bring all agency headquarters personnel under one roof. Until that time, the CIA's divisions had been spread out all over Washington and surrounding communities, and Congress had been sold on the consolidation because of problems this created. But, according to this talkative, glib young man, whole divisions began moving out shortly after moving in when construction was completed. When this came to the attention in 1968 of then director Richard Helms, he was furious and decreed that no one was to make a move without his personal approval. Somehow, that didn't deter division chiefs who found being under one roof to be stifling and, if nothing else, boring. The exodus continued.

Cahill often wondered how you ran an organization

with that kind of discipline, and whether the young tour guide's loose tongue had cut short his agency career. It wasn't like the FBI, where public relations and public tours were routine, conducted by attractive young men and women hired solely for that purpose. The CIA did not give tours to outsiders; the guide was obviously a full-fledged employee.

She reached the end of the tunnel where two other young men awaited her. "Miss Cahill?" one asked.

"Yes."

"May I see your pass?"

She showed him.

"Please take the elevator. Mr. Fox is expecting you." He pushed a button and a set of the stainless-steel doors slid open quickly and silently. She stepped into the elevator and waited for them to close. She knew better than to look for a button to push. There weren't any. This elevator knew its destination.

Hank Fox was waiting for her when the doors opened a floor above. He hadn't changed. Though older, he'd always looked old, and the changes weren't quickly discernible. His craggy face broke into a smile and he extended two large, red, and callused hands. "Collette Cahill. Good to see you again."

"Same here, Hank. You look terrific."

"I feel terrific. At my age you might as well or, at least, lie. Come on, Fox's special blend of coffee awaits you." She smiled and fell in step with him down a wide hallway carpeted in red, its white walls providing a backdrop for large, framed maps.

Fox, Cahill noticed, had put on weight and walked with a slower, heavier gait than the last time she'd seen him. His gray suit, its shape and material testifying to its origins in a Tall and Big (read Fat) Man's clothing shop, hung gracelessly from him.

He stopped, opened a door, and allowed her to enter. The corner office's large windows looked out over the woods. His desk was as cluttered as it had always been. The walls were covered with framed photos of him with political heavyweights spanning many administrations, the largest one of him shaking hands with a smiling Harry S. Truman a few years before the President's death. A cluster of color photographs of his wife and children stood on his desk. A pipe rack was full; little metal soldiers stood at attention along the air-conditioning and heating duct behind the desk.

"Coffee?" he asked.

"If it's as good as it used to be."

"Sure it is. The only difference is that they told me I have a fast and irregular pulse. The doc thought I was drinking too much coffee and said I should use de-caf. I compromised. I mix it half and half now, half the amaretto from that fancy coffee and tea shop in Georgetown, the other half de-caf. Never know the difference." Hank Fox's special blends of coffee were well known throughout the agency, and being invited to share a pot carried with it the symbolism of acceptance and friendship.

"Sensational," Cahill exclaimed after her first sip. "You haven't lost your touch, Hank."

"Not with coffee. Other things, well . . ."

"They moved you."

"Yeah. That's right, the last time I saw you was when I had that office in with Personnel. I liked it better there. Being up here in Miscellaneous Projects is another world. The director said it was a promotion, but I know better. I'm being eased out, which is okay with me. Hell, I'm sixty."

"Young."

"Bull! All this crap about being only as old as you think is babble from people who are afraid of getting old. You may feel young, but cut you open and the bones and arteries don't lie." He sat in a scarred leather swivel chair, propped his feet on the desk, and reached for a pipe, leaving Cahill staring at the soles of his shoes, both of which sported sizable holes. "So one of my prize pupils has returned to see the aging prof. How've you been?"

"Fine."

"I got a BIGOT from Joe Breslin saying you were coming home." Fox often used intelligence terms from his early days, even though they'd passed out of common usage over the years. "BIGOT" stemmed from secret plans to invade France during World War II. Gibraltar had been established as a planning center, and orders for officers being sent there were rubber-stamped "TO GIB." BIGOT was the reverse, and the term came into being: sensitive operations were known to be *bigoted*, and personnel given knowledge of them were on the *bigot list*.

"Any reason for him doing that?" she asked.

"Just an advisory. I was going to call but you beat me to it. This your first leave from Budapest?"

"No. I took a few short ones to Europe, and got back home once about a year ago for a favorite uncle's funeral."

"The boozer?"

She laughed. "Oh, God, what a memory. No, my hard-drinking Uncle Bruce is still very much with us, rotted liver and all. Having him in the family almost blew my chances here, didn't it?"

"Yeah. That prissy little security guy raised it during your clearance investigation." He belched and excused himself, then said, "If having an alky in the family ruled you out for duty around here, there'd only be a dozen temperance-league types running intelligence for the good ol' U.S. of A." He shook his head, "Hell, half the staff drinks too much."

She laughed and sipped more coffee.

"Let me ask you a question," he said in a serious tone. She looked up and raised her eyebrows. "You here strictly for R & R?"

"Sure."

"The reason I ask is that I thought it was strange . . . well, maybe not strange, but unusual for Joe to bother using a BIGOT to tell me you were coming."

She shrugged. "Oh, you know Joe, Hank, the perpetual father figure. It was nice of him. He knows how fond I am of you."

" 'Fond.' Pleasant term to use on an old man."

"*Older* man."

"Thank you. Well, I'm fond of you, too, and I just thought I'd raise the question in case you were involved in something official and needed an inside rabbi."

"Rabbi Henry Fox. Somehow, Hank, it doesn't go with you. Priest, yes. They still call you that?"

"Not so much anymore since they shifted me."

His comment surprised Cahill. She'd assumed he'd only been physically moved, but that his job had remained the same. She asked.

"Well, Collette, I still keep a hand in training, but they've got me running an operation to keep track of the Termites and Maggots. It's an Octopus project."

Cahill smiled, said, "I never could keep it straight, the difference between Termites and Maggots."

"It really doesn't matter," Fox said. "The Termites are media types who don't carry a brief for the Communists, but who always find something wrong with *us*. The Maggots follow the termites and do whatever's popular which, as you know, means taking daily shots at us and the FBI and any other organization they see as being a threat to their First Amendment rights. Between you and me, I think it's a waste of time. Take away their freedom to write what they want and there goes what the country's all about in the first place. Anyway, we've got them on the computer and we plug in everything they write, pro or con." He yawned and sat back in his chair, his arms behind his head.

Cahill knew what he'd meant by it being an "Octopus project." A worldwide computer system to track potential terrorists had been termed Project Octopus, and had become a generic label for similar computer-rooted projects. She also thought of Vern Wheatley. Was he a Maggot or a Termite? It caused her to smile. Obviously, he was neither, nor were most of the journalists she knew. It was a tendency of too many people within the CIA to apply negative terms to anyone who didn't see things their way, a tendency that had always bothered her.

She'd debated on her way to Langley whether to open up a little to Fox and to bring up Barrie Mayer. She knew it wasn't the most prudent thing to do—Need-to-know coming to the fore—but the temptation was there, and the fact that Joe Breslin had alerted Fox to her arrival gave a certain credence to the notion. There were few people within the Pickle Factory that she trusted. Breslin was one; Fox was another. Mistake! Trust no one, was the rule. Still . . . how could you go through life viewing everyone with whom you worked as a potential enemy? Not a good way to live. Not healthy. In Barrie Mayer's case, it had worked the other way around. Whose confidence had she trusted that turned against her? Had Tolker been right, that her death might have been at the hand of a Soviet agent? It was so difficult to accept, but that was another rule that her employer instilled in every employee: "It's easy to forget that we are at war every day with the Communists. It is their aim to destroy our system and our country, and a day must never pass when that reality isn't at the forefront of your thinking."

"You know what I was just thinking, Collette?" Fox asked.

"What?"

"I was thinking back to when this whole organization was started by President Truman." He shook his head. "He'd never recognize it today. I met Truman, you know."

She glanced at the photograph on the wall before saying, "I remember you talked about that during training." He'd talked about it often, as she recalled.

"Hell of a guy. It was right after those two Puerto Ricans tried to assassinate him in 'fifty. They did their best to do him in, botched it, got death sentences, and then Truman turns around at the final minute and commutes their sentences to life. I admired him for that."

Along with cabinet building, winemaking, jewelry design and crafting, and a dozen other interests, Hank Fox was a history buff, especially the Harry Truman presidency. During Cahill's training, it was obvious that the Truman hand in creating the CIA in 1947 was being deliberately glossed over. She hadn't understood the reasons for it until Fox had sat down with a few favorite recruits over dinner at Martin's Tavern in Georgetown and explained.

When Truman abolished the OSS following World War II, he did so because he felt that such wartime tactics as psychological warfare, political manipulation, and paramilitary operations that had been practiced during the war by the OSS had no place in a peacetime, democratic society. He did, however, recognize the need for an organization to coordinate the collection of intelligence information from all branches of government. As he said, "If such an organization had existed within the United States in 1941, it would have been difficult, if not impossible, for the Japanese to have launched their successful attack on Pearl Harbor."

And so the Central Intelligence Agency was born—to collect, assimilate, and analyze intelligence, not to engage in any other activity.

"He got snookered," Fox had told his handful of students that night at dinner. "Allen Dulles, who ended up running the CIA six years later, thought Truman's views on intelligence were too limited. Know what he did? He sent a memo to the Senate Armed Services Committee undercutting Truman's view of what the CIA was supposed to be."

Fox had produced a copy of that memo for his students:

> Intelligence work in time of peace will require other techniques, other personnel, and will have rather different objectives. . . . We must deal with the problem of conflicting ideologies as democracy faces communism, not only in the relations between Soviet Russia and the countries of the West but in the internal political conflicts with the countries of Europe, Asia, and South America.

Dulles went on to contribute a concept to what would eventually become intelligence law, and which gave the CIA its ultimate power. It called for the agency to carry out "such other functions and duties related to intelligence as the National Security Council may from time to time direct." This took it out of the realm of congressional control and helped establish the atmosphere under which the CIA could function autonomous from virtually all control, including manpower and financing. The director had only to sign a voucher and the funds were there, something President Truman had never envisioned happening.

Cahill and the other students at that dinner with Hank Fox later discussed his somewhat irreverent view of the agency and its history. It was refreshing; everyone else with whom they'd come into contact seemed rigidly bound to a party line, no room for deviation, no patience with frivolity or casual remarks that could be construed as less than sanctified.

"Well, on to other functions and duties," Cahill said. "I lost a very good friend recently."

"I'm sorry. Accident?"

"No one is sure. It's been ruled a heart attack but she was only in her thirties and . . ."

"She work with us?"

Cahill hesitated, then said, "Part time. She was a literary agent."

He removed his feet from the desk and replaced them with his elbows. "Barrie Mayer."

"Yes. You know about her, about what happened?"

"Very little. The rumor mill swung into full gear when she died, and the word was that she did some part-time carrying for us."

Cahill said nothing.

"Did you know she was affiliated?"

"Yes."

"Did she carry to you in Budapest?"

"Not directly but yes, she carried to Budapest."

"Banana Quick."

"I'm not sure about that, Hank."

"Is that what you're on these days?"

"Yes. I turned someone."

"So I heard."

"You did?"

"Yeah. Whether you know it or not, Miss Cahill, your Hungarian friend is viewed around here as the best we've got at the moment."

She resisted a smile of satisfaction and said, "He's been cooperative."

"That's a mild way to put it. Your girlfriend's demise has a lot of people reaching for the Tums bottle."

"Because of Banana Quick?"

"Sure. It's the most amibitious project we've had since the Bay of Pigs. Unfortunately, it has about half as much chance of succeeding, and you know how successful the Cuban fiasco was, but the timetable's been pushed up. Could be anytime now."

"I wouldn't know about the overall project, Hank. I get information from my source and I feed it back. One spoke. I'm not privy to what the wheel does."

"Operation Servo?"

"Pardon?"

"Haven't heard of it?"

"No."

"Just as well. Another act of genius by our army of resident geniuses. I hope death is final, Collette. If it isn't, Harry S. Truman has been twisting and turning ever since he left us the day after Christmas, 1972." He drew a deep breath and his face seemed to sink, to turn gray. He pressed his lips together and said in a low voice lacking energy, "It's no good here anymore, Collette. At best, it's disorganized and ineffectual. At worst, it's evil."

She started to respond but he quickly said, "You'll have to pardon a tired, disgruntled old man. I don't mean to corrupt your enthusiasm with my jaded grumbling."

"Please, Hank, no apologies." She glanced around the office. "Are we secure?"

"Who knows?"

"You don't care?"

"No."

"Why?"

"It's a perk of becoming old. Lots of things don't matter anymore. Don't get me wrong. I do my job. I give them my best effort and loyalty for the check. I want to retire. Janie and I bought a pretty house on some land down in West Virginia. Another year and that's where we head. The kids are doing nicely. We bought another dog. That's three. The five of us, Janie, me, and the canine trio, need West Virginia."

"It sounds great, Hank," Cahill said. "Should I leave now?"

"You have to?"

"I have a luncheon appointment in Rosslyn."

" 'Appointment.' " He smiled. "Not a date?"

"No. I'm meeting Barrie Mayer's mother."

"Only kid?"

"Yes."

"Tough."

"Yes."

"Come on. I'll walk you out. I need fresh air."

They stood next to her small red rented car and Fox looked up at the building, then out over the woods that shielded other buildings from view. "Rosslyn? I spend a lot of time over there."

"Really?"

"Yeah. One of the Octopus computer centers moved to Rosslyn. Half this joint is empty now."

Cahill laughed as she thought of the tour guide who'd talked about that. She mentioned him.

"I remember him," Fox said. "He was an idiot which, we've all come to realize, doesn't preclude you from working here. He was a running joke around here, and his boss was told to get him out. He hit him with fifty demerits in a week, and you know what that means. Fifty in a *year* is automatic dismissal. The kid was really broken up. He came to me and begged for another chance. I felt sorry for him but he *was* an idiot. I told him I couldn't do anything and he slunk away. He's probably a millionaire four times over now."

"Probably. Hank, it was wonderful seeing you, touching base like this."

"Good to see you, too, kid. Before you take off, listen carefully to me."

She stared at him.

"Watch that pretty little rear end of yours. The Barrie Mayer thing is hot. So's Banana Quick. It's trouble. Watch who you talk to. Banana Quick is a mess, and anybody associated with it goes down the tube along with all the rest of the dirty water." He lowered his voice. "There's a leak in Banana Quick."

"Really?"

"A big one. Maybe that's why your friend isn't with us anymore."

"Oh, no, Hank, she'd never . . ."

"I didn't say she'd do anything, but maybe she got too close to the wrong people. Understand?"

"No, but I have a feeling you're not about to continue my education."

"I would if I could, Collette. I've been kicked upstairs, remember? Need-to-know. I don't have that need any-more. Be careful. I like you. And remember Harry Tru-man. If they could screw the President of the United States, they can screw anybody, even bright, pretty girls like you who mean well." He kissed her on the cheek, turned, and disappeared inside the building.

CHAPTER 12

"It was sweet of you to come," Mrs. Mayer said as they sat at a window table in Alexander's III in Rosslyn, just over the Key Bridge from Georgetown. Rosslyn had grown rapidly. Their view of Georgetown and Washington from the penthouse restaurant was partially obscured by the latest in a series of high-rise office and apartment buildings.

"Frankly, I dreaded it, Mrs. Mayer," Collette said, running a fungernail over the starched white linen tablecloth.

Melissa Mayer placed her hand on Collette's, smiled, and said, "You shouldn't have. It means a great deal to me that one of Barrie's closest friends cared enough to see me. I've felt very lonely lately. I don't today."

Her words boosted Cahill's spirits. She smiled at the older woman, who was impeccably dressed in a light blue jersey suit, white blouse with lace at the neck, and mink stole. Her hair was white and pulled back into a severe chignon. Her face had a healthy glow, aided by makeup that had been expertly applied. She wore a substantial strand of pearls around her neck and pearl earrings with tiny diamond chips. Her fingers, gnarled by arthritis, supported heavy gold and diamond rings.

"I had all sorts of things I'd planned to say when I saw you but . . . "

"Collette, there really is very little to say. I'd always heard that the saddest thing in life was to have a child predecease a parent and I never debated it. Now I *know* it's true. But I am also a believer in the scheme of life. It was never meant to be perfect. The odds are that children will outlive their parents, but it certainly isn't set in stone. I've grieved, I've cried, I've cried a great deal, and now it's time to stop those things and continue with my life."

Cahill shook her head. "You're an amazing woman, Mrs. Mayer."

"I'm nothing of the sort, and please call me Melissa. 'Mrs. Mayer' creates too wide a gap."

"Fair enough."

A waiter asked whether they'd like another drink. Cahill shook her head. Mayer ordered a second perfect Manhattan. Then Collette said, "Melissa, what happened to Barrie?"

The older woman frowned and sat back. "Whatever do you mean?"

"Do you believe she died of a heart attack?"

"Well, I . . . what else am I to believe? That's what I was told."

"Who told you?"

"The doctor."

"Which doctor?"

"Our family doctor."

"He examined her, did an autopsy?"

"No, he received confirmation from a British physician, I believe. Barrie died in . . . "

"I know, in London, but there's . . . there's some reason to question whether it really was her heart."

Mayer's face hardened. She said in a voice that matched her expression. "I'm not sure I understand what you're getting at, Collette."

"I'm not sure what I'm getting at either, Melissa, but I'd like to find out the truth. I simply can't buy the notion that Barrie had a coronary at her age. Can you?"

Melissa Mayer reached into an alligator purse, took out a long cigarette, lighted it, seemed to savor the smoke in her lungs and mouth, then said, "I believe that life revolves around accepting, Collette. Barrie is dead. I must accept that. Heart attack? I must accept that, too, because if I don't, I'll spend the rest of my days in torment. Can't you accept *that*?"

Cahill winced at the intensity in her voice. She said, "Please don't misunderstand, Melissa, I'm not trying to raise questions that would make Barrie's death more painful to you than it is right now. I realize losing a friend is not as traumatic as losing a daughter, but I've been suffering my own brand of torment. That's why I'm here, trying to lessen my own pain. I suppose that's selfish, but it happens to be the truth."

Cahill watched the older woman's face soften from the hard mask it had become, for which she was thankful. She was feeling an increasing amount of guilt. There she was sitting with a grieving mother under false pretenses, pretending only to be a friend but, in actuality, functioning as an investigator for the CIA. That damned duality, she thought. It was the thing that bothered her most about the work, the need to lie, to withhold, to be anything but the basic person that you were. Everything seemed based upon a lie. There was no walking in the sunshine because too much was conducted in shadows and safehouses, messages written in code instead of plain English, strange names for projects, a life of looking over your shoulder and watching your words, and suspicions about everyone with whom you came in contact.

"Melissa, let's just have a pleasant lunch," Cahill said. "It was wrong of me to use this occasion to salve my own feelings about losing my friend."

The older woman smiled and lighted another cigarette. "Barrie was always chiding me for smoking. She said it would take ten years off of my life but here I sit, very much alive, smoking like a chimney and talking about my health-conscious daughter who's very much dead." Collette tried to change the subject but Mrs. Mayer shook her off. "No, I would like to talk about Barrie with you. There really hasn't been anyone since it happened that I could turn to, be open with. I'm very glad you're here and were close to her. There didn't seem to be many people close to her, you know. She was so outgoing, yet . . . yet, she had so few friends."

Cahill looked quizzically at her. "I would have thought the opposite was true. Barrie was so gregarious, full of life and fun."

"I think that was more show than anything, Collette. You see, Barrie had a lot of nasty things to deal with."

"I know she had occasional problems but . . . "

The smile on Melissa Mayer's face was a knowing one. She said, "It was more than just normal problems, Collette. I'm afraid I'll go to *my* grave regretting those aspects of her life in which I played a part."

Cahill felt uncomfortable at what seemed to be Mayer's apparent intention to delve into some cavern of secrets about Barrie and her. Yet she was as curious as she was uncomfortable, and did nothing to hinder the conversation.

Mayer asked, "Did Barrie ever mention her father to you?"

Cahill thought for a moment. "I think so but I can't remember in what context. No, I'm not even sure she did." In fact, it had struck Cahill a few times during her years of friendship with Barrie Mayer that she didn't mention her father. She remembered a conversation during college with Barrie and some other girls about fathers and their impact on daughters' lives. Barrie's only contribution to the conversation had been sarcastic comments about fathers in general. Later that night, Cahill asked about her own father and was met with the simple response, "He's dead." The tone of Barrie's voice had made it plain that the conversation was over.

Cahill told Melissa Mayer about it and the older woman nodded. Her gaze drifted across the dining room as though in search of a place to which she could anchor her thoughts.

"We don't have to talk about this, Melissa," Cahill said.

Mayer smiled. "No, I was the one who introduced the subject. Barrie's father died when Barrie was ten."

"He must have been a young man," said Cahill.

"Yes, he was young and . . . he was young and not missed."

Cahill said, "I don't understand."

"Barrie's father, my husband, was a cruel and inhuman person, Collette. I wasn't aware of that when I married him. I was very young and he was very handsome. His cruelty started to come out after Barrie was born. I don't know whether he resented that a child came between us or whether it just represented a warped aspect of his character, but he was cruel to her, abusive physically and psychologically."

"That's terrible," Cahill said.

"Yes, it was."

"It must have been terrible for you, too."

A pained expression came over Mrs. Mayer's face. She bit her lip and said, "What was terrible was that I did so little to stop it. I was afraid of losing him and kept finding reasons for what he was doing, kept telling myself that he would change. All that did was to prolong it. He . . . *we* virtually destroyed Barrie. She had to find ways to escape the pain of it and went into her own private little world. She didn't have any friends then, just as she didn't as an adult—except you, of course, and some love interests—so she created her own friends, imaginary ones who shared her private world which was, Lord knows, better than her real one."

Collette felt a lump develop in her throat. She thought back to spending time with Barrie and tried to identify some sort of behavior that would indicate such a childhood. She came up empty, except for Barrie's tendency sometimes to drift off into her own thoughts, even in the middle of a spirited conversation with a group of people. But that hardly constituted strange behavior. She'd done it herself.

Melissa Mayer interrupted Cahill's thoughts. "Barrie's father left on her ninth birthday. We had no idea where he went, didn't hear from him again until Barrie was ten and we received a call from the police in Florida. They told me that he'd died of a stroke. There wasn't even a funeral because I didn't want one. He was buried in Florida. I have no idea where." She sighed. "He certainly lived on in Barrie, though. I've carried the guilt and shame of what I allowed to be done to my daughter all these years." Her eyes filled up and she dabbed at them with a lace handkerchief.

Collette felt a twinge of anger at the woman across from her, not only because of her admission that she did nothing to help her daughter, but because she seemed to be looking for sympathy.

She quickly told herself that wasn't fair and motioned for a waiter. They both ordered lobster bisque and Caesar salads.

The conversation took a decided upturn in mood. Melissa wanted Cahill to talk about experiences she'd had with Barrie, and Collette obliged her, some of the stories making Melissa laugh heartily, aided, in Cahill's mind, by the second drink.

When lunch was over, Cahill brought up the subject of the men in Barrie's life. Her question caused Barrie's mother to smile. She said, "Thank God the experience with her father didn't sour her on men for the rest of her life. She had a very active love life. But you must know more about that than I do. It's not the sort of thing daughters routinely share with their mothers."

Cahill shook her head. "No, Barrie didn't tell me about her male friends in great detail, although there was one, a yacht charter captain from the British Virgin Islands." She waited for a response from the mother but got none. "Eric Edwards. You didn't know about him?"

"No. Was it a recent relationship?"

Cahill nodded. "Yes, I think she was seeing him right up until the day she died. She shared her feelings about him with me. She was madly in love with him."

"No, I didn't know about him. There was that psychiatrist she was seeing."

Cahill almost said the name but held herself in check. "Seeing professionally?" she asked.

The mother made a sour face. "Yes, for a while. I was very much against it, her going into therapy where she'd have to bear her soul to a stranger."

Cahill said, "But, considering Barrie's childhood, that might have been the best thing she could do. Hadn't she had any professional help up until seeing this psychiatrist? You said his name was . . . ?"

"Tolker, Jason Tolker. No, I never saw the need for it. I think I was the one who should have had therapy, considering the grief it caused me all these years, but I don't believe in it. People should be able to handle their own emotional lives. Don't you agree?"

"Well, I suppose . . . I gather from what you've said that Barrie saw him socially as well."

"Yes, and I found that appalling. Imagine going to someone like that for more than a year and telling your most intimate secrets and then going out with him. He must have considered her a fool."

Cahill thought for a moment, then said, "Was Barrie in love with this psychiatrist?"

"I don't know."

"Did you meet him?"

"No. Barrie kept her personal life very separate from me. I suppose that goes back to her childhood needs to escape her father."

"I really don't know of any other men in Barrie's life," Cahill said, "except for fellows she dated in college. We fell out of touch for a while, as you know."

"Yes. There is that fellow at the office, David Hubler, who I think she was interested in."

That was news to Cahill, and she wondered whether the mother had it straight. She asked whether Barrie had actually dated Hubler.

"Not that I know of, and I suppose the fact that she freely introduced him to me means there was not romantic interest." She suddenly looked older than she had at the beginning of lunch. She said, "It's all water over the dam, isn't it, now that she's dead? All so wasted." She sat up straight, as though she'd suddenly realized something. She looked Cahill in the eye. "You really don't believe Barrie died of a heart attack, do you?"

Cahill slowly shook her head.

"What, then? Are you saying someone killed her?"

"I don't know, Melissa, I just know that I can't accept the fact that she died the way they say she did."

"I hope you're wrong, Collette. I know you're wrong."

"I hope so. I'm glad we could get together for this lunch. I'd like to keep in touch with you while I'm back here in Washington."

"Yes, of course, that would be lovely. Would you come for dinner?"

"I'd like that."

They went to the basement parking garage and stood next to Melissa Mayer's Cadillac. Cahill asked, "When was the last time you saw Barrie?"

"The night before it happened. She stayed with me."

"She did?"

"Yes, we had a nice quiet dinner together before she took off on another journey. She traveled so much. I don't know how she managed to keep her sanity with all the trips."

"It was a hectic schedule. Did she have her luggage with her at your house?"

"Her luggage? Yes, she did, as a matter of fact. She was going to go directly to the airport but decided to stop at the office first to take care of some things."

"What kind of luggage did Barrie have?"

"Regular luggage, one of those hang-up garment bags and a nice leather carry-on. Of course, there were always the briefcases."

"Two of them?"

"No, only the one that she always used. I bought it for her birthday a few years ago."

"I see. Did she act different that night at your house? Did she complain about feeling ill, display any symptoms?"

"Goodness, no, we had a delightful evening. She seemed in very good spirits."

They shook hands and drove off in their respective automobiles. A third car left the garage at the same time and fell in behind Cahill.

She returned to the hotel and called David Hubler. They made a date for drinks at the Four Seasons at four. She then called the British Virgin Islands, got the number of the Edwards Yacht Charter Company, and reached a secretary who informed her that Mr. Edwards was away for a few days.

"I see," Cahill said. "Do you have any idea when he'll be back? I'm calling from Washington and . . . "

"Mr. Edwards is in Washington," said the young woman, whose voice had an island lilt.

"That's wonderful. Where is he staying?"

"At the Watergate."

"Thank you, thank you very much."

"What did you say you name was, ma'am?"

"Collette Cahill. I was a friend of Barrie Mayer." She waited; the name didn't trigger a response from the girl.

She hung up, called the Watergate Hotel, and asked for Mr. Edwards's room. There was no answer. "Would you like to leave a message?"

"No, thank you, I'll call again."

CHAPTER 13

Cahill sat in the lavish lobby of Georgetown's Four Seasons Hotel waiting for David Hubler. A pianist played light classics, the delicate notes as muted as the conversations at widely spaced tables.

Cahill took in the faces of the well-dressed men and women. They were the faces of power and money, cause and effect, probably in reverse order. Dark suits, furs, highly polished shoes, minimal gestures, and comfortable posture. They belonged. Some people did and others didn't, and nowhere was the distinction more obvious than in Washington.

Were the people around her involved in politics and government? It was always assumed that everyone in Washington worked in its basic industry, government, but that had changed, Cahill knew, and for the better.

It had seemed to her during her college days that every eligible young man worked for some agency or congressman or political action committee, and that all conversation gravitated toward politics. It had become boring for her at one point, and she'd seriously considered transferring to another college in a different part of the country to avoid becoming too insular. She didn't, and ended up in government herself. What if? A silly game. What was reality for her was that she worked for the Central Intelligence Agency, had lost a friend, and was now in Washington trying to find out what had happened to that friend, for herself and for her employer.

She realized as she waited for Hubler that she'd been forgetting or, at least, ignoring that second reason for being there.

Her official assignment to take "leave" and to use it "unofficially" to find out more about Barrie Mayer's death had been handed her so casually, as though it really didn't matter what she discovered. But she knew better. Whatever underlying factors contributed to Mayer's death, they had to do with Banana Quick, perhaps the most important and ambitious clandestine operation the Company had ever undertaken. The fact that it had been compromised in some way by Mayer's death, and its implementation had been accelerated, added urgency—an urgency that Cahill now felt.

She lost track of time, and of the Four Seasons as she reflected on what had transpired over the past few weeks, especially what had been said to her by her Hungarian agent, Árpád, and what Hank Fox had said that morning about a leak in Banana Quick.

Tolker? Hegedüs had hinted that he might be "friendly" to the other side. But, she wondered, what information could he have on Banana Quick that would threaten the project and, if he did, where did he get it?

Barrie Mayer? It was the only source that made any sense to her, but that raised its own question—where would Mayer have learned enough about the project?

Eric Edwards? Possible. They were lovers, he was CIA, and he lived in the British Virgins.

If Mayer *was* killed because of what she was carrying that pertained to Banana Quick, who had the most to gain, the Soviets, or someone working with or within the CIA with something to hide?

She checked her watch. Hubler was a half hour late. She ordered a white wine and told the waitress she had to make a phone call. At Barrie's agency, Marcia St. John answered. "I was supposed to meet David at the Four Seasons a half hour ago," Collette said.

"I don't know where he is," St. John said. "I know he planned to meet you but right after you called, he got another call and tore out of here like an Olympic sprinter."

"He didn't say where he was going?"

"No. Sorry."

"Well, I'll wait another half hour. If he doesn't show and checks in with you, ask him to call me at the Hotel Washington."

"Shall do."

■ ■ ■

As Collette resumed her seat in the Four Seasons and quietly sipped her wine, David Hubler parked his car in front of a hydrant in Rosslyn, got out, locked the door, and looked up the street. He had to squint, finally to shield his eyes with his hand from the harsh, direct rays of a blazing setting sun that was anchored at the far end of the busy road. There was a heavy, dirty haze in the air that compounded the blinding effect.

He said aloud the address he'd been given by the caller who'd prompted him to run from the office, and to break his date with Collette. He checked his watch; he was ten minutes early. Street signs at the corner told him he was within half a block of his destination, an alley between two nondescript commercial buildings.

A group of teenagers passed, one carrying a large portable radio and cassette player from which loud rock 'n' roll blared. Hubler watched them pass, turned, and started for the corner. The sidewalk was busy with men and women leaving their jobs and heading home. He bumped into a woman and apologized, circumvented a young couple embracing, and reached the corner. "What the hell," he said as he turned left and walked halfway down the block until reaching the entrance to the alley. He peered down it; the sun was anchored at its end, too. He cocked his head, focused his eyes on the ground, and took a few steps into the narrow passageway. It was empty, or appeared to be. Steel doors that were rear entrances to businesses were closed. Occasional piles of neatly bagged garbage jutted out into the alley; two motorcycles and a bicycle were securely chained to a ventilation pipe.

Hubler continued, his eyes now searching walls on his left for a large red sign that would say NO PARKING. He found it halfway into the alley, above a bay of sorts. A narrow loading dock with a roll-down corrugated door was below the sign. Large drums, probably having contained chemicals or some other industrial product, were stacked three high and five deep, creating a pocket invisible to people on the streets at either end.

He looked at his watch again. It was time. He skirted the drums and went to the loading dock, placed his hands on it, and listened. The alley was a silent refuge from the distant horns of the streets, the boom boxes, and the animated conversations of people happily escaping nine-to-five.

"On time," a male voice said.

Hubler, hands still on the loading dock, raised his head and turned in the direction of the voice. His pupils shut down as his eyes tried to adjust from shadows to the stream of sunlight pouring into the alley. The man to whom the voice belonged took three steps forward and thrust his right hand at Hubler's chest. A six-inch, needle-thin point of an ice pick slid easily through skin and muscle and reached Hubler's heart, the handle keeping it from going through to his back.

Hubler's mouth opened wide. So did his eyes. A red stain bloomed on the front of his shirt. The man withdrew the pick, leaned his head closer to Hubler, and watched the result of his action, like a painter evaluating an impetuous stroke of red paint on his canvas. Hubler's knees sagged and led his body down to the cement. His assailant quickly knelt and pulled Hubler's wallet from his pants pocket and shoved it into his tan rain jacket. He stood, checked both ends of the alley, and walked toward the sun, now in the final stage of its descent.

■ ■ ■

When Hubler didn't arrive, Cahill paid for her drink and returned to her hotel. There were two messages, one from Vern Wheatley, the other from the British literary agent, Mark Hotchkiss. She tried Dave Hubler at home. No answer. Hotchkiss, the message said, was staying at the newly renovated Willard. She called; no answer in his room. Vern Wheatley was staying in his brother's apartment on Dupont Circle. She reached him.

"What's up?" she asked.

"Nothing much. I just thought you might be free for dinner."

"I'm not, Vern, wish I were. Rain check?"

"Tomorrow?"

"Sounds good. How's the assignment going?"

"Slow, but what else is new? Trying to pin down bureaucrats is like trying to slam a revolving door. I'll give you a call tomorrow afternoon and set things up."

"Great."

"Hey, Collette?"

"Huh?"

"You have a date tonight?"

"I wouldn't call it that unless the fact that I'm having dinner with a man makes it so. Business."

"I thought you were home to relax."

"A little relaxation, a little business. Nothing heavy. Talk to you tomorrow."

She hung up and chided herself for the slip. As she took off her clothes and stepped into the shower, she found herself wishing she were on a vacation. Maybe she could tack on a week of leave when she was done snooping into Barrie Mayer's death. That would be nice.

After her shower, she stood naked in front of a full-length mirror and looked herself over from head to toe. "Strictly a salad, no bread," she said to her reflection as she pinched the flesh at her waist. She certainly wasn't overweight, but knew the possibility was always there should she neglect her sensible eating habits and go on a binge.

She chose one of two dresses she'd brought with her from home, a mauve wool knit she'd had made for her in Budapest. Her hair had grown longer and she debated with herself whether she liked it that way. It didn't matter at the moment. She wasn't about to get a haircut that evening. She completed her ensemble with tan pumps, a simple, single-strand gold necklace, and tiny gold pierced earrings, a gift to her from Joe Breslin on the first anniversary of her assignment to Budapest. She grabbed her purse and raincoat, went to the lobby, and told the doorman she needed a cab. She wasn't in the mood to drive and have to search for parking spaces.

It had started to rain, and the air had picked up a chill from a front that was passing through Washington. The doorman held a large golf umbrella over her as he opened the door to a taxi that pulled up. She gave the driver Jason Tolker's address and, a few minutes later, was seated in his reception area. It was six forty-five; Tolker's group session was still in progress.

Fifteen minutes later, the participants in the group filed past her. Tolker emerged moments later, smiling. "Spirited group tonight. You watch them argue with each other over trivialities and understand why they don't get along with colleagues and spouses."

"Do they know you're that cynical?"

"I hope not. Hungry?"

"Not especially. Besides, I've put on a few pounds and would just as soon not compound it tonight."

He looked her up and down. "You look perfect to me."

"Thank you." He didn't waste time, she thought. She'd never responded to men who came up with lines like that, found them generallly to be insecure and immature. Vern Wheatley flashed through her mind, and she wished she hadn't accepted Tolker's dinner invitation. Duty! she told herself, smiled, and asked what restaurant he had in mind.

"The best in town, my house."

"Oh, wait a minute, doctor, I . . ."

He cocked his head and said in serious tones, "You're stereotyping me, Miss Cahill, aren't you, assuming that because I suggest dinner at my place the seduction scene is sure to follow?"

"It crossed my mind."

"Mine, too, frankly, but if you'll come to dinner at my house, I promise you that even if you change your mind, you'll get no moves by me. I'll throw you out right after coffee and Cognac. Fair enough?"

"Fair enough. What's on the menu?"

"Steaks and a salad. Skip the dressing and you'll lose a pound or two."

His champagne-colored Jaguar was parked outside. Cahill had never been in one; she enjoyed the smell and feel of the leather seats. He drove swiftly through Foggy Bottom, turned up Wisconsin Avenue and passed the Washington Cathedral, then took smaller streets until reaching a stretch of expensive houses set back from the road. He turned into a driveway lined with poplar trees and came to a stop on a gravel circle in front of a large stone house. A semicircular portico decorated with egg-and-dart detail protected the entrance. There were lights on in the front rooms that shed soft, yellow illumination through drapes drawn over the windows.

Tolker came around and opened Collette's door. She followed him to the front door. He pushed a buzzer. Who else was there? she wondered. The door opened and a young Chinese man wearing jeans, a dark blue short-sleeved sweatshirt, and white sneakers greeted them.

"Collette, this is Joel. He works for me."

"Hello, Joel," she said as she entered the large foyer.

To the left was what looked like a study. To the right was a dining room lighted by electrified candelabra.

"Come on," Tolker said, leading her down a hall and to the living room. Floor-to-ceiling windows afforded a view of a formal Japanese garden lighted by floodlights. A high brick wall surrounded it.

"It's lovely," Cahill said.

"Thanks. I like it. Drink?"

"Just club soda, thank you."

Tolker told Joel to make him a kir. The young man left the room and Tolker said to Cahill, "Joel's a student at American University. I give him room and board in exchange for functioning as a houseboy. He's a good cook. He's been marinating the steaks all day."

Cahill went to a wall of books and read the titles. They all seemed to be on the field of human behavior. "Impressive collection," she said.

"Most of them pop garbage, but I wanted them all. I'm a collector by nature." He came up beside her and said, "Publishers have been after me to write a book for years. Frankly, I can't imagine spending that much time on anything."

"A book. I imagine that would be an ego-booster, not that . . ."

He laughed and finished her sentence. "Not that I need it."

She laughed, too, said, "I sense you're not lacking in it, Doctor."

"Ego is healthy. People without egos don't function very well in society. Come, sit down. I'd like to learn more about you."

She wanted to say that she was the one who wanted to

learn something from the evening. She sat on a small, gracefully curved Louis XV sofa upholstered in a heavy bloodred fabric. He took a seat on its mate, across an inlaid leather coffee table. Joel placed their drinks in front of them and Tolker said, "Dinner in an hour, Joel." He looked to Cahill for approval, and she nodded. Joel left. Tolker lifted his glass and said, "To dinner with a beautiful woman."

"I can't drink a toast to that, but I won't argue."

"See, you have a healthy ego, too."

"Different from yours, Doctor. I would never toast myself. You would."

"But I didn't."

"It wouldn't have offended me if you had."

"All right, to a beautiful woman *and* to a handsome, successful, bright, and impossibly considerate gentleman."

She couldn't help but laugh. He got up and started a tape that sent soft sounds of a modern jazz trio into the room. He sat again. "First of all, how about calling me Jason instead of Doctor?"

"All right."

"Second, tell me about your life and work in Budapest."

"I'm on leave," she said.

"Spoken like a true Company employee."

"I think we ought to drop any conversation along those lines."

"Why? Make you nervous?"

"No, just aware that there are rules."

"Rules. I don't play by them."

"That's your choice."

"And your choice is to rigidly adhere to every comma and period. I'm not being impudent, Collette. I just find it amazing and wonderful and damned ironic that you and Barrie and I have this uncommon common bond. Think about it. You and your best friend both end up doing work for our country's leading spook agency, you because of a sense of patriotism, or the need for a job with a pension and a little excitement, Barrie because she became close to me, and I, as I've already acknowledged, have been a consultant to the spooks a time or two. Remarkable when you think of it. Most people go through their lives not knowing the CIA from the Audubon Society and never meeting a soul who works for them."

"Small world," she said.

"It turned out that way for us, didn't it?"

He arranged himself comfortably on his couch, crossed his legs, and asked, "How well did you know Barrie?"

"We were good friends."

"I know, but how well did you know her, *really* know her?"

Cahill thought of her luncheon conversation with Mayer's mother and realized she didn't know her friend well at all. She mentioned the lunch to Tolker.

"She was more disturbed than you realize."

"In what way?"

"Oh, what we call a disturbed myth-belief pattern."

"Meaning?"

"Meaning that she lived by a set of troublesome beliefs caused by childhood myths that were not tied to normal childhood patterns."

"Her father?"

"Her mother mentioned that to you?"

"Yes."

He smiled. "Did she indicate her role in it?"

"She said she felt guilty for not putting a stop to it. She was very candid. She admitted that she was afraid to lose her husband."

Another smile from him. "She's a liar. Most of Barrie's adult problems stemmed from her mother, not her father."

Cahill frowned.

"The old lady's a horror. Take it from me."

"You mean from Barrie. You've never met the mother."

"True, but Barrie was a good enough source. What I'm suggesting to you, Collette, is that you become a little more discriminating about who in Barrie's life you turn to for information."

"I'm not looking for information."

"You said you were trying to find out what went on with her just before she died."

"That's right, but I don't consider that 'looking for information.' I'm curious about a friend, that's all."

"As you wish. More club soda?"

"No, thank you. You obviously aren't including yourself in that restricted list."

"Of course not. I was the best friend she had . . . excluding you, of course."

"You were lovers, too."

"If you say so. Barrie didn't have any trouble attracting men."

"She was beautiful."

"Yes. Her problem was she couldn't tell the white hats from the black. Her choice in men was terrible, self-destructive to say the least."

"Present company excepted."

"Right again."

"Eric Edwards?"

"I wondered whether you knew about Barrie's macho yacht captain."

"I know a lot about him," Cahill said. "Barrie was very much in love with him. She talked about him a great deal."

"Excuse me, I need a drink." He returned a few minutes later. "Joel's started the steaks. Let me give you a quick tour before dinner."

The house was unusual, an eclectic assortment of rooms, each decorated in a different style. The master bedroom had been created from three rooms. It was huge. While the other rooms in the house smacked of an Early American influence, this room was modern. The thick carpet was white, as was the bedspread on a king-size round bed that stood in the middle of the room like a piece of sculpture, spotlights in the ceiling focusing all attention on it. One wall housed a huge projection screen television and racks of state-of-the-art sound equipment. Besides a black lacquered nightstand that held controls for the audio and video equipment, the only other furniture was black leather director's chairs scattered about the room. There wasn't a piece of clothing, a shoe, or a magazine.

"Different, isn't it?" he said.

"From the rest of the house, yes." She pictured Barrie Mayer in the bed with him.

"My apartment in New York is different, too. I like different things."

"I suppose we all do," she said, walking from the room at a pace just under a run.

Dinner was relaxed, the food and talk good. The subject of Barrie Mayer was avoided. Tolker talked a great deal about his collections, especially wine. When dinner was finished, he took Cahill to the basement where thousands of bottles were stored in temperature-controlled rooms.

They came upstairs and went to his study, which had the look of a traditional British library, books on three walls, polished paneling, carpet in warm earth tones, heavy patinated furniture, pools of gentle light from floor lamps next to a long leather couch and leather armchairs. Tolker told Joel to bring them a bottle of Cognac, then told him he was finished for the night. Cahill was glad the young Chinese man wouldn't be around any longer. There was something unsettling about him, and about the relationship with Tolker. Joel hadn't smiled once the entire evening. When he looked at Tolker, Cahill could see deep anger in his eyes. When he looked at her, it was more resentment she sensed.

"Brooding young man, isn't he?" she said, as Tolker poured their drinks.

Tolker laughed. "Yes. It's like having a houseboy and guard dog for the price of one."

They sat on the couch and sipped from their snifters. "Do you really think you're overweight?" Tolker asked.

Cahill, who'd been staring down into the dark, shimmering liquid, looked at him and said, "I know I can be if I'm not careful. I love food and hate diets. Bad combination."

"Ever try hypnosis?"

"No. Oh, that's not true. I did once, in college. So did Barrie."

It had been a fraternity party. A young man claimed to know how to do hypnosis and everyone challenged him to try it on them. Cahill was reluctant. She'd heard stories of how people can be made to act foolish at the hands of a hypnotist. It represented giving up control and she didn't like the idea.

Mayer, on the other hand, eagerly volunteered and convinced Cahill to give it a try. She eventually agreed and the two of them sat next to each other on a couch while the young man dangled his fraternity ring from a string in front of their eyes. As he talked about how they would begin to feel sleepy and relaxed, Cahill realized two things: She was feeling anything except sleepy, and was finding the whole situation funny. Mayer, on the other hand, had sagged into the couch and was actually purring. Cahill diverted her eyes from the ring and glanced over at her friend. The hypnotist realized he'd lost Cahill and devoted all his attention to Mayer. After a few more minutes of soothing talk, he suggested to Mayer that her hands were tied to helium balloons and would float up. Cahill watched as Mayer's arms began to tremble, then slowly drifted toward the ceiling. They remained there for a long time. Others in the room were watching intently. They were quiet; only the hypnotist's voice invaded the silence.

"I'm going to count from one to five," he said. "When I reach five, you'll be awake, will feel real good, and won't remember anything from the last few minutes. Later, someone will say to you, 'The balloons are pretty.' When you hear that, your arms will feel very light again and they'll float up into the air. You won't try to stop it because it will feel good. Ready? One—two—three—four—five."

Mayer's eyes fluttered open. She realized her arms were high in the air, quickly stretched them, and said, "I feel so good and rested."

Everyone applauded and the beer keg became the center of attention again.

Twenty minutes later, a friend of the hynotist who'd been prompted casually said to Mayer, "The balloons are pretty." Others at the party knew it was coming and were watching. Barrie Mayer yawned. A contented smile crossed her face and her arms floated up toward the ceiling.

"Why are you doing that?" someone yelled.

"I don't know. It just . . . feels good."

The hypnotist told her to lower them. "No," she said, "I don't want to."

He quickly went through the induction again, then told her that her arms were normal and that there weren't any balloons filled with helium. He counted to five, she shook her head, and that was the end of it.

Later, as Collette and Barrie sat in a booth in an all-night diner drinking coffee, Collette said, "You're such a phony."

"Huh?"

"That business with hypnosis and your arms being light and all. You were going along with it, right?"

"I don't know what you mean."

"You were acting. You weren't asleep or hypnotized."

"No, I really was hypnotized. At least I *think* I was. I don't remember much about it except feeling so relaxed. It was great."

Collette sat back and looked closely at her friend. "The balloons are pretty," she said softly.

Barrie looked around the diner. "What balloons?"

Collette sighed and finished her coffee, still convinced that her friend had been playacting for the sake of the hypnotist.

When she was finished telling the story to Jason Tolker, he said, "You shouldn't be so skeptical, Collette. Just because you weren't receptive doesn't mean Barrie wasn't. People differ in their ability to enter an altered state like hypnosis."

"Barrie must have been *very* receptive. It was incredible what that student was able to get her to do unless . . . unless she was just going along with it for fun."

"I don't doubt you're not hypnotizable, Collette," Tolker said, smiling. "You're much too cynical and concerned about losing control."

"Is that bad?"

"Of course not, but . . . "

"Did you ever hypnotize Barrie?"

He paused as though thinking back, then said, "No, I didn't."

"I'm surprised," Cahill said. "If she was that susceptible and . . . "

"Not susceptible, Collette, receptive."

"Whatever. If she was that receptive, and you use it in your practice, I would have thought that . . . "

"You're crossing that line of doctor-patient confidentiality."

"Sorry."

"You might be more hypnotizable than you think. After all, your only brush with it was with a college amateur. Want me to try?"

"No."

"Could help you resist fattening food."

"I'll stick to willpower, thank you."

He shrugged, leaned forward, and said, "Feel like turning on?"

"With what?"

"Your choice. Pot. Coke. Everything I have is the best."

An invitation to drugs wasn't new to Cahill, but his suggestion offended her. "You're a doctor."

"I'm a doctor who enjoys life. You look angry. Never turn on?"

"I prefer a drink."

"Fine. What'll you have?"

"I don't mean now. I really should be going."

"I really *have* offended you, haven't I?"

"Offended? No, but I am disappointed you choose to end the evening this way. I've enjoyed it very much. Would you take me home now?"

"Sure." His tone was suddenly surly, his expression one of annoyance.

They pulled up in front of her hotel and shut off the engine. "You know, Collette, Barrie wasn't the person you thought she was. She enjoyed drugs, used them with some frequency."

Cahill turned and faced him, her eyes narrowed. "One, I don't believe that. Two, even if it's true, it doesn't matter to me. Barrie was tall, slender, and her hair was sandy. I'm short, could be chubby, and have black hair. Thanks for a nice evening."

"I kept my promise, didn't I?"

"Which one?"

"Not to put moves on you. Can I see you again?"

"I don't think so." It swiftly crossed her mind that maybe she should keep in touch with him as a potential source of information. She had learned things about Barrie that were previously unknown to her and that, after all, was the purpose for her being in Washington. She softened her rejection with, "Please don't misunderstand, Jason. I'm a little confused these days, probably a combination of lingering jet lag, still grieving about Barrie's death, and a lot of other things. Let me see how my schedule goes the next few days. If I'm free, I'll call you. All right?"

"Don't call us, we'll call you."

She smiled. "Something like that. Good night."

"Good night." His face was hard and angry again, and she could see a cruelty behind his expression that caused her to flinch.

She stepped from the car—he didn't bother getting out to open the door for her this time—and started toward the hotel's entrance where the doorman, taken by surprise by her sudden exit, quickly pushed open the door for her. Across the lobby, she could see Vern Wheatley. He was seated in a wing chair facing the door. When he spotted her, he jumped up and met her just inside.

"Vern, what are you doing here?" she asked.

"I have some news, Collette, and I think we'd better discuss it."

CHAPTER 14

Cahill sat with Vern Wheatley the next morning in his brother's apartment. "Good Morning America" was the program on television. The morning paper sat on a coffee table. The lead story on page one seemed to be set in gigantic type; it virtually sprang off the page at Cahill.

D.C. LITERARY AGENT MURDERED

David Hubler, 34, a literary agent with the Georgetown firm of Barrie Mayer Associates, was found murdered last night in an alley in Rosslyn. A spokesman for the Rosslyn Police Department, Sergeant Clayton Perry, said that the cause of death appeared to be a sharp object driven into the victim's heart.

According to the same police spokesman, robbery was the apparent motive. The victim's wallet was missing. Identification was made from business cards in his pocket.

The story went on to provide sketchy details about Hubler. Barrie Mayer's death was mentioned in the final paragraph: "The agency for which Hubler worked suffered another recent loss when its founder and president, Barrie Mayer, died in London of a coronary."

Collette sat on a couch in the living room. She wore Wheatley's robe. Her eyes were focused on the newspaper. Wheatley paced the room.

"It could be a coincidence," Cahill said in a monotone.

Wheatley stopped at the window, looked out, rolled his fingertips on the pane, turned, and said, "Be reasonable, Collette. It can't be. Both of them within such a short period of time?"

A local news cutaway came on TV and they turned their attention to it. It was the second lead story. Nothing new. Just the facts of Hubler's death—apparent robbery—a thin, sharp object the weapon. No suspects. "Back to Charles Gibson in New York and his guest, a former rock star who's found religion."

Collette clicked off the set. They'd been up all night, first in her room at the hotel, then to the apartment at 4:00 A.M. where Wheatley made coffee. She'd cried, much of it out of sympathy for David Hubler, some of it because she was frightened. Now her tear tank, she thought, was empty. All that was left was a dry throat, stinging eyes, and a hollow feeling in her stomach.

"Tell me again how you found out David was dead."

"That's a *real* coincidence, Collette. I happened to be over at Rosslyn police headquarters trying to run down some leads for this assignment I'm on. I was there when the report came in about Hubler. Because of you, I knew right away who he was. You talked a lot about him the night of your party, how that guy Hotchkiss claims he ended up owning the agency and what it would mean to Hubler."

"You just happened to be there?" There was disbelief in her voice.

"Yeah. The minute I heard, I came looking for you at the hotel."

She blew a stream of breath through her lips and pulled on a clump of her hair. "It's scary, Vern, so scary."

"You bet it is, which is why you can't go around viewing it as some dumb coincidence. Look, Collette, you don't buy the fact that your friend Barrie dropped dead of a heart attack. Right?"

"I never said that."

"You didn't have to. The way you talked about it said it all. If you're right—if she was killed by someone—Hubler's death means a hell of a lot more. Right?"

"I don't know how Barrie died. The autopsy said . . ."

"What autopsy? Who did it, some London doctor, you said? Who's he? Did anybody back here connected with her family confirm it?"

"No, but . . ."

"If Barrie Mayer didn't die of natural causes, who do you think might have killed her?"

"Damn it, Vern, I don't know! I don't know anything anymore."

"More coffee?" Wheatley asked.

"No."

"Let's view it rationally," Wheatley said. "Whoever killed Hubler might have killed Barrie, right? The motive could have to do with the agency, with a client, a publisher, or with this character Hotchkiss. What do you know about him?"

"That I didn't particularly like him, that he had dinner with Barrie in London the night before she died, and that he claims to have entered into a partnership agreement with her."

"Did he show you papers?"

"No."

"Do you know where he lives, where his office is in London?"

"I have it written down. He's not there, though. He's in Washington."

Wheatley's eyes widened. "He's here."

"Yes. He left a message for me. He's at the Willard."

"You talked to him?"

"No. He wasn't there when I returned his call."

Wheatley started pacing again. He paused at the window. "Let me talk to Hotchkiss," he said.

"Why would you want to do that?"

"I'm interested."

"Why? You didn't know any of these people."

"I feel like I did because of you." He sat next to her and put his hand on her arm. "Look, Collette, you check out of the hotel and come stay here with me. My brother won't be back for another couple of weeks."

"I thought . . ."

"So did I, but he called from Africa yesterday. He finished the photo assignment but he wants to do some shooting for himself."

She pondered his suggestion. "You seem to think *I* might be in danger," she said.

He shrugged. "Maybe, maybe not, but you're a link, too, to both of them. You've met Hotchkiss. He knows you were close to Barrie and that you know about Barrie's will that sets Hubler up to run the agency. I don't know, Collette, I just think being safe is better than being sorry."

"This is all silly, Vern. I could go back to Mom's house."

"No, I want you here."

She looked up into his slender, chiseled face and realized he was giving an order, wasn't suggesting anything. She got up, went to the window, and watched people on the street below scurrying to work, briefcases and brown paper bags of coffee and Danish in their hands. There was something comforting about seeing them. It was normal. What was happening to her wasn't.

Wheatley said, "I'm going to take a shower. I have some appointments this morning. What are you up to?"

"I don't have any definite plans. I have some calls to make and . . ."

"And we check you out of the hotel. Right?"

"Okay. Can I use the phone?"

"Use anything you want. And let's get something straight right now, up front. You stay here, but it doesn't mean you have to sleep with me."

She couldn't help but smile. "Did you really think I'd assume that?" she asked.

"I don't know, but I just want it understood."

"Understood, sir."

"Don't be a wise guy."

"And don't you be a male chauvinist."

"Yes, ma'am. I'll do my best."

She heard the shower come on, picked up the phone in the living room and called her mother.

"Collette, where have you been? I tried you many times at the hotel and . . ."

"I'm okay, Mom, just a change of plans. I'll tell you all about it when I see you. Is anything wrong with you?"

"No, but Mr. Fox called. He was the one you liked so much, wasn't he?"

"Yes. What did he want?"

"He said it was very important that you call him. I promised I'd get the message to you but I couldn't reach you."

"That's okay, Mom. I'll call him this morning. Anything else new?"

"No. Your Uncle Bruce fell last night. He broke his arm."

"That's terrible. Is he in the hospital?"

"He should be but he wouldn't stay. That's the problem with drinking like he does. He can't go to the hospital because he can't drink there. They set his arm and sent him home."

"I'll call."

"That would be nice. He's such a good man except for all the drinking. It's a curse."

"I have to go, Mom. I'll call you later in the day. By the way, I'll be staying at Vern's brother's apartment for a few days."

"With him?"

"Vern? Well . . ."

"His brother."

"Oh, no. He's in Africa on a photo assignment. Vern will be here but . . ."

"You be careful."

"Of Vern?"

"I don't mean that, I just . . ."

"I'll be careful."

"Give him my best. He's a nice boy."

"I will." She gave her the apartment phone number.

Wheatley came from the shower wearing a big, fluffy red towel around his waist. His hair was wet and fell over his forehead. "Who'd you call?" he asked.

"My mother. She says hello."

"The bathroom's all yours."

"Thanks."

She closed the bathroom door, hung the robe on the back of it, and turned on the shower. A radio inside the stall was tuned to a light rock station. She reached through the water and steam and found WGMS-FM, where Samuel Barber's *Adagio for Strings* was being performed by the New York Philharmonic. She turned up the volume, withdrew her hand, stood in front of the mirror, wiped condensation from it with her palm, and peered at herself.

"Out of control," she said. "Everything's out of control."

The poignancy of the music drew her into the shower, where she eased herself under the torrent of hot water until her body had acclimated, then thrust her face beneath it. As fatigue was driven from her by the pulsating stream, she thought of her decision—*his* decision—to stay with him. Maybe she shouldn't. There was no need. She wasn't in any danger.

She absently wondered why Wheatley was so interested? Of course . . . how stupid not to realize it immediately. There's a story in it, possibly a big one. He wanted her close in case she could contribute to it by knowing Mayer and Hubler. She'd undoubtedly be finding out more about their deaths, and he could use that knowledge. It didn't anger her that she might be used by him. In fact, it set her mind at ease.

She took a plastic bottle of shampoo from a white wire rack, poured some into her hand, and vigorously worked it into her hair. It relaxed her; she felt ready to start the day. She'd call Hank Fox, then go to Barrie Mayer's agency where she'd find out what she could from her associates. There was Mark Hotchkiss to call, and Eric Edwards. It would be a busy day but she welcomed it. She'd been floundering too long, flopping between the role of concerned, grieving friend and unofficial investigator. It was time to pull everything together, accomplish what she could, grab a legitimate week's vacation and get back to Budapest where, no matter how much intrigue existed, there was a sense of order and structure.

She didn't hear the door open. It was only an inch at first, then wider. Wheatley stuck his head inside the bathroom and said softly, "Collette."

The water and music blotted out everything for her.

"Collette," he said louder.

She sensed rather than heard him, looked through the glass door and saw him standing there. She gasped; hot water instantly filled her throat and caused her to gag.

"Collette, I have some clean jockey shorts if you want a pair. Socks, too."

"What? *Shorts?*"

"Yeah. Sorry to barge in." He backed out and closed the door.

She quickly finished showering, stepped out and stood immobile, her heart pounding, her lips quivering. "Shorts," she said. "Jockey shorts." She began to calm down and started to laugh as she dried her hair. He'd left a clean pair of shorts and white athletic socks on a hamper. She put them on, slipped the dress she'd worn the night before over her head, and went to the bedroom where he was finishing dressing in jeans, a turtleneck, and a corduroy sport jacket.

"Thanks for the shorts and socks," she said. "They don't exactly go with the dress, but they'll do until I can get back to the hotel."

"We'll go right now," he said. "Hope I didn't scare you?"

"Scare me? Of course not. I thought you were making a move."

"I promised, remember?"

She thought of Jason Tolker's similar promise. She tried to slip her pumps over the heavy socks, gave up, and slipped bare feet into them. "Can't use these," she said, tossing the socks on the bed.

They drove to the hotel in her rented car, checked out, and an hour later were back in the apartment. "Got to go," Wheatley said. "Here's an extra key to the place. Catch up later?"

"Sure."

"Who are you seeing today?"

"I'm going over to Barrie's agency."

"Good idea. By the way, who was that guy you were with last night?"

"Just a friend. A doctor, friend of the family."

"Oh. We're on for dinner tonight, right?"

"Right."

"Take care. Maybe I'm being paranoid but I'd move easy," he said. "Don't take chances."

"I won't."

"Not worth it. After all, murder isn't your business. You help stranded tourists, right?"

"Right." There was a playful, disbelieving tone in his voice, and it irked her.

After he'd gone, she picked up the phone and called Hank Fox in Langley.

"You took your time," he said.

"I just got the message. My mother couldn't track me last night."

"One of those nights, huh?"

"Not in the least. Why did you call me?"

"A need to talk. Free now?"

"Well, I . . ."

"Be free. It's important. You have a car?"

"Yes."

"Good. Meet me in an hour at the scenic overlook off the G.W. Parkway, the one near the Roosevelt Bridge. Know it?"

"No, but I'll find it."

"An hour."

"I'll be there."

CHAPTER 15

Collette dressed in a gray skirt, low shoes, red-and-white striped button-down shirt and blue blazer. She went to a coffee shop around the corner from the apartment and had bacon and eggs, then got in her car and headed for her rendezvous with Hank Fox.

She kept to the speed limit on the George Washington Memorial Parkway, but her mind was going faster. Had Fox found a link between Barrie Mayer's and David Hubler's deaths? That possibility opened up another avenue of thought—David Hubler might have been involved with the CIA, too. That hadn't occurred to her before but, now that it had, it didn't seem far-fetched. Hubler and Mayer worked closely together at the agency. Mayer's frequent trips to Budapest, and the constant contact with authors like Zoltán Réti, could easily have opened up areas of discussion between them. Even if it hadn't, there had to be some tangible vestige of Mayer's part-time work for the CIA kicking around the office. Maybe she'd actually recruited Hubler into her second life. If that were the case, Cahill hoped she'd done it with agency blessing. Taking others into the fold without being ordered to do so was bound to cause major trouble, big enough, she realized, to have caused their deaths. She'd heard of agents who'd been "terminated" by the CIA itself, not for revenge or punishment as with the Mafia, but as an expedient means of closing leaks on a permanent basis.

Traffic was light this morning, so light that she noticed a green sedan that had fallen in behind her as soon as she turned onto the parkway. It stayed a considerable distance from her, but occasional glances in the rearview mirror confirmed that it was still there. She decided not to proceed to the location given her by Hank Fox until the green sedan was no longer an issue. She reached the scenic overlook Hank Fox had mentioned but passed it, her eyes quickly surveying the area. There were two cars, one a four-door pale blue Chevrolet Caprice, the other a white station wagon with paneling. A young woman holding a baby on her hip walked a dalmatian on a leash. A pit stop for the dog, Cahill thought, as she got off at the next exit and made a series of sharp turns on local streets until finding her way back onto the parkway. She checked her watch; she was ten minutes early but that time would be eaten by having to exit the parkway again and circling back. She checked behind her in the mirror. No green sedan. So much for that.

Precisely an hour after she'd talked to Fox she turned into the parking area. The woman, baby, and dog were gone, leaving the Caprice sitting by itself. Cahill pulled up next to it, put her car into PARK, turned, and peered into the Caprice. Hank Fox looked back at her through the glass. She noticed there was someone else in the car.

She stiffened; why would he bring someone else? Who was it? She tried to see, but glare on the window left only a vague image in the passenger seat.

Both doors on the Caprice opened. Hank Fox stepped out of the driver's side, Joe Breslin the other. Collette breathed a sigh of relief, and surprise. What was Breslin doing there?

Fox slid in next to her and Breslin got in the rear.

"Joe, what a surprise," Cahill said, turning and smiling.

"Yes, for me, too," Breslin said, slamming the door.

"Let's go," Fox said.

"Where?" asked Cahill.

"For a ride, that's all. Head out toward the airport."

Cahill did her turnaround again and headed south on the parkway, along the Potomac, until reaching National Airport. Fox told her to pull into the metered parking area. When she was at a meter and had turned off the engine, he said, "You two go inside. I'll stay with the car."

They entered the terminal and Breslin led the way to the observation deck entrance. They paid, went through the door, and stood at a railing. Below them was the aircraft ramp area and active runways. A brisk wind whipped Collette's hair. She gently pressed her middle fingers against her ears to muffle the whine of jet engines.

"Just right," Breslin said.

"What?"

"Just the right amount of ambient noise." He moved closer to her, turned, and said inches from her ear, "Plans have changed."

Cahill looked quizzically at him.

"How would you like a little time in the sun?" he asked.

"Sounds nice. I was going to ask about a vacation."

"It's not a vacation. It's an assignment."

When he didn't say more, she asked.

"They want you in the BVI."

"Why?"

"To get to know Eric Edwards. They want you to get close to him, see what he's up to."

Cahill looked to the runway where a Boeing 737 was slicing into a gray sky. Breslin, his hands shoved into his raincoat pockets, a dead pipe clenched in his teeth, paused for what he'd said to sink in, then removed the pipe and leaned toward her. "Banana Quick has been badly compromised, Collette. We have to know how and why."

"Edwards is in Washington, not the BVI," she said.

"We know that, but he'll be returning there in a couple of days. They want you to make contact with him here and do whatever you have to do to . . . to get inside him. See if you can wangle an invitation from him to go down there."

"Wait a minute," she said, her face reflecting her anger, "you want me to sleep with him?"

"The orders don't stipulate that. They just say . . ."

"To do anything I have to do to 'get inside him.' No dice, Joe. Hire a hooker. The Pickle Factory's ripe with them."

"You're overreacting."

"I'm underreacting," she said sharply.

"Call it what you will, the order has come down and you're it. You don't have a choice."

"Ever hear of quitting?"

"Sure, but you won't. I don't want you to. You don't have to sleep with anybody, just get to know a little about his operation and tell us about it. He's too independent, not enough controls."

"What if he doesn't invite me to the BVI?"

"Then you will have failed. Try not to let that happen."

"Where are you getting your information about the leak?"

Breslin glanced around before saying, "From your man in Budapest, Árpád Hegedüs."

"It's definitely Edwards?"

"We don't know, but he's a logical place to start. He's our eyes and ears down there. We know he's a drinker and a talker. Maybe he's been drinking and talking with the wrong people."

"The Russians know everything?"

Breslin shrugged. "They know too much, that's for sure." Some other people came onto the observation deck and stood close to them. "There are two tickets at the Concert Theater box office for some dance recital tomorrow night at the Kennedy Center," Breslin told her. "Go to it. I'll be on the terrace at intermission. Check in with me then."

Collette let out a deep sigh and placed her hands on the railing. "Why did they send you all the way from Budapest to tell me this?" she asked.

"Why do they do anything, Collette? Besides, sending me indicates how important the project is. When the stakes are big, they care enough to send their very best." He smiled.

She couldn't help but smile, too. "They sent you because they knew you could get me to do it."

"Did I?"

"I'll do my best, no promises."

"Can't ask for more than that," he said, touching her arm and turning.

A half hour later they were back at the overlook. Before

Fox and Breslin got out of her car, Fox asked, "How was your evening with Jason Tolker?"

"You know about that?"

"Yes."

"It was pleasant enough. He and Barrie were close. I wanted to find out what I could from him."

"Did you? Find out anything?"

"A little."

Breslin said from the back seat, "Save it for tomorrow night on the terrace, Collette." He slapped Fox on the shoulder and said, "Let's go."

They got into Fox's car and drove off, neither man looking back. When they were gone, Cahill felt alone and vulnerable. She gripped the bottom of the steering wheel and saw her eyes in the rearview mirror. Somehow, they didn't belong to her. She tapped the mirror so that it no longer reflected her face, started the engine, and drove as quickly as she could to the apartment, remembering to check her mirror a few times. No green sedan.

CHAPTER 16

"Eric Edwards?"

"Yes."

"This is Collette Cahill, Barrie Mayer's friend."

"Hi, how are you? My secretary told me you'd called. I assume you got my message in Budapest?"

"Yes, I did. I'm sorry I didn't contact you sooner but I've been busy."

"I understand."

"I still can't believe she's dead."

"Hard for any of us to believe it. Barrie talked a lot about you. I suppose you were her best friend?"

"We were close. I was wondering if we could get together for a drink, or lunch, or whatever works for you. Will you be in Washington long?"

"Leaving tomorrow. You on vacation?"

"Yes."

"How's things in Budapest?"

"Fine, except for when I heard about Barrie. Are you free for lunch?"

"No, unfortunately I'm not. I'm on a tight schedule."

"Time for a fast drink this afternoon? I'm free all day."

"Well, I suppose . . . how about six? I have a dinner date at seven."

"That'd be fine." She realized she was not about to generate enough interest from him in an hour to result in an invitation to the BVI. "Actually," she said, "I'm not being completely honest. I do want to talk to you about Barrie, but I also would love some good advice on the BVI. I'm spending part of my vacation there and thought you could recommend a good hotel, restaurants, that sort of thing."

"Happy to. When are you leaving?"

Some quick thinking. "In a few days."

"I'll give it my best shot when we meet tonight. On a budget?"

"Sort of, but not too tight."

"Fine. Like sailing?"

Collette had never been out in a sailboat. "Yes," she said, "I love it." She knew she should qualify her answer. "I really don't know much about it, though. I've only been a few times."

"Let's see if we can't arrange a day trip for you. I'm in the yacht-chartering business."

"I know. It sounds . . ." She laughed. "It sounds wonderful and romantic."

"Mostly hard work, although it does beat a suit and tie and nine to five, at least for me. Any suggestion where to meet tonight?"

"Your choice. I've been away from Washington too long."

"Might as well come over here to the Watergate. Would make my life a little easier. Come to my room. I'll have something sent up. What do you drink?"

"Scotch and soda?"

"You got it. See you at six, Room 814."

She drove to Barrie Mayer's literary agency where Marcia St. John and Carol Geffin were behind their desks. Tony Tedeschi, one of the associate agents, was burrowing through a file cabinet in the corner.

St. John, a lanky, attractive mulatto, who'd been there the longest, greeted Cahill soberly.

"I heard," Cahill said.

St. John shook her head. "First Barrie, now David. It's incredible."

Tedeschi said, "How are you, Collette?"

"Okay, Tony. The question is how are *you*?"

"We're holding up. Have you heard anything new about David?"

"No, just the TV and newspapers. What are the funeral plans?"

"Not set yet," St. John said. "How's Budapest?"

"Fine, last I saw it." Collette looked at the door leading to Barrie's private office. It was open a crack and she saw a figure cross the room, then disappear. "Who's in there?" she asked.

"Our new leader," St. John said, raising her eyebrows.

"New leader?"

"Mark Hotchkiss."

"Really?" Cahill went to the door and pushed it open. Hotchkiss, in shirtsleeves, bow tie, and yellow suspenders, was seated behind what had been Barrie Mayer's desk. A pile of file folders were on his lap. He looked up over half-glasses, said, "Be with you in a minute, Miss Cahill," and went back to leafing through the files.

Cahill closed the door and stood at the edge of the desk.

She waited a few moments before saying, "I find this arrogant, at best."

He looked up again and smiled. "Arrogant? I'd hardly call it that. Due to unforeseen circumstances, there's been a dreadful gap created at this agency. I'm being decisive. If that represents arrogance, so be it."

"Mr. Hotchkiss, I'd like to see the partnership agreement you and Barrie signed."

He smiled, exposing his yellow teeth, pushed the glasses up to the top of his head and leaned back in Mayer's chair, arms behind his head. "Miss Cahill, I have no reason whatsoever to show you anything. The partnership arrangement Barrie and I constructed is quite sound, quite legal. I suggest that if your curiosity is that strong, you contact Barrie's solicitor . . . attorney, Richard Weiner. Would you like his address and phone number?"

"No, I . . . yes, I would."

Hotchkiss found a slip of paper on the desk and copied it onto another slip. "Here you are," he said, a smug smile on his face. "Call him. You'll find that everything is quite in order."

"I'll do that."

"Now," he said, standing and coming to her, "I believe we had tentative plans for dinner here in Washington. What night is good for you?"

"I'm afraid I'm all booked up."

"Pity. I'm sure we have a great deal to talk about. Well, if you change your mind, give me a call. I suspect I'll be here day and night trying to sort things out." His face suddenly sagged into a sympathetic expression. "I am so sorry about that poor chap, Hubler. We had our differences, but to see such a personable young man snuffed out at such an early age is bloody awful. Please give my deepest sympathies to his family."

Cahill's frustration level made further talk impossible. She spun around and left the office. Tedeschi was the first to see her. "You, too, huh?"

"This is absurd," Cahill said. "He just walks in and takes over?"

"Afraid so," Tedeschi said. "He's got the piece of paper. He ran it through Dick Weiner. Weiner doesn't believe it, either, but it looks legit. Why Barrie would have hooked up with this bozo is beyond me, but it looks like the lady made a mistake."

"She made it, we live with it," said Marcia St. John, who'd overheard the conversation.

"Barrie had a will," Cahill said. "She turned things over to David in the event of her death."

Tedeschi shook his head. "The will's invalid, according to Weiner. The partnership agreement takes precedence for some legal reason, the way it was worded, who knows? It's all foreign language to me."

"I'm going to see Weiner."

"You know him?" Tedeschi asked.

"No, but I will."

"He's a nice guy and a good lawyer, but you're wasting your time. Hotchkiss has the agency as the surviving partner. Excuse me, Collette, I gotta work on my résumé."

"I just don't believe this," Collette said, shaking her head and knowing it was a pathetically ineffective statement.

"Life in the fast lane," Carol Geffin said.

"How's David's family holding up?" Collette asked.

"The way they're supposed to, I guess. God, he was

young." St. John started to cry and went to the ladies' room.

Collette asked again about funeral arrangements, and was told a decision was to be made later that afternoon. She left the office and went to a phone booth from which she called the attorney, Richard Weiner. She explained her relationship; he was on the line in seconds.

"This can't be right," she said. "Barrie would never have signed an agreement with Hotchkiss making him a full partner so that he'd inherit the agency if she died."

"I feel the same way, Miss Cahill, but the papers do seem in order. Frankly, I can't take any further steps without the prompting of her family. They'd have to challenge it, go after expert handwriting analysis, probe the background of the deal."

"Her only family is her mother."

"I know that. I spoke with her earlier this morning after hearing about David Hubler."

"And?"

"She said she was too old to become involved in something like this."

"What about Dave's family? Her will took care of him. Wouldn't it be in their interest to challenge Hotchkiss?"

"Probably not. Barrie didn't leave the agency to him. She simply stipulated that he be retained on a specified compensation package for five years. She left him key-man insurance, too, fifty thousand dollars."

"Who gets that now that *he's* dead?"

"The agency."

"Hotchkiss."

"Ultimately, not directly. It goes in the corporate coffers. He's the corporation."

She banged her fist against the booth and said, "First her, now David. Do you think . . . ?"

"Think what, that Hotchkiss might have killed David? How can I think that, Miss Cahill?"

"I can. I have."

"Well, I suppose you're . . . but what about Barrie? She died of natural causes."

Cahill had to fight with herself to keep from telling him that Barrie hadn't died of natural causes, that she'd been murdered. Instead, she said, "I'm glad I had a chance to talk with you, Mr. Weiner."

"Let's talk more. If you come up with any information that bears on this, call me day or night." He gave her his home phone number. She pretended to write it down but didn't bother. She knew she wouldn't be calling him at home, or at his office again either. Barrie Mayer's business affairs really didn't interest her, unless Mark Hotchkiss were involved in both deaths. She doubted it. Weiner was right; Hotchkiss wasn't the type.

Still, there was the question of how he'd enticed Mayer into signing such a binding partnership agreement. Had he held something over her head? What could it be? Wrong road, Cahill decided. She'd pursue it later, after taking care of primary business, her initial meeting with Eric Edwards.

That brought up another whole series of thoughts as she returned to the apartment, stopping first at a bookstore to buy a travel guide to the British Virgin Islands.

Did Edwards know for whom she was working? That was one of the biggest problems in tracking Mayer's life prior to her death. Who knew what? Tolker knew. She had to assume that Edwards knew, too. He hadn't indicated it on the message he left on her answering machine in Budapest, or during their brief telephone conversation that morning. But *he knew;* she had to operate under that assumption.

It also began to lean heavily on her that she'd been hopelessly naive in this matter. She'd never once questioned the motives or activities of people like Joe Breslin, Hank Fox, Stan Podgorsky, or any of the others with whom she'd developed a "father-daughter" relationship. The fact was that they responded to a higher calling than Collette Cahill's personal needs and future. They were Company men, fully capable of selling anyone down the river to further the cause for which they'd been hired, or to perpetuate their own careers and lifestyles. "Damn it," she mumbled as she parked the car and headed for Vern Wheatley's brother's apartment, "I hate this."

Those feelings were forgotten as she spent an hour reading the travel guide and formulating questions for Eric Edwards about her "vacation." It took her into the early afternoon. She called Mayer's office and asked whether there'd been any word on funeral plans for David.

"Private," St. John told her. "Just family."

"Why?"

"Because that's the way they want it."

"Who's in the family?"

"His mother and father, a sister who's flying in from Portland, cousins, others, I guess."

"You were his family, too, at least part of it."

"Collette, I only work here. There's a man in Barrie's office with a funny way of talking and yellow fangs. One of the nicest guys I ever knew is being buried. Tony's grinding out résumés like it was the State of the Union address, and Carol is dwelling on which disco will have the best collection of hunks tonight. I miss you, David. I'd be there if they let me. Understand, Collette?"

"Sure. Sorry. I can keep in touch?"

It was a hollow laugh. "P-l-e-a-s-e," St. John said. "Make sure *I'm* alive on a day-to-day basis."

Collette hung up and wrapped her arms about herself as the meaning of St. John's final remark sent a chill through her body. Two dead out of the same office. That realization caused her to begin rethinking everything that had happened. Maybe Barrie Mayer's death had absolutely, positively nothing to do with spies and governments. Maybe it had to do with commerce, pure and simple. Maybe . . . maybe . . .

There were so many of those.

CHAPTER 17

Edwards answered his door wearing a white hotel-provided terrycloth robe with a "W" on the breast pocket. "Miss Cahill, come in. I'll only be a minute. I managed to get in a little workout at the end of the day." He disappeared into the bedroom, leaving her alone in the suite's living room.

A small set of barbells rested on towels on the floor. Written on them in black was PROPERTY OF WATERGATE HOTEL. A rock station blared the day's latest hits. Clothing was strewn on every piece of furniture.

She answered a knock on the door. A young Hispanic bellhop rolled a cart into the room, opened its leaves, fussed with napkins and silverware, and handed Collette the check. "I'm not . . . Sure." She signed Edwards's name and included a dollar tip.

Edwards came from the bedroom wearing slacks. Cahill couldn't help but take immediate note of his bare upper body—heavily muscled arms and chest, trim waist, and all of it the color of copper. "It arrived," he said. "I owe you anything?"

"No. I signed."

"Good. Well, let me finish dressing. Help yourself."

"Can I pour you something?"

"Yes, please. Just gin on the rocks. The bottle's over there." He pointed to a cabinet on which a half-empty bottle of gin sat. He returned to the bedroom and Cahill fixed the drinks. When he again joined her he'd put on a monogrammed white silk shirt and yellow loafers. She handed him his glass. He held it up and said, "To the memory of Barrie Mayer, one hell of a fine lady." He drank. She did, too, the Scotch causing her mouth to pucker.

"I'm sorry to be in a rush." He cleared clothing and magazines from the couch and they sat on it. "Tell me, is there anything new about Barrie?"

"New? No. I assume you heard about her associate being murdered last night?"

"No, I didn't. Which associate?"

"David Hubler."

"I don't believe it. She really liked him. He was murdered?"

"That's what the police say. It happened in Rosslyn. Somebody rammed a sharp object into his heart."

"Jesus."

"They say robbery was the motive because his wallet and credit cards were missing, but that doesn't prove anything to me."

"No, I guess not. What irony, the two of them dying so close together."

Collette nodded.

He looked directly at her and said, "I miss Barrie. We were getting close to making it official."

Cahill was surprised. "You were planning marriage?"

"Maybe 'planning' isn't the word, but we were headed in that general direction." He smiled. It was a charming, engaging, little boy's smile. "You must have thought I was some college sophomore with that message I left on your answering machine. It took me forever to get a line to Budapest. When I did and was faced with that infernal machine, I just started babbling. I was very upset. *Very* upset."

"I can imagine," said Cahill. "When had you last seen her?"

"A week or so before. Frankly, we'd been having a few problems and were looking forward to getting away for a few days to straighten things out. She was planning a trip to the BVI when she got back from Hungary. She'll never make that trip now, will she?"

Cahill reacted by filling up. She took a deep breath and forced a smile. Her thoughts were on the situation that existed at the moment, the same old one that characterized every meeting she'd had during the past few days. Did he know she worked for the CIA? She reminded herself that *she'd* decided the answer to that earlier in the day. He knew. Still, should she bring everything up, Barrie's courier life, Jason Tolker, her job in Budapest, and her knowledge of his job in the British Virgins?

Not yet, she decided. The wrong time.

"So, to get onto a lighter note," Edwards said, "you're coming to my little part of the world for a rest."

"Yes, that's right." She'd forgotten that aspect of her visit.

"Made any plans yet?"

"Not really. It's a last-minute decision. I thought I'd go to a travel agent but then I remembered you. Barrie said you know the BVI better than anyone."

"That's not true, but I have learned a lot sailing those islands. Want to go posh? Peter Island, Little Dix, Biras Creek. Want a little more action? The Tradewinds, Bitter End. Looking for a real native feel? Andy Flax's Fischer's Cove, Drake's Anchorage on Mosquito Island. Lots of choices, with even more in between."

Mosquito Island, she thought, the site of Banana Quick's highest-level meetings. "What would you recommend?"

"There's always my place."

Would it be this easy?

"Or," he said, "one of my yachts, if one is available. I promised you a day's sailing. Might as well stay on board and save yourself some money."

"That's much too generous."

"I wouldn't be offering it to just anyone. Barrie stayed with me so many times, at my house and on the yachts. I'd really be privileged to have you, Collette. I can't promise I'll be around much. It depends on bookings, but we're still out of season down there and, at least when I left, things were slow." He stood and refilled his glass. "Another?"

She checked her watch. "You have to leave," she said, "and I have things to do. I feel as though I should be doing something to repay your generosity."

"Don't be silly," he said, walking her to the door.

"If you weren't going back tomorrow, I'd invite you to join me at the Kennedy Center. I ended up with two tickets to a marvelous performance and there's just me to use them."

"Damn, I wish I could," he said, "but it's impossible. I have appointments back home in the afternoon. You'll find somebody else."

She was glad he turned her down. It had been an

impetuous offer, one she thought might help bring them closer together in a hurry. But then, she realized, it would be awkward, if not impossible, to meet with Joe Breslin at intermission. Did Edwards know Breslin, and Hank Fox? Probably by name, not by sight. Agents like Edwards operated as rogues, seldom coming into contact with administrative types. They had their single contact in Langley, some operatives in place, and that was it. The nature of the beast. Whether he knew about her was another matter, a bridge to be crossed when . . .

"How's things at the embassy?" he asked as they stood at the door.

"Fine, last I heard."

"You still with the same division?"

What division was that? She said, "Yes."

"When are you planning to come to the BVI?"

"I thought maybe . . . maybe Saturday." It was Wednesday.

"Great. Pan Am goes into San Juan and you can catch an Air BVI flight from there. There's a new direct service out of Miami, too."

"I'd rather leave from New York." She made a mental note to check out the Miami flight. "Thanks for the offer."

"I look forward to it. You have my phone number. Let me know when you're due to arrive and I'll have you picked up."

"This is all overwhelming."

"It's for Barrie. See you in the sun in a couple of days."

CHAPTER 18

The Dance Theatre of Harlem ended its first act to thunderous applause from twenty-five hundred people in Kennedy Center's concert hall. Cahill joined in enthusiastically from her twelfth-row-center seat. She picked up her raincoat from the empty seat next to her and moved with the crowd as it spilled out into the Grand Foyer, the Hall of States, and the Hall of Nations. It had been raining when the audience arrived, but had stopped during the first act.

She went to one of the doors leading to the broad terrace on the Potomac and looked out. A few people had gone outside and stood in small groups separated by puddles. She looked toward the railing on the river side and saw Joe Breslin. His back was to her. Blue smoke from his pipe drifted up into the damp night air.

She came up behind him. "Hello, Joe."

He didn't turn as he said, "Nice night. I like it just after it rains."

She joined him at the railing and they looked out over the river and toward National Airport. A jet screamed over them as it sought the solid safety of the runway, its landing gear extended like a large bird's talons reaching for a tree branch. After its engine noise had faded, Breslin asked, "Enjoying the performance?"

"Very much. You?"

"It's not my favorite entertainment but I suppose it has its place."

She started to discuss the dance troupe but knew it wasn't why they were standing there. "I made contact with Eric Edwards," she said.

"And?"

"I'm joining him in the BVI on Saturday."

He swiveled his head and stared at her, smiled, raised his eyebrows, and returned his gaze to the river. "That was fast," he said, sounding disapproving.

"It was easy," she said. "Barrie paved the way."

"Barrie?"

"The common bond between us. I didn't have to do any seducing. We're a couple of friends because of her."

"I see. Are you staying with him?"

"Yes, either at his home or on one of his yachts."

"Good. How did you meet up with him?"

"I called. He invited me for a drink at his suite at the Watergate. Actually, I invited myself. I told him I was planning a vacation in the BVI and asked for recommendations."

"Good tactic."

"I thought so. Anyway, it worked. Now, what's the next step?"

"Meaning what?"

"Meaning, what are you looking for while I'm there?"

Breslin shrugged and drew on his pipe. "I don't know, anything that looks interesting."

"It can't be that vague, Joe."

"I don't mean it to be." His sigh was deep and prolonged. He looked around at others on the terrace. The nearest people were fifteen feet away—two couples who'd come to the railing to see the river. Breslin positioned his body so that he leaned on the rail with his back to them, and was facing Cahill. "Why are you staying with your former boyfriend?"

His directness took her aback. "Vern Wheatley? How do you know about him?"

"It's not so much knowing about him, Collette, it's knowing about you."

"I'm being followed?"

"You're being protected."

"From what?"

"From harm."

"I resent this, Joe."

"Be grateful. What about Wheatley?"

"What about him? We went together in high school, that's all. When I came home, my mom threw a party and he showed up. He's down here on assignment for *Esquire* magazine."

"I know that. Why are you staying with him?"

"Because . . . Christ, Joe, what business is it of yours?"

"You're right, Collette, it's not my business. It's the Company's business."

"I'd debate that."

"Don't bother."

He looked at her and said nothing. She said, "Vern was the one who told me about David Hubler being killed."

"And he convinced you to leave the hotel and move in with him for . . . for your own safety?"

"Yes, as a matter of fact, that's exactly what happened."

She shook her head and made a sound by blowing air past her lips. "Boy, I am some protected girl, huh, Joe? What are you doing now, trying to get me to distrust, Vern, too? Trust nobody, right? Everybody's a spy or a double agent or a . . ."

Breslin ignored her rising emotions and said flatly, "You do know that your high school beau is in Washington researching a story on us?"

It hit her in the chest like a fist. "No, I did not know that," she said in a controlled voice.

"Hank Fox's unit has been tracking your friend."

"So?"

"Maybe he wants you close to him for information."

"I doubt that."

"Why?"

"Because . . ."

"I think you should be aware of the possibility."

"Thank you." She wasn't proud of the snippy way she answered, but it was the best she could manage.

"About Edwards. There's a possibility that he's the leak in Banana Quick."

"So I heard."

"If so, he's potentially dangerous."

"In what way?"

"Physically. To you. It's something else I thought you'd appreciate knowing."

"Of course I do."

"It's possible he's been turned."

Another fist in the chest. "I thought it was just a matter of drinking too much and a loose tongue."

"Could be those things, too, but the possibility of a turn can never be overlooked. It isn't prudent to overlook such possibilities."

"I certainly won't. Anything else you think I should know?"

"Lots of things. Your man, Árpád Hegedüs, is on his way to Russia."

"He is? They did it?"

"Yes. We had one final meeting with him before he left. It wasn't easy. He wouldn't talk to anyone except 'His Miss Cahill.' We managed to convince him that it was in his interest to talk with somebody else."

"How is he?"

"Frazzled, afraid of what's in store for him once he's back in Mother Russia. He almost bolted, came over to us."

"He wanted that."

"I know, I went over the transcript of the session with Stan. The woman he's met complicated things for him. He was ready to defect and bring her with him."

"He didn't."

"We dissuaded him."

"Because we need him." Now it was scorn she didn't intend to come from her mouth.

"We suspect he'll be all right. There's nothing to indicate he's in trouble."

"The woman?"

"She's a clerk in a Hungarian food-processing plant. No use to us."

"I don't think we'll ever see Hegedüs again."

"We'll see. What's really important is that casual, last-minute comment he made at the end of your session with him about Dr. Tolker."

"I know. I never had a chance to discuss it with anyone before I left. I figured the transcript would tell the tale."

"We think Tolker's okay."

"Why?"

"Because . . . because he's never done anything to raise anyone's doubts. Still . . ."

"Still, he was Barrie Mayer's contact, and she was intimate with Eric Edwards which, according to Logic 101, means a link with Banana Quick. Maybe Tolker's the leak."

"Maybe, maybe not. We're watching him. What concerns us more at the moment is his link with your former beau, Mr. Wheatley."

The fists to the breastbone were beginning to hurt. "What link?" she asked.

"Wheatley is digging into a program that we abandoned years ago. Project Bluebird? MK-ULTRA?"

"Means nothing to me."

"It was covered in your training. Mind control. Drug experimentation."

"Okay, I remember vaguely. Why would Vern be interested if it's past tense?"

Breslin hunched his shoulders beneath his raincoat against a sudden cool breeze that whipped in from the river. "That's what we'd like to know. Maybe you could . . . ?"

"Nope."

"Why not? He's using you as a source of information for *his* ends."

"That's your interpretation, not mine."

"Do him a favor, Collette, and ask some questions. He's swimming in deep water."

"Why do you say that?"

"Look at Mr. Hubler."

Cahill started to respond, pushed away from the railing, and took steps toward the door leading back into the Kennedy Center. Breslin said, "Collette, come here."

She stopped; lights flashed indicating the second act was about to begin. She turned, hands in her blazer pockets, head cocked, eyes narrowed.

Breslin smiled and made a small motion with his index finger for her to return to him. She looked down into a wavy reflection of herself in a large puddle on the terrace, brought her eyes back up to him, and retraced her steps. Another jet, this time taking off from National, shattered the moment with its crescendo of full throttle.

Breslin said once she was again at his side, "David Hubler came over to Rosslyn because he'd been told there was a book to be offered on an inside story about us." She started to say something but he raised his finger to silence her. "He was to meet someone on the corner where we have a facility. This unnamed person was to talk to him about selling inside information which, in turn, would be turned into a book, a best seller no doubt."

Cahill just stared at him and blinked.

"This facility in Rosslyn is the one Hank Fox directs."

Another blink. Then, the question, "And David was killed by this person who was going to sell him information?"

"David was killed by . . . we don't know."

"Not robbery?"

"Not likely."

"Us? Someone from . . . *us*?"

"I don't know. Your friend, Vern Wheatley, was there when it happened."

"He was with the Rosslyn police looking for information on a story he's doing about Washington and . . ."

"He was there." His words were stone-hard.

"Good God, Joe, you're not suggesting that Vern had anything to do with David's murder?"

"I stopped suggesting things a long time ago, Collette. I just raise possibilities these days."

"You're damn good at it."

"Thanks. By the way, one of Barrie Mayer's clients, Zoltán Réti, was in to see us." He laughed. "Talk about a poor choice of words. He contacted Ruth Lazara from Cultural Exchange at a party, said he had to talk to someone. We arranged a meet."

"What did he say?"

"He said that he was convinced that he'd been sent to London for a conference because they knew he was supposed to meet Barrie Mayer when she arrived in Budapest."

"Meaning what?"

"Meaning . . . that the Soviets evidently knew not only that she was carrying something important, but that they wanted her point man out of the way."

"You think the Soviets killed her?"

"No idea."

"Joe."

"What?"

"What was Barrie carrying?"

"As far as I can ascertain, nothing."

"Nothing?"

"Nothing."

"She was killed for *nothing*?"

"Looks like it."

"Great. That gives real value to her life."

He re-ignited his pipe.

"We have to go in," Cahill said. "It's starting again."

"Okay. One more thing, Collette. Keep these things in mind. One, choosing you to follow up on the Banana Quick leak isn't a frivolous choice. You have the perfect reasons for asking questions, and now you've got an invitation from one of our primary people. You've met Tolker. Don't drop that contact. You're living with someone who's poking his nose into our affairs, which means you have as much access to him as he has with you. Be a pro, Collette. Drop all the personal reactions and do the job. You'll be rewarded."

"How?"

He grunted. "You want figures?"

"No, I want some sense of being able to return to a routine life."

"Meeting Hungarian turncoats in secret safehouses?"

"Right now, Joe, that's like working nine to five as a switchboard operator."

"Do the job and you can have what you want. They told me."

"Who?"

"The brain trust."

"Joe."

"What?"

"I don't know you."

"Sure you do. When this whole thing settles, it'll be like old times, dinners at Gundel, the Miniatur, heartburn, out-of-tune violins. Trust me."

"They say that in L.A."

"Trust me. I'm a fan."

"I'll try."

Cahill skipped the second act and returned to the apartment where Vern Wheatley was waiting. He was in his shorts, a can of beer in his hand, his bare feet propped up on the coffee table. "Where've you been?" he asked.

"The Kennedy Center."

"Yeah? Good concert?"

"Dance recital."
"Never could get into dance."
"Vern."
"What?"
"Let's talk."

CHAPTER 19

By the time Saturday rolled around and Cahill was settled into a seat on a Pan Am flight to San Juan, she was more than ready to escape Washington, and to spend some time on an island. She had no illusions. Her trip to the BVI was just an extension of everything else she'd been doing since returning from Budapest but, for some reason (probably the concept of hitting your foot with a hammer to make you forget a headache), there was a vacation air to the trip.

There hadn't been time to visit her mother before leaving, but she did squeeze in a frantic shopping spree in search of warm-weather clothing. She didn't buy much; sunny islands didn't demand it—two bathing suits, one a bikini, the other a tank suit, both in shades of red; a multicolored caftan, white shorts, sandals, a clinging white dress, and her favorite item, a teal blue cotton jumpsuit that fit perfectly, and in which she felt comfortable. She wore it that morning on the plane.

Once airborne, and breakfast had been served, she removed her shoes, reclined in her seat, and tried to do what she'd promised herself—use the flight to sort things out without interruption, off by herself, some time alone in her own private think tank.

She'd had one additional contact with Langley before leaving. It was with Hank Fox. During their meeting on the Kennedy Center's terrace, Breslin had verbally given her a special telephone number to call, and suggested she check in each day, saying to whoever answered, "This is Dr. Jayne's office calling for Mr. Fox." She did as instructed and Fox came on the line a moment later. All he said was, "Our friend's gone back to Budapest. You're all set to go south?"

"Yes, Saturday."

"Good. In the event you get homesick and want to talk to someone, there's always a large group of friends at Pusser's Landing. They congregate in the deck bar and restaurant. Feed the big bird in the cage between noon and three. You'll have all the conversation you need."

She'd been on the receiving end of enough double-talk since joining the CIA to understand. Obviously, they kept a bird in a cage at this place called Pusser's Landing, and if she fed it at the right time, she'd be approached by someone affiliated with the CIA. It was good to know.

"Call this number when you get back," Fox said. "I'll be here."

"Right. Thanks."

"My best to Dr. Jayne."

"What? Oh, yes, of course. He sends his regards, too."

Silly games, she used to think, until she was in the field and understood the thinking behind such codes. *Need-to-know*; unless the person receiving the call was certain to answer, there was no need for whoever else picked up the phone to know who was calling. They carried it to extremes at times, especially those who loved intrigue, but it made sense. You had to adopt that attitude, she'd reasoned during her training, or you'd never take anything seriously, and that could get you in trouble.

Had Barrie Mayer not taken it seriously enough? Cahill wondered. She had been shockingly cavalier at times, and Cahill had called her on it. Had she joked at the wrong time, when the thing she was carrying was no joke? Had she taken too lightly the need to use a code name, or failed to contact someone through circuitous routes rather than directly?

The possible link between Mayer's and Hubler's deaths remained at the top of her list of thoughts. Dave Hubler had been killed in an alley adjacent to a CIA facility in Rosslyn, the one run by Hank Fox. Supposedly, Hubler had gone there to meet with someone who'd indicated he, or she, was willing to sell inside Company information that could be used in a book. That certainly drew Hubler in enough to validate a possible *mutual* reason for both murders.

She tried to stretch her mind to accommodate all the possibilities. She was hindered in this exercise by the most pervasive thought of all, the last thirty-six hours with Vern Wheatley.

She'd returned from the dance recital and decided to force a conversation. They talked until three o'clock the next morning. It was a frustrating discussion for Cahill. While Wheatley had been open to an extent, it was clear that there was more he was holding back than offering.

Collette had started the discussion with, "I'd like to know, Vern, exactly what this assignment is you're on for *Esquire*."

He laughed; Rule Number One, he told her, was never

to discuss a story in progress. "You dilute it when you do that," he said. "You talk it out and the fire's gone when you sit down to write it."

She wanted to say, "Rule Number One for anyone working for the CIA is to stay far away from journalists." She couldn't say that, of course. As far as he knew, she'd left Central Intelligence for a mundane job with the United States Embassy in Budapest.

Or *did* he believe that? If Hank Fox's insinuations were correct, Wheatley had made contact with her again not to rekindle their romance, but to get close to a potential inside source to feed the story he was working on about a program that had been dropped long ago.

There it was again, *the* dilemma. Who knew what about whom? On top of that, could she believe Hank Fox? Maybe Wheatley wasn't pursuing a story about the CIA. The agency's paranoia wasn't any secret. There were people within it who found conspiracies behind every garage door in Georgetown.

She realized as she sat with Wheatley that night in his brother's apartment that she'd have to be more direct if anything near the truth were to be ferreted out. She took the chance and said, "Vern, someone told me today that you weren't in Washington doing a story on social changes here. This person told me you were digging into a story about the CIA."

He laughed and shook his empty beer can. "I think I'll have another. Can I get you something?"

"No, I . . . sure, any Scotch in there?"

"Probably. My brother has been known to take a drink now and then. Neat?"

"A little water."

She used his absence to go to the bedroom, where she

undressed and got into one of his brother's robes. Three of her could have been enfolded in it. She rolled up the sleeves and returned to the living room where her drink was waiting. Wheatley raised his beer can. "Here's to the basic, underlying distrust between man and woman."

Cahill started to raise her glass in a reflex action. She stopped herself and looked at him quizzically.

"Great scenario, Collette. Some clown tells you I'm down here doing a story on the CIA. You used to work for the CIA so you figure I showed up at your house to get close to a 'source.' That's my only interest in Collette Cahill, hoping she'll turn into a Deep Throat—hey, maybe that wouldn't be so bad—and now she confronts me with the naked facts." He threw up his hands in surrender. "Your friend is right."

Wheatley put his beer can down on a table with considerable force, leaned forward, and said with exaggerated severity, "I've come into information through a highly reliable source that the Director of the CIA is not only having a wild affair with a female member of the Supreme Court—naturally, I can't mention her name—but is, at the same time, engaged in a homosexual liaison with a former astronaut who has been diagnosed at a clinic in Peru as having AIDS."

"Vern, I really don't see. . . ."

"Hold on," he said, his hand raised as a stopper. "There's more. The CIA is plotting the overthrow of Lichtenberg, has permanently wired both of Dolly Parton's breasts, and is about to assassinate Abe Hirschfeld to get control of every parking lot in New York City in case of a nuclear attack. How's it play for you?"

She started to laugh.

"Hey, Collette, nothing funny here."

"Where's Lichtenberg? You meant Liechtenstein."

"I meant Lichtenberg. It's a crater on the moon. The CIA wouldn't bother with Liechtenstein. It's the moon they want."

"Vern, I'm being serious," she said.

"Why? You still work for our nation's spooks?"

"No, but . . . it doesn't matter."

"Who told you I'm working on a CIA story?"

"I can't say."

"Oh, that's democratic as hell. I'm supposed to bare my soul to you, but the lady 'can't say.' Not what I'd expect from you, Collette. Remember the yearbook line I wrote."

"I remember," she said.

"Good. Anything new about your friend Hubler?"

"No."

"You talk to that Englishman, Hotchkiss?"

"Yes, I ran into him at Barrie's agency. He's taken over. He owns it."

"How come?"

She explained the partnership agreement and told him of her call to Mayer's attorney.

"Doesn't sound kosher to me."

"To me, either, but evidently Barrie saw fit to make such a deal."

"She was that impetuous?"

"Somewhat, but not to that extent."

He joined her on the couch and put his arm around her. It felt good, the feel of him, the smell of him. She looked up into his eyes and saw compassion and caring. He lightly brushed her lips with his. She wanted to protest but knew she wouldn't. It was preordained, this moment, in the cards, an inevitability that she welcomed . . .

■ ■ ■

They slept late the next morning. She awakened with a start. She looked over at Vern, his face calm and serene in sleep, a peaceful smile on his lips. Are you being legit with me? she questioned silently. All thoughts of their discussion the night before had been wiped away by the wave of passion and pleasure they'd created for themselves in bed. Now sunlight came through the windows. The passion was spent, the reality of beginning another day took center stage. It was depressing; she preferred what she'd felt under the covers where, someone once said, "They can't hurt you."

She got up, crossed the room, and sat in a chair for what seemed to be a very long time. It was only minutes, actually, before he woke up, yawned, stretched, and pushed himself to a sitting position against the headboard. "What time is it?" he asked.

"I don't know. Late."

Another yawn, legs swung over the side of the bed. He ran his hand through his hair and shook his head.

"Vern."

"Yeah?"

"I loved last night but . . . "

He slowly turned his head and screwed up his face. "But *what*, Collette?"

She sighed. "Nothing. I guess I just hate having to wake up, that's all. I'll be away a few days."

"Where you going?"

"The British Virgin Islands."

"How come?"

"Just to get away. I need it."

"Sure, I can understand that, but why that place? You know people there?"

"One or two."

"Where are you staying?"

"Ah . . . probably on a chartered yacht a friend of mine is arranging."

"You have rich friends." He stood, touched his toes, and disappeared into the bathroom.

Cahill realized she was sitting in the chair naked. She picked up her robe from where she'd tossed it on the floor and started a pot of coffee.

When he returned, he'd turned cold. He'd showered and dressed. He went through papers in a briefcase and started to leave.

"Don't you want coffee?" Cahill asked.

"No, I have to go. Look, I may not see you before you leave."

"Won't you be back tonight?"

"Probably, only I may end up going out of town overnight. Anyway, have a nice vacation."

"Thanks, I will."

He was gone.

He didn't return that night, and it bothered her. What had she done to turn such a warm, loving night into a frosty morning? Because she was going away? He was jealous, imagining that she'd be sleeping with someone else, an old or current boyfriend in the BVI. She wished she could have confided in him about the nature of her trip, but as that thought caused a jolt of sadness and frustration in her, it was tempered by knowing that he probably wasn't being open with her, either.

She got up early Saturday morning and packed. At the last minute she looked for a paperback book to take with her. There were piles of them everywhere. She picked up a half dozen from a nighttable next to the bed and scanned the covers. One immediately caught her eye. Its title was *Hypnotism*, by someone named G. H. Estabrooks. She put it in a shoulder bag she intended to carry on board, called a local cab company, and was on her way to National Airport.

After the Pan Am flight attendant had served Collette a cup of coffee, she pulled the book from her bag and opened it to a page on which was a brief biographical sketch of the author. Estabrooks had been a Rhodes Scholar, held a 1926 doctorate in educational psychology from Harvard, and was a professor of psychology, specializing in abnormal and industrial psychology at Colgate University. The book she held was first published in 1943, and had been revised in 1957.

The first few pages dealt with a murder trial in Denmark in which a man had hypnotized another to commit a murder. The chief state witness, Dr. P. J. Reiter, an authority on hypnotism, stated that any man is capable of any act while hypnotized.

She continued skimming until reaching page sixteen, where Estabrooks discussed the use of hypnotism in modern warfare. She read his thesis carefully.

> Let us take an illustration from warfare, using a technique which has been called the "hypnotic messenger." For obvious reasons the problem of transmitting messages in wartime, of communication within an army's own forces, is a first-class headache to the military. They can use codes, but codes can be lost, stolen or, as we say, broken. They can use the dispatch carrier, but woe betide the messages if the enemy locates the messenger. They can send by word of mouth, but the third degree in any one of its

many forms can get that message. War is a grim business and humans are human. So we invent a technique which is practically foolproof. We take a good hypnotic subject in, say, Washington, and in hypnotism we give him the message which we wish transferred. This message can be long and complicated, for his memory is excellent. Let us assume the war is still on and that we transfer him to Tokyo on a regular routine assignment, say, with the Army Service Corps.

Now note a very curious picture. Awake, he knows just one thing as far as his transfer to Tokyo is concerned; he is going on regular business which has nothing whatever to do with the Intelligence Department. But in his unconscious mind there is locked this very important message. Furthermore, we have arranged that there is only one person in all this world outside ourselves who can hypnotize this man and get this message, a Major McDonald in Tokyo. When he arrives in Tokyo, acting on posthypnotic suggestion, he will look up Major McDonald, who will hypnotize him and recover the message.

With this technique, there is no danger that the subject in an off-guard moment will let drop a statement to his wife or in public that might arouse suspicions. He is an Army Service Corps man going to Tokyo, that is all. There is no danger of getting himself in hot water when drunk. Should the enemy suspect the real purpose of his visit to Tokyo, they would waste their time with third-degree methods. Consciously, he knows nothing that is of any value to them. The message is locked in the unconscious and no amount of drugs, no attempts at hypnotism, can recover it until he sits before Major McDonald in Tokyo. The uses of hypnotism in warfare are extremely varied. We deal with this subject in a later chapter.

Collette went to the chapter on using hypnotism in warfare but found little to equal what she'd read on page sixteen. She closed the book, and her eyes, and replayed everything having to do with hypnosis and Barrie Mayer. Their college experience. Mayer had been such a willing and good subject.

Jason Tolker. He obviously had delved deeply into the subject, and had been Mayer's contact. Had she been hypnotized in her role as a courier? Why bother? Estabrooks's theory sounded exactly that—a theory.

MK-ULTRA and Project Bluebird—those CIA experimental programs of the sixties and early seventies that resulted in public and congressional outrage. Those projects had been abandoned, according to official proclamations from the agency. Had they? Was Mayer simply another experimental subject who'd gone out of control? Or had Estabrooks's theories, refined by the CIA, been put to practical use in her case?

For a moment, she lost concentration and her mind wandered. She'd soon need hypnosis to focus on the subject. Her eyes misted as she thought of Vern Wheatley—and then they opened wide. Why did Vern have Estabrooks's book at his bedside? Hank Fox had said that Wheatley was digging into the supposedly defunct ULTRA and Bluebird projects. Maybe Fox was right. Maybe Wheatley was using her as a conduit for information.

"Damn," she said to the back of the seat in front of her. She took a walk up and down the aisles of the aircraft, looking into the faces of other passengers, women and children, old and young, infants sleeping on mothers' laps, young lovers wrapped around each other, businessmen toiling over spread sheets and lap-top computers, the whole spectrum of airborne humanity.

She returned to her seat, loosely buckled her seat belt and, for the first time since she'd joined the CIA, considered resigning. The hell with them and their cops-and-robbers games, hiding behind vague claims that the fate of the free world depended upon their clandestine behavior. Destroy the village to save it, she thought. The Company's budgets were beyond scrutiny by any other branch of government because it was in "the national interest" to keep them secret. President Truman had been right when he'd eventually railed against the animal he'd created. It *was* an animal, free of all restraints, roaming loose in the world with men whose pockets were filled with secret money. Buy off someone here, overthrow someone there, turn decent people against their own countries, reduce everything to code words and collars turned up in the night. "Damn," she repeated. Send her off to dig into the lives of other people while, undoubtedly, people were delving into her life. Trust no one. A Communist threat exists under every pebble on the shore.

The flight attendant asked if Cahill would like a drink. "Very much," Cahill said; "a bloody Mary."

She drank half the drink and her thoughts went to the reason for her trip to the British Virgin Islands. That was the problem, she realized. Some things were important, not only for America but for people in other parts of the world. Like Hungary.

Banana Quick.

She hadn't been allowed access to all aspects of the plan—Need-to-know—but had learned enough to realize that the stakes were enormous.

She also knew that Banana Quick had been named after a tiny BVI bird, the bananaquit, and that someone within the CIA, whose job it was to assign names to projects, had decided to change it to Banana Quick. Quit was too negative, went the reasoning. Quick was more like it, positive, promising action and speed, more in line with the agency's vision of itself. There'd been laughter and snide remarks when the story had gotten around, but that was often the case in Central Intelligence. The international stakes might be high, but the internal machinations were often amusing.

Banana Quick was designed to set into motion a massive uprising by Hungarians against their Soviet keepers. The '56 attempt had failed. No wonder. It was ill-conceived and carried out by poorly armed idealists who were no match for Soviet tanks and troops.

Now, however, with the backing of the major powers—the United States, Great Britain, France, and Canada—there was a good chance that it would succeed. The climate was right. The Soviets had lost control over Hungary in a social and artistic sense. Hungarians had been gradually living freer lives, thumbing their noses at the young men in drab uniforms who wore red stars on their caps. What had Árpád Hegedüs told her when she asked how to distinguish Hungarian soldiers from Russian soldiers? "The dumb-looking ones are Russian," he'd answered.

Hungary had slowly turned in the direction of capitalism. Graft and corruption were rampant. Pay someone off and you'd have your new automobile in a month instead of six years. Condominiums were rising in the fashionable hills, available to anyone with enough hidden, hoarded illegal cash to buy in. More shops had been opened that were owned by individual entrepreneurs. They, too, had to pay some Russian, in some department, for the privilege, and that Russian was buying his own condo in the hills.

Banana Quick. A small bird flying free in the simple, excruciating beauty of the BVI. Stan Podgorsky had told her that they'd chosen the idyllic Mosquito Island as a planning center because, in his words, "Who'd ever think of looking there for planning a major uprising in an Eastern European country? Besides, we're running out of remote places to meet, unless we go to Antarctica or Ethiopia, and I, for one, am not going to those hellholes."

Who would look to the BVI for the brain trust behind a Hungarian uprising?

The Russians, for one. They'd taken over the private island because they knew something was up, knew the gray-haired men in dark suits flying in were anything but Canadian businessmen going over marketing strategies for a new product. The Soviets were many things; dumb wasn't one of them. Something was up. They'd play the game, too, lie, claim they needed a place for their weary bureaucrats to unwind in the sun. They'd watch. We'd watch.

Eric Edwards. He was there to *watch.* To look into their telescopes through his own, eye to eye, think one step ahead, as each man reported back to the dark suits in his own country.

Games.

"Games!" she said as she finished her drink.

As she deplaned in San Juan, she'd come to peace with the fact that she was a player in this game, and would give her all. After that, she'd see. Maybe . . .

Maybe it was time to get out of the business.

In the meantime, she'd apply her father's philosophy. "You take someone's money, you owe them a decent day's work."

CHAPTER 20

Hello, my name is Jackie, I work for Mr. Edwards," the slight native girl said in a loud voice.

"Yes, he told me you'd be here," Cahill said. Edwards had also told her during the telephone conversation that the girl he was sending for her was almost totally deaf. "Talk loud and let her see your lips," he'd said.

Jackie drove a battered yellow Land Rover. The back seat was piled high with junk, so Cahill sat in front with her. Edwards needn't have bothered instructing her how to communicate with Jackie. There was no conversation. The girl drove on the left side of the road with a race car driver's grim determination, lips pressed together, foot jamming the accelerator to the floor, one hand on the wheel, the heel of the other permanently against the horn. Men, women, children, dogs, cats, goats, cattle and other four-legged animals either heeded the horn or were run over.

The ride took them up and over steep hills. The views were spectacular—water like a painter's palette, every hue of blue and green, lush forests that climbed the sides of mountains and, everywhere, white slashes in the water that were yachts, big and small, sails raised or lowered. It was, at times, so breathtaking—their perch so high—that Cahill gasped.

They came down into Road Town, skirted Road Harbor, and then headed up a steep incline that took them through a clump of trees until reaching a plateau. A single house stood on it. It was one story and pristine white. The roof was covered with orange tiles. A black four-door Mercedes stood in front of a black garage door.

Collette got out and took a deep breath. A breeze from the harbor below rippled her hair and the elephant ears, kapok, white cedar, and manalikara trees that surrounded the house. The air was heavy with hibiscus and bougainvillea, and with the sound of tree frogs. Bananaquits flew from tree branch to tree branch.

Jackie helped bring the luggage into the house. It was open and airy. Furniture was at a minimum. The floors were white and yellow tile, the walls stark white. Flimsy yellow curtains fluttered in the breeze through the open windows. A huge birdcage that stood floor to ceiling housed four brilliantly colored, large parrots. "Hello, goodbye, hello, goodbye," one of them repeated over and over.

"It's just beautiful," Cahill said from behind Jackie. She remembered, came around in front of the girl, and said, "Thank you."

Jackie smiled. "He'll be back later. He said for you to be comfortable. Come." She led her to a rear guest bedroom with a double bed covered in a white-and-yellow comforter. There was a closet, dressing table, two cane chairs, and a battered steamer trunk. "For you," Jackie said. "I have to go. He'll be here soon."

"Yes, thanks again."

"Bye-bye." The girl disappeared. Cahill heard the Land Rover start and pull away.

Well, she thought, not bad. She returned to the living room and talked to the parrots, then went to the kitchen, opened the refrigerator, and took out one of many bottles of club soda. She squeezed half a lime into it, walked to a terrace overlooking the harbor, closed her eyes, and purred. No matter what was in store for her, this particular moment was to be cherished.

She sat on a chaise longue, sipped her drink, and waited for Edwards to arrive.

It was a longer wait than she'd anticipated. He rolled in an hour later on a Honda motorcycle. He'd obviously been drinking. Not that he was overtly drunk, but there was a slur to his speech. His face glowed; he'd been in the sun.

"Hello, hello, hello," he said, taking her hand and smiling.

"As long as you don't say, 'Hello, goodbye, hello, goodbye,' " she said with a laugh.

"Oh, you met my friends. Did they properly introduce themselves?"

"No."

"Bad manners. I'll have to speak to them. Their names are Peter, Paul, and Mary."

"The fourth?"

"Can't decide. Prince, Boy George, some bloody rock-'n'-roll star. I see you've helped yourself and are well into limmin'."

"Limmin'?"

"Native for loafing. Pleasant trip?"

"Yes, fine."

"Good. I've made plans for dinner."

"Wonderful. I'm famished."

They left an hour later in his Mercedes and drove to a small local restaurant ten minutes away where they dined on native food; she passed up what he ordered as a main course, souse, a boiled pig's head with onion, celery, hot peppers, and lime juice. She chose something more conventional, *kallaloo*, a soupy stew of crab, conch, pork, okra, spinach, and very large pieces of garlic. The soup was *tannia*, their before-dinner drinks rum in a fresh coconut split open at the table.

"Delicious," she said when they were through, and after she'd tasted "bush tea," made of soursop.

"Best cure for a hangover ever invented," he said.

"I may need it," she said.

He laughed. "I think I probably spill more in a day than you drink."

"Probably so."

"Game for a little sightseeing?"

She looked through the window at darkness. Only a few flickering lights on distant hills broke the black.

"Beautiful time to be out on the water. Can't sail . . . wind's always down about now, but we can loaf along on the engine. I think you'd like it."

She looked down at the slinky white dress she was wearing. "Hardly sailing clothes," she said.

"No problem," he said, getting up and pulling out her chair. "Plenty of that on board. Let's go."

During the short drive to where Edwards's yachts were docked, Cahill pleasantly realized that she was totally relaxed, something she hadn't been in far too long a time. She was all for limmin' if it made you feel the way she felt at that moment.

The man behind the wheel, Eric Edwards, had a lot to

do with it, she knew. What was it in men like him that made a woman feel important and secure? His thoroughly masculine and slightly dissipated looks contributed, of course, but there was more to it. Chemical? Some olfactory process at work? The climate, the sweet fragrances in the tropical night air, the food and rum in the belly? Who knew? Cahill certainly didn't, nor did she really care. Pondering it was just a way of intensifying the feeling.

Edwards helped her to board the Morgan 46. He started the engine and generator, and turned on a light in the cabin. "Take what you want from under that bench," he said.

Cahill picked up the bench top and saw an assortment of female clothing. She smiled; along with everything else, he was practiced at enticing women on impetuous night-time sailings. She pulled out a pair of white terrycloth shorts and a sleeveless, navy blue sweatshirt. Edwards had gone up on deck. She quickly kicked off her shoes, slipped out of her dress, and put on the shorts and shirt. She hung her dress behind a door that led to a lavatory and joined him as he freed his dock lines.

Edwards skillfully manipulated engine and wheel and backed away from the dock, then reversed power and slowly guided the large, sleek vessel past other secured boats until reaching open water. "Here, you take it," he said, indicating the wheel. She started to protest but he said, "Just keep aiming for that buoy with the light on it. I'll only be a minute." She slid behind the wheel as he went forward and took a breath against her nervousness, then smiled and relaxed into the seat cushion.

If she'd felt relaxed before, it had been nothing compared to the euphoria she now experienced.

He came back to her a few minutes later and they

settled into a leisurely sightseeing journey, moving smoothly on an eastern tack through Sir Francis Drake Channel, the lights of Tortola, and the silhouette of the "Fat Virgin"—Virgin Gorda Island—their land markers.

"What are you thinking?" he said in a soft voice.

Her smile was one of pure contentment. "I was just thinking that I really don't know how to live."

He chuckled. "It isn't always this peaceful, Collette, not when I have a charter with three or four couples all hell-bent on having a good time and guzzling booze as fast as I can stock it."

"I'm sure that's true," Cahill said. "But you have to admit it isn't always that way. Obviously, you have time to . . ."

"Time to take moonlight sails with beautiful young women? True. You don't hold that against me, do you?"

She turned and looked into his face. He was wearing a broad smile. His teeth, very white, seemed phosphorescent in the light of the moon. She said, "How could I hold it against you? Here I am enjoying it to the hilt." She was about to throw in a disclaimer that she wasn't necessarily a "beautiful woman," but she decided not to bother. She'd never felt more beautiful in her life.

They continued their cruise for another hour, then headed back, reaching the dock at two in the morning. She'd fallen asleep next to him, her head on his shoulder. She helped him secure the Morgan and they went to the house, where he poured nightcaps of straight Pusser's Rum into large brandy snifters.

"You look tired," he said.

"I am. It's been a long day . . . and night."

"Why don't you get to bed? I'll be out early, but you sleep in. The house is yours. We'll catch up when I get back. I'll leave the keys to the Mercedes in the kitchen. Feel free."

"That's generous, Eric."

"I like having you here, Collette. Somehow, it makes me feel a little closer to Barrie." He studied her face. "You aren't offended at that, are you? I don't want you to feel used, if you understand what I mean."

She smiled, stood, and said, "Of course not. Funny, but while we were out on the water I thought a lot about Barrie and realized that I was feeling closer to her, too, by being here. If there is any using, we're both guilty. Good night, Eric. Thanks for a lovely evening."

CHAPTER 21

She heard Edwards leave and took his advice: rolled over and went back to sleep. When she awoke again, she didn't know what time it was but the room had become hot. She looked up into a gently revolving ceiling fan, then slipped on her jumpsuit and strolled out to the kitchen. A heavy black woman was polishing countertops. "Good morning," Collette said.

The woman, who wore a flowered dress and straw sandals, smiled and said in a singsong voice, "Good morning, lady. Mr. Edwards, he gone."

"Yes, I know. I heard him. My name is Collette."

The woman evidently did not want to extend the conversation to that level of intimacy because she turned away and went back to making circles on the counter.

Collette took a pitcher of fresh-squeezed orange juice from the refrigerator, filled a large glass, and took it to the terrace. She sat at a round white table with an orange umbrella protruding from a hole in the middle and thought about the exchange in the kitchen. Her interpretation was that Edwards had so many young women walking into the kitchen and introducing themselves that the housekeeper had decided it wasn't worth getting to know them. Chances were they never stayed around long enough to become part of the household.

The marina and harbor below bustled with activity. Cahill squinted against the sun and picked out the section of the complex where Edwards's yachts were situated. She was too far away to see whether he was there, but she assumed he'd left early to take out a charter. Then again, he hadn't specified that, so maybe he had other business on the island.

She got the Estabrooks book on hypnotism from the bedroom and returned to the terrace, settled in the chair, and picked up reading where she'd left off on the plane.

She was fascinated as she read that certain people have a heightened ability to enter the hypnotic state, and that these people, according to the author, were capable of remarkable feats while under hypnosis. Estabrooks cited examples of men and women undergoing major surgery, with hypnotism as the only anesthesia. To such special people, total amnesia about the hypnotic experience was not only possible, it was easily accomplished by a skilled hypnotist.

She also learned that contrary to popular perception, those who enter a hypnotic state are anything but asleep. In fact, while under hypnosis, the subject enters a state of awareness in which it is possible to focus most intently, and to block out everything else. Memory "inside" is enhanced; it's possible under hypnosis to compress months' worth of material into an hour and to retain virtually everything.

Collette found particularly fascinating the chapter on whether it was possible to convince someone under hypnosis to perform a degrading or illegal act. She remembered high school chatter when boys used to kid about hypnotizing girls to get them to take off their clothes. One boy had sent away for a publication advertised on the back of a comic book promising "total hypnotic, seductive power over women." The girls in school had giggled, but the boys kept trying to get them to submit to their new-found power. No one did, and it was forgotten in the wake of the next fad which was, as she recalled, the ability to "throw your voice through ventriloquism."

According to Estabrooks, it was not possible to blatantly convince people in hypnosis to act against their moral and ethical codes. It was, however, possible to achieve the same end by "changing the visual." He went on to explain that while you could not tell a moral young lady to take off her clothes, you could, with the right subject, convince that person under hypnosis that she was alone in an impossibly hot room. Or, while you could not persuade someone, even the most perfect hypnotic subject, to murder a close friend, you could create a visual scenario in which when that friend came through the door, it was not that person. Instead, it was a rabid bear intent upon killing the subject, and the subject would fire in self-defense.

Cahill looked up into the vivid blue sky. The sun was above her; she hadn't realized how long she'd been reading. She returned the glass to the kitchen, took a shower, dressed in the loosest, coolest clothing she had, and got into the Mercedes, through the wrong door. The steering wheel was on the right side. She'd forgotten that the islands were British. No problem, she thought. She'd had plenty of experience driving on the other side of the road in England.

She drove off without the slightest idea of where she

was going. That pleased her. The lack of destination or timetable would give her a chance to leisurely explore the island and to find her own adventures and delights.

She drove into Road Town, the BVI's only thoroughly commercial area, parked, and strolled its narrow streets, stopping to admire classic examples of West Indian architecture painted in vivid colors, hip roofs glistening in the midday sun, heavy shutters thrown open to let in air and light. She stopped in shops, many of which were just opening, and bought small gifts to bring home.

At two, she drove on again. Once she left the town, she was lost, but it didn't bother her. The vistas in every direction were spectacular, and she stopped often along the side of a mountain road to drink in their natural beauty.

Rounding a sharp curve, she looked to her right and saw a large sign: PUSSER'S LANDING. She'd forgotten what Hank Fox had told her. She checked her watch; it was almost three, but she reasoned that since everything else started late on the island, lunch hour would probably still be in progress. She parked, entered beneath the sign, passed a gift shop, and reached the outdoor dining deck that overlooked a gentle, protected bay.

As she headed for a vacant table near the water, she came to a large birdcage. In it was a big, docile parrot. She glanced around. There were perhaps twenty people on the deck, some at tables, others standing in small clusters sipping rum drinks. She decided to go to the table first and order, then feed the bird to see if someone approached her. She ordered a hamburger and a beer and went to the cage. "Hello there, fella," she said. The bird looked at her with sleepy eyes. A tray of bird food was in front of the cage. She picked up a piece of fruit and extended her hand through the open cage door. The bird took the fruit from her fingers, tasted it, then dropped it to the cage floor.

"Fussy, huh?" she said, picked up some seed, and extended her open palm. The bird picked at the seed and swallowed it. "Want some more?" she asked. She was so engrossed in feeding the bird that she'd forgotten the real reason for doing it.

"Like him?" a male voice asked.

The voice startled her, and the snap of her head toward it testified to that fact. So she smiled. "Yes, he's beautiful."

The man to whom the voice belonged was tall and heavy. He wore baggy overalls and a soiled tan shirt. His black hair was thinning and swirled over his head without direction. His round face bore the scars of childhood acne. He was light-skinned, obviously the child of mixed parentage, and his eyes were pale blue. An interesting-looking man, Cahill thought.

"I call him Hank," the man said.

"He looks like a fox to me," she said intuitively.

The man laughed. "Yes, a Fox called Hank. Are you visiting the islands?"

"Yes, I'm from the States."

"Have you found our people pleasant and helpful?"

"Very." She fed the bird more seeds.

"We have that reputation. It's important for tourism. If there's anything I can do for you while you visit us, please do not hesitate to let me know. I have lunch here every day."

"That's kind of you. Your name is . . . ?"

He grinned and shrugged. "Call me Hank."

"Like the fox."

"Look at me. Bear would be more like it. Have a good day, miss, and enjoy your stay."

"Thank you; now I know I will."

CHAPTER 22

Have a good day?" Eric Edwards asked as he came to the terrace where Collette was sitting. She'd bathed and slipped into her caftan, found a glass pitcher in the refrigerator filled with a dark liquid and decided to try it. "What is this?" she asked Edwards as he joined her at the table.

"Oh, you found my daily supply of *maubi*. The housekeeper whips it up for me. It's non-alcoholic, but if you let it age long enough it ferments into something that knocks your socks off. It's got tree bark, ginger, marjoram, pineapple, stuff like that in it."

"It's delicious."

"Yeah, only I'm ready for a real drink. Let me get it and I'll brief you on the next couple of days of your vacation."

When he returned, he carried a large vodka martini on the rocks. "How would you like a *real* sail?" he asked.

"I'd love it," she said. "What does a *real* sail mean?"

"Two days and a night. Jackie's provisioning the boat first thing in the morning. We'll spend the day with sails up and I'll really show you the BVI. We'll find a pleasant place to anchor overnight, and spend the days catching beautiful winds and seeing one of God's gifts to the world. Sound good?"

"Sounds religious," she said. This didn't reflect what she was thinking at first. The sail would mean being out of touch, particularly with her contact at Pusser's Landing. Somehow, that brief encounter had been comforting.

Still, she knew that her job was to stay close to Edwards and to find out what she could. So far, she'd been successful only in discovering that he was handsome, charming, and a generous host.

He took her for dinner that night to the Fort Burt Hotel, and they stopped for a drink at Prospect Reef before returning to the house. She assumed this warm, pleasant evening would culminate in some attempt at seduction. Later, she had to laugh quietly in bed when she realized that the absence of any attempt at seduction left her ambivalent. She didn't want to be seduced by Eric Edwards. On the other hand, there was a side of her, part psychological and part physical, that yearned for it.

She heard Edwards walking about the house and tried to determine from her bedroom what he was doing. She heard him go outside, then return, listened to the dishwasher start and begin its cycles. She closed her eyes and focused on sounds from outside her window. The tree frogs were especially noisy. A pleasant sound. She allowed waves of contemplation of two days on that magnificent yacht to carry her into a blissful sleep.

■ ■ ■

Edwards, who'd poured himself a glass of rum over ice, sat on the terrace. The harbor below was peaceful and dark, except for occasional lights shining through tiny portholes on the yachts docked there. One of those lights came from his Morgan. Inside, Edwards's shipmate, Jackie, was putting the finishing touches on a vegetable tray she'd prepared for the sail. She covered it with plastic wrap and placed it in the galley's refrigerator along with the other food and drinks Edwards had ordered.

She went to the companionway, took two steps up, and surveyed the deck and dock. Then she returned to the cabin and went to a low door that led to a large hanging locker containing extra gear, flotation cushions, and snorkeling equipment. She opened the door. A flashlight's movement threw a sudden ray of light on her. "Are you done yet?" she asked.

A young native scrambled toward her on his knees, shone the light on his face, and nodded. She motioned for him to come. He took a final look back into the black corner of the stowage locker. She, of course, could hear nothing, but if he concentrated hard enough, he could hear the regular, rhythmic ticking in the silence of the night.

He joined her in the main cabin and they turned out the interior lights. She went up the companionway again, looked around, saw that it was clear, waved for him to follow, and they quickly climbed onto the dock. They looked at each other for a moment, then separated, Jackie heading in the direction of the main buildings, the young man following a narrow strip of wooden walkway until he reached a small beach and disappeared into the trees.

CHAPTER 23

"Good job, Jackie," Eric Edwards said, as the slender girl in tight shorts and a T-shirt tossed him the last line from the dock.

She smiled and waved.

Once Edwards had backed the yacht away from the dock and was proceeding toward the same water they'd traveled two nights ago, he turned over the wheel to Cahill. This time she took it with confidence, eager to guide the sleek vessel with enough proficiency to make him proud.

"I don't know how much you know about sailing," Edwards said, "but you're going to have to help me."

"I don't know much," Cahill said, raising both hands in defense, "but I'll do what you tell me to do."

"Fair enough," Edwards said. "Let's kill that noisy engine and get some sail up."

The difference between sailing up Sir Francis Drake Channel in the daytime and at night, Cahill realized, was literally as different as day and night. The sun on the water turned it into a glistening turquoise and silver fantasy. She sat at the helm and watched Edwards, who wore only white duck pants, scurry back and forth over the coach roof and foredeck adjusting halyards and running rigging. The huge white sails billowed in the wind, the sound of them flapping against the yacht's spar like a giant bird's wings. When Eric was satisfied, he stood, hands on hips, and looked up at the full white sheets pressed into perfect symmetry by the 20-knot Caribbean breeze. Like something out of a movie, Cahill thought, as she took deep breaths and raised her face to the sun. A spy movie—or a romance?

"Where are we going?" she asked as he joined her at the wheel.

"We'll go right up the channel past Beef Island—that's where you flew in—and then up through the Dogs."

"The dogs?"

"Yeah. Why they're called that depends on who you talk to. Somebody told me once Sir Francis Drake dropped his dogs off on them. Some people think the islands look like dogs. The way I figure it, they named them the Dogs the way they name most things down here. Somebody just liked the name. There's three of them. Once we're past them, we'll be up off the northwest tip of Virgin Gorda. I thought we'd come around and go into Mosquito Island."

Was he testing her? Cahill wondered. Looking for a sign of recognition when he mentioned Mosquito Island? It didn't seem that way because the minute he finished telling her of their sailing plans, he left her side and busied himself again up front.

They reached the Dogs a little after three and anchored near Marina Cay, where they took a swim in the warm, incredibly clear water and had lunch. Eating made her sleepy, but once they were under way again, her spirits and energy picked up and she threw herself into the role of mate. They sailed between West Dog and Great Dog, came around a tiny bump in the water that Edwards said was Cockroach Island, then sailed almost due east toward Anguilla Point, which jutted out from the Fat Virgin. Far in the distance was Mosquito Island.

"See that island over there?" Edwards said, pointing to his left. "That's really the dogs, or gone to the dogs." Cahill shielded her eyes and saw a small island dominated by a large house built on its highest point. Edwards handed her a pair of binoculars. She peered through them and adjusted the lenses until the island and its structure were sharp. Virtually the entire island was surrounded by a high metal fence, with barbed wire stretched along its top. Two large black Dobermans ran along the perimeter of the property. On top of the building were elaborate antennas, including a huge dish.

She lowered the binoculars to her lap. "Is that a private island?"

Edwards laughed. "Yes, privately owned. The owner leased it out to the Soviet Union not long ago."

Collette feigned surprise. "Why would the Soviet Union want an island down here?"

Another laugh from Edwards. "They say it's to provide rest and recreation for its top bureaucrats. There's some debate about that."

Cahill looked at him quizzically. "Do people think it's a military installation?"

Edwards shrugged and returned the binoculars to the clip on the taffrail. "Nobody knows for sure," he said. "I just thought you'd be interested in seeing it."

"I am," she said.

behind the reef and crossed below them, so close that Cahill was able to probe the middle of the school with her hand.

Edwards brought his head out of the water and spit the breathing tube from his mouth. Cahill raised her head, too. He said, "Let's go around the reef that way," indicating the direction with his head. "There's a great . . ."

The sound started with a low rumble that was more felt than heard from where they were. Thunder? On such a day? They looked around, then back in the direction from which they had come. A microsecond later, Edwards's 46-foot Morgan rose into the brilliant blue BVI sky in a giant, ferocious fireball. Out of the top of the cloud came thousands of shreds and shards of what had been a magnificent sailing vessel.

The explosion was deafening, but more potent was what the impact did to the water below the surface. Cahill and Edwards were suddenly engulfed in a swirl of water gone mad. She was flipped on her back and water rushed into her mouth. Her arms and legs flailed for something to grab on to, something to help her combat the violent force in which she was trapped.

Then, as quickly as it had begun, the water's surge ebbed. Debris rained down from the sky above, flaming pieces of the yacht hitting the water with a vicious sizzle, large hunks of fiberglass and wood, steel and plastic falling like meteorites. A piece of burning material struck Cahill on her back, but she quickly turned over and the pain was gone.

She'd now regained enough of her senses to begin to think about what had happened, and about what to do next. She looked for Edwards, saw him close to the reef. He was on his side. One hand reached into the sky as

He guided the vessel around Anguilla Point and approached Mosquito Island from the south. He went below and called Drake's Anchorage, the only resort on Mosquito, on VHF Channel 16 to inform them they would be mooring in the bay and would like a launch to bring them in for drinks and dinner. The pleasant female voice asked Edwards what time he estimated dropping anchor. He looked at his watch. "About an hour, hour and a half," he said. He flicked off the microphone switch, said to Cahill, "Feel like another swim before we go ashore?"

"Love it," she said.

"Make it an hour and a half," Edwards said to the young woman on the other end of the radio.

Ordinarily, Edwards would have brought the Morgan in closer, but he wanted Cahill to see a prime snorkeling reef a few miles to the east, near Prickly Pear Island. He headed for it, dropped anchor, went below, opened the door to the stowage locker, and pulled out two sets of masks and flippers. He helped Collette fit her feet into her flippers, adjusted the mask on her face, then put on his own set. "Ready?" he asked.

She nodded.

"Let's go."

Edwards climbed up onto the stanchion and threw himself over backwards into the water. Cahill managed a minor variation on the technique and soon they were paddling along, side by side, toward the coral reef he'd pointed out.

Edwards moved in front of her and began pointing beneath the water to a spectacular staghorn reef, its multicolored polyps beckoning as though they were millions of fingers. A thick school of yellow snapper appeared from though looking for a hook to grasp. There was blood coming from the exposed side of his face, and his mouth was open like that of a dying fish.

Cahill swam to him. "Are you all right?" she asked foolishly, her hand instinctively going to the wound on his temple.

His whole body heaved as he discharged water from his mouth and throat. He shook his head and said, "I think my arm is broken."

Cahill turned in the water and looked back to where the yacht had been. All that was left were random pieces, smoke drifting lazily from them. A large motor launch pierced the smoke, skirted the debris, and came directly at them.

The three young natives in the launch helped Cahill into it, then carefully brought Edwards on board. Cahill looked at his arm and asked, "Can you move it?"

He winced as he tried to extend the arm. "I think I can. Maybe it isn't broken."

Now, safe in the launch, Cahill was suddenly assaulted by the mental and physical horror of what had happened. She fell against the back of one of the wooden seats and began to breathe deeply and quickly. "Oh, my God. My God, what happened?"

Edwards didn't answer. His eyes were wide and fixed upon the remains of the Morgan.

"We take you back?" one of the natives asked.

Edwards nodded and said, "Yes, take us to the island. We need to make a phone call."

CHAPTER 24

After Cahill applied first aid to his arm and head in the manager's office of Drake's Anchorage, Edwards made a call to his office on Tortola and told them to send a motor launch to pick them up on Virgin Gorda. The Mosquito Island shuttle boat took them there and they went to a clinic where more sophisticated aid was given Edwards, including an X ray of his arm. It wasn't broken. The gash on his head, the result of a falling piece of metal, was deeper than they'd realized. It took eleven stitches to close.

They were driven to a dock where one of Edwards's native staff was waiting with a large powerboat. An hour later they were back at Edwards's house.

Throughout the return to Tortola, they said little to each other. Collette was still in mild shock. Edwards seemed to have his wits about him, but he made the journey with his face set in a pained, brooding expression.

They stood together on his terrace and looked down on the harbor.

"I'm sorry," he said.

"Yeah, sorry, me, too," she said. "I'm just glad to be alive. If we hadn't taken that swim . . . "

"There are a lot of *ifs*," he mumbled.

"What could have caused it?" Cahill asked. "A gasoline leak? I've heard about that happening with boats."

He said nothing, stared instead at the marina far below. Then he slowly turned his head and said, "It was no gasoline leak, Collette. Somebody wired the yacht. Somebody planted explosives on a timer."

She took a few steps back until her bare calves touched a metal chair. She collapsed into it. He continued looking out over the harbor, his hands on the terrace railing, his body hunched over. Finally, he turned and leaned against the rail. "You damn near lost your life because of things you don't know, and I'm going to tell you about them, Collette."

As much as she wanted to hear what he had to say, she was gripped with a simultaneous, overwhelming wave of nausea and shaking, and her head had begun to pound. She stood and used the arm of the chair for support. "I have to lie down, Eric. I don't feel well. Can we talk later?"

"Sure. Go rest. Whenever you feel up to it we'll sit down and hash out what happened."

She gratefully climbed into bed and fell into a troubled sleep.

When she awoke, she was facing the window. It was dark outside. She sat up and rubbed her eyes. The tree frogs were performing their usual symphony. They provided the only sound.

She looked toward the door, which was open a crack. "Eric?" she said in a voice that could be heard by no one. "Eric," she said louder. No response.

She'd slept in what she'd been wearing that day, removing only her shoes. She placed her bare feet on the cool tile floor, stood, and tried to shake away her lingering sleepiness and the chill that had turned her flesh into a pattern of tiny bumps. She said it again: "Eric?"

She opened the door and stepped into the hallway. A light from the living room spilled over to where she stood. She followed it, crossed the living room, and went to the open terrace doors. No one. Nothing.

She was met with the same situation when opening the front door. The Mercedes and motorcycle were there, but no sign of their owner.

She went to the car and looked inside, then walked to the side of the house where a large tree created a natural roof above a white, wrought-iron love seat.

"Sleep good?"

A burst of air came from her mouth. She turned and saw Eric standing behind the tree.

"All rested?" he asked as he approached her.

"Yes, I . . . I didn't know where you'd gone."

"Nowhere. Just enjoying the evening."

"Yes, it's . . . lovely. What time is it?"

"Nine. Feel like some dinner?"

"I'm not hungry."

"I'll put it out anyway, nothing fancy, a couple of steaks, local vegetables. A half hour okay?"

"Yes, that will be fine, thank you."

A half hour later she joined him on the terrace. Two plates held their dinner. A bottle of Médoc had been opened, and two delicately curved red wineglasses stood on the table.

"Go ahead, eat," he said.

"Funny, but I am hungry now," she said. "Some people

eat when they're upset, others can't bear the thought of it. I was always an eater."

"Good."

She asked how his arm felt, and he said it was better. "A bad sprain," the doctor at the clinic had said. Edwards had been told to keep it in the sling the doctor had provided, but he'd discarded it the minute they left the clinic. There was a large compression bandage on his left temple. A spot of dried blood that hadn't washed off remained on his cheek.

Cahill pushed her plate away, sat back, and said, "You said you wanted to share something with me. Sorry I wasn't in any shape to listen before, but I'm ready now. Do you still want to tell me?"

He leaned forward, both forearms on the table, took a breath and looked down into his plate, as though debating what to say.

"You don't have to," she said.

He shook his head. "No, I want to. You almost lost your life because of me. I think that deserves an explanation."

Cahill thought: Barrie Mayer. Had *she* lost her life because of him?

He repositioned his chair so that there was room for him to cross his legs and to face her. She adopted a similar posture, her hands in her lap, her eyes trained on his.

"I really don't know where to begin." A smile. "At the beginning. That makes sense, doesn't it?"

She nodded.

"I suppose the best way to get into this, Collette, is to tell you that I'm not what I appear to be. Yes, I have a yacht-chartering service here in the BVI, but that's a front." She told herself to offer nothing, take in what he had to say and make decisions later.

He continued. "I work for the Central Intelligence Agency."

It struck her that he was being completely honest, that he had no idea that she knew about his involvement. Obviously, Barrie hadn't told him what her close friend Collette did for a living. That realization was refreshing. On the other hand, it put Cahill in a position of being the dishonest one. It made her squirm.

Her turn to say something. "That's . . . interesting, Eric. You're an . . . agent?"

"I suppose you could call it that. I'm paid to keep my eyes and ears open down here."

Cahill took a moment to appear as if she were looking for the next question. In fact, she had a list of a dozen. She said, "The CIA has people everywhere in the world, doesn't it?" She didn't want appear too naive. After all, he knew she had once worked for the CIA. She certainly would be somewhat knowledgeable about how things worked.

"It's more than just having people plopped in places around the globe to report back on what's going on. I was sent down here for a specific purpose. Remember the island I pointed out to you, the one the Russians have taken over?"

"Yes."

When he didn't say anything else, she leaned forward. "Do you think the Russians blew up the yacht?"

"That would be the logical explanation, wouldn't it?"

"I suppose it's possible, considering you're an agent for the other side. But you don't seem convinced."

Edwards shrugged, poured more wine into each of their glasses, held his up in a toast. "Here's to wild speculation."

She picked up her glass and returned the gesture. "What wild speculation?"

"I hope you don't misunderstand why I would say something like I'm about to say. I mean, after all, we both work for the United States government."

"Eric, I'm not a recent college graduate having her first taste of bureaucracy."

He nodded. "Yeah, well, here goes. I think the CIA set the charge aboard the yacht, or arranged for someone to do it."

It hadn't occurred to her for a moment since the incident that the people *she* worked for would do such a thing. She'd thought of the Russians, of course, and also wondered whether it hadn't been the act of a competing yacht-chartering company. She'd also had to question whether anyone else *had* been involved at all. There was no more evidence to link the explosion to a plot than there was to rule out a natural cause.

But those thoughts had little value at the moment. She asked the only obvious question: "Why do you think that?"

"I think it because . . . because I know things that the CIA would prefer not be told to anyone else."

"What things?"

"Things about individuals whose motivations are not in the best interests of not only the Central Intelligence Agency but the United States as well. In fact . . ."

Collette's body tensed. She was sure he was about to say something about Barrie Mayer's death.

He didn't disappoint her. "I'm convinced, Collette, that Barrie was murdered because she knew those same damaging things." He pulled his head back a little and raised his eyebrows. "Yes, she knew them from me. I suppose that's why I'm talking to you this way. Being responsible for the death of one person is bad enough. Seeing a second person come this close"—he created a narrow gap between his thumb and index finger—"to losing her life is too much."

Cahill leaned back and looked up into a sky that had, like her mind, clouded over. Her brain was short-circuited with thoughts and emotions. She got up and went to the edge of the terrace, looked down on the harbor and dock. What he was saying made a great deal of sense. It represented the sort of thing her instincts had pointed to from the beginning.

A new thought struck her. Maybe he was wrong. Assuming that the explosion had been the result of someone's having planted a device on board, who was to say the intended victim hadn't been herself? She turned to him again. "Are you suggesting that someone from the CIA murdered Barrie?"

"Yes."

"What about Dave Hubler, her associate at the literary agency?"

He shook his head. "I don't know anything about that, unless Barrie gave him the same information she'd gotten from me."

Collette returned to her chair, took a sip of wine, and said, "Maybe I was to be the victim."

"Why you?"

"Well, I . . . " She'd almost stepped over the line she'd drawn for herself in terms of how much she would reveal to him. She decided to stay on her side. "I don't know, you were the one who toasted 'wild speculation.' Maybe somebody wanted to kill me instead of you. Maybe the engine just blew up by itself."

"No, nothing blew up by itself, Collette. While you were sleeping, the authorities were here questioning me. They're filing a report that the destruction of the yacht resulted from an accidental electrical discharge into a fuel tank because that's what I want them to think. No, I know better. It was deliberate."

Cahill was almost afraid to ask the next question but knew she had to. "What was it that Barrie learned from you that caused her death, and that prompted somebody to try to kill you?"

He gave forth a throaty laugh, as though saying to himself, "My God, I can't believe I'm doing this." Collette felt for him. Obviously, the event near Mosquito Island, and Barrie's death, had brought him to a level of candor that every bit of his training cautioned against; in fact, prohibited. Her training, too, for that matter. She touched his knee. "Eric, what was it that Barrie knew? It's terribly important for me to know. As you said, I came this close to losing my life."

Edwards closed his eyes and puffed out his cheeks. When he exhaled through his lips and opened his eyes again, he said, "There are people within the CIA whose only interest is their own *self*-interest. Ever hear of Project Bluebird?"

Back to that again. Jason Tolker. Was that what he was getting at? She said, "Yes, I've heard of it, and MK-ULTRA, too." The minute she'd said it, she knew she'd offered too much.

His surprised look indicated she was right.

"How do you know about those projects?" he asked.

"I remember them from my training days with the CIA, before I quit and went to work for the embassy."

"That's right, they did talk about such projects in

training, didn't they? You know, then, that they involved experimentation on a lot of innocent people?"

She shook her head. "I don't know the details of it, just that those projects had been operative and were abandoned because of public and congressional pressure."

Edwards narrowed his eyes. "Do you know how Barrie got involved with the CIA?"

Collette did a fast mental shuffle. Should she acknowledge knowing about Mayer's life as a courier? She decided to continue playing the surprised role.

"Did Barrie ever mention someone named Tolker?"

Cahill raised her eyes as if thinking back, then said, "No, I don't think so."

"He's a psychiatrist in Washington. He was the one who recruited her."

"Really?"

"You didn't know that? She never told you any of this?"

"No, I don't remember anyone named Tolker."

"How much did she tell you about what she was doing for the CIA?"

Her laugh was forced. "Not much. It certainly wouldn't have been professional for her to tell me, would it?"

Edwards shook his head. "No, it wouldn't, but Barrie wasn't necessarily the most professional of intelligence couriers." He seemed to be waiting for Cahill to respond. When she didn't, he said, "I suppose it doesn't matter what she told you. The fact is that she'd been seeing this guy Tolker professionally. She was a patient of his. He used that opportunity to bring her into the fold."

"That isn't so unusual, is it?" Cahill asked.

"I suppose not, although I really don't know a hell of a lot about that end of the business. The point is, Collette, that Dr. Jason Tolker was deeply involved in Operation

Bluebird and MK-ULTRA—and continues to be involved in experimentation programs that spun out of those projects."

"The CIA is still doing mind-control experimentation?"

"Sure as hell is, and Tolker is one of the top dogs. He manipulated Barrie, brought her into the CIA as a courier, and that's why she's dead today. More wine?"

It seemed an absurd thing to say considering the tenor of the conversation, but she said, "Yes, please." He poured.

Collette thought about what she'd read in the book by G. H. Estabrooks, about how people could be persuaded to do things against their will if the hypnotist changed the visual scenario. Was that what Edwards was suggesting, that Barrie had been seduced into the role of CIA courier against her will? She asked him.

"Barrie evidently was an unusual hypnotic subject," Edwards answered, "but that really isn't important. What *is* important is that when she left on her most recent trip to Budapest, she carried with her information that would hang Jason Tolker by his thumbnails."

"I don't understand."

"Tolker is a double agent." He said it flatly and matter-of-factly. It left Cahill stunned. She got up and crossed the terrace.

"He's a goddamn traitor, Collette, and Barrie knew it."

"How did she know it? Did you tell her?"

Edwards shook his head. "No, she told me."

"How did *she* learn he was a double agent?"

He shrugged. "I really don't know, Collette. I pumped her, but all she'd say was that she had the goods and was going to blow him out of the water." He grinned. "That's an apt way to put it considering our little snorkeling excursion today, huh?"

Her smile was equally rueful. She asked the next obvious question. Who was Barrie going to tell about what she knew of Tolker's supposedly traitorous acts?

He answered, "My assumption was that she'd tell somebody back in Washington. But it didn't take me long to realize that that didn't make any sense. She didn't know anybody at Langley. Her only contact with the CIA *was* Jason Tolker. . . ."

"And whoever her contact was in Budapest."

Edwards nodded and joined her at the edge of the terrace. The strains of a fungee band, with its incessant island rhythms, drifted up to them.

They stood close together, their hips touching, both lost for a time in their individual thoughts. Then Edwards said in a monotone, "I'm getting out. I don't need boats blown out from under me."

She turned and looked into his face. Lines that had always been there now seemed more pronounced. "Was the yacht insured?" she asked.

His face broke into a wide smile. "Insured by the richest insurance company in the world, Collette, the Central Intelligence Agency."

"That's something to be thankful for," she said, not meaning it. It was something to say. Money meant nothing in this scenario.

He turned grim again. "The CIA is run by evil men. I never wanted to accept that fact. I never even acknowledged it until recently. I was filled with the sort of patriotism that leads people into working for an intelligence agency. I believed in it and its people, *really* believed in what the CIA stood for and what I was doing." He shook his head. "No more. It's filled with the Jason Tolkers of this world, people who only care about themselves and who don't give a damn who gets trampled in the process. I . . ." He placed his hand on her shoulders and drew her to him. "You and I have lost something very special in Barrie Mayer because of these people. I didn't know David Hubler, but he just joins the list of people who've had to pay with their lives because of them."

She started to say something but he cut her off. "I told Barrie to stay away from Tolker. The projects that he's involved in are at the root of what's rotten about the Company and the government. It uses innocent citizens as guinea pigs without any regard for their fate. They've lied to everyone, including Congress, about how they abandoned Operation Bluebird and MK-ULTRA. Those projects never missed a beat. They're more active today than they ever were."

Cahill was legitimately confused. "But what about funding? Projects like that cost money."

"That's the beauty of an organization like the CIA, Collette. There's no accountability. That's the way it was set up in the beginning. That was one of the reasons Truman had serious thoughts about establishing a national intelligence-gathering organization. The money is given to individuals and they're free to spend it any way they want, no matter who it hurts. There's got to be a thousand front groups like mine, shipping companies and personnel agencies, little airlines and weapons brokers, university labs and small banks that do nothing but launder Company money. It stinks. I never thought I'd get to this point but it *does* stink, Collette, and I've had it."

She stared at him for a long time before saying, "I understand, Eric, I really do. If you're right, that whoever blew up the yacht today did it on orders from people in my own government, I don't know how I can keep working for it, even in State."

"Of course you can't. That's the whole point. I'm glad to be an American, always have been, always considered it a rare privilege to have been born American, but when I end up as part of a series of systematic abuses that result in the murder of a woman I loved very much, it's time to draw the line."

The band down the hill began a slow, sensuous rendition of an island song. Edwards and Cahill looked at each other until he said, "Care to dance?"

Again, the absurdity of the request, considering the circumstances, caused her to burst out laughing. He joined her, slipped his right arm around her waist, took her left hand in his, and began leading her across the terrace.

"Eric, this is ridiculous."

"You're right, it is so ridiculous there is only one thing left to do—dance."

She stopped protesting and gracefully followed his lead, thinking all the while of how ludicrous it was yet at the same time how romantic and beautiful. The feel of his hardness against her sent a succession of tiny sexual electric bursts through her body. He kissed her, tentatively at first, then with more force, and she returned his hunger.

As they danced by the table, he deftly took the wine, led her through the open doors and into the bedroom. There, he released her and his fingers began opening the bottons on the front of her blouse. She knew it was the last opportunity to protest, or to step away, but she moved closer. They made love, and soon her intensely pleasurable response merged with his, and with visions of the fireball in the blue skies of the British Virgin Islands.

■ ■ ■

The next day, Edwards was out early. He said he had a number of officials on the island with whom he had to speak about the explosion.

After he was gone, Cahill grappled with conflicting thoughts. What he'd said last night had caused her to rethink everything she'd done since coming to work for Central Intelligence. She certainly didn't share his passionate disgust with the CIA. She wasn't even sure that what he'd said was true. All she knew was that it was time to do some serious thinking, not only about this assignment, but about who she was.

She considered placing a call to Hank Fox in Washington but was afraid of breaching security. Phone calls from the islands went to the United States via satellite; conversations were open to the world, including the Russians on their small, private island.

Pusser's Landing.

She drove Edwards's Mercedes there at noon, took a table, ordered a sandwich and a Coke, then went to the birdcage where she fed the parrot. She'd noticed the big man from the day before. He was down on the dock repairing an outboard engine on a small runabout. Soon, he had casually made his way to her side.

"I thought I'd come back for lunch again," she said. "It was so pleasant last time."

"It is a pleasant place, miss," he said. He looked about to ensure no one was near them before adding, "It is even nicer in Budapest. You should go there immediately."

"Budapest? Who . . . ?"

"As quickly as possible, miss. Today."

Cahill asked, "Does my travel agent know about this?"

The big man smiled and said, "Ask him yourself. You are to go to Washington first."

She left Pusser's Landing, telling the waiter that an emergency had arisen, found her way back to Edwards's house, quickly packed, and left him a note.

> Dear Eric,
> I won't even try to explain why I've rushed away but I assure you it's urgent. Please forgive me. There are so many things I want to say to you about last night, about feelings it generated in me, about—well, about a lot of things. There's no time now. Thank you for providing a wonderful vacation in your beloved BVI. I hope I'll be able to share it with you again soon.
>
> Collette

CHAPTER 25

Cahill got off the plane at Dulles Airport, rented a car, and drove directly to her mother's house where she was met with a barrage of questions about where she'd been and why she was running off again in such a rush. Cahill explained, "They're having some kind of a budget crisis at the embassy at Budapest and I have to get back right away."

"What a shame," her mother said. "I thought I might get to see you for at least a day."

Collette stopped rushing for a moment, hugged her, said she loved her and yes, she would have coffee, and ran upstairs to pack.

She shared the next hour with her mother in the kitchen and felt a desperate yearning to stay, to retreat into childhood where the world was wondrous and the future bright when viewed from the protective custody of family and home. She had to force herself to say goodbye, leaving her mother standing at the front door with a poignant expression on her face. "I'll be back soon," Cahill yelled through the open car window. She knew her mother's smile was forced but she appreciated the effort.

She drove back to Washington, went to a phone booth, and dialed the special number Hank Fox had given her. When a young woman answered, Cahill said, "This is Dr. Jayne's office calling for Mr. Fox." The woman told her to hold. A minute later Fox came on the line and said, "I heard about the accident. I'm glad you're all right."

"Yes, I'm fine. I made friends with someone at Pusser's Landing. He told me . . . "

Fox said sharply, "I know what he told you. The Fisherman is restless in Budapest."

"The Fisherman?" Then, it dawned on her. Code name Horgász—Árpád Hegedüs. She said, "I thought he went to . . . ?"

"He didn't, and he wants to talk to his friend. It's important that he see her as soon as possible."

"I understand," she said.

"How is your boyfriend in the British Virgin Islands?"

"He's . . . he's not my boyfriend."

"How is he?"

"Fine." She started to think of the last conversation she'd had with Edwards but Fox didn't give her enough time to complete the thought.

"You can leave tonight?"

Cahill sighed. More than anything she didn't want to get on a plane for Budapest. What she really wanted was to return to the BVI and be with Eric Edwards, not only because of the intimacy that had developed between them, but because she wanted to talk more about this thing she was doing, this organization she'd placed so much trust in. That trust wasn't there anymore. Now she knew: She wanted out, too.

"I'll be hearing from Joe," Fox said. Breslin.

"I'm sure you will. I have to go. Goodbye." She slammed the receiver into its cradle, gripped the small shelf beneath the phone and shook it, muttering as she did, "The hell with you, the hell with it all."

She caught a flight out of Washington to New York and barely made the Pan Am flight to Frankfurt, Germany, where she could make a direct connection for Budapest. She'd called Vern Wheatley at his brother's apartment but there was no answer. She needed to talk with him. Somehow, she had the sense that if she didn't talk to someone outside the organization, someone who wasn't intrinsically bound up in its intrigues, she'd go to pieces. And that, she knew, would be the worst thing that could happen.

▪ ▪ ▪

By the time she left the plane in Budapest she was exhausted but, at least, more in control of herself and her circumstances. She realized as she went through Customs that she was now back in her official status as an employee of the United States Embassy. It didn't matter that her real employer was the CIA. What *did* matter was that things were familiar now; not quite as comforting as the bosom of her mother, but certainly better than what she'd been through the past week.

She took a cab to her apartment and called Joe Breslin at the embassy.

"Welcome back," he said. "You must be beat."

"I sure am."

"It's five o'clock. Think you can stay awake long enough for dinner?"

"I'll make myself. Where?"

"Légrádi Testvérek."

Cahill managed a smile despite her fatigue. "Going fancy, are we? Is this in honor of my return?"

"If it makes you feel good thinking that, then that's what it's for. Actually, my stomach is in need of a good meal, and I get a kick out of the chubby little violin player."

"I'll consider it in my honor. What time?"

"I prefer late but, considering your condition, maybe we should make it early. How's eight sound?"

"Eight? I'll be dead to the world by then."

"Okay, tell you what. Take a good long nap and meet me there at ten."

She knew there was little sense in trying to negotiate a different time. He said he'd make a reservation under his name. She opened the door of her small refrigerator and remembered she'd cleaned it out before leaving. The only thing in it was two bottles of Szamorodni, the heavy dessert white wine, a half dozen bottles of Köbanyai világos beer, a tin of coffee, and two cans of tuna fish her mother had sent in a "care package" a month ago. She opened the tuna fish, realized she was out of bread, ate it directly from the can, stripped off her clothing, set her alarm clock, climbed into bed, and was asleep in seconds.

They sat across from each other in a small room at Légrádi Testvérek. The oval table betwen them was covered with a white lace tablecloth. Their chairs were broad, had high backs covered in a muted tapestry. A single silver candle epergne with ruffled glass dishes on two protruding arms dominated the center of the table. One of the dishes held fresh grapes and plums, the other apples and pears. The walls were stark white, the ceiling low and curved. Gypsy music emanated from a short, fat violinist and a tall, handsome cimbalom player who used tiny mallets to delicately strike the strings on his pianolike instrument.

"You look good," Breslin said, "considering the schedule you've been on."

"Thank you. Nothing like a can of American tuna fish and a nap to put color back in a girl's cheeks."

He smiled and looked up at the owner, who'd come to take their order. They decided to share a dish of assorted appetizers—caviar, tiny shrimps on salmon mousse stuffed into an egg, three kinds of pâté, and marinated oysters. Breslin ordered beef with pâté as his entrée; Cahill opted for chicken layered with a paprika sauce and little pools of sour cream. They skipped wine; Breslin had a Scotch and soda, Cahill mineral water.

"So?" he asked.

"So?" she mimicked. "You don't want a litany here, do you?"

"Why not?"

"Because . . ." She made a small gesture with both hands to indicate the public nature of the restaurant.

"Skip the names, and I don't need details. First, what about your boyfriend in the pretty place?"

She shook her head and sat back. "Joe, what do you and Hank do, talk every twenty minutes?"

"No, just two or three times a day. What about him? Did you enjoy your vacation?"

"Very much, except for a minor mishap out in the water."

"I heard. What were you doing, snorkeling or something?"

"Exactly, and that's why I'm sitting here tonight. As for my so-called boyfriend, he's terrific. Want to know something? A lot of our *friends* have said bad things about him. . . ." She raised her eyebrows and adopted an expression to reinforce she was talking about her employer. "People are wrong. If there's a problem, it's not with my 'boyfriend.' "

"I see," Breslin said, scratching his nose and rubbing his eyes. "We can discuss that at length another time. Did you see your shrink while you were back?"

"My— Oh, you mean Dr. Jayne."

"Who?"

"Don't worry, Joe, we're talking about the same person. I didn't see him again after I saw you in Washington. I felt no need to. My mental health is getting better all the time."

He narrowed his eyes as he scrutinized her across the flickering candle. "Something up with you, Collette? You okay?"

"I think I'm beginning to be more than okay, Joe. I think I grew up this past week."

"What does that mean?"

"It means . . ." She realized she was on the verge of tears and told herself that if she cried, she would never forgive herself. She looked around the restaurant. A waiter brought the appetizers on a white china platter. He filled their glasses with water and asked if they needed anything else.

"No, *köszönöm szepen,*" Breslin said politely. The waiter left and Breslin gave his attention to Cahill. "You're not happy, are you?"

Cahill shook her head in wonder and laughed. She leaned forward so that her face was inches from the candle's flame and said, "What the *hell* am I supposed to be happy about, Joe?"

He held up his hands and said, "Okay, I won't press it.

You've been under a lot of strain. I realize that. Come on, enjoy the food. It's costing me a month's salary."

Throughout the meal, Cahill was on the verge a dozen times of telling him how she felt. She resisted the temptation and contented herself with light conversation.

The doorman got Breslin's car for him. When he and Cahill were in it, Breslin asked, "Feel up to a little nightlife?"

"Joe, I . . . the Miniatur?"

"No, I ran across another spot while you were away. Change is good for the soul, right?"

"If you say so, Joe. Might as well catch up on what's new in Budapest, but not too late, huh? One drink and get me home."

"Trust me."

She always had, but wasn't so sure anymore.

He drove slowly through the narrow, winding streets of the Pest side of the city until reaching Vörösmarty tėr, with its statue of the famed Hungarian poet for whom the square was named. They passed a succession of airline offices and government buildings until they reached Engels Square and its large bus terminal. Ahead of them was St. Stephen's basilica. Breslin made a sharp turn north and, five minutes later, entered an especially narrow street made worse by cars hanging off their sidewalk parking spots. He found a place, wedged his small Renault between two other cars, and they got out. Cahill looked up the street to the huge red star atop the Parliament Building. She was back. Hungary. Budapest. Red stars and Soviet tanks. She was glad. Oddly, it was as close to home as she'd ever be outside of her mother's house in Virginia.

The bar wasn't marked, no sign, no windows. Only the

faint tinkling of a piano heralded its location, and that was confused by a dozen dark doors set into the long concrete wall that formed the front of the street's buildings.

Breslin rapped with a brass knocker. The door opened and a large man in a black suit, with long greasy black hair and sunken cheeks, scrutinized them. Breslin nodded toward Cahill. The man stepped back and allowed them to enter.

Now the music was louder. The pianist was playing "Night and Day." Female laughter in the air mingled with his notes.

Cahill looked around. The club was laid out much like the Miniatur—bar as you entered, a small room just off it in which customers could enjoy the piano.

"*Jó napot* (How are you?)," Breslin said to an attractive woman with hair bleached white, wearing a tight red satin dress.

"*Jó estét* (Good evening)," she said.

"*Fel tudya ezt váltani?* (Can you change this?)," Breslin asked, handing her a Hungarian bill of large denomination.

She looked at the bill, at him, then stepped back to give them access to a door hidden in shadows beyond the bar. Breslin nodded at Cahill and she followed him. He hesitated, his hand poised over the knob, then turned it. The door swung open. Breslin indicated that Cahill should enter first. She took a step into a small room lighted only by two small lamps on a battered table in the middle. There were no windows, and heavy purple drapes covered all walls.

Her eyes started to adjust to the dimness. A man, whose face was vaguely familiar, was the first object she focused on. He had a thick, square face. Bones beneath bushy eyebrows formed hairy shelves over his cheeks. His black hair was thick and curly and streaked with gray. She remembered—Zoltán Réti, the author, Barrie Mayer's author.

Next to Reti sat Árpád Hegedüs. One of his hands on the table covered a female hand. A plain, wide-faced woman with honest eyes and thin, stringy hair.

"Árpád," Cahill said, the surprise evident in her voice.

"Miss Cahill," he said, standing. "I am so happy to see you."

CHAPTER 26

Collette looked across the table at Hegedüs and Réti. Hegedüs's presence was the more easily understood. She'd known that the purpose of her return to Budapest was to meet with him. Réti was another matter. She'd forgotten about him in the rush of the past weeks.

"Miss Cahill, allow me to introduce you to Miss Lukács, Magda Lukács," Hegedüs said. Cahill rose slightly and extended her hand. The Hungarian woman reached out tentatively, then slipped her hand into Cahill's. She smiled; Cahill did too. The woman's face was placid, yet there was fear in her eyes. She wasn't pretty, but Cahill recognized an earthy female quality.

"I mentioned Miss Lukács to you the last time we were together," Hegedüs said.

"Yes, I remember," said Cahill, "but you didn't mention her name." She again smiled at the woman. Here was Hegedüs's lover, the woman Cahill had fervently hoped would not deter him from continuing to provide information. Now, as she observed the happiness in Hegedüs's face, she was glad he'd found Magda Lukács. He was happier and more relaxed than Cahill could ever remember seeing him.

As for Réti, she knew him only from photographs, and from having seen him on Hungary's state-controlled television network. Barrie had often spoken of him but they'd never met. "I'm glad to finally meet you, Mr. Réti," she said. "Barrie Mayer spoke so often and enthusiastically of you and your work."

"That is flattering," said Réti. "She was a wonderful woman and a fine literary agent. I miss her very much."

Cahill turned to Breslin. "Joe, why are we here?"

Breslin glanced at the others before saying, "First of all, Collette, I should apologize for not telling you up front how the evening would play. I didn't want to lay a lot of tension on you at dinner. From what I've heard, there's been enough of that in your life already."

She half smiled.

"Mr. Hegedüs has come over to our side."

Collette said to Hegedüs, "You've defected?"

He gave her a sheepish smile. "Yes, I have. My family is in Russia and I am now one of you. I am sorry, Miss Cahill. I know that was not what you or your people wished."

"No need to apologize, Árpád. I think it's wonderful." She looked at Magda Lukács. "You have defected, too?"

Lukács nodded. "I come with Árpád."

"Of course," said Cahill. "I'm sure that . . ." She swung around to Breslin. "But that isn't why we we're sitting here, is it?"

Breslin shook his head. "No, it's not. The defection has already taken place. What we *are* here for is to hear what Mr. Hegedüs and Mr. Réti have to tell us." He smiled. "They wouldn't say a word unless you were here, Collette."

"I see," Cahill said, taking in the table. "Well, go ahead. Here I am, and I'm all ears."

When no one spoke, Breslin said, "Mr. Hegedüs."

Now Hegedüs seemed more like his old nervous self. He cleared his throat and squeezed his lover's hand. He ran a finger beneath his shirt collar and said with a forced sense of gaiety, "We are in a bar, yes? Could I possibly have some whiskey?"

His request visibly annoyed Breslin, but he got up with a sigh and went to the door, opened it, and said to the woman in the red satin dress who was seated at the bar, "Could we have a bottle of wine, please?"

Hegedüs said from behind Breslin, "Would bourbon be all right?"

Breslin turned and screwed up his face. *"Bourbon?"*

"Yes, Miss Cahill always . . ."

Breslin shook his head and said to the woman in red, "A bottle of bourbon." He then laughed and added, "And some Scotch and gin, too." He closed the door and said to Cahill, "Never let it be said that Joe Breslin didn't throw as good a defector party as Collette Cahill."

"You're a class act, Joe," Collette said. She looked at Zoltán Réti and asked, "Have you defected too, Mr. Réti?"

Réti shook his head.

"But have you . . . ?" She checked Breslin before continuing. His expressionless face prompted her to go ahead. "Have you been involved with our efforts all along, Mr. Réti, through Barrie Mayer?"

"Yes."

"Were you Barrie's contact here in Budapest?"

"Yes."

"She would hand you what she was carrying for us?"

He smiled. "It was a little more complicated than that, Miss Cahill."

There was a knock at the door. Breslin opened it and the woman in red carried in a tray with the liquor, a bucket of ice and glasses. After she'd placed it on the table and left, Collette cocked her head and listened to the strains of piano music and the laughter of patrons through the wall. Was this place secure enough for the sort of conversation they were having? She was almost ashamed for even questioning it. Breslin had a reputation of being the most cautious intelligence employee within the Budapest embassy.

"Maybe I'd better lead this conversation," Breslin said.

Cahill was momentarily taken aback, but said, "By all means."

Breslin pointed a finger across the table at Zoltán Réti and said, "Let's start with you." To Hegedüs, "You don't mind, do you?"

Hegedüs, busy pouring a tall glass of bourbon, quickly shook his head and said, "Of course not."

Breslin continued. "Mr. Réti, Miss Cahill has been back in the United States trying to find out what happened to Barrie Mayer. I don't know if you're aware of it, but they were best of friends."

"Yes, I know that," said Réti.

"Then you know that we've never believed that Barrie Mayer died of natural causes."

Réti grunted. "She was assassinated. Only a fool would think otherwise."

"Exactly," said Breslin. "One of the pieces we've had trouble with has to do with what she could have been carrying that was important enough for her to have been murdered. Frankly, we weren't even aware of her final trip to Budapest until after the fact. We expected nothing from Washington. But you evidently knew she was coming."

Réti nodded, and his heavy eyebrows came down even lower over his eyes.

Cahill said, "But you weren't *here*, Mr. Réti. You were in London."

"Yes, I was sent there by the Hungarian Arts Council to make an appearance at an international writers' conference."

"Didn't Barrie know that you wouldn't be here to meet her?" Cahill asked.

"No, I had no time to contact her. I was not allowed access to any means of communication with her before she left the United States."

"Why?" Cahill realized she had taken the meeting from Breslin. She cast a glance at him to see if he were annoyed. The expression on his face showed that he wasn't.

Réti shrugged. "I can only assume that they . . . the government had become aware that she and I were more than simply agent and author."

Cahill processed what he'd said, then asked, "And they didn't do more to you than just keep you from telling Barrie that you wouldn't be here to meet her? They knew that you were involved in some sort of activity on our behalf, but only kept you from calling her?"

Réti smiled, exposing a set of widely spaced teeth. He said, "That is not so surprising, Miss Cahill. The Russians . . . and my government . . . they are not so foolish to punish someone like myself. It would not look so good in the world, huh?"

His explanation made sense to Cahill, but she said, "Still,

if Barrie *had* arrived and didn't find you here, what would she do with what she was carrying? Who would she hand it to?"

"This time, Miss Cahill, Barrie was not to hand me anything."

"She wasn't?"

"No."

"What was she to do, then?"

"She was to tell me something."

"Tell?"

"Yes. This time what she carried was in her head."

"Her mind, you mean."

"Yes, in her mind."

The room was hot and stuffy, yet a chill radiated through Collette that caused her to fold into herself. Was it all coming true now—Jason Tolker, Estabrooks's theories on using hypnosis to create the perfect intelligence courier, programs like Operation Bluebird and MK-ULTRA, supposedly scrapped years ago but still going strong—everything Eric Edwards had told her, every bit of it?

She looked at Breslin. "Joe, do you know what Barrie was supposed to tell Mr. Réti?"

Breslin, who'd just lighted his pipe, squinted through the smoke and said, "I think so."

Cahill hadn't expected an affirmative answer. Breslin said to Hegedüs, "Perhaps it's time for you to contribute to this conversation."

The Hungarian psychiatrist looked at Magda Lukács, cleared his throat with a swallow of bourbon, and said, "It has to do with what I told you the last time, Miss Cahill."

Collette said it quietly, almost to the table: "Dr. Tolker."

"Yes, your Dr. Tolker . . ."

"What about him?"

A false start from Hegedüs, then, "He had given Miss Mayer information of the gravest importance to the Banana Quick project."

"What sort of information?" Cahill asked.

"The source of the leak in the British Virgin Islands," Breslin said.

Cahill raised her eyebrows. "I thought that . . ."

Breslin shrugged. "I think you're beginning to understand, Collette."

"You told me the last time we were together, Árpád, that Tolker was not to be trusted."

"That is correct."

"But now I'm to understand that he's the one who is identifying a security leak in Banana Quick."

"Right," said Breslin. "You know who we're talking about, Collette."

"Eric Edwards."

"Exactly."

"That's ridiculous," Collette said.

"Why?" Breslin asked. "Edwards has been a prime suspect from the beginning. That's why you were . . ." He stopped. The rules were being broken. Take everything you could from the other side but offer nothing.

Collette was having trouble controlling her emotions. She didn't want to mount an impassioned defense of Edwards because it would only trigger in Breslin the question of why she was doing it. She imposed calm on herself and asked Breslin, "How do you know what Barrie was carrying? Maybe it had nothing to do with Banana Quick . . . or Eric Edwards."

Breslin ignored her and nodded at Hegedüs, who said regretfully, "I was wrong, Miss Cahill, about Dr. Tolker."

"Wrong?"

"I was misled, perhaps deliberately by certain people within my professional ranks. Dr. Tolker has not been disloyal to you."

"Just like that," Cahill said.

Hegedüs shrugged. "It is not such a crime to be wrong, is it, not in America?"

Cahill sighed and sat back. "Collette," Breslin said, "the facts are written on the wall. Barrie was coming here to . . ."

She said, "Coming here to deliver a message that had been implanted in her mind by Jason Tolker."

"That's right," said Breslin. "Tell her, Mr. Réti."

Réti said, "I was to say something to her when she arrived that would cause her to remember the message."

"Which was?" Collette asked.

"That this Eric Edwards in the British Virgin Islands has been selling information to the Soviets about Banana Quick."

"How do we know that's what she was carrying?"

"Tolker has been contacted," Breslin said.

Cahill shook her head. "If Tolker can simply tell us what he knows about Eric Edwards, why did he bother sending Barrie with the information? Why didn't he just go to someone at Langley with it?"

"Because . . ." Breslin paused, then continued. "We can discuss that later, Collette. For now, let's stick to what Mr. Réti and Mr. Hegedüs can provide us."

"Well?" Cahill said to the two Hungarians.

"Miss Cahill," Réti said, "first of all, I did not know what Barrie was to tell me when I said to her the code words."

"What were those words?" Cahill asked.

Réti looked to Breslin, who nodded his approval. "I was to say, 'The climate has improved.' "

"The climate has improved," Cahill repeated.

"Yes, exactly that."

"And she was then to open up to you like a robot."

"I do not know about that. I was simply following instructions."

"Whose instructions?"

"Mr. . . ." Another look at Breslin.

"Stan Podgorsky," Breslin said. "Stan's been the contact for Barrie and Mr. Réti since the beginning."

"Why wasn't I told that?" Cahill asked.

"No need. Barrie's courier duties had nothing to do with you."

"I wonder about that."

"Don't bother. It's the way it is. Accept it."

"Árpád, who has caused you to change your opinion of Jason Tolker?"

"Friends." He smiled. "Former friends. There are no longer friends for me in Hungary."

"Collette, Mr. Réti has something else to share with us," Breslin said.

Everyone waited. Finally, Réti said in a low, slow monotone, "Barrie was bringing me money, too."

"Money?" Cahill said.

"Yes, to pay off one of our officials so that the earnings from my books could reach me here in Hungary."

"This money was in her briefcase?"

"Yes."

"Joe, Barrie received her briefcase from Tolker. Why would he . . . ?"

"He didn't," Breslin said. "The money wasn't from Mr. Réti's fund in the States. It was Pickle Factory money."

"Why?"

"It's the way it was set up."

"Set up . . . with Barrie?"

"Right."

"But she had Réti's own money, didn't she? Why would she need CIA money?"

Breslin lowered his eyes, then raised them. "Later," he said.

"No, not later," Cahill said. "How about now?"

"Collette, I think you're becoming emotionally bound up in this. That won't help clarify anything."

"I resent that, Joe,"

What she was really feeling was a sense of being a woman, and disliking herself for it. Breslin was right. He'd read her; she wasn't taking in and evaluating what was being said at the table like a professional. She was bound up in protecting a man, Eric, a man with whom she'd slept and, incredibly, with whom she'd begun to fall in love. It hadn't seemed incredible at the time, but it did now.

She took in everyone at the table and asked, "Is there anything else?"

Hegedüs forced a big smile, his hand still resting on his lover's hand. He said, "Miss Cahill, I would like you to know how much I appreciate . . . how much Magda and I appreciate everything you have done for us."

"I didn't do anything, Árpád, except listen to you."

"No, you are wrong, Miss Cahill. By spending time with you, my decision to leave the oppression of the Soviets was made clear, and easier." He stood and bowed. "I shall be forever grateful."

Cahill found his demeanor to be offensive. "What about your family, Árpád, your beautiful daughter and bright young son? Your wife. What of her? Are you content to abandon them to the tenuous life you know they'll lead in Russia?" He started to respond but she went on. "You told me you wanted more than anything else for your son to have the advantage of growing up in America. What was that, Árpád, all talk?" Her voice was now more strident, reflecting what she was feeling.

"Let's drop it," Breslin said with finality. Collette glared at him, then said to Réti, "What happens to you now, Mr. Réti? The money never reached you."

"Réti shrugged. "It is the same now as it was before. Perhaps . . . "

"Yes?"

"Perhaps you could be of help in this matter."

"How?"

"We're working on it, Mr. Réti," Breslin said. To Cahill, "It's one of the things I want to discuss with you when we leave here."

"All right." Collette stood and extended her hand to Magda Lukács. "Welcome, Miss Lukács, to freedom." Hegedüs beamed and offered his hand to Cahill. She ignored it, said to Breslin, "I'm ready to leave."

Breslin got up and surveyed the bottles on the table. "Souvenirs?" he asked, laughing.

"If you would not be offended I would . . . "

"Sure, Mr. Hegedüs, take it with you," Breslin said. "Thank you for being here, all of you. Come on, Collette, you must be exhausted."

"That, and more," she said, opening the door and walking into the smoky barroom. The lady in red was standing at the door.

"*Jó éjszakát,*" Breslin said.

"*Jó éjszakát,*" she said, nodding at Cahill.

Collete said "Good night" in English, walked past her, and stood in the cool, refreshing air outside the club.

Breslin came to her side. Without looking at him, she said, "Let's go somewhere and talk."

"I thought you were beat," he said, taking her arm.

"I'm wide awake and I'm filled with questions that need answering. Are you up to that, Joe?"

"I'll do my best."

Somehow, she knew his best wouldn't be enough, but she'd take what she could get.

■ ■ ■

They'd driven out of the city to the Római fürdö, the former Roman baths that now constituted one of Budapest's two major camping sites. The sky had clouded over and was low. It picked up the general glow of the city's lights and was racing over them, pink and yellow and gray, a fast-moving scrim cranked by an unseen force.

"You said you had questions," Breslin said.

Cahill had opened her window and was looking out into the dark. She said into the night, "Just one, Joe."

"Shoot."

She turned and faced him. "Who killed Barrie Mayer?"

"I don't know."

"Know what I think, Joe?"

"No, what?"

"I think everybody's lying."

He laughed. "Who's *everybody*?"

"*Everybody!* Let's start with Réti."

"Okay. Start with him. What's he got to lie about?"

"Money, for one thing. I knew Barrie was supposed to pay off some government bigwig on Réti's behalf, but I didn't know until tonight that Barrie was actually carrying the money with her in the missing briefcase. Oh, that's right, you said you'd discuss with me later why the Company used its money to buy off the official, instead of Barrie using what she'd already collected of Réti's earnings. This is later, Joe. I'm ready."

He scrutinized her from where he sat in the driver's seat, ran his tongue over his lips, then pulled a pipe from his raincoat pocket and went through the ritual of lighting it. This was all too familiar to Cahill, using the pipe to buy thinking time, and tonight was especially irritating. Still, she didn't interrupt, didn't attempt to hasten the process. She waited patiently until the bowl glowed with fire and he'd had a chance to inhale. Then she said, "Réti's money. Why the Company?"

"To make sure he knew who he owed," Breslin answered.

"That doesn't make sense," she said. "Why would he owe anyone? The money is his. His books earned it."

"That's what he said, but we educated him. He's Hungarian. His big money is earned out of the country. Puts him in a tough position, doesn't it? All we did was to set up a system to help him get his hands on some of it."

"If he played the game with us."

"Sure. He thought Barrie would take care of it as his agent." Breslin smiled. "Of course, he didn't know up front that she worked for us, and would do what we told her to do. We struck a nice deal. Réti cooperates with us, and we see that he gets enough money to live like a king here."

"That is so . . . goddamned unfair. He earned that money."

"I suppose it is unfair, unless you're dealing with a Socialist writer and a capitalist agent. Come on, Collette, you know damn well that nothing's fair in what we're called upon to do."

" 'Called upon to do.' You make it sound so lofty."

"Necessary. Maybe that's more palatable to you."

She drew a sustained, angry breath. "Let's get to Hegedüs and Jason Tolker. Why do you buy Hegedüs's change of mind about Tolker?"

"Why not buy it?"

"Why *not?* Joe, hasn't it occurred to you that Árpád might have come over to feed us disinformation? What if Tolker has been cooperating with the other side? How convenient to have Hegedüs defect and get us to look the other way. No, I can't buy it. When Hegedüs told me earlier that Tolker was not be to trusted, he meant it. He doesn't mean what he's saying now. He's lying."

"Prove it."

"How do you prove anything in this stupid game?"

"Right, you don't. You look at everything you've got—which sure as hell never amounts to much—and you feel what your gut is saying and listen to what your head says and you make your decisions. My decision? We've got ourselves a defector, a good one. Sure, we'd all prefer he'd stayed in place so he could keep feeding us from the inside, but it's okay that he's with us now. He's loaded with insight into the Soviet and Hungarian psychological fraternity. You did a good job, Collette. You turned him nicely. He trusted you. Everybody's pleased with the way you've handled him."

"That's terrific. Why don't *you* trust me?"

"Huh?"

"Why can't you put some stock in what my gut feels and my head says? He's lying, Joe, maybe to protect his family back in the Soviet Union, maybe to play out his own brand of patriotism to his government. Don't you question why the Soviets have let him off the hook? He was supposed to go back to Russia because they didn't trust him. He doesn't go, and he neatly defects. He's lying. They've plopped him into the middle of us, and one of his jobs is to get Jason Tolker off the hook."

"Pure speculation, Collette. Ammunition. Give me something tangible to back it up."

She spread her hands. "I don't have any, but I know I'm right."

"What about Réti?" Breslin asked. "What's he got to lie about?"

"I don't know. But remember, he was in London when Barrie died."

"Meaning?"

"Meaning maybe he killed her because he knew her briefcase was loaded with cash."

"His cash. Why kill her for it?" A long, slow drag on his pipe.

"Did he know how much she was bringing to him?"

"Not sure. Probably not."

"Maybe Mr. Réti figured out that he was never going to get a square count from us. Maybe he figured out that he'd only get a small piece of what she was carrying. Maybe he wanted to get his hands on the money while he was outside Hungary and stash it."

"Interesting questions."

"Yes, aren't they?"

"What about Hubler back in Washington? Réti sure as hell didn't kill him, Collette."

"He could have arranged it if Hubler knew what had happened. The Soviets could have done it. Then again, maybe it was pure coincidence, nothing to do with Barrie."

"Maybe. What other theories do you have?"

"Don't dismiss what I'm saying, Joe. Don't treat me like some schoolgirl who's spewing out plots from bad TV shows she's watched."

"Hey, Collette, back off. I'm a white hat, remember? I'm a friend."

She wanted to question what he'd said but didn't. Instead, she asked if he had a cigarette.

"You don't smoke."

"I used to, back when I was a schoolgirl watching bad TV shows. Got any?"

"Yeah, in the glove compartment. Every once in a while I get the urge."

She opened the compartment and reached inside, found a crumpled pack of Camels, and pulled one from the pack. Breslin lighted it for her. She coughed, exhaled the smoke, then took another drag, tossed the cigarette out the window, and said, "You think Eric Edwards is a double agent?"

"Yes."

"Do you think he killed Barrie?"

"Good chance that he did."

"Why would he do that? He was in love with her."

"To save his skin."

"What do you mean?"

"Barrie knew he was a double agent."

"Because Tolker told her."

"No, because she told Tolker." He reached across the seat and grabbed her arm. "You ready for some heavy stuff, Collette?"

"Heavy stuff? The last week hasn't exactly been lightweight, Joe, has it?"

"No, it hasn't." He paused, used his pipe to fill a few seconds, then said, "Your friend Barrie sold out, too."

"Sold out? What do you mean? Sold out to whom?"

"The other side. She was in it with Edwards."

"Joe, that's . . . "

"Hey, at least hear me out."

She didn't, jumped in with, "If she was in it with Edwards, why would she be off to Hungary to blow the whistle on him?"

"Ever hear of the woman scorned?"

"Not Barrie."

"Why not?"

"Because . . . she wouldn't do something like that." Now there was only a modicum of conviction behind her words. What spun through her mind was the kind of control someone like Jason Tolker could exercise over a good subject like Barrie Mayer. What she'd read in Estabrooks's book was there, too, about changing the "visual" in order to get people to behave in a manner foreign to their basic personality and values.

"What if Tolker programmed her to come up with a story about Eric Edwards out of . . . I don't know, out of jealousy or pique or to save his own hide? Maybe Tolker is a double agent and used Barrie to cover up. Maybe he poisoned Barrie against Edwards."

"Yeah, maybe, Collette. Who poisoned you against Tolker?"

"I'm not . . . "

"Put another way, how come you're so hell-bent on defending Edwards?"

"I'm not doing that, either, Joe."

"I think you are."

"Think again, and get off treating me like some pathetic

woman defending a lover to the death. I am a woman, Joe, and I am an agent of the CIA. Know what? I'm good at both."

"Collette, maybe . . . "

"Maybe nothing, Joe. You and Stan have wrapped everything up in what you think is a neat little package, no loose ends, no doubts. Why? Why is it so damn important to resolve Barrie's murder by laying it on Edwards?" He raised his eyebrows as though to say, "There you go again." She shook her head. "I don't buy it, any of it, Joe."

"That's a shame," he said quietly.

"Why?"

"Because that attitude will get in the way of your next assignment."

She stared quizzically at him, finally asking, "What assignment?"

"Terminating Eric Edwards."

She started to speak but all that came out was breath.

"You understand what I'm saying, don't you?"

"Terminate Eric? Kill him."

"Yes."

It was hardly an accurate reflection of what was on her mind, but it happened anyway: She laughed. Breslin did, too, and continued until she stopped.

"They mean it," he said.

"They?"

"Up top."

"*They* . . . they told you to assign me to kill him?"

"Uh-huh."

"Why me?"

"You can get close to him."

"So can lots of people."

"Easier and neater with you, Collette."

"How do 'they' suggest I do this?"

"Your choice. Go by Tech in the morning and choose your weapon."

"I see," she said. "Then what?"

"What are you talking about, what happens after it's done?"

'Right."

"Nothing. It's over, the double agent in Banana Quick is no longer a problem and we can get back to normal, which can't be too soon. Banana Quick is close to popping."

"Back to normal for me, here in Budapest?"

"If you wish. It's customary for anyone carrying out a wet affair to have their choice of future assignment, even to take a leave of absence, with pay, of course."

"Joe, I'm sorry but . . ." She started to laugh again, but it did not become laughter, and this time he didn't join her. Instead, he puffed on his pipe and waited for her nervous, absolutely necessary reaction to subside.

"They're serious, Collette."

"I'm sure they are. I'm not." She paused, then said, "Joe, *they* blew up the yacht, didn't they?" When he didn't respond, she added, "Eric knew it."

Again, no reply from him.

"I was on that yacht, Joe."

"It wasn't us."

"I don't believe you."

"It was the Soviets."

"Why would they do that if he's on their side?"

A shrug from Breslin. "Maybe he started holding out for more money. Maybe they thought he was feeding them bad information. Maybe they didn't like him carousing around with a pretty CIA agent."

Cahill shook her head. "You know what's remarkable, Joe?"

"What?"

"That 'they' means the same people . . . the Soviets, the CIA . . . all the same, same morality, same ethics, same game."

"Don't give me the moral equivalency speech, Collette. It doesn't play, and you know it. We've got a system to preserve that's good and decent. Their system is evil. I'll tell you something else. If you do want to view it that way, keep it between us. It wouldn't go over to big with . . . "

"The hell with *them*."

"Suit yourself. I've given you the assignment. Take it?"

"Yes."

"Look, Collette, you realize that . . . ?"

"Joe, I said I'd do it. No need for more speeches."

"You'll really do it?"

"Yes, I'll really do it."

"When?"

"I'll leave tomorrow."

"I get the feeling that . . . "

"Take me home, Joe."

"Collette, if there's any hesitation on your part, I'd suggest you sleep on it."

"I'll do that. I'll sleep just fine."

"Why?"

"Why what?"

"Why the sudden willingness to kill Edwards?"

"Because . . . I'm a pro. I work for the CIA. I do what I'm told. It's obviously for the good of the country, *my* country. Someone has to do it. Let's go."

He pulled up in front of her apartment building and said, "Come talk to me in the morning."

"What for?"

"To go over this a little more."

"No need. You'll tell Tech I'll be by?"

He sighed, said, "Yes."

"Know something, Joe?"

"What?"

"For the first time since I joined the CIA, I feel part of the team."

CHAPTER 27

She awoke the next morning feeling surprisingly refreshed. There was no hangover from jet lag or from the late evening and its drinks. She showered quickly, chose her heather wool tweed suit and burgundy turtleneck, and called for a taxi. A half hour later she walked through the front door of the United States Embassy on Szabadság tér, flashed her credentials at the security guard who knew her well, was buzzed into the inner lobby, and went directly to the transportation office. There she booked an afternoon Malev flight to London, and a connecting flight to New York the following evening.

"Good morning, Joe," she said brightly to Breslin as they approached each other in the hall.

"Hello, Collette," he said somberly.

"Can we get this over with now?" she asked.

His was a deep, meaningful sigh. "Yeah, I suppose so," he said.

He closed the door to his office. "Got a cigarette, Joe?" she asked pleasantly.

"No. Don't start the habit."

"Why not? Looks like I'm about to start a whole new set of bad habits."

"Look, Collette, I talked to Stan late last night. I tried to . . ." He looked up at the ceiling. "Let's take a walk."

"No need. You've arranged for me to go to Tech this morning?"

"Yes, but . . ." He got up. "Come on."

She had little choice but to follow him out of the embassy and across Liberation Square to a bench on which he propped a foot and lighted his pipe. "I tried to get you off it, Collette," he said.

"Why? I didn't balk."

"Yeah, and that worries me. How come?"

"I thought I explained myself last night. I want to be a pro, part of the team. You join an organization like this because, no matter how much you want to—need to—deny your fascination with James Bond movies, it's always there. Right, Joe?"

"Maybe. The point is, Collette, I went to Stan's house after I dropped you and tried to persuade him to cancel the order from Langley."

"I wish you hadn't. I don't want to be treated different from anyone else because I'm a woman."

"That wasn't what I pegged my request upon," Breslin said. "I don't think you're the one to go after our friend in the BVI because of your relationship with him."

"I don't have a *relationship* with him, Joe. I went down there on business and did what I was told to do. I got close to him and damn near ended up fish food in the bargain. It makes perfect sense for me to do this."

"Hank thinks so, too."

"Fox? I'm flattered. All I seem to end up with are father figures, and want to know something, Joe?"

"What?"

"I don't need a father, and that includes you."

"Thanks."

"No gratitude necessary. All my fathers seem to do—including you—is to send their daughters into battle. New definition of fatherhood, I guess. Female liberation. I'm glad. Now, let's get back to basics. You tried to get me off, you failed. That's good because I'm committed to this. Everything is right in my mind. One thing I don't need is a set of doubts implanted." She laughed. "Besides, I'm a lousy hypnotic subject. It's a shame Barrie wasn't."

Breslin nodded toward a far corner of the square where two men in overcoats and hats stood, conspicuously not watching them. "I think we've talked enough," Breslin said.

"I think you're right," Cahill said. "I have a plane reservation for this afternoon. Better get inside and pick up my supplies."

"All right. One other thing, though." He walked away from her and toward a corner where a line of taxicabs waited for fares. He slowed down and she caught up with him. "When you get home, Collette, contact no one involved with us. No one. Understand?"

"Yes." The order didn't surprise her. The nature of her mission would preclude touching base with anyone even mildly associated with the CIA and Langley.

"But," he said, "if you need help in a real emergency, there's been a control established for you in D.C."

"Who?"

"It doesn't matter. Just remember that it's available in an emergency. You make contact any evening for the next two weeks at exactly six o'clock. The contact point is the statue of Winston Churchill just outside the British Embassy on Massachuetts Avenue. Your contact will hold for ten minutes each evening, no more. Got it?"

"Yes. Do I still have my contact in the BVI, at Pusser's Landing?"

"No."

"All right."

She had nothing more to say, just followed him back inside the embassy, went to her office, closed the door, and stood at the window peering out at the gray, suddenly bleak city of Budapest. Her phone rang but she ignored it. She realized she was in the midst of an unemotional void: no feelings, no anxiety or anger or confusion. There was nothing, and it was pleasant.

Ten minutes later she went to the embassy's basement where a closed door bore the sign TECHNICAL ASSISTANCE. She knocked; a latch was released and Harold Sutherland opened the door.

"Hi, Red," she said.

"Hi. Come on in. I've been expecting you."

Once the door was closed behind them, Sutherland said, "Well, kid, what do you need?"

Cahill stood in the middle of the cramped, cluttered room and realized he was waiting for an answer. What was the answer? She didn't know what she "needed." Obviously, there were people who did for a living what she was about to do. For a death. *They* knew what was needed in their job. She didn't. It wasn't her job to kill anyone, at least not in the lengthy job description that accompanied her embassy employment. But those specifications were a lie, too. She didn't work for the embassy. She worked for the Central Intelligence Agency, the CIA, the Company, the Pickle Factory, whose stated purpose was to gather and assimilate intelligence from all over the world and . . . and to kill when it was necessary to keep doing its job.

She'd had courses during her CIA training at the Farm that dealt with killing, although it was never labeled as such. "Self-protection," they called it. There were other terms—"Termination Techniques," "Neutralization," "Securing the Operation."

"You flying somewhere?" Sutherland asked.

His gravel voice startled her. She looked at him, forced a smile, and said, "Yes."

"Come here."

He led her past his desk, past rows of floor-to-ceiling shelving stocked with unmarked boxes and to a tiny separate room at the rear. It was a miniature firing range. She didn't even know it existed. She'd participated in firing exercises on the embassy's main range, which wasn't much bigger, just longer.

There was a table, two chairs, and a thick, padded wall ten feet away. The pads were filled with holes. She glanced up; the ceiling was covered with soundproofing material. So were the other walls.

"Have a seat," Sutherland said.

She took one of the chairs while he disappeared back into the shelves, returning moments later carrying a white cardboard box. He placed it on the table, opened it, and removed a purple bag with a drawstring. She watched as he opened the bag and lifted from it a piece of white plastic that was shaped like a small revolver. He pulled a second bag from the box. It contained a plastic barrel. The only metal item was a small spring.

"Nine millimeter," he said as he weighed the components

in his large, callused hand. "It's like the Austrian Glock 17, only the barrel is plastic, too. It's U.S.-made. We just got it last week."

"I see."

"Here, put it together. Simple."

He watched as she fumbled with the pieces, then showed her how to do it. When it was assembled, he said, "You stick the spring in your purse and pack the rest in your suitcase. Wrap it in clothes, only that's not even necessary. X-ray picks up nothing.

She looked at him. "Bullets?"

He grinned. "Ammunition, you mean? Pick it up in any sporting goods store where you're traveling. Want to try it?"

"No, I . . . Yes, please."

He showed her how to load it and told her to shoot at the padded wall. She placed two hands on it and squeezed the trigger. She'd expected a kick. There was virtually nothing. Even the sound was small.

"You need a silencer?"

"Ah, no, I don't think so."

"Good. It's developed but we don't have it yet. Break it down. I'll watch."

She disassembled and assembled the small plastic weapon four times.

"Good. You've got it down. What else?"

"I . . . I'm not sure, Red." What she wanted to say was that she was about to go off on an assignment to kill someone, to kill a man she'd slept with, to terminate him for the good of her country and the free world. She didn't say anything, of course. It was too late for that. It wouldn't be professional.

"Red."

"Yeah?"

"I'd like some prussic acid and a detonator."

His eyebrows went up. "Why?" he asked.

"I need it for my assignment."

"Yeah? I ought to . . ." He shrugged and heaved his bulk to its feet. "Joe said give you anything you wanted. Sure you want this?"

"Yes, I'm sure."

It took him a few minutes to assemble her request. When he handed it to her, she was amazed at the smallness of it. "Know how to use it?" he asked.

"No."

He showed her. "That's all there is to it," he said. "You get it close to the nose and trip this spring. Make sure it's not your own nose. By the way, if it is, use this stuff fast." He handed her a package of two glass ampules. "Nitro. If you get a whiff of the prussic, break this under your nose or . . ." He grinned and patted her on the shoulder. "Or I lose a favorite of mine."

His words cut into her, but then she smiled, too, and said, "Thanks, Red. Any last words of wisdom?"

"Yeah, I got a few."

"What are they?"

"Get out of the business, kid. Go home, work for a bank, get married and raise a couple of good citizens."

She wanted to cry but was successful in fighting the need. "Actually," she said, "I was going to become the Attorney General of the United States."

"That's not much better than what you're doing now." He shook his head and asked, "You want to talk?"

She did, desperately, but what she said was, "No, I have to get going. I haven't packed. The other stuff, that is." She looked down at the white box she held in her hands.

Sutherland had put the revolver, the prussic acid vial, and detonator in it, packing it carefully, like a bridal gift.

"Good luck, kid," he said. "See you back here soon?"

"Yeah, I guess so. Unless I decide to go work for a bank. Thanks, Red."

"You take care."

CHAPTER 28

It was a running joke among embassy employees—Malev airlines, the national Hungarian airline, sold a first-class section on its flights, but its seats, food, and service were identical to those in the rear of the plane. A Communist compromise with free enterprise.

It was also unusual, Cahill knew, for her to be flying first class. Company policy put everyone in coach, with the exception of chiefs-of-station. But when Cahill had walked into the Transportation Department, she was handed first-class tickets on every leg of the trip. The young woman who handled embassy travel arrangements lifted a brow as she handed the tickets to Cahill. It had amused Cahill at the time, and she was tempted to say, "No, there hasn't been a mistake. Assassins always ride first class."

Now, at thirty thousand feet between Budapest and London, it was not as amusing. It carried with it a symbolism that she would have preferred to ignore, but couldn't. Like a last meal, or wish.

She passed through Heathrow Customs and went to the

approximate place where Barrie would have been standing when the prussic acid was shoved beneath her nose. She stared at the hard floor for a long time, watching hundreds of pairs of shoes pass over it. Didn't they know what they were walking on? What a horrible place to die, she thought as she slowly walked away, took a taxi outside the terminal, and told the driver to go to 11, Cadogan Gardens.

"Yes, we have a room," the manager on duty told her. "I'm afraid the room you enjoyed last time isn't available, but we have a nice single in the back."

"Anything will be fine," Cahill said. "This was a last-minute trip, no time to call ahead."

She ordered a dinner of cold poached salmon and a bottle of wine. When the hall porter had left, she securely latched the door, undressed, removed the small plastic revolver from her suitcase, did the same with the spring and prussic acid detonator from her purse, and placed everything on the table next to the tray. She tasted the white wine the porter had uncorked. It was chilled and tart.

She ate the salmon with enthusiasm, and finished half the wine, her eyes remaining for most of the meal on the mechanical contraptions of death with which she'd traveled.

The phone rang. "Was dinner satisfactory?" the porter wished to know.

"Yes, fine, thank you," said Cahill.

"Do you wish anything else?"

"No, no, thank you."

"Shall I remove the tray, madam?"

"No, that won't be necessary. In the morning. Will you arrange a wake-up call for me at ten, please?"

"Yes, madam."

"And breakfast in the room. Two eggs over easy, bacon and toast, coffee, orange juice."

"Yes, madam. Have a pleasant evening."

"Thank you."

She stood at the window and watched a brisk wind whip leaves from the trees on the street below. People walked their dogs; someone was attempting to squeeze a too-large automobile into a too-small parking space.

She went to the table and picked up the white plastic revolver, assembled its components and, with two hands, aimed at an oil of a vase of roses that hung on the far wall. There was no ammunition in the weapon; she'd have to buy it when she got to the British Virgin Islands. She'd never bought bullets before and wondered whether she'd be able to do it with aplomb. Like a teenage boy sheepishly buying contraceptives, she thought.

She squeezed the trigger several times, sat on the couch and took the weapon apart, put it back together again, and repeated the process a dozen times. Satisfied, she carefully picked up the detonator and tested the spring, making sure before she did that the ampule of prussic acid wasn't in it.

She dialed a local number. It was answered on the first ring.

"Josh, this is Collette Cahill."

"Collette, great to hear your voice. How've you been?"

"It's good to hear your voice, too, Josh. I've been fine. I'm in London."

"Hey, that's great. Can we get together? How about dinner tomorrow? I'll round up some of the troops."

"I'd love it, Josh, but I'm here on business and have to leave early tomorrow evening. Actually, I'm calling for a favor."

"Anything. What is it?"

"I need a photograph."

"You're looking for a photographer?"

"No, I need an existing photograph of someone. I thought maybe you could pull one out of the files for me."

He laughed. "Not supposed to do that, you know."

"Yes, I know, but it really would be a tremendous help to me. I won't have to keep it, just have it for an hour or so tomorrow."

"You've got it—if we have it. Who do you want a picture of?"

"A literary agent here in London named Mark Hotchkiss."

"I don't know whether we'd have anything on a literary agent, but I'll check. You'd probably do better through a newspaper morgue."

"I know that, but I don't have time."

"I'll check it out first thing in the morning. Where can I meet up with you?"

She gave him the address of the hotel. "At least I'll get to see you tomorrow," he said. "If I come up with the photo, you owe me the chance to buy you a quick lunch."

"That'll be great. See you around noon."

Josh Moeller and Collette had worked closely together during her previous CIA assignment to the listening post in England. They'd become fast friends, sharing a mutual sense of humor and a quiet disdain for much of the bureaucratic rules and regulations under which they lived and worked. Their friendship evolved into a brief affair shortly before Cahill's reassignment to Budapest. Her move concluded the affair with finality, but they both knew it had effectively died by its own hand before that, one of those situations in which the friendship was stronger and more important to both parties than the passion. They'd initially kept in touch, mostly through letters delivered by way of the diplomatic pouch between Budapest and London. But then their correspondence tapered off, too, as will happen with the best of friends, especially when the friendship is strong enough to preclude any need for frequent contact.

Her next call was long-distance. It took ten minutes for it to go through to the BVI. Eric Edwards's secretary answered.

"Is Mr. Edwards there?" Cahill asked, glancing at her watch to reconfirm the time difference.

"No, ma'am, he is not. He is in the United States."

"Washington?"

"Yes, ma'am. Is this Miss Cahill?"

Cahill was surprised to be asked. "Yes, it is."

"Mr. Edwards told me that if you called I should inform you that he is staying at the Watergate Hotel in Washington, D.C."

"How long will he be there?"

"One more week, I think."

"Thank you, thank you very much. I'll contact him there."

One final call, this one to her mother in Virginia.

"Collette, where are you?"

"London, Mom, but I'll be coming home in a few days."

"Oh, that will be wonderful." A pause: "Are you all right?"

"Yes, Mom, I'm fine. I think . . . I think I might be coming home for good."

Her mother's gasp was audible even over the poor connection. "Why?" she asked. "I mean, I'd love for that to happen but . . . are you sure everything is all right? Are you in some sort of trouble?"

Collette laughed loudly to help make the point that she wasn't. She simply said, "Lots of things have been happening, Mom, and maybe the best of them all is to come home and stay home."

The connection was almost lost, and Cahill said quickly, "Goodbye, Mom. See you in about a week."

She knew her mother was saying something but couldn't make out the words. Then the line went dead.

She stayed up most of the night, pacing the room, picking up and examining the weapons she'd brought with her—thinking—her mind racing at top speed, one person after another in her life taking center stage—Barrie Mayer, Mark Hotchkiss, Breslin, Podgorsky, Hank Fox, Jason Tolker, Eric Edwards—all of them, the chaos and confusion they'd caused in her small world. Was it that simple to restore order, not only to her life but to so complex and important a geopolitical undertaking as Banana Quick? The ultimate solution, they said, lay on the coffee table—a white plastic revolver that weighed ounces and a spring-loaded device that cost a few dollars to make, devices whose only purpose was to snuff out life.

She could almost understand now why men killed on command. Women, too, in this case. What value has a single human life when wrapped in multiple layers of "greater good"? Besides, eliminating Eric Edwards wasn't her idea. It didn't represent what she was really all about, did it? "But wait, there's more," she told herself as she paced the room, stopping only to look out the window or to stare at the tools of the trade on the table. She was avenging the death of a good friend. Barrie had died at the hand of someone who viewed life and death from the same perspective as she was being called upon to accept. In the end, it didn't matter who the individual was who'd taken Barrie's life—a Soviet agent, a doctor named Tolker, very different characters like Mark Hotchkiss or Eric Edwards—whoever did it answered to a different god, one it was now necessary for her to invoke if she were to go through with this act.

As she continued trying to deal with the thoughts that had invaded her ever since Joe Breslin told her to kill Eric Edwards, she became fascinated with the process going on inside her, as though she were a bystander watching Collette Cahill come to terms with herself. What she'd been asked to do—what, in fact, she was actually setting out to do—represented so irrational an act that had it been suggested to her at any other point in her life, it would have immediately gotten lost in her laughter. That was no longer true. What had evolved, to the bystander's amusement and amazement, was a sense of right and reason responsive to the act of murder. More important, it could be done. *She* could do it. She hadn't thrown up her hands, raced from Breslin's car, hid in her apartment, or hopped the first flight out of Budapest. She'd accepted the mission and chosen her weapons carefully, no different from selecting a typewriter or pencil sharpener for an office job.

She was numb.

She was confused.

And she was not frightened, which was the most frightening thing of all for the bystander.

In the morning, a series of taps on her door. She'd forgotten; she'd ordered breakfast. She scrambled out of bed and said through the door, "Just a minute," then went to the living room and hastily took the tools from the coffee table and slid them into a desk drawer.

She opened the door and a hall porter carried in her tray. He was the same porter she'd talked to during her last visit to the hotel, the one who'd told her about the three men coming to collect Barrie Mayer's belongings. "Will you be on duty all day?" she asked him.

"Yes, madam."

"Good," she said. "I'd like to show you something a little later."

"Just ring, madam."

Josh Moeller arrived at a quarter of twelve carrying an envelope. After they'd embraced, he handed it to her, saying in slight surprise, "We had this in our own files. I don't know why, although there's been a push for the past year to beef up the general photo files. You'd think Great Britain had become the enemy the way we've been collecting on everybody."

Collette opened the envelope and looked into the black-and-white glossy face of Mark Hotchkiss. The photo was grainy, obviously a copy of another photograph.

Moeller said, "I think this came from a newspaper or literary magazine."

Cahill looked at him and said, "Any dossier on him?"

Moeller shrugged. "I don't think so, although I have to admit I didn't bother checking. You said you wanted a photograph."

"Yes, I know, Josh, that's all I needed. Thanks so much."

"Why are you interested in him?" he asked.

"A long story," she replied, "something personal."

"Got time for the lunch you promised me?"

"Yes, I do. I'd love it, but first I have to do one thing."

She left him in the suite and went downstairs to where the hall porter was sorting mail. "Excuse me," she said, "do you recognize this man?"

The porter adjusted half-glasses on his large nose and moved the photo in and out of focus. "Yes, madam, I believe I do, but I can't say why."

She said, "Do you remember those three men who came to collect the belongings of my friend, Miss Mayer, right after she died?"

"Yes, that's it. He was one of the gentlemen who came here that day."

"Is this a photograph of Mr. Hubler, David Hubler?"

"Exactly, madam. This is the gentleman who introduced himself as a business associate of your lady friend. He said his name was Hubler, although I can't quite recall what his first name was."

"It doesn't matter," Cahill said. "Thank you."

Cahill and Moeller had lunch in a pub on Sloane Square. They promised to keep in touch, and hugged before he climbed into a taxi. She watched him disappear around the corner, then walked briskly back to the hotel where she carefully packed, had the desk call a taxi, and went directly to Heathrow Airport for a first-class ride home.

CHAPTER 29

Cahill deplaned in New York and went to the nearest public telephone where she dialed Washington, D.C., information. "The number for the Watergate Hotel," she asked.

She placed the call and said to the hotel operator, "Has Mr. Eric Edwards changed suites yet?"

"Pardon?"

"I'm sorry. I'm here in Washington with the French contingent of Mr. Edwards's investors. When I tried to reach him before, I realized he'd changed suites. Is he still in 845?"

"Well, I . . . no, he's still in 1010 according to my records. I'll connect you."

"Oh, don't bother. I just didn't want to bring the French group to the wrong suite." She laughed. "You know how the French are."

"Well . . . thank you for calling."

Collette hung up and sighed. Hotel operators didn't give out room numbers, but there were ways. Dazzle 'em with confusion. She picked up the phone again, dialed the Watergate number, and asked whether there were any suites available.

"How long will you be staying?" she was asked.

"Three days, possibly more."

"Yes, we have two diplomat suites available at $410 a night."

"That will be fine," Cahill said. "Do you have one on a low floor? I have a phobia about high floors."

"The lowest we would have is on the eighth floor. Our diplomat suites are all higher up."

"The eighth floor? Yes, I suppose that will be all right." She gave her name, read off her American Express card number, and said she would be taking the shuttle to Washington that evening.

It took her longer to get from Kennedy Airport to La Guardia than it did for the flight to Washington's National Airport. The minute she stepped off the plane, she went to a telephone center, pulled out a Washington Yellow Pages, and scanned the listing for sporting goods stores. She found one in Maryland within a few blocks of the district line and took a cab to it, catching the owner as he was about to close. "I need some bullets," she told him sheepishly, the teenager buying condoms.

He smiled. "Ammo, you mean."

"Yes, ammunition, I guess. It's for my brother."

"What kind?"

"Ah, let's see, ah, right, nine millimeter, for a small revolver."

"Very small." He rummaged through a drawer behind the counter and came up with a box. "Anything else?"

"No, thank you." She'd expected questioning, a demand for an address, for identification. Nothing. Just a simple consumer purchase. She paid, thanked him, and returned to the street, a box of bullets in her purse.

She walked to the Watergate and checked in, her eyes scanning the lobby.

The moment she was in her suite, she unpacked, took a hot shower and, wearing a robe provided by the hotel, stepped out onto a wraparound balcony that overlooked the Potomac River and the oversized, gleaming white Kennedy Center. It was a lovely sight, but she was too filled with energy to stand in any one place for more than a few seconds.

She went to a living room furnished with antique reproductions, found a scrap of paper in her purse, and dialed the number on it. The phone at Vern Wheatley's brother's apartment rang eight times before Wheatley answered. The minute he heard her voice, he snapped, "Where the hell have you been? I've been going crazy trying to find you."

"I was in Budapest."

"Why didn't you tell me you were leaving? You just take off and not even tell me?"

"Vern, I tried to call but there was no answer. It wasn't a leisurely trip I took. I had to leave immediately."

His voice indicated that he'd ignored her words. He said flatly, "I have to see you right away. Where are you?"

"I'm . . . why do you want to see me?"

He snorted. "Maybe the fact that we slept together is good enough. Maybe just because I want to see you again. Maybe because I have something damned important to discuss with you." She started to say something but he quickly added, "Something that might save both our lives."

"Why don't you just tell me on the phone?" she said. "If it's that important . . ."

"Look, Collette, there are things I haven't told you because . . . well, because it wasn't the right time. The right time is *now*. Where are you? I'll come right over."

"Vern, I have something I have to do before I can talk to you. Once it's done, I'll *need* to talk to someone. Please try to understand."

"Damn it, Collette, stop . . ."

"Vern, I said I have other things to do. I'll call you tomorrow."

"You won't catch me here," he said quickly.

"No?"

"I'm getting out right now. I was on my way when the phone rang. I almost didn't bother answering it."

"You sound panicked."

"Yeah, you might say that. I always get a little uptight when somebody's looking to slit my throat or blow up my car."

"What are you talking about?"

"What am I talking about? I'll tell you what I'm talking about. I'm talking about that freaky outfit you work for. I'm talking about a bunch of psychopaths who start out ripping wings off flies and shooting birds with BB guns before they graduate to people."

"Vern, I don't work for the CIA anymore."

"Yeah, right, Collette. That one of the courses down on the Farm? Lying 101? Goddamn it, I have to see you right now."

"Vern, I . . . all right."

"Where are you?"

"I'll meet you someplace."

"How about dinner?"

"I'm not hungry."

"Yeah, well I am. I'm in the mood for Greek. Like

drama or tragedy. Meet me at the Taverna in an hour."

"Where is it?"

"Pennsylvania Avenue, Southeast. An hour?"

She almost backed out but decided to go through with the date. After all, she'd called him. Why? She couldn't answer. That weakness coming through, that need to talk with someone she knew and thought she could trust. Talk about *what*, that she was back in Washington to assassinate someone? No, there'd be no talk of that. He sounded desperate. It was *he* who needed to talk. Okay, she'd listen, that's all.

As she dressed, she went over in her mind what she'd been told about Vern by Joe Breslin. He'd come to Washington to do an exposé of one sort or another on the CIA, particularly its mind-control experimentation programs. If that was true—and she was sure it was, based upon their brief conversation a few minutes ago—he was to be as distrusted as the rest of them. Nothing was straightforward anymore. Living a life of simple truth must be reserved for monks, nuns, and naturalists, and it was too late to become any of those.

She rode the elevator to the tenth floor and walked past Suite 1010, her heart tripping in anticipation of running into Edwards. It didn't happen; she retraced her steps, got in the elevator, and went to the lobby. The Watergate was bustling. She stepped through the main entrance to where a long line of black limousines stood, their uniformed drivers waiting for their rich and powerful employers or customers to emerge. A cab from another line moved forward. Cahill got in and said, "The Taverna, on Pennsylvania Avenue, South. . . ."

The driver turned and laughed. "I know, I know," he said. "I am Greek."

She walked into what the cabbie had said was a "goud

Grick" restaurant and was immediately aware of bouzouki music and loud laughter from the downstairs bar. She went down there in search of Wheatley. No luck. He hadn't specified where he would meet her but she assumed it would be the bar. She took the only vacant stool and ordered a white wine, turned and looked at the bouzouki player, a good-looking young man with black curly hair who smiled at her and played a sudden flourish on his instrument. She was reminded of Budapest. She returned his smile and surveyed others in the room. It was a loud, joyous crowd and she wished she were in the mood—wished she were in the position—to enjoy something festive. She wasn't. How could she be?

She sipped her wine and kept checking her watch; Wheatley was twenty minutes late. She was angry. She hadn't wanted to meet him in the first place but he'd prevailed. She looked at the check the bartender had placed in front of her, laid enough money on it to take care of it plus tip, got up and started for the stairs. Wheatley was on his way down. "Sorry I'm late," he said, shaking his head. "I couldn't help it."

"I was leaving," she said icily.

He took her arm and escorted her up the stairs to the dining room. Half the tables were vacant. "Come on," he said. "I'm starved."

"Vern, I really don't have time to . . ."

"Don't hassle me, Collette, just spend an hour while I get some food for my belly and feed you some food for your thoughts."

The manager showed them to a corner table that put them at considerable distance from other patrons. Collette took the chair that placed her back against the wall. Wheatley sat across from her.

After they'd ordered a bottle of white wine, Wheatley shook his head and grinned. "You could drive a guy crazy."

"I don't mean to do that, Vern. My life has been . . ." She smiled. "It's been chaotic lately, at best."

"Mine hasn't been exactly run-of-the-mill, either," he said. "Let's order."

"I told you I'm not hungry."

"Then nibble."

He looked at the menu, motioned for the waiter, and ordered moussaka, stuffed grape leaves, and an eggplant salad for two. After the waiter was gone, Wheatley leaned across the table and said, his eyes locked on hers, "I know who killed your friend Barrie Mayer, and I know why. I know who killed your friend David Hubler, and I know why he was killed, too. I know about the people you work for but, most of all, I know that you and I could end up like your dead friends if we don't do something."

"You're going too fast for me, Vern," she said, her excitement level rising. A large "What if?" struck her. What if Breslin and the rest of them were wrong? What if Eric Edwards was not, in fact, a double agent, had not killed Barrie Mayer? It was the first time since she left Budapest that she acknowledged to herself how much she hoped it was the case. . . .

Wheatley said, "All right, I'll slow down for you. In fact, I'll do even better than that." He had a briefcase on the floor at the side of his chair. He pulled from it a bulging envelope and handed it to her.

"What's this?" she asked.

"That, my friend, is the bulk of an article I'm writing about the CIA. There's also the first ten chapters of my book in there."

She immediately thought of David Hubler and the call that brought him to Rosslyn and to his death. She didn't have to ask. Wheatley said, "I was the one who called Hubler and asked him to meet me in that alley."

His admission hit her hard. At the same time, it wasn't a surprise. She'd always questioned the coincidence of Wheatley having been there at the time. The look on her face prompted him to continue.

"I've been working through a contact in New York for months, Collette. He's a former spook—I hope that doesn't offend you, considering you're in the same business. . . ." When she didn't respond, he continued. "This contact of mine is a psychologist who used to do work for the CIA. He broke away a number of years ago and almost lost his life in the bargain. You don't just walk away from those people, do you?"

"I don't know," Cahill said. "I've never walked away," which was only half true. She'd left Budapest committed to never returning, not only to that city but to any job within Central Intelligence once her present assignment was completed.

"When someone tried to kill my contact, he did some fast thinking and came to the conclusion that his best protection was to offer up everything he knew for public consumption. Once he did that, why bother killing him? Eliminating him would only make sense if it were to avoid disclosure."

"Go on," she said.

"A mutual friend got us together and we started talking. That's what brought me to Washington."

"Finally, some simple honesty," Cahill said, not particularly proud of the smugness in her voice.

"Yeah, that must be refreshing for you, Collette, considering that you've been dishonest with me all along."

She was tempted to get into that discussion but resisted. Let him continue talking.

"My contact put me in touch with a woman who'd been an experimental subject in the Operation Bluebird and MK-ULTRA projects. They pulled out all the stops with her and, in the process, manipulated her mind to the extent that she doesn't know who she is anymore. Ever hear of a man named Estabrooks?"

"A psychologist who did a lot of work with hypnosis." She said it in a bored tone of voice.

"Yeah, right, but why should I be surprised? You probably know more about this than I ever imagined,"

She shook her head. "I don't know much about those CIA projects from the past."

He guffawed. "From the *past*? Those projects are going on stronger than ever, Collette, and someone you know pretty well is one of the movers and shakers in them."

"Who would that be?"

"Your friend Dr. Jason Tolker."

"He's not a friend. I simply . . . "

"Simply slept with him? I don't know, maybe I've got my definition of friendship all screwed up. You slept with me. Am I your friend?"

"I don't know. You used me. The only reason you got together with me again was to get close to someone involved with the . . . "

"The CIA?"

"You were saying?"

"What you just said, about me making contact with you because you're with the CIA, is only partially true. You're acknowledging that you're with the CIA, right? The embassy job is a front."

"That doesn't matter, and I resent being put in the position of having to explain what I do with my life. You have no right."

He leaned toward her, and there was a harsh edge to his voice. "And the CIA has no right to go around screwing up innocent people, to say nothing of killing them, like your friend Barrie, and Hubler."

Collette leaned away from him and glanced about the restaurant. The sounds of the bar crowd downstairs mingled with the strains of the bouzouki music as it drifted up the stairs. Upstairs, where they sat, it was still relatively quiet and empty.

Wheatley sat back. His was a warm, genuine smile and his voice matched it. "Collette, I'll level with you one hundred percent. After that, you can decide whether you want to level with me. Fair enough?"

She knew it was.

"This woman I mentioned, the one who was a subject in the experimentation, is a prostitute. The CIA is big on hookers. They use them to entice men into apartments and hotel rooms that have been wired for sight and sound. They slip drugs in their drinks and the shrinks stand behind two-way mirrors and watch the action. It's a nasty game, but I suppose they rationalize it by saying that the other side does it, too, and that 'national defense' is involved. Whether those things are true or not I don't know, but I do know that a lot of innocent people get hurt."

Cahill started to add to the conversation but stopped herself. She simply cocked her head, raised her eyebrows, and said, "Go on."

Her posture obviously annoyed him. He quickly shook it off and continued. "I came down to Washington to see what I could find out about whether these experimental projects were still in operation. The day before Hubler was killed, I got a call from this lady, the prostitute, who told me that someone within the CIA was willing to talk to me. No, that isn't exactly accurate. This person was willing to *sell* information to me. I was told to meet him in that alley in Rosslyn. I figured the first thing I ought to do was to test the waters with a book publisher, see if I could raise the money I needed to pay the source. I knew the magazine wouldn't pay, and I sure as hell don't have the funds.

"I was trying to think of people back in New York to call when Dave Hubler came to my mind. You'd told me all about him, how Barrie Mayer put a lot of faith in him and had actually left the agency to him. I figured he was my best move, so I called him. He was very receptive. In fact, he told me that if the kind of information I was talking about was valid, he could probably get me a six-figure advance. The problem was he wanted to hear with his own ears what this source was selling. I invited him to meet with me. I knew the minute I hung up that it was a mistake. Having two of us show up would probably scare the guy off, but I figured I'd go through with it anyway. Want to know what happened?"

"Of course."

"I ran late, but Hubler got there on time. Obviously, there was nobody selling information. It was a setup, and if I'd arrived when I was supposed to and alone, I would have had the ice pick in my chest."

His story had potency to it, no doubt about that. If what

he'd said were true, it meant . . . "You've got problems," she told him.

"That's right," he said. "I'm being followed everywhere I go. The other night I was driving through Rock Creek Park and a guy ran me off the road. At least he tried to. He botched it and took off. I think they've thrown a tap on my brother's phone, and my editor back in New York told me he'd received a call from a personnel agency checking my references for a job I was applying for with another magazine. I didn't apply for a job with another magazine. There's no legitimate personnel agency checking on me. These guys will stop at nothing."

"What do you plan to do?" she asked.

"First of all, keep moving. Second, I'm going to adopt the philosophy of my shrink friend back in New York, get everything I know on paper, and make sure it's in the proper hands as fast as possible. No sense killing somebody once they've spilled what they know."

Cahill looked down at the heavy envelope. "Why are you giving me this?"

"Because I want it in someone else's hands in case anything happens to me."

"But why *me*, Vern? You seem filled with distrust where I'm concerned. I'd think I'd be the last person you'd give this to."

He grinned, reached across the table, and held her hand. "Remember what I wrote in the yearbook, Collette?"

She said softly, "Yes, of course I do. I'm the girl in this world who would never sell out."

"I still feel that way, Collette. You know something else I feel?"

She looked in his eyes. "What?"

"I'm in love with you."

"Don't say that, Vern." She shook her head. "You don't know me."

"I think I do, which is why I'm throwing in with you. I want you to hold on to this, Collette," he said, tapping the envelope. "I want you to read it and look for any gaps."

She shoved the envelope back across the table at him. "No, I don't want that responsibility. I can't help you."

His face, which had settled into a slack and serene expression, now hardened. His voice matched it. "I thought you took some oaths when you became a lawyer, silly things like justice and fairness and righting wrongs. I thought you cared about innocent people being hurt. At least, that was the line you used to give. What was it, Collette, high school rhetoric that goes down the drain the minute you hit the real world?"

She was stung by his words, assaulted by hurt and anger. Had she succumbed to the hurt, she would have cried. Instead, her anger overrode the other feeling. "Don't preach to me, Vern Wheatley, about ideals. All I'm hearing from you is journalist's rhetoric. You're sitting here lecturing me about right and wrong, about why everybody should jump on your bandwagon and sell out our own government. Maybe there is justification for what an organization like the CIA does. Maybe there are abuses. Maybe the other side does it, only worse. Maybe national defense *is* involved, and not just a slogan. Maybe there are things going on in this world that you or I have no idea about, can't even begin to conceive of the importance of them to other people—people who don't have the advantages we have in a free society."

The eggplant salad had gone untouched. Now the waiter

brought the stuffed leaves and moussaka. The moment he left, Collette said to Vern, "I'm leaving."

Wheatley grabbed her hand. "Please don't do that, Collette," he said with sincerity. "Okay, we've each made our speech. Now let's talk like two adults and figure out the right thing to do for both of us."

"I already have," she said, pulling her hand away.

"Look, Collette, I'm sorry if I shot off my mouth. I didn't mean to, but sometimes I do that. The nature of the beast, I guess. If spies are out in the cold, journalists need friends, too." He laughed. "I figure I have one friend in this world. You."

She slumped back in her chair, stared at the envelope, and suffered the same sensation she'd been feeling so often lately, that she had become increasingly dishonest. She was perfectly capable of taking a stand at the table, yet, more than anything, she wanted that envelope and its contents. She was desperate to read it. Mayb it contained factual answers to events that had shrouded her in confusion.

She deliberately softened as she said, "Vern, maybe you're right. I'm sorry, too. I just . . . I don't want, alone, the responsibility for that envelope."

"Fine," he said. "We'll share the responsibility. Stay with me tonight."

"Where?"

"I've taken a room in a small hotel over in Foggy Bottom, around the corner from Watergate. The Allen Lee. Know it?"

"Yes, friends who used to visit me at college stayed there."

"I figured it was low class enough that they wouldn't

look for me there, although that's probably naive. I used a phony name when I checked in. Joe Black. How's that for a pseudonym?"

"Not very original," she said, realizing that she shouldn't have checked into the Watergate under her own name. Too late to worry about that now. "Vern, I think it's better if I left now and we both did some thinking on our own." He started to protest but she grabbed his hand and said earnestly, "Please. I need time alone to digest what you've said. I can use it to read your article and book. Okay? We'll catch up tomorrow. I promise."

Dejection was written all over his face but he didn't argue.

He slid the envelope back toward her. She looked at it, picked it up, and cradled it in her arms. "I'll call you at the Allen Lee, say around four tomorrow afternoon?"

"I guess that's the way it will be. I can't call you. I don't know where you're staying."

"And that's the way it will have to be until tomorrow."

He forced himself to lighten up, saying pleasantly, "Sure you don't want some food? It's good."

"So my cab driver said. He told me this was 'goud Grick.' " She smiled. "I'm not a fan of Greek food, but thanks anyway." When his expression sagged again, she leaned over and kissed him on the cheek, said into his ear, "Please, Vern. I've got a lot of thinking to do and I'll do it best alone." She straightened up, knew there was nothing more to say, and quickly left the restaurant.

A taxi was dropping off a couple. Cahill got in.

"Yeah?"

"I'd like to go to . . ." She'd almost told him to take her to Dr. Jason Tolker's office in Foggy Bottom.

How silly. Like giving the name of an obscure restaurant and expecting the driver to know it.

She spelled out Tolker's address.

CHAPTER 30

Lights were on in Tolker's building. Good, she thought, as she paid the driver. She hadn't wanted to call ahead. If he weren't there, she'd go to his house. She'd find him someplace.

She rang the bell. His voice came through the intercom. "Who is it?"

"Collette. Collette Cahill."

"Oh. Yes. I'm tied up right now. Can you come back?" She didn't answer. "Is it an emergency?" She smiled, knew he was asking it for the benefit of whoever was with him. She pressed the "Talk" button: "Yes, it is an emergency, doctor."

"I see. Well, please come in and wait in my reception area, Miss Cahill. It will be a few minutes before I can see you."

"That will be fine, Doctor. Thank you."

The buzzer sounded. She turned the knob and pushed the door partially open. Before entering, she patted her raincoat pocket. The now familiar shape of the small revolver resisted her fingers' pressure. A deep breath pumped any lost resolve back into her.

She stepped into the reception area and looked around. Two table lamps provided minimal, soft lighting. A light under his office door, and muffled voices, indicated at least two people in there. She stepped close and listened. She heard his voice, and then a woman. Their words were only occasionally audible: ". . . Can't help that . . . Hate you . . . Calm down or . . ."

Collette chose a chair that allowed her to face the office door. She'd started to pull the revolver from her raincoat pocket when the office door suddenly opened. She released the weapon and it slid back to its resting place. A beautiful and surprisingly tall young Oriental girl, dressed in tight jeans, heels, and wearing a mink jacket, came into the reception area, followed by Tolker. The woman strained to see Collette's face in the room's dimness. "Good night," Tolker said. The girl looked at him; there was hatred on her face. She crossed the room, cast a final, disapproving look at Collette, and left. Moments later the front door closed heavily.

"Hello," Tolker said to Collette.

"Hello. A patient?"

"Yes. You thought otherwise?"

"I thought nothing. It's nice of you to see me on such short notice."

"I try to accommodate. What's the emergency?"

"Severe panic attack, free-floating anxiety, paranoia, an obsessive-compulsive need for answers."

"Answers to what?"

"Oh, to . . . to why a friend of mine is dead."

"I can't help you with that."

"I disagree."

He conspicuously looked at his watch.

"This won't take long."

"I can assure you of that. Ask your questions."

"Let's go inside."

"This is . . ." He stopped when he saw her hand come out of her raincoat holding the revolver. "What's that for?"

"A persuasive tool. I have a feeling you might need persuasion."

"Put it away, Collette. James Bond never impressed me."

"I think I can . . . *impress* you."

He blew through his lips and sighed resignedly. "All right, come in, *without* the gun."

She followed him into his office, the revolver still in her hand. When he turned and saw it, he said sharply, "Put the goddamn thing away."

"Sit down, Dr. Tolker."

He made a move toward her. She raised the weapon and pointed it at his chest. "I said sit down."

"You've gone off the deep end, haven't you? You're crazy."

"That's professional."

"Look, I . . ." She nodded toward his leather chair. He sat on it. She took the matching chair, crossed her legs, and observed him. He certainly hadn't overreacted, but she could discern discomfort, which pleased her.

"Go ahead," she said. "Start from the beginning, and don't leave anything out. Tell me all about Barrie, about how she came to you as a patient, how you hypnotized her, controlled her, got her involved in the CIA and then . . . I'll say it . . . and then killed her."

"You're crazy."

"There's that professional diagnosis again. Start!" She raised the revolver for emphasis.

"You know everything, because I told you everything. Barrie was a patient. I treated her. We had an affair. I suggested she do some courier work for the CIA. She gladly and, I might add, enthusiastically agreed. She carried materials to Budapest, things she got from me, things I didn't know. I mean, I would hand her a briefcase, a *locked* briefcase, and off she'd go. Someone killed her. I don't know who. It wasn't me. Believe that."

"Why should I?"

"Because . . ."

"When Barrie made her last trip to Hungary, whatever it was she carried wasn't in a briefcase. It was in her mind, because you implanted it there."

"Wait a minute, that's . . ."

"That's the truth, Dr. Tolker. I'm not the only one who knows it. It's common knowledge. At least it is now."

"What of it? The program calls for it."

"What was the message?"

"I can't tell you that."

"I think you'd better."

He stood. "And I think you'd better get out of here."

Collette held up the envelope she'd been given by Vern. "Know what's in this?"

He tried for levity. "Your memoirs of a clandestine life."

She didn't respond in kind. "A friend of mine has been researching the projects you're involved with. He's done quite a job. Want an example?"

"You're talking about Vern Wheatley?"

"Right."

"He's in deep water."

"He's a strong swimmer."

"Not with these tides. Go ahead. I know all about him, and about you. Bad form, Collette, for an intelligence agent to sleep with a writer."

"I'll let that pass. Vern knows, and so do I, that you programmed Barrie to claim that Eric Edwards, from the BVI, was a double agent. Correct?"

To her surprise, he didn't deny it. Instead, he said, "That happens to be the truth."

"No, it's not. You're the double agent, Doctor."

The accusation, and the weight of the envelope despite neither of them knowing what was in it, stopped the conversation. Tolker broke the silence by asking pleasantly, "Drink, Collette?"

She couldn't help but smile. "No."

"Coke? The white kind?"

"You're disgusting."

"Just trying to be sociable. Barrie always enjoyed my sociability."

"Spare me that again."

"Like to spend some intimate moments with our deceased friend?"

"What?"

"I have her on tape. I'm reluctant to expose myself to you because, naturally, I'm on the tape too. But I will."

"No thanks." Collette didn't mean it. Her voice betrayed her true feelings.

He did exactly the right thing. He said nothing, simply sat back down, crossed his legs, folded his hands in his lap, and smirked.

"What kind of tape? While she was hypnotized?"

"No, nothing concerning therapy. That would be highly

unprofessional of me. The tape I'm talking about is more *personal.*"

"When she was . . . with you?"

"When she was very much with me, right here in this office, after hours."

"You recorded it?"

"Yes. I'm recording us, too."

Cahill's head snapped left and right as she took in the room in search of a camera.

"Up there," Tolker said casually, pointing to a painting at the far end of the room.

"Did Barrie know?"

"Shall we see it?"

"No, I . . ."

He went to bookshelves where hundreds of videotapes were neatly lined up and labeled. He pulled one from the collection, knelt before a VCR hooked up to a 30-inch NEC monitor, inserted the tape, pushed buttons, and the screen came alive.

Collette turned her head and watched the screen from an angle, like a child wanting to avoid a gruesome scene in a horror movie, yet afraid to miss it. Tolker resumed his seat and said smugly, "You came here demanding answers. Watch closely, Collette. There's lots of answers on the screen."

Cahill looked away, her eyes going to where Tolker indicated there was a camera recording them. Out of the corner of her eye, a naked form appeared on the TV monitor. She focused on the screen. It was Barrie, walking around Tolker's office, a glass in her hand. She went to where he sat fully dressed in his chair. "Come on, I'm ready." Her words were slurred; her laugh was that of a drunken woman. When he didn't respond, she sat on his lap and kissed him. His hands ran over her body . . .

"You slime," Collette said.

"Don't judge me," Tolker said. "She's there, too. Keep watching. There's more."

A new scene appeared on the screen. Barrie was seated cross-legged on the carpet, still nude. A man's naked form—presumably Tolker—was in shadows. He obviously knew where to position himself so that he was out of the camera's direct focus, and out of the lighting.

Barrie held a clear plate on which cocaine was heaped. She put a straw to her nose, leaned forward, placed the other end in the powder, and inhaled.

Cahill stood. "Turn that damn thing off," she said.

"It's not over. It gets even better."

She went to the VCR and pushed the "Stop" button. The screen went blank. She was aware that he'd come up behind her. She quickly fell to her knees, spun around, and pointed the revolver up at his face.

"Easy, easy," he said. "I'm not out to hurt you."

"Get away. Back up."

He did as she requested. She stood, was without words.

"See?" he said. "Your friend was not the saint you thought she was."

"I never considered her a saint," Collette said. "Besides, this has nothing to do with how she died."

"Oh, yes, it does," Tolker said. He sat in his chair and tasted his drink. "You're right, Collette, this is kid's stuff. Ready for the adult version?"

"What are you talking about?"

"Barrie was a traitor. She sold out to Eric Edwards, and to the Soviets." He sighed and drank. "Oh, God, she was so innocent in that situation. She didn't know a Soviet from a Buddhist monk. A great literary agent, a lousy intelligence agent. I should have known better than to get her involved. But that's water over the dam."

"She wasn't a traitor," Collette said, again without conviction. The truth was that she knew little about her close friend. The video she'd seen—so unlike the image she had of Barrie—caused anger to swell in her. "How dare you record someone in their . . ."

Tolker laughed. "In their *what*, most intimate moments? Forget the tape, think about what I just told you. She was going to turn Edwards in, and that's what got her killed. I tried to stop her but . . ."

"No you didn't. You were the one who poisoned her against Eric."

"Wrong. You're wrong a lot, Collette. Sure, she told me that Edwards was working both sides of the street, and I encouraged her to blow the whistle on him. Want to know why?" Cahill didn't answer. "Because it was the only way she had a chance to get herself off the hook. They knew about her."

"Who?"

"The British. Why do you think that buffoon, Hotchkiss, came into the picture?"

Cahill was surprised. "What do you know about him? Why . . . ?"

"You came here for answers," Tolker said, standing. "I'll give them to you, *if* you give me the gun, sit down, and shut up!" He extended his hand; his expression said he'd lost patience.

For a moment, Collette considered handing the revolver to him. She started to, but when he went to grab it from her hand, she yanked it away. Now his expression indicated he'd progressed beyond impatience. He was angry. He would do whatever he had to do. He would hurt her.

Collette glared at him; there was an overwhelming desire to use the small plastic revolver—to kill him. It had nothing to do with having determined his responsibility for Barrie's death, nor was it bound up in some rational thought process involving her job or mission. Rather, it represented what had become an obsession to take action, to push a button, place a phone call, pull a trigger to put an end to the turmoil in her life.

Then again, it occurred to her, there *was* a certain order to what was being played out, a Ramistic logic that said, "Enjoy the pragmatic role you're in, Collette. You're a CIA agent. You have the authority to kill, to right wrongs. Nothing will happen to you. You're expected to act with authority because it is your country that is at stake. You're a member of law enforcement. The gun has been given to you to use, to enforce a political philosophy of freedom and opportunity in order to keep evil forces from destroying a precious way of life."

The thoughts cleared her mind and calmed her down. "You underestimate me," she said.

"Get out."

"When I'm ready. Hotchkiss. What role did he play?"

"He . . ."

"Why are you knowledgeable about him?"

"I have nothing more to say to you."

"You said the British knew about Barrie being a . . . traitor. That's why Hotchkiss is here?"

"Yes."

"You convinced Barrie to become his partner?"

"It was best for her. It was the understanding."

"Understanding?"

"The deal. It saved her. Our people agreed with it."

"Because they believed you, that she and Eric Edwards were traitors."

"No, Collette, because they *knew* they were. They gave Barrie's mother money not to pursue any interest in the agency. Barrie's will left operating control to Hubler, but her mother was to receive Barrie's share of profits. The old bitch was happy for cash."

"How much?"

"It doesn't matter. Any amount was too much. She created the person Barrie became, a muddled, psychotic, pathetic human being who spent her adult life hiding from reality. It's not unusual. People with Barrie's high capacity for hypnotic trance usually come out of abused childhoods."

A smirk crossed Collette's face. "Do you know what I want to do, Dr. Tolker?"

"Tell me."

"I either want to spit on you, or kill you."

"Why?"

"You never tried to help Barrie get over her abused childhood, did you? All you were interested in was exploiting it, and her. You're despicable."

"You're irrational. Maybe it's a female thing. The agency ought to reconsider hiring women. You make a good case against the policy."

Collette didn't respond. She wanted to lash out. At the same time, she couldn't mount an argument against what he'd said. Somehow, defending equality between the sexes didn't seem important.

His voice and face had been cold and matter-of-fact up until now. He softened, smiled. "Tell you what," he said.

"Let's start over, right now, this night. No silly guns, no nasty remarks. Let's have a drink, dinner. Good wine and soothing music will take care of all our differences. We are on the same side, you know. I believe in you and what you stand for. I like you, Collette. You're a beautiful, bright, talented, and decent woman. Please, forget why you came in here tonight. I'm sure you have other questions that I can answer, but not in this atmosphere of rancor and distrust. Let's be friends and discuss these matters as friends, the way you used to discuss things with Barrie." His smile broadened. "You *are* incredibly beautiful, especially when that anger forces its way to the surface and gives your face a . . ."

He went for her. She'd shifted the revolver to her left hand minutes before. As he lunged, she dropped Vern's envelope, stiffened her right hand, and brought the edge of it against the side of his neck. The blow sent him sprawling to the carpet. A string of four-letter words exploded from him as he scrambled to his feet. They stood facing each other, their breathing rapid, their eyes wide in anger and fear.

Collette slowly backed toward the door, the revolver held securely in two hands, its tiny barrel pointed directly at his chest.

"Come here," he said.

She said nothing, kept retreating, her attention on controlling the damnable shaking of her hands.

"You've got it all screwed up," he said. She sensed the tension in his body as he prepared to attack again, a spring being compressed to give it maximum velocity and distance when released. The restraint on the spring was disengaged. It uncoiled in her direction. Her two fingers on the trigger contracted in concert; there was an almost silly "pop" from the revolver—a Champagne cork, a dry twig being snapped, Rice Krispies.

She stepped back and he fell at her feet, arms outstretched. She picked up the envelope, ran through the door and to the street where, once she realized the revolver was still in her hands, she shoved it into her raincoat and walked deliberately toward the nearest busy intersection.

The message light on her telephone was on when she returned to her suite at the Watergate. She called the message center. "Oh, yes, Miss Cahill, a gentleman called. He said"—the operator laughed. "It's a strange message. The gentleman said, 'Necessary that we discuss Winston Churchill as quickly as possible.' "

"He didn't leave a name?"

"No. He said you'd know who he was."

"Thank you."

Collette went to the balcony and looked out over the shimmering lights of Foggy Bottom. What had Joe Breslin told her? She could make contact with someone at the Churchill statue any evening for the next two weeks at six o'clock, and that the contact would remain there for no more than ten minutes.

She returned to the living room, drew the drapes, got into a robe, and sat in a wing chair illuminated by a single floor lamp. On her lap was Vern Wheatley's envelope. She pulled the pages from it, sighed, and began reading. It wasn't until the first shaft of sunlight came through a gap in the drapes that she put it down, hung the DO NOT DISTURB sign on the door, and went, soberly, to bed.

CHAPTER 31

Sleep. It was what she'd needed most. The small travel alarm clock on the nightstand next to her bed read 3:45. She'd slept almost ten hours, and it had been easy. The events earlier in the evening seemed not to have happened or, at least, had happened to someone else.

It was four-thirty when she got out of the shower. As she stood in front of the bathroom mirror drying her hair, she remembered she was supposed to call Vern. She found the number for the Allen Lee Hotel and dialed it, asked for Mr. Black's room. "Sorry to be late calling," she said. "I slept all day."

"It's okay. Did you read what I gave you?"

"Read it? Yes, two or three times. I was up all night."

"And?"

"You make some remarkable accusations, Vern."

"Are they wrong?" he asked.

"No."

"Okay, talk to me. How did you react to . . . ?"

"Why don't we discuss it in person?"

He whooped. "This is called progress. You mean you're actually going to initiate a date with me?"

"I wasn't suggesting a date, just some time to discuss what you've written."

"Name it. I'm yours."

"I have to meet someone at six. How about getting together at seven?"

"Who are you meeting?" he asked. It irked her but she said nothing. He said, "Oh, that's right, Miss Cahill operates incognito. Known in high school as the girl most likely to succeed dressed in a cloak and dagger."

"Vern, I'm in no mood for your attempts at sarcasm."

"Yeah, well, I'm not in any mood for jokes, either. You ever hear of Operation Octopus?"

She had to think. Then she started to mention Hank Fox, cut off her words, and said, "No."

"It's a division of the CIA that keeps computer tabs on writers, at least the ones who don't carry briefs for the goddamn agency. I'm at the top of the list." When she didn't respond, he added, "And they take care of writers like me, Collette. Take care." He guffawed. "They goddamn kill us, that's what they do."

"Where shall we meet at seven?" she asked.

"How about picking me up here at the hotel?"

"No, let's meet at the bar in the Watergate."

"You buying? Drinks there cost the national debt."

"If I have to. See you here . . . there at seven."

She found a vacant cab and told the driver to take her to the British Embassy on Massachusetts Avenue. As they approached it, she kept an eye out for a statue. There it was, less than a hundred yards from the main entrance, set into clumps of bushes just off the sidewalk. The driver made a U-turn and let her off in front of the embassy gate. It had started to rain, and the air had taken on a distinct chill. She brought the collar of her raincoat up around her neck and slowly walked toward the statue of Winnie. It was imposing and lifelike, but the years had turned Churchill green, blending into the foliage. He would not have liked that.

Traffic was heavy on Massachusetts Ave. It was raining harder, too, which slowed the traffic. There were few pedestrians, those scurrying past her coming from jobs at the British Embassy. She checked her watch; exactly six. She looked up and down the street in search of someone who might be interested in her but saw no one. Then, across the broad avenue, a man emerged from Normanstone Park. It was too dark and he was too far away for her to see his face. His trench-coat collar was up, his hands deep in his pockets. It took him some time to cross the street because of the traffic but, eventually, there was a break and he took advantage of it with long, loping strides. Good.

She sensed someone approaching from her right, turned, and saw another man coming down the sidewalk. He wore a hat, and had hunched his shoulders and lowered his head against the rain. She'd forgotten the rain and realized her hair and shoes were soaked. She quickly looked to her left again. The man from the park was gone. Another look to the right. The man in the hat was almost abreast of her. She poised, waiting for him to look up and say something. Instead, he walked by, his head still lowered, his eyes on the sidewalk.

She took a deep breath and wiped water from her nose and eyes.

"Miss Cahill." It came from her left. She knew immediately who it was from the accent. British. She turned and looked into the long, smiling face of Mark Hotchkiss.

"What are you doing here?" she said quickly. The question represented the only thought on her mind at the moment. What *was* he doing there?

"You arrived precisely on time," he said pleasantly. "Sorry I'm a few minutes late. Traffic and all that, you know."

As difficult as it was to accept, she had no choice. The contact who was to meet her here at the Winston Churchill statue. "I suggest we get out of this bloody rain and go somewhere where we can talk."

"You left the message at my hotel?"

"Yes, who else? Let's go to my office. I have some things to say to you."

"Your office? Barrie's, you mean?"

"As you wish. It's one and the same. Please, I'm getting damn well drenched standing here. Not much of a Londoner, forgetting my umbrella this way. Too long in the States, I suppose."

He took her arm and led her back toward the entrance of the British Embassy. They passed it and turned left on Observatory Lane, the U.S. Naval Observatory on their right, and walked a hundred yards until reaching a champagne-colored Jaguar. Tolker's Jaguar. Hotchkiss unlocked the passenger door and opened it for her. She became rigid and stared at him.

"Come on, now, let's go." His voice was not quite as pleasant as earlier.

She started to bend to get in, stopped and straightened, took a few steps back, and fixed him in a hard look. "Who *are* you?"

His face testified to his exasperation. "I don't have time to answer your silly questions," he said harshly. "Get in the car."

She backed farther away, her right hand up in a gesture of self-defense. "Why are you here? You have nothing to do with . . ." He'd been standing with his hands outstretched as he attempted to convince her. Now his right hand slipped into his raincoat pocket.

"No," she said. She spun around and ran back toward Massachusetts Avenue. She stumbled; one shoe fell off but she kept going, an increasing wind whipping her face with water. She looked over her shoulder without breaking stride, kicked off her second shoe, and saw that he had started after her but had stopped. He shouted, "Come back here!"

She kept going, reached the avenue and ran, retracing her route toward the statue of Winston Churchill, passing other embasssies and racing through puddles that soaked her feet. She kept going until she was out of breath, stopped, and looked back. Hotchkiss's Jaguar came up to the corner and waited for a break in traffic to make a right. A vacant taxi approached her. She leaped into the gutter and frantically waved it down. The driver jammed on his brakes, causing others behind him to do the same. Horns blew and muffled curses filled the air. She got in the back, slammed the door, and said, "The Watergate, please, the hotel, and if a light Jag is behind us, please do everything you can to lose him."

"Hey, lady, what's the matter? What's going on?" the young driver asked.

"Just *go*—please."

"Whatever you say," he said, slapping the gearshift and

hitting the accelerator, causing his wheels to spin on the wet pavement.

Cahill looked through the rear window. Vision was obscured but she could see a dozen car-lengths behind. The Jaguar wasn't to be seen.

She turned around and said to the driver, "Get off this street, go through the park."

He followed her order and soon drove up to the main entrance to the Watergate Hotel.

Cahill was drained. Once she was certain that Hotchkiss wasn't behind them, her energy had abandoned her and she slumped in the back seat, her breath still coming heavily.

"Lady, you all right?" the driver asked over the seat.

She'd closed her eyes. She opened them and managed a small smile. "Yes, thank you very much. I know it all seems strange but . . ." There was no need to explain any further. She handed him a twenty-dollar bill and told him to keep the change. He thanked her. She got out and suddenly realized the condition she was in. Her shoeless feet were bleeding from cuts on the soles. The bottoms of her stockings were in shreds.

"Evening," the doorman said from beneath the protection of a canopy.

Cahill mustered all the dignity she could and said, "Messy night," proudly walked past him and into the lobby, aware that he'd turned and was taking in her every step.

The lobby was busy as usual which, Cahill reasoned, was to her advantage. People were too engaged in coming and going and in conversations to care about a shoeless, wet woman.

She went to the elevator bank serving her floor and pushed the "Up" button. Because she was in a hurry, it was a series of eternities as she watched the lights above the elevator door indicate a slow descent from the top of the hotel. "*Damn,*" she muttered as she glanced left and right to see whether there was any interest in her. There wasn't. She looked up again; the elevator had stopped at the tenth floor. She thought of Eric Edwards and Suite 1010. Had it stopped to pick him up? Coincidence but . . .

She moved away from the door so that she was not in the line of anyone's vision coming through it. She could still see the lighted numbers. The elevator had stopped at Five, had skipped Four and stopped at Three. A large party of conventioners who'd flooded the center of the lobby ever since Cahill entered moved out en masse, affording her a clear view of a cluster of small tables and stuffed chairs at which well-dressed people enjoyed predinner cocktails. The sight didn't seem real at first, but it took her only a second to realize that it was. He was sitting at a table by himself, a glass in his hand, legs casually crossed, his attention directed at a woman seated at an adjacent table. Cahill quickly turned her head so that only her back was visible to him.

The sudden opening of the elevator door startled her. A dozen people filed out. Collette faced the wall and took each of them in with her peripheral vision. No Eric Edwards.

The moment the elevator was empty, she sidestepped into it, her back still to the cocktail area. She pushed Eight, then the "Close Door" button. She kept punching it, silently cursing the fact that it had no effect on what the elevator did. Like "Walk" buttons at intersections, she thought. Placebos.

A man in a tuxedo and a woman in a gown and furs joined her in the elevator. She ignored their glances at her feet and kept her eyes trained on the control buttons. The doors started to close; a man suddenly reached in and caused them to open again. He stepped in, followed by two teenage girls. One of them looked down at Cahill's shoeless dishabille, nudged her friend, and they both giggled.

The doors finally closed and the elevator made its ascent. The teenagers got off first, glancing back, then the man who'd stopped the doors with his arm. At the eighth floor, Cahill hobbled out. The man in the tux and the woman in furs whispered something unintelligible to each other. Oh, to be respectable.

She went to her door and opened it. A maid had been in and turned down the bed, leaving two small pieces of foil-wrapped chocolate on the pillow. Cahill locked the door from inside and attached the chain. She quickly got out of her raincoat, which was soaked through, and dropped it on the floor. The rest of her clothes followed. A tiny smear of blood on the carpet from her foot was dissolved by the wet clothing. She turned on the shower and, when it was as hot as she could stand it, stepped in. Ten minutes later she emerged, dried herself, found a Band-Aid in her purse and applied it to the small cut on her foot.

She hadn't noticed upon entering her room that her message light was on. She picked up the phone and identified herself. "Yes, Miss Cahill, you have a message from a Dr. Tolker. He said he was anxious to speak with you and would be in the hotel this evening. You can have him paged."

"No, I . . . Yes, thank you very much, I'll do that later, not now."

The message from Tolker was no surprise. Seeing him sitting in the lobby with a glass of wine had been. She'd assumed she'd killed him. Unless his CIA-funded research had resulted in perfect clone development, he was very much alive. She was glad for that. And frightened.

She picked up the phone again, dialed the number for the Allen Lee Hotel, and asked for Mr. Black's room. There was no answer. Then the operator asked, "Do you happen to be Miss Collette Cahill?"

"Yes, I am."

"Mr. Black had to run out but he left a message in case you called. He said he would return at ten. He said he had some urgent business that came up at the last minute."

Collette's sigh of frustration was, she was certain, audible to the operator even without the benefit of a telephone. She closed her eyes and said dejectedly, "Thank you."

Naked while on the phone, she suddenly felt cold and vulnerable. She pulled out a pair of jeans from the suitcase that she hadn't bothered to unpack, and a furry pink sweater. She got into them and slipped her feet into white sneakers.

She turned on all the lights, looked at the suitcase on the floor, hesitated, then went to it and unlocked an inside compartment. She reached in and came out with the ampules of prussic acid and nitro, and the cigar-shaped detonator. She sat in a chair beneath a lamp and assembled it, then reloaded the small white plastic revolver. She slipped everything into her purse and sat quietly, her fingers playing with the purse's shoulder strap, her ears cocked for sound, her eyes skating over every inch of the large room.

It was intensely quiet, which unnerved her. She was getting up to turn on the television set when the phone rang. The sound of it froze her in the middle of the room. Should she answer? No. Obviously, Tolker and Mark Hotchkiss knew that she was staying at the Watergate, and she didn't want to speak to either of them. Vern didn't know where she was. "How stupid," she chided herself. Why had she played it so secret with him? He loomed large as the only human being in Washington that she could trust. That was ironic, she realized, considering how deceitful he'd been up until their dinner last night.

What suddenly imbued him with trustworthiness was that of everyone in her recent life, only Vern was outside the Company. In fact, he was outside trying to break in, dedicated to exposing and harming it. So much of what he'd written was accurate, at least to the best of her knowledge. Although he hadn't stated it in so many words, the pattern that emerged from his pages gave considerable weight to the idea that it was Jason Tolker who was responsible for Barrie Mayer's and David Hubler's deaths. It all seemed so clear to her now, as though a brilliant light illuminated the truth as she stood in the center of the room.

Árpád Hegedüs *had* lied in that small bar in Budapest. What he'd told her earlier in their relationship was the truth, and what she'd suggested to Joe Breslin made sense. Hegedüs had come over as a defector in order to spread disinformation to the Americans. Tolker had been selling information to the Soviets about the results of mind-control experimentation in the United States. More than that, according to Wheatley's manuscript, he'd used various hypnotized subjects to transmit that information.

Wheatley hadn't mentioned Eric Edwards in his pages. Chances were he didn't even know about him. But Cahill quickly created a scenario in which Tolker, viewing Edwards as a threat because of his close relationship with the too-chatty Barrie, had convinced those involved in Banana Quick that Edwards was a double agent selling information to the other side. What other explanation could there be for his having been accused of double-dealing? Again, there was no tangible evidence to support her thesis, but the cumulative weight of everything that had happened, of every scrap of input she'd taken in, supported her notion.

She knew that she might be justifying her initial instincts about Tolker, but that didn't matter now. The picture she'd painted was good enough. The paramount thing in her mind at this point was to avoid Tolker and Hotchkiss, find Vern and, together, make contact with someone within the CIA who could be trusted. Who could that be? she wondered. The only name she could come up with was Eric, but that posed a risk. He was surrounded by controversy. Still, he represented for Cahill the one person besides Wheatley who seemed to deal with things in a straightforward manner. Hank Fox also came to mind but she dismissed the thought. He was too much one of *them*, despite his fatherly approach.

The phone stopped ringing. Collette returned to the chair, opened her purse, and ran her fingers over the revolver's smooth, plastic finish. Mark Hotchkiss! The confrontation with him had shaken her. What was he, MI-6? A contract agent. There were lots of them in the global system. Hotchkiss's obvious close working relationship with Tolker both puzzled and dismayed her. It made sense, in a way, she reasoned. Tolker wouldn't have physically killed Barrie and Dave Hubler. Too messy, not his style, or role. But Hotchkiss might have been the actual killer, working under Tolker's direction. Yes, that played for her.

She squeezed her eyes shut and shook her head. Why was she bothering trying to make sense out of a system that depended, to a great extent, upon being nonsensical? Too many things in the gray world of intelligence were inscrutable, begging answers, defying the common man's logic. Friends. Enemies. You needed a scorecard to tell the players on opposing teams. Hotchkiss had been in place geographically to kill both Barrie and David. Of course, it was possible that he had no connection with Tolker at all. If he'd killed Mayer and Hubler, he might have been acting strictly on behalf of British intelligence. They'd preached during her training days that there were no allies in the spy business, no forbidden, hands-off nations. The Israelis had proved that recently, and it was well known that the British had dozens of agents in place within the United States.

The phone rang again. Cahill ignored it for a second time. Then another sound intruded upon her thoughts.

Someone was knocking at her door.

CHAPTER 32

She went slowly, quietly to the door and placed her ear against it. A male voice said, "Collette?" She couldn't place it. It wasn't Hotchkiss; no trace of a British accent. "Collette."

She remained silent and motionless, the small revolver at her side, her senses acutely tuned. She pressed her eye against the peephole in the door, saw no one. Whoever had been calling her name was against a wall, out of range of the wide-angle lens. She had no way of knowing whether he was still there. The halls were carpeted; no footsteps to give a clue.

She went to the phone and called Vern again on the chance that he might have returned early. He hadn't.

Pacing the living room of her suite, she tried to sort out her next move. She was tempted to abandon the safety of the locked room, but that very safety kept her from doing it, at least for now. Still, she knew she'd have to leave sometime to go to the Allen Lee. Should she, could she wait until Wheatley returned and ask him to come to the Watergate? She answered no to both questions.

She looked down at the phone and read the instruction for calling another room in the hotel. She debated it, then picked up the receiver, dialed the required prefix, and punched in 1010. It rang a long time. She was about to hang up when Eric Edwards came on the line. He sounded out of breath.

"Eric. It's Collette."

"I don't believe it. Mystery lady surfaces. Let me get my breath. I've been working out. Where are you?"

"I'm . . . I'm in the vicinity."

"I knew you were in Washington. My secretary told me. How long will you be here?"

She wanted to say forever, said instead, "I really don't know. I'd like to see you."

"I hoped you'd want to see me," he said. "I was really upset the way you disappeared on me down in the BVI."

"I couldn't help it. I'm sorry."

"Nothing to be sorry about, and thanks for the note. I have a dinner engagement later this evening but . . ."

"I really need to see you tonight, Eric."

"Could you come by now? We can have a drink before I have to get dressed."

Collette paused before saying, "Yes, I can be there in ten minutes."

"Hope you don't mind a sweaty host."

"I won't mind that at all. Will we be alone?"

"Sure. What are you suggesting?"

"Nothing. Ten minutes."

"Fine, I'm in Suite 1010."

"Yes, I know."

After hanging up, she put on her raincoat and slipped the revolver into its pocket. She slung her purse over her shoulder and went to the door, her ear again cocked against the cool metal. There wasn't a sound outside. Then she heard the rattling of dishes and someone whistling—a hotel employee going past her room with a serving cart. She listened to the jangle as it faded into the distance, and until everything was silent again. She undid the chain as quietly as possible, turned the lock on the knob and opened the door, looking out into the hallway right and left. Empty. She made sure she had her key, stepped through the opening, and closed the door behind her.

The elevators were to her left, about a hundred feet away. She started swiftly toward them when Mark Hotchkiss stepped from around a bend in the hallway beyond the elevators. She stopped, turned, and saw Jason Tolker approaching from the opposite direction. His right arm was in a sling, that side of his suit jacket draped over his shoulder. She hadn't noticed that downstairs. "Collette," Tolker said. "Please, I want to talk to you."

"Get away," she said, backing toward the elevators, her hand slipping into her pocket.

Tolker continued to walk toward her, saying, "Don't be foolish, Collette. You're making a big mistake. You must listen to me."

"Shut up," she said. Her hand came out of the pocket holding the revolver and she pointed it at him. It stopped him cold. "I won't miss you this time."

"Miss Cahill, you're being bloody unreasonable," Hotchkiss said from behind.

She glanced over her shoulder and showed him the weapon. "I'm telling you to stay away from me or I'll kill you both. I mean it."

Both men stopped their advance and watched as she moved toward the elevators, her head moving back and forth like a spectator's at a tennis match, keeping them both in view.

"Get her," Tolker yelled.

Hotchkiss extended his arms and stumbled toward her. She waited until he was about to grab her, then brought her knee up sharply into his groin. His breath exploded from him as he sank to his knees, his hands cupping his wounded genitals.

Collette ran to the elevators and pushed the "Down" button. Almost immediately one of the doors opened. The elevator was empty. She backed into it. "Don't come after me," she said, the doors sliding closed and muffling her words.

She looked at the control panel and pushed Seven. The elevator moved a floor lower. She got out, ran along the hall, and turned a corner until she came to another bank of elevators. She frantically pushed the button until one of them arrived. In it were two couples. She stepped inside and pressed Ten.

The couples got out with her at the tenth floor. She waited until they'd entered a room, then walked past it and went directly to 1010. She knocked. The door was immediately opened by Eric Edwards. He wore blue gym shorts and a gray athletic shirt with the sleeves cut off at the shoulders. His hair was damp with perspiration and hung over his tanned forehead.

"Hello, Eric," she said.

"Hello to you," he said, stepping back so that she could enter. He closed the door and latched it.

She went to the center of the room and looked down at a pair of hotel barbells and a couple of towels tossed in a pile on the floor. She kept her back to him.

"Not even a kiss hello?" he asked from behind. She turned, sighed, lowered her eyes, and her body began to shake. Large tears instantly ran down her cheeks.

He put his arms around her and held tight. "Hey, come *on* now, it can't be that bad. Some reaction to me. I should be offended."

She controlled herself, looked up, and said, "I'm so confused, Eric, and frightened. Do you know why I'm here in Washington?"

"No, except you said you had some business to attend to."

"But do you know what that business was?"

He shook his head and smiled. "No, and unless you tell me, I never will."

"I was sent here to kill you."

He looked at her as though she were a small child caught in a lie. She said, "It's true, Eric. They wanted me to kill you, and I said I would."

"Telling you to kill me is one thing," he said as he went to a chair near the window, "agreeing to it is another. Why would you want to kill me?"

She tossed her raincoat on a couch. "I don't. I mean, I didn't. I never intended to."

He laughed. "You're incredible, you know that?"

She shook her head, went to him, and sank to her knees in front of the chair. "Incredible? No, I'm anything but. What I am is a terribly mixed up and disillusioned woman."

"Disillusioned with what, our good friends at Langley?"

She nodded. "The so-called Company, everyone in my life, life itself I guess." She took a deep breath. "They wanted me to kill you because they think you're a double agent, selling information to the Soviets about Banana Quick."

He grunted, shrugged.

"When I came to you and asked for advice about a vacation in the BVI, it was all a lie. They told me to do it. They wanted me to get close to you so that I could find out what you were doing down there."

He leaned forward, touched her cheek, and said, "I knew that, Collette."

"You did?"

"Well, not for certain, but I had a pretty strong feeling about it. It really didn't bother me for a couple of reasons. One, I fell in love with you. Two, I figured that when you almost went up with me and the yacht, you'd lost your taste for doing their dirty work. Was I right?"

"Yes."

"Having something like that happen puts things in perspective, doesn't it? You can see how little you or I mean to them. We can go out and put our necks on the line for their crazy sense of duty and patriotism, but when push comes to shove, we're all expendable. No questions asked, just 'terminate' some people and get on with the sham."

His words had considerable impact on her, as words always do when they say what you've already been thinking. She thought of Tolker and Hotchkiss and their confrontation. "There are two men in the hotel who tried to stop me in the hall."

He sat up. "Who are they? Do you know them?"

"Yes. One is Jason Tolker, the psychiatrist who was Barrie's control. He brainwashed her, Eric. The other is an Englishman named Mark Hotchkiss, the one who took over Barrie's agency."

Edwards's placid face turned grim as he looked out the window. "You know him?" Collette asked.

"I know of him. He's British intelligence, an old buck who supposedly did some hits for MI-6, the Middle East, I think."

Cahill said, "I think Tolker is the one who killed Barrie and David Hubler, maybe not directly, but I'm convinced he was behind it."

Edwards continued to stare silently at the window. Finally, he turned to her and said, "I have a proposal for you, Collette."

"A proposal?"

He managed a thin smile. "Not that kind of proposal, although maybe that's in the cards down the road. As it would have been with Barrie if . . ." She waited for him to finish his thought. Instead, he said, "For all her intelligence, Barrie didn't have one tenth the smarts you have, Collette."

"If there's one thing I don't consider myself these days, it's smart."

He placed his hands on her shoulders and kissed her gently on the forehead. "You've seen more in your lifetime than most people can only imagine. You've not only witnessed the rotten underbelly of the CIA, what they call Intelligence, you've been a victim of it, like me. Barrie didn't understand that. She never realized how she was being used by them."

Cahill sat back on her haunches. "I don't understand," she said.

"I suppose it doesn't matter anymore about Barrie. She's dead. It's different for you, though. You could . . . you could step in where she left off, sort of in her memory." His face lit up as though what he'd just said represented a profound revelation. "That's right, you could view it that way, Collette, as doing something in Barrie's memory."

"View *what* that way?"

"Doing something to right wrongs, to avenge all the things that have happened because of them, including the loss of your good friend, and that young man who worked for her. You could do something very worthwhile for the world, Collette."

"What do you mean?"

"Come in with me," he said.

She had no idea what he meant, and her face indicated it.

He hunched forward and spoke in low, paternal tones. "Collette, I want you to think carefully about everything that's happened over the past weeks, beginning with the death of Barrie Mayer." He scrutinized her face. "You know why Barrie died, don't you?"

"Sometimes I think I do, but I've never been sure. Do you know . . . for sure?"

His expression was one of bad taste in his mouth. He said in the same measured tones, "Barrie died because she wouldn't listen to me. She did in the beginning, and it was good for her, but then she started listening to others."

"Tolker?"

"Yes. He had remarkable control over her. I warned her. I tried to reason with her, but every time she'd see him, he'd capture another small piece of her mind."

"I knew that was the case, but . . . "

"But what?"

"Why would he have killed her if she were so obedient to him?"

"Because that's the flaw in their whole stupid mind-control program, Collette. They spend millions, screw up one life after the other, but still can't—and never will—

create a person they can *totally* control. It's impossible, and they know it."

"But they . . . "

"Yeah, they keep spending and trying. Why? The freaks who work in those projects, like Tolker, get off on it. They exaggerate results and keep promising a breakthrough, while the ones who control funding rationalize the millions by claiming the other side is doing it, and in a bigger way. Barrie might have been manipulated by Tolker, but he didn't own her. Maybe it would have been better if he did. Or thought he did."

Collette said nothing as she thought about what he'd said.

"Tolker filled Barrie with a lot of lies that turned her against me," Edwards continued. "It was a tragic mistake on her part. She didn't know who to trust, and ended up putting all her cards in the wrong player's hand."

Cahill went to a table. She leaned her hands on it and peered down at its surface. As hard as she tried, she couldn't fully process what he was saying. Everything was so indirect, raising more questions than answers.

"Eric, why was Barrie killed? What did she know that made it necessary to murder her? Who would have been so hurt if she stayed alive that they'd be driven to such an act?"

He came closer to her. "You have to understand, Collette, that Barrie knew the risks involved in what she was doing."

"Being a courier? Occasionally carrying things to Budapest shouldn't pose that much of a risk, Eric."

"Not unless what she was carrying could be construed as being destructive to the Company."

"Why would it be destructive? She was working *for* it, wasn't she?"

"In the beginning, then . . . Look, let me level with you, Collette, the way I've been doing right along. I won't try to soften it, mince words. Barrie eventually saw the wisdom in cooperating with—the other side."

Collette shook her head. "No, I can't believe that Barrie would double-deal. No, sorry, I can't accept that."

"You have to, Collette. Open your mind. Don't automatically make it negative. What she was doing was noble in its own way."

"Noble? You're saying she was a traitor."

"Semantics. Is trying to achieve a balance of sanity in this world a traitorous act? I don't think so. Is saving the lives of thousands of innocent people, Hungarians in this case, traitorous? Of course it isn't. Banana Quick was ill-conceived from the beginning, doomed to failure, like the Bay of Pigs and the rescue attempt in Iran and all the other misguided projects we undertake in the name of freedom. If Banana Quick is implemented, it will only result in the death of innocent people in Hungary. Barrie didn't see that at first, but I eventually convinced her of it."

"*You* convinced her?"

"Yes, and I want to convince you of the same thing. This is something I've wanted to do ever since I met you, but I was never sure you'd be receptive. Now I think you will be, just as Barrie was, once she understood."

"Go ahead."

"I want you to work with me to fend off this madness. I want you to pick up where Barrie left off. I want you to . . . to help me feed information to where it will do the most good, to what you call 'the other side.' "

Cahill's stomach churned and she felt light-headed. What they'd said was true. He *was* a double agent, and had recruited Barrie. She didn't know what to say, how to respond, whether to lash out at him physically or to run from the room. She held both instincts in check. "I defended you at every turn. I told them they were wrong about you. I was the one who was wrong." She'd said it with a calm voice. Now she exploded. "Damn it, damn you! I thought Tolker was the double agent leaking information about Banana Quick. I really believed that, but now you're admitting to me that you are. You bastard! You set Barrie up to be killed, and now you want me to put myself in the same position."

He shook his head slowly. "Collette, you have a lot more to offer than Barrie did. She was so naive. That's what got her in trouble, what led to her death. When I took Barrie into my confidence, I had no idea of her potential for control by someone like Tolker. She told him everything, and he convinced her to inform on me. She'd learned too much. I never should have let her get that close, but I fell in love. I do that too easily and often for my own good."

"Love? You call it love for a woman to recruit her into selling out her country?"

"Love comes in all forms. It was a nice partnership, personally and professionally, until Tolker soured everything. Barrie made a lot of money from our partnership, Collette, a lot more than she was getting from the CIA."

"Money? That matters to you?"

"Sure. It mattered to her, too. There's nothing inherently evil with money, is there? Let me suggest something. Climb down off your high horse and hear me out. I'll cancel my date tonight and we'll have dinner right here in the room. We'll get to know each other better." He laughed. "And we can pick up where we left off in the BVI. No strings, Collette. You don't have to fall in with me. Nothing lost by talking about it."

"I don't want to talk about it," she said.

"You don't have much choice."

"What do you mean?"

"You're already in because you know too much. That makes sense, doesn't it?"

"Not at all."

He shrugged, leaned over and picked up a barbell, lifted it a few times over his head. "I'll make a deal with you. All you have to do is go back to Budapest and tell them I'm clean. I'll give you materials that make a case against Tolker as having thrown in with the Soviets. That's all you have to do, Collette, tell them you dug up this material and are turning it over like a good Company employee. They'll take care of Tolker and . . . "

"And what, terminate him?"

"That's not our concern. You knew, didn't you, that Barrie was carrying almost two hundred thousand dollars to pay off some Hungarian bureaucrat?"

She didn't reply.

"I have it."

"You took it from her after you killed her." She was amazed at how matter-of-factly she was able to say it.

"It doesn't matter how I got it. What's important is that half is yours for clearing me. After that, there'll be plenty more if you decide to help me on a long-term basis. Think about it, lots of money stashed away for your retirement." Another laugh as he did curls with the barbell. "I figure I've got maybe another year at best before it's time for me to get out. I want enough money to start my own charter service, not a front I don't own. What do you want in a year, Collette? A house in Switzerland, an airplane, enough money in a foreign bank so that you'll never have to work again? It's yours." He dropped the barbell to the floor and said, "How about it? Dinner? Champagne? We'll toast anything you want, anybody, and then we can . . . "

"Make love?"

"Absolutely. I established a rule with myself years ago that I'd never let anything get in the way of that, especially when it's a beautiful and bright woman like you who . . . " He shook his head. "Who made me fall in love again."

She went for her raincoat on the couch. He jumped in front of her and gripped the back of her neck, his fingertips pressing hard against her arteries. She could see the muscles rippling in his bare arms, and the red anger on his face. "I'm through being nice," he said, pushing her across the room and into the bedroom. He flung her down on the bed, grabbed the front of her sweater, and tore it off.

She rolled off the bed and scrambled across the floor toward the door, got to her feet, and raced into the living room. She swiped at her raincoat and tried to get behind the couch where she'd have time to retrieve the revolver. He was too quick; she'd barely managed to pull the weapon from the pocket when he grabbed her wrist and twisted, the white plastic gun falling to the floor.

"You bitch," he said. "You would kill me, wouldn't you?"

His ego was so damaged momentarily that he relaxed his grip on her wrist. She sprang loose and ran to where she'd left her purse on top of a large console television set, grabbed it, and tried to find something to get behind, a haven where she could catch her breath and ready the detonator. There wasn't any such place—her only escape route was into the master bedroom. She ran there and tried to slam the door behind her, but he easily pushed it open, the force sending her reeling toward the bed. Her knees caught it, and she was suddenly on her back, her hands frantically seeking the device in her purse.

He stood over her and glared. "You don't understand the game, do you? What did you think would happen when you decided to get some excitement in your life by joining up? What did you think, you can play spy but run home to Mommy when it hurts?"

"I'm . . . please don't hurt me," she said. Her purse had fallen to the floor, but she'd grasped the loaded detonator and cupped it in her right hand, her arms flung back over the edge of the bed.

"I don't want to," he said. "I don't hurt people for fun. Sometimes, though . . . sometimes it's necessary, that's all. Don't make it necessary for me to hurt you."

"I won't." His eyes were focused on her bare breasts. He smiled. "A beautiful woman. You'll see, Collette, we'll end up together. It'll be nice. We'll stash the money, then go away somewhere and enjoy the hell out of it—and each other."

He leaned forward and put a hand on either side of her head. His face was inches from her face. He kissed her on the lips, and she managed to return it, mimicking the memory of their night together, until he pulled his head back and said, "You're beautiful."

Then she brought her hand up and jammed the detonator against his lips. Her thumb pulled the switch and the ampule exploded, sending the acid and a thousand fine fragments of glass into his face. He gasped and fell back to his knees, his hands ripping at his sweatshirt, his face contorted.

Cahill, too, felt the effect of the acid. Her face had been too close to his. She reached down and shoved her hand into her open purse, found the small glass vial of nitro and broke it beneath her nose, breathing deeply, praying it would work.

"Me . . . " Edwards said. He was now writhing on the floor, one hand outstretched, his last living expression one of pleading. Cahill lay on her stomach, her head at the foot of the bed, her eyes wide as she watched him breathe and then, with one last convulsion, his head twisted to one side and he was dead, his open eyes looking up at her.

CHAPTER 33

She made her final trip to Budapest a week later, to process out and to arrange for the shipment of her things back to the United States.

Joe Breslin met her Malev flight and drove her to her apartment. "I really don't have much," she said. "It was probably silly for me even to come here."

"You didn't have to bother with packing," Breslin said, lighting his pipe. "We would have done it for you. Got a beer?"

"Go look. I don't know."

He returned from the tiny kitchen with a bottle of the Köbányai világos and a glass. "Want one? There's plenty."

"No."

He sat on a deep window bench and she leaned against a wall, her arms folded across her chest, ankles crossed, her head down. She sighed, looked at him, and said, "I'll hate you and everybody in the CIA for the rest of my life, Joe."

"I'm genuinely sorry about that," he said.

"So am I. Maybe if I grow up someday and begin to

understand everything that's happened, I won't feel quite so filled with hatred."

"Maybe. You know, none of us likes doing what we have to do."

"I don't believe that, Joe. I think the agency's filled with people who love it. I thought I did."

"You did a good job."

"Did I?"

"Your handling of Hegedüs was as masterful as any I've ever seen."

"He was telling the truth about Tolker, wasn't he?"

"Yeah. I wish the Fisherman were still in place. He's no good to us now."

She made a sound of displeasure.

"What's the matter?" he asked.

" 'He's no good to us now.' That's the way it is, isn't it, Joe? People are only worthwhile as long as they have something to give. After that . . . instant discard."

He didn't respond.

"Tell me about Hotchkiss," she said.

Breslin shrugged and drew on his pipe. "MI-6, an old-timer who hung in. They—the Brits—set Hotchkiss up in the literary agency business years ago. Nice cover, good excuse to travel and get a pulse on what's happening in the literary fraternity. In most countries, literary means political. Having him in that business paid off for them. They're not talking, at least to us, but somehow they got wind that Barrie had turned, and was working with Edwards. They sicced Hotchkiss on her." Breslin's laugh was one of admiration. "Hotchkiss did a better job than they'd hoped for. He actually got Barrie to consider going into partnership."

"Consider? They did become partners."

"Not really. The papers were bogus. We figure your friend told Hotchkiss to get lost the night before she died. That eventuality had been considered for a long time. Those papers were drawn, and her signature forged, in anticipation of the deal going down the tube."

"But why . . . ?"

"Why what? Go through all that? The British have been complaining from the first day about Banana Quick. They felt we were running the show, and that they were being left in the dark about too many things. Answer? Get someone on the inside, in this case Barrie Mayer. Knowing what she was up to was as good as sleeping with Edwards."

"And Jason Tolker?"

A long draw on his pipe. "Funny about Tolker. He really was in love with Barrie Mayer, but he found himself between a rock and a hard place. The British suspected she was double-dealing, but never knew for certain. Tolker knew. He was the only one, besides Edwards, but what does he do with the information? Turn them in and destroy the woman? He couldn't do that, so he went to work on her and tried to convince her to drop Edwards, turn him in, and hope that they'd let her off the hook. He was effective, *too* effective. She finally decided to do it. Edwards couldn't allow that. That's why he killed her. All such a waste. They've scrapped Banana Quick."

Cahill stared at him incredulously, then quickly went to a closet. She would not allow him to see that her eyes were moist. She waited until she was under control before pulling out a blue blazer and slipping it on over her white blouse. "Let's go," she said.

"Stan wants to talk to you before you leave," said Breslin.

"I know. What is it, a debriefing?"

"Something like that. He'll lay down the rules. He has

to do that with anyone leaving. There are rules, you know, about disclosure, things like that."

"I can live with rules."

"What about your friend, the journalist?"

"Vern? Don't worry, Joe, I won't tell him what happened, what *really* happened."

"The book he's writing."

"What about it?"

"You've seen it. Is it damaging?"

"Yes."

"We'd like to know what's in it."

"Not from me."

"Do him a favor, Collette, and get him to drop it."

"That sounds like an order."

"A strong request."

"Denied."

She started to open the door but he stopped her with "Collette, you sure you want to make such a clean break? Hank Fox told you what your options were before you came here. The outfit takes good care of those who do special service, and do it well. You could have six months anywhere in the world with all expenses paid, a chance to get your head together and for enough time to pass so that it all doesn't seem so terrible. Then a nice job back at Langley, more money, the works. People who . . ."

"People who carry out an assassination are taken care of. Joe, I didn't assassinate Eric Edwards. He tried to rape me. I was like any other woman—except I had a plastic gun, a vial of lethal acid, and the blessing of my country's leading intelligence agency. I killed him to save myself, no other reason."

"What does it matter? The job got done."

"I'm glad that makes everyone happy. No, Joe, I want

ten thousand miles between me and the CIA. I know there are a lot of good people in it who really care about what happens to their country, and who try to do the right thing. The problem is, Joe, that not only are there lots of people who *aren't* like that, but the definition of 'right thing' gets blurred all the time. Come on. Let me go and have the rules explained to me, and then let's have dinner. I'm really going to miss Hungarian food."

ABOUT THE AUTHOR

MARGARET TRUMAN is the author of seven successful mystery thrillers. Born in Independence, Missouri, she now lives with her husband, Clifton Daniel, in New York City.